The Girl I Used to Know

FAITH HOGAN lives in the west of Ireland with her husband, four children and a very busy Labrador. She has an Hons Degree in English Literature and Psychology, has worked as a fashion model and in the intellectual disability and mental health sector.

Also by Faith Hogan

My Husband's Wives
Secrets We Keep
What Happened to Us?

The Girl
I Used to
Know

Faith Hogan

HEAD
of ZEUS

An Aria Book

First published in the UK in 2017 by Aria,
an imprint of Head of Zeus Ltd
This paperback edition published by Head of Zeus Ltd in 2019

9 7 5 3 1 2 4 6 8

A CIP catalogue record for this book is available from the
British Library.

Printed and bound in Great Britain by
CPI Group (UK) Ltd, Croydon CR0 4YY

ISBN (PBO): 9781788549882
ISBN (E): 9781786692863

Aria
c/o Head of Zeus
First Floor East
5–8 Hardwick Street
London EC1R 4RG

WWW.ARIAFICTION.COM

For Bernadine Cafferkey, super sister,
first editor and fashionista—

Love always xx

'*A good neighbour is a priceless treasure.*'

Chinese Proverb.

Prologue

Forty-eight years ago...

The sun began to empty its rays across the bay earlier each morning now. Finally, it seemed Ballycove was drifting towards the summer months. May had been clement, and it looked as if June could surge, blazing into summer with long hot days reminding them all how lucky they really were to have the Irish Sea wash cool spray onto the doorstep of their little village. It was confirmed when day tourists from Dublin arrived, half-baked already from the twenty-minute train journey south to escape the dusty city. Tess Cuffe listened to their voices, sing-songing across the little village streets and cast like stray nets, fragments of sentences, on the sea breeze. With a bit of luck, she would be one of them, one day. She imagined herself, joining a tribe and returning for short holidays with worldly eyes to find a picturesque village. And, even as a youngster, Tess could see that Ballycove was quaint, but she was ready to leave it behind. She was already tired of its narrow streets and blinkered people. She craved the anonymity of the city, where you weren't known as the headmaster's daughter, or just the girl who sang in church each week, the second sister who was nothing like her mother.

Her parents, Harold and Maureen Cuffe, lived in Ballycove all their lives. Quietly, perhaps a little oddly, their cottage set apart, just enough to let the neighbours know that they were somehow better than the rest. Harold was a man who had an education; it would surely be marked on his headstone, one day: *Harold Cuffe, B.A. National Teacher and Headmaster*. It was unlikely there'd be room for much more, *sadly missed*, and *pray for his soul* would have to be taken as agreed. Maureen, well, unless she died first, it would be on the toss of a coin as to whether she would even get a mention, beyond being the wife of Harold Cuffe. It was good enough in life; she might have to settle for the same in death as well.

Tess could think of nothing worse than being like her mother. It wasn't that she didn't love her. Maureen was kind, giving and stoic in her faith in Harold, but it seemed to Tess that she had no passion and so that made her into a diluted version of what she might have otherwise been. Whereas Tess, from the first moment she realised she could sing, had been lost to a different world. Every amateur show in the village, every party, wedding or funeral wake, Tess would make a stand and sing until her father told her that it was time to stop. She was at the front of every choir and knew the words to any song that managed to make it onto the top of the pops or the weekly hymn sheets. If there were words and music, Tess would sing along.

This morning, Tess was first up, waiting for the familiar squeak of the letter box. Nancy still slept soundly in her twin bed, unaware her sister had tiptoed across the threadbare circular rug that bled a colour wheel of faded purples, wines and reds across their tiny bedroom. Sometimes, Tess wondered if Nancy ever dreamed. Tess's sleep crowded with dreams of lyrics and music and her voice carrying to the rooftops of some unknown city, where even the pigeons craned taller on their roosts to hear her sing. Tess didn't just dream about singing, she breathed it with every cell in her body, and the letter that she so longed to hold was as dear to her as a king's pardon. In many ways, she had always felt her life would properly begin once she shook the dust of Ballycove from her awkward schoolgirl shoes.

Tess stood before the mirror for a moment. In the dim light it was hard to make out her reflection, but the sleep was long gone from her eyes and her lips and cheeks were plump from a good night's rest. She smoothed down her soft chestnut hair, straightened up her blouse so the collar sat high on her neck. She loved this blouse, cobalt blue, it brought out the colour of her eyes, which were dark-ringed with eyelashes long and heavy. She looked back once more at Nancy, perhaps she dreamed of baking cakes, or typing letters or… it was beyond Tess. Nancy was a full year older than Tess and she seemed to have no desire to go anywhere or do anything. The boys in the village would never be good enough for Harold Cuffe's daughter, so maybe going to Dublin with Tess was the best option for her. It was hardly the most exciting prospect, a secretarial course and then perhaps the chance to gain entry to the civil service for a few years. Was it very bad to feel sorry for your older sister? Perhaps the bonds between them were all the stronger because of this affection that cloaked over Tess when she thought of how differently their futures seemed mapped out before them.

Tess sighed; they were just so different, close as peas in a shell, but poles apart. She waited now for that whisper of envelope as it glided onto the tiled floor her mother fretted over with polish for as long as Tess could remember. Maureen Cuffe was a mouse of a woman, forever playing small to augment her husband's supremacy. Tess had decided long ago that she would be different, even if her older sister Nancy was happy to fall into that spiritless mould.

It was six days now. Six days since she'd attended the interview in the prestigious College of Music, in Dublin's' Trinity College. That was the most exhilarating day of her life. The college itself was as old as any building in the city and hushed with the reverence of a church. It was like nowhere she'd ever been before and yet, it was exactly as she expected. The grandeur intimidated as much as it impressed. The rooms were imposing, tall and echoing so her voice sprang back at her with unexpected vigorous fluency. Even that, just attending for her audition, it tasted like the start of where she was meant to be. She walked through halls lined with heavy oak, beneath the glare of past teachers and students of that selective school. It was all she'd ever wanted and she was too keyed up to care about pretending it didn't matter. That audition was all she thought of. All her work, her hopes and her future were pinned on just less than eight minutes. She'd sang her best, timed every single note, waited, buttoned up her soul so she could unleash it as her voice ascended to heights she'd only hoped for. The panel, a bunch of stuffy, whiskered men and a woman who hardly greeted her, had been entranced before she finished. She knew it, from the moment she paced into the aria – pens were suspended, words only half written and smiles, fighting against muscles determined not to let them escape, drew half-expressions across otherwise weary faces and now, all she could do was wait.

The cottage was silent this morning, apart from the continuing marking of time; the Swiss carriage clock wore seconds across rooms that no longer paid any heed. Although the village children were on holiday for weeks on end, her father would walk down to the schoolhouse this morning. Sometimes, she wondered what he did there, each day. She suspected he just went because he didn't know what else to do with his time – her mother talked of his impending retirement with a sense of doom worthy of an undertaker. 'Not long now,' she would say when he left the house. Everything about their family was tied up in that school. Even this cottage, 'the Master's house', long ago gifted to the family. Her father would have his ties cut in two years' time, three if they were lucky. Finding a replacement who'd want to settle in a little village like Ballycove might not be easy. As for her father, a pillar of the community, he would have to find some other way of being proper or drift into old age with only the past to buoy him towards the end.

Then, Tess heard it. A creak that meant she was not alone. She skipped into the little hallway, the sunlight reaching dusty rays down to dance upon the silky blue envelope that lay composed on the floor. Tess picked it up, her parents' names in flowing font gave nothing away. The stamp, measured into the corner, seemed to wink at her, impish in all that hid within. She rushed into the kitchen, placed it carefully in the centre of the table and went about making as much noise as she could. First, she boiled the kettle and set about emptying the stove that burned in all weather, it worked harder than her mother did, but it seemed to get more care.

'It's here,' Nancy carolled her words so they filled the kitchen, she was still in her night clothes, wakened perhaps by Tess's soft movements or the early morning birds intent on starting a new day before anyone else. 'I can't believe you've waited, it's...' Nancy inspected the envelope in her hand. 'Are you nervous?' Almost identical eyes found each other and Tess realised that this affected Nancy as much as it affected her. If she got a place in Trinity, Nancy would be uprooted too. Nancy was older by just eleven months, it gave her the advantage when it came to being the one her parents credited with having 'sense and moral fibre.'

'I...' Everyone knew it was all she wanted, but the fear of failure drove Tess back from saying the words aloud. 'No, of course not, as they say, que sera, sera?' Then she laughed a nervous tickle that stretched into tight silence between them. She couldn't fool Nancy.

'Oh, come on. I don't believe you for a minute; let's get Mamma and Father up here.' Nancy skipped down to the door that led into her parents' room. 'Mamma, Tess's letter has arrived.' Her voice bubbled with a lighter version of the nerves playing at the back of Tess's throat. In the kitchen, Nancy came over to Tess now, reached towards her arm and squeezed it because maybe, she could feel the longing too. It had always been that way for them. Tess thought, they knew each other inside out. Of course, the similarities were only on the surface, but a deeper connection skirted about the everyday; a connection that went beyond sisterhood. Their mother believed it came from long before they were born. Nancy said it would be there long after they died – wherever life took them on the way and, somehow, this made Tess feel warm inside.

'Right,' her mother said as she took the last hairclip from her lips and slid it into hair that grew greyer with every passing day. She patted back the stray ribs that no longer settled with a comb. By the time her parents arrived in the kitchen, nerves had almost gotten the better of Tess, what if they didn't want her after all? 'Let's see what they have to say.' She handed the envelope to her husband with a reverence that came as much from respect as expectation.

Tess passed him one of the ivory-handled knives that she'd placed on the table earlier.

'I dare say, this'll be the end of having the table set before we all start our day,' their mother smiled. Tess would not be quite so earnest tomorrow morning if this letter contained the invitation she'd worked so hard to get. Maureen peered across her husband's shoulder, narrowed her eyes to read the embellished font. 'Now that you're going to be a…' she didn't get to finish off the sentence. They wanted her in the College of Music and as her father read out the letter, Tess and Nancy started to dance around the kitchen – Tess had never been so happy.

Tess wound her way up the steep little road to Aunt Beatrice's house as soon as it was respectable to call. Beatrice lived in a little cottage; on a ledge that overhung the Irish Sea. Strictly speaking, Aunt Beatrice wasn't her aunt at all. She was a cousin of her mother's. No one was entirely sure how they were related, but as with many connections in the village, they were wrought with time and affection as much as any blood ties. Tess loved this cottage. She'd come here for years, marking out the hours before she had to return to the austerity of her father's overbearing appropriateness. Aunt Beatrice said she was far too old to think about what was proper anymore. Tess wasn't sure when Aunt Beatrice had become old, it was something that had stealthily overtaken them at some point. Tess could imagine her being very young and vibrant, a darker-haired version of herself. There was no picturing her in that middle ground between youth and old age, making that steady journey to this point through mildly greying hair and soft discrepancy between what was and what would be. Perhaps she'd always been young, until once when they'd looked away for a moment too long and time had stolen its place without any word of warning. 'You get to a stage in life, when really, you have to take your happiness as it is. I'd be a very disappointed old lady now if I waited for everything to come along in the packaging that I'd wished for.' Beatrice spoke of her love affairs with the honesty of one who cared little for the po-faced propriety of her peers and less for the double standards of the Sunday pulpit. She was thrilled with the news of the letter.

'I will miss you of course, but oh, Tess, think of all that lies ahead of you. I'm so pleased for you.'

'I will miss you too, and our little heart-to-hearts,' Tess looked around the cottage, feeling nostalgic already for its cosy homeliness.

'Ach, go on with you,' Beatrice smiled and Tess knew that for all that she'd enjoyed Beatrice's unfailing love and support over the years, soon the time would come when Beatrice would no longer be here. This little cottage would be half a world without her, but it was the most important connection she had with Ballycove. Tess put the thought from her mind quickly.

'I will come and visit, as often as I can,' Tess said then, touching Beatrice's feathery-skinned hand.

'You've always been a good girl, Tess, but I'm happy to see you go and chase your dreams. I'll always be here, long after you think I'm gone, looking out over the water, perhaps dancing on the waves with some handsome young officer that I've kept a secret all these years.' Beatrice smiled now and reached for the dresser at her back. 'Come on, we should have some cake while you tell me all about your plans until you finally go.'

There was very little to tell. She would have to find a place to live, but Beatrice said that perhaps she could help there. 'And Nancy. How's Nancy with all of this good news?'

'Well, she's thrilled, of course she is,' Tess said, but

she found the uncertainty in her words that excitement had concealed before.

'She won't want to leave Maureen,' Beatrice whispered.

'We can't stay home forever, though Mum wouldn't want that.'

'No, it's not what your mother wants; it's what Nancy feels she needs. She's afraid to leave…' Beatrice shook her head. The words silently tacked between them. Nancy wanted nothing more than a husband to look after her and a house to mind. The idea of holding her own in the city was probably as much to be endured as enjoyed. 'Of course, you must both go to Dublin, your mother wants that more than anything, I think.'

'It's only for a year, but maybe…' Tess smiled, she didn't need to fill in any blanks. They both hoped that Nancy would find some kind of work that might put her in the way of a nice young man. Tess on the other hand wanted adventure. She wanted to leave behind the little village where respectability pinned you into holes that smothered. She wanted to sing and feel her voice soar high and far as the seagulls threading stitches across the vista of her world. Nancy wanted to be here, not here in this cottage – this was Tess's refuge. She wanted to be here, in Ballycove, with someone who would keep her safe, make her feel matchless, assure the world edged out into the perimeters of her life. Nancy wanted to be taken care of, to live a life that didn't punish her for being less. She wanted everything their mother had and none of it. 'Nancy doesn't have to come, you know.' The words were defensive, but the truth was, Tess was looking forward to it being just the two of them.

'She doesn't get to choose, she feels your happiness depends upon her.' Beatrice spoke softly. It wasn't a reprimand, just a reminder that Nancy was giving up a year to go and live in Dublin, just to pacify their father. It was out of the question, as far as he was concerned, that Tess would live in the city on her own, or worse, with strangers. 'She has no interest in pursuing any secretarial work, we both know that,' Beatrice said. 'But you're right, it's exactly what she needs the most.'

'It will be good for her – you see that too.' Tess shook her head. 'She might find that there's more to life than Ballycove and living like my mother for the rest of her days.' Tess fidgeted with a ball of wool that lay unravelled across the table between them. She offered to roll it up, but still it lay, unfurled lazily on the lacy cloth that soaked up the midday sun searing through the little windows.

'Hmm. Well, don't forget, it's just a year – you'll be taking care of her probably more than she'll be taking care of you.' Beatrice smiled across her half-moon glasses and they both knew that whatever her parents believed, it had always been that way. Nancy would always need minding. She was similar to their mother: pliant, self-deprecating, the people-pleaser of the pair. Tess only hoped that didn't mean she took after her father. Tess could see no happiness for someone as proud as Harold Cuffe, he was far too tied up with the importance of being right to understand the meaning of being loved.

Tess did not answer. Instead, she looked out onto the glassy black water below, biting and shifting glints upon unending waves. It seemed to Tess that the waves below them could not mark out the time quickly enough to enter this new world that beckoned so forcefully.

December 29 – Monday

Coffee with the girls just wore Amanda King out these days. She pulled up onto the Italian pebble drive of her home, exhausted, which of course was ridiculous – it was just coffee after all. First-world problems, that's what Richard called it, and he must be right.

Richard was always right, he was a banker, her successful husband of twenty-two years; the love of her life. Richard fell in love with her when she was a flighty art student with notions probably far beyond her talent. She could thank him for saving her from the delusions of herself. He fell in love with her in spite of her permanently charcoaled fingernails. Sometimes it seemed like a lifetime ago, but it was twenty-two years in a few weeks' time. Life had been generous to them, giving them a perfect family – Casper and Robyn – well, they were teenagers now, in that awkward phase of no man's land between rebellion, tears and needing her. She could thank Richard too for their lovely home, a three-storey over basement Georgian townhouse; after all, he had paid for it. They had been captivated by it together, perhaps for different reasons. Richard liked the address – you don't get more exclusive in Dublin than an intact Georgian square, with a private shared park in the centre, on the right side of town. Amanda adored everything about it, from the intricate cornicing and ceiling roses, to the buttery windowpanes that rattled in their frames. She loved the light that shone through every inch of the house at the precise moment when you needed it. Their breakfast bar faced east, their dining room benefited from the western evening sun. She threw herself headlong into a sympathetic restoration project that managed to extend beyond the house to the communal square and more. Amanda spent almost a year researching the history of the square, from the first stone laid on a grey Dublin day in 1798 to each mistress of the house, before she arrived to steer it into its third century.

She sighed now, as much from exhaustion as the notion of all those women who went before. They suffered on through famine, land wars, world wars and countless other ups and downs; she had not yet lost the grace to feel a little prickly when she complained about her trifling niggles.

What was she doing? She was complaining about going for coffee in one of Dublin's smartest hotels, with some of the most glamourous women in the city? She had fallen into this charmed, if somewhat vacuous life.

Coffee morning was a ritual at this stage, two hours spent dissecting the lives of everyone outside their circle – people of interest, who hadn't quite managed to make it in yet. They sat at the same table each week, Amanda and the other wives, feasting on the morsels of gossip gleaned from husbands who only cared in an offhand way.

Amanda opened the button of her pants and groaned her disappointment. Once again, she had tucked into the plate of sweet biscuits, croissants and scones. Single-handedly, she was a one-woman scoffing machine; she'd cleared the lot. She never remembered eating them, but, as usual, she had found herself reaching for something to nibble and before she knew it, the tiered plate was empty. Ah, well, no point crying over spilled milk or eaten pastries, she thought regretfully.

Amanda sat for a moment, looking up at her beautiful home. If she only looked up, past the granite steps, the glossy black handrails, she could convince herself that everything was perfect. It was her dream home, her lovely Georgian house, with its original fanlight and reconstructed glossy front door, brasses glinting in the afternoon unseasonable sunshine. It still made her so proud that she had pulled this place back from the brink. Well, she had refurbished it thanks to Richard's money and an army of specialist builders and advisors. Unfortunately, it took just a glimpse to the lower left to catch sight of the only blight on the vista of their lovely mansion. A sturdy little porch jutted out of what they called the basement, although the windows and door appeared to be at ground level. Tess Cuffe, their sitting tenant, had hung a line of washing out again.

Amanda tried to block it out of view, but it was hard to ignore an orange clothes line clipped with neat green pegs, a sail of freshly washed, if very worn linen flapping on the icy afternoon breeze. Indeed, you had to wonder, when you looked at those almost threadbare sheets, if they might not be considered vintage at this point. On the end of the line, a couple of blouses fluttered mournfully, their flowers long faded by hot washes and too much cheap detergent. My God, but they probably didn't even sell blouses like those anymore. They were truly ancient, outmoded – collectibles that no one would ever want to collect. Amanda wondered who wore them in this day and age. The answer of course was Tess Cuffe – she was the only person Amanda had ever known to wear clothes that might have fallen off a shelf in Woolworths forty years before. Presumably, they were her work clothes, although, for the life of her Amanda couldn't fathom who would want to employ a woman like Tess Cuffe.

Oh, God. Amanda could feel the familiar swell of dread in her stomach. Richard would be incandescent if he arrived home to see Tess was hanging out her washing again. They all knew she only did it because Amanda had expressly written it in their residents' association code of conduct. It was clear as day, residents were not to lower the tone of Swift Square by embarking on any activity more suited to the rear of their properties. It went for barbecues as much as pottering about and, certainly, it went for drying clothes. She made the mistake of mentioning it to Tess, just once, years before, and ever since, as soon as the sun shone, lines of washing were pegged out with spiteful haste at the front of number 4, Swift Square.

It annoyed Richard more than anyone; it was like a rebellious one finger to all the money he had wasted over the years trying to get Tess out. Amanda hated to use the word *evicted*, it was all too messy and unthinkable, even now. Still, after all these years, Richard could spend an entire evening whining and complaining about Tess. Funny, but in the beginning, Amanda believed it would pass. After all, Tess Cuffe was the reason they picked this place up at a bargain price. Tess knew that too and perhaps resented them all the more for it. Richard did everything he could think of to induce her to leave. When bullying her did not work, he tried money. He offered her enough to put a down payment on a nice cosy flat. She could have her own place in a neighbourhood where her underwear would not be the only washing hanging on clothes lines along a veranda designed for that purpose. Tess had been unyielding. It seemed to Amanda, the more Richard made it plain he wanted her out, the more Tess dug herself in to stay. There had been so many small squabbles over the years, but then in a moment of fury, Richard instigated legal proceedings. He wanted her gone and he could call it anything the judges preferred to hear, but in the end, they lost. Tess was still here; still paying her legally agreed ten bob a week rent. It was a covenant agreement, based on some old law that Tess managed to unearth with free legal aid. The amount meant nothing in terms of financial gain for the Kings but gave immense satisfaction to Tess, who left the old coins on the doorstep each Friday afternoon, just at the end of the working week.

For her ten bob or, in new money, less than two euros a week, Tess had the entire basement of the house. It consisted of a two-bedroom flat, which although it hadn't been modernised, was very generous by today's rental proportions in the city. A separate entrance squeezed within a small add-on porch just left of the impressive granite steps to Amanda's imposing front door. The judge held firm when Richard went back with the second case to increase the rent. Amanda knew there was no repairing the damage the courts had wreaked on what should have been a neighbourly relationship.

Still, Amanda adored Swift Square; it was one of only five intact Georgian squares dotted about Dublin. Sometimes, when the square was silent, she loved to stand on the doorstep and look about. Four storeys of preserved history surrounded them on all sides. Each building had a unique history of its own, and yet the fact that they stood shoulder to shoulder for over two hundred years connected them in an enduring way that added so much to the square that was greater than the sum of all its parts. At its heart, the garden she had set her sights on when she first arrived. It had been a labour of love and at times back-breaking work, but she and a fiery old Italian called Antonio had undertaken a complete restoration of the shared garden. It was worth it. Now, on any given day, it was dotted with flowering shrubs each blooming and giving way for the next colour of the season.

For the last month, standing taller and prouder than any other time of the year, they had decorated the huge conifer that stood in the northernmost point. The decorating had become a square tradition. Some of Amanda's happiest memories with Casper and Robyn were around the dressing of that tree. It dripped with glinting sepia white lights and oversized wooden trinkets depicting the twelve days of Christmas rising up its furry branches to a superb silvery star on top.

In the centre of the garden, there was ample space for kids to kick about a ball or throw Frisbees on a summer's day. There were plenty of dark-stained garden chairs for tired au pairs or gossiping young mothers to watch their little darlings as they played. They kept it locked at night, but even now, looking across at the light frosty haze gathered about it, she felt proud.

The square was home mainly to smart offices these days, but there were a handful of private homes and quite a few basement flats too. Not that Amanda knew all the renters by name, but everyone smiled and acknowledged each other. She felt it was important, so the square held onto that small town feeling that Celtic tiger greed and overzealous development had sucked out of the big city.

Amanda cleared her throat as though she might be getting ready to say something important to the emptiness before her. Perhaps she could say something, about the washing. Amanda peered towards the little flat. The windows at ground level opposite, she knew, were high within the flat. She took a step towards them, gingerly; it was so hard to know what to do, most of the time. If only Richard hadn't insisted on having the court case.

Amanda stood for a moment; perhaps she could get someone in to put up a rotary line in a small corner of the garden. Of course, she'd have to say it to Richard, and really, she already knew what he'd think of that idea.

She wouldn't do it, of course. Not just because she couldn't listen to Richard's tirade. No. Rather, she wouldn't do it, because she knew, that letting Tess into the garden was just giving her another opportunity to bleed her dislike of them even further into their lives. The truth was that she was in the slow lane if it came to a game of tit for tat. Tess Cuffe had all the time in the world to plan a tactical campaign to drive Amanda to sheer distraction, whereas Amanda was a busy woman. She had coffee to drink, lunches to attend, committees to organise, magazines to read, hairdressing appointments and, of course, a husband and family to keep happy.

She was just turning towards the steps to her front door when she heard the porch door open in the basement flat opposite. The sound of it splintered a sneer behind her.

'Measuring up for curtains, are you?' Tess Cuffe cackled as she fingered the washing on her line. She looked towards the grey sky and sighed, as though confirming what she already knew – it was not a day for drying clothes outside. 'Ah, sure, that's lovely for you.'

'No, of course not, I was just…' Amanda didn't look at the woman, eye contact always led to more wrath, but she couldn't help noticing a hard plaster on her hand. If it was anyone but Tess Cuffe, she would have enquired what had happened, but with Tess, such concern could go either way. Honestly, it was more likely to go the wrong way.

'Well, you better put your measuring tape away for a while yet.' She pulled the belt of her unfashionable coat tighter around her middle – everything about Tess seemed bitter to Amanda, from the way her mouth turned sourly down, to her bitten voice; she was irritated by a life she chose only to drift through. Tess was probably pretty, once. She still had the features to whisper that she might have been a stunner in her day. She was tall and graceful and if her anger pushed aside a sunny nature, it couldn't hide the striking colour of her eyes.

'I had no intention of...' Amanda cast a glance about the square uncertainly. The last thing she wanted was to have Tess Cuffe scorning at her again; you never knew quite what she was thinking of you. Perhaps that was the most unsettling thing of all. They'd lived as neighbours for over two decades and Amanda knew so little of this proud and private spinster who still managed to get the better of them, even with all that money could buy on their sides.

'Not content with taking a poor old woman to court, now you're just going to have to wait for me to die, I suppose,' Tess sighed in mock resignation; she enjoyed making Amanda squirm, that much was certain.

'Look here,' Amanda straightened up to her full half-pint size, her voice rising an octave higher than she promised herself it would. 'I'll have you know...' she was eyeballing her now, but of course, there was nothing she could say. Sometimes, Amanda wondered if they could roll back time and start again. Could doing things differently have made things any better? Of course, she'd never mention that to another living soul, it was too late now. She was never going to say that the court case was Richard's idea, or that she would quite happily have let things lie after they had offered to buy her out. She had a feeling Tess would see her wifely support as just more evidence of her not having a brain or backbone of her own. In that way, when Amanda thought about it, they were total opposites – Tess had enough backbone for both of them and plenty to spare. Amanda often wondered if being a good wife always meant surrendering to your husband's wishes, but then she was very lucky with Richard, because he really did know best. And, that was it, there was no point having an argument with Tess Cuffe, because, Amanda knew she wouldn't win. Instead, she turned on her heel and left the woman standing there with her infuriating knowing eyes mocking everything about Amanda. At least in her exquisite, immaculate home, she could pretend Tess Cuff did not exist and her world was just perfect.

2

December 31 – Wednesday

'It's just a scrape, that's all.' Tess hated that her voice sounded so small here. It was the machines of course, buzzing, humming and occasionally beeping, eating up the static silence of her little cubicle. The A&E at St. Mel's city hospital was hushed, ready for impending invasion by the Dublin City revellers, wounded in various, often-unaccountable ways for the sake of *auld lang syne*.

It was New Year's Eve and this was not where she planned to spend it; not that she had any plan at all. It was a long time since Tess had anywhere she wanted to be for New Year's, Christmas, or indeed her birthday. These days she told herself it suited her, but she was too wise not to remember what it was like to be part of something more.

Tess eyeballed the doctor. He was young, maybe a bit of a smart-arse, but she put him in his place when he mispronounced her name and again when he stumbled over her prescription. 'I'm going home now. Either stitch me up, or give me a needle and I'll do it myself.' She swung her legs as smoothly as she could off the trolley that they had allocated to her almost three hours earlier. 'For goodness sake, you'll have all sorts in here soon.'

It was fuss over nothing. So, there was a bit of blood, but nothing broken on this occasion. Tess had tripped, that was all there was to it. A bloody cat wandering through her legs in the dark. It could happen to anyone. Of course, the fact that she had a broken wrist made her look as though she was always in the wars. The broken wrist had occurred just over a month before, but she had been sensible, had the X-ray, got the bandage and gone on her not so merry way. She blamed the damned heavy cast for throwing her off balance. It had made her feel a little light-headed. It had been dark and the last thing she'd expected was to have a cat in her little porch. That was how she'd ended up in here again. For the second time in the same emergency ward; same flipping cat, only this time when she fell she managed to land against the front door and shattered every last piece of glass in the long thin side panel. Nothing broken, this time, but there was plenty of blood and, Tess knew, you couldn't be too careful with old glass. She'd called the bugger every name under the sun; if she got her hands on him there was no telling what she might have done to him. In the ambulance, she'd groaned at her own stupidity and the zealous EMT began to check for everything from aneurism to zinc deficiency. She cursed under her breath, she was just a stupid old woman and there was no cure in this hospital for that particular condition.

'So, you live on your own, Mrs, ah, Miss… Tess?'

'On my own, of course I…' then it dawned on her. They were treating her as if she was in shock, a head injury. They would never let her home if they thought she was on her own. It was the New Year, even if she wasn't inundated with social invitations, she was damned if she was spending it in this place. 'Of course, I don't, my… husband will be so worried about me, so will you let me go home now?' There was never a husband, but there might have been, once, long ago – but then he'd married Nancy and that was that.

'Ah, Tess.' A vaguely familiar-looking older man arrived, clipboard in hand. 'You won't remember me, Dr Kilker, I treated you last time round.' He smirked at the hard plaster on her wrist. She disliked him instantly, had a feeling he knew something she didn't and that just got up her nose. 'So, you've been in the wars again? What was it this time, kissing the ground instead of kicking it?' He moved closer to her, inspected the wound. He smelled of garlic mixed with a hint of tobacco, and aftershave clinging to survive on a ten-hour hospital shift, it drifted from him being so close.

'No, for your information, I was the victim of an intruder,' Tess snapped.

'Half a dozen stitches should see you straight.' He raised a sceptical eyebrow.

'Finally,' Tess grunted towards the younger doctor.

'Now, be a good girl and sit still while I put it right.' Dr Kilker silenced her while he tacked up the wound.

It was infuriating to be spoken to as if she were a child.

'How did you really manage it, Tess?' He asked as he stood back to admire his neat stitches.

'There was a flipping cat in a dark porch; it could happen to the Pope himself.'

'I suppose it could, but then, he's not wearing a cast, is he?' he said lightly. 'No dizziness or blackouts? Nothing odd or strange going on that we should hear about?'

'No, nothing like that.' Tess glared at him. She wasn't stupid. She knew when to see a doctor. 'Maybe just a little too much seasonal cheer for my own good.' She had just had a small nip before she went to lock up the flat for the night.

'Hmm.' From the shuffling, it was obvious none of them could visualise a cheerful Tess, seasonal or otherwise. 'Well, stay away from the brandy bottle until those painkillers wear off.' He handed her a prescription. 'I'll get a few of these to bring home with you, tide you over for a few days, okay?' He counted out a half dozen small white tablets, placed them in a blue container then squinted while he scribbled some illegible instructions on the label. When he finished, he looked at her oddly over reading glasses that perhaps might be fashionable on someone decades younger.

'Oh, I won't need any of those,' Tess said and then felt the blood rush from her head as she sat forward. 'On second thoughts.' She took the pills and folded the prescription into her bag.

'There's definitely someone to take care of you?' Dr Kilker kept his eyes on the notes he was making to her records. 'You'll need to rest well for a day or two, let those stitches knit.'

'Of course I have people to look after me, I'll be tucked up in bed as soon as I get home and then...' She left the words hanging. The truth was that some nights, she settled down on the old sofa in her little flat. Somehow, making the effort of getting ready for bed seemed to be beyond her too often lately. It was as though she was giving in that another day was over, same as the last, same as the next, until one day there would be no more.

One of the nurses suggested diplomatically that older women could be even more exhausted while convalescing; Tess just nodded wordlessly at her. Convalescing was for other people, not for Tess.

'And then, there's the neighbours,' she said as if there was a chance she'd let that snooty wagon from upstairs over her threshold even if Amanda *did* decide to come check that she was still alive.

'Retired yet?' He tapped the pen on her file; she presumed he was looking at her age.

'Not yet, shouldn't you be thinking about it too?' she

said acerbically. Just because he was a doctor did not mean he could take liberties.

'Oh, believe me, I think about it all the time.' He looked around the hectic emergency ward and she caught a weary sound to his words. 'Can't come soon enough.'

'Well for some,' she said. 'They're still putting the finishing touches on my villa in Spain, if you want to know the truth of it,' she shook her head. 'Oh, yes, you'd be surprised at how us old girls plan to live it up when we retire, Dr Kilker.'

'Well, you have to call a halt sometime.' He smiled wryly, before beckoning to an ambulance driver who was just folding up a wheelchair. 'Ted, are you heading back across town now?'

'Yep, no calls, just a nice cup of tea back at the base.' He smiled sadly. Perhaps, without the action of the job, it would be a long and boring night with far too much tea.

'Any chance you'd give Tess a lift,' he looked at her notes again, 'to Swift Square?' He raised an eyebrow, as though he was familiar with the place, then smiled sadly when he caught her eye.

'Sure.' Ted put out a hand to steady her before she got to her feet.

'I'm well able to walk, young man.' Tess saw Dr Kilker smile as she shrugged off the help. The distraction caught her off balance and in what felt like a slow-motion exaggerated dance move she ended up falling clumsily on her bottom.

'Ah, Tess, I'm afraid you're staying here for the night.' The words floated about over her head; she blamed the painkillers this time round.

The city bells woke her at midnight. New Year's Eve. Well, this was a first. She'd never spent it in hospital before. Looking on the bright side, it turned out, she was not alone for the ringing in of the new, even if her company were all old biddies snoring loudly and unaware that they had made it into the next year, albeit, if from the sounds of some of them, it could be their last.

Tess yanked herself up higher in the bed. She looked out across the Dublin rooftops. It was surreal to see the city so quiet, and as if on cue, a loud bang heralded the start of a twenty minute fireworks' display. She had never watched the festivities before. Usually, Tess made sure she was fast asleep before people could get too nostalgic. Anyway, she was a morning person – liked to get a start at the day.

Now, watching each exploding colour bomb hit the inky sky, she regretted missing them over the years. They really were quite beautiful. Intoxicating.

She heard the thrum of modern loud music and the roars and claps from the city dwellers when the last golden burst faded into the smoky black night. Then, the oddest thing, she started to cry. This was not a raging upset, but more of a slow-releasing sadness at how her life had turned out. She was truly alone – not a friend to call on her over the Christmas holidays. No one missed her for ten whole days. At the various offices around the city, she'd temped in on and off for the last few years, they hadn't even sent a card or enquired how she was when she returned. Her wages just arrived in her bank account. Ten days she'd not turned up. The agency had just replaced her – and nobody had noticed anything different. She was an old woman now. She was only sixty-six, which was nothing these days. Women her age were winning marathons, running countries, and doing all sorts of marvellous things all over the world. She was younger than Meryl Streep for God's sake. Tess knew, though, that those women were not like her. They had young hearts, souls that sang with love and joy. It was many years since Tess had known what it was to be moved by passion for something that filled her soul. These last few weeks, she realised that she was, to all extents, invisible – could it be that she had allowed herself to become sidelined in her own life? That seemed neither possible nor practical, and yet, it had become an overwhelming sense within her. No one noticed if she didn't turn up, apart from the plants that she watered each day, because if she didn't, she believed no one else would. She temped in offices throughout the heart of the business centre in Dublin. Tidied up the mess left behind by the bright young things that couldn't quite manage to get their work completed. She found it mind-numbingly dull, of course, but she had shown up and for too many years to count, it was all she had to push her into each new day.

In this moment, Tess, all alone in the world, knew that it had been too long since she had loved. It was two score and more since she felt the kind of joy that she knew with certainty was still outside that window tonight.

What if it wasn't too late to change things? She considered herself a brave and resilient woman; was she courageous enough to turn things around, if there was time? And how on earth would she go about it? It was time to take a good hard look at her life.

In the near silence of the hospital ward, the only punctuating sounds were easily drowned to quiet when Tess began to sit up and think. This unease, this gulf that had become her whole existence, wasn't just about taking stock of herself, it was her health, her happiness. Could she honestly move forward if she didn't first resolve the harm done in the past?

God, Tess shuddered. She couldn't go back.

There was Nancy, the sister that she'd treasured. Her parents, long dead now, she never really said goodbye. And then, of course, there was Douglas, the man she had so prized, all those years ago. It was a love that cost too much in the end. Should she have let it steal her life away? That thought jolted her now, or was it the sound of some buzzer, muted and unending far off, letting nurses know that they were needed once again? Tess knew, with the certainty of time and sudden blinding clarity, that was what she'd done. She'd allowed life to slip through her fingers, just a little with each passing year, until the gossamers of time had pulled so finally away that it was almost too late to make anything of what was left.

How could someone who started with so much have ended up with so little in life? Tess had an uncomfortable feeling that learning the truth of this might be the only way to make a life that was worth something more than another decade of loneliness.

Tess knew with certainty, in this moment, surrounded by women who were much older than she was, they would give their false teeth to have another ten years before them. She should have that, and surely, if she had, then she just had to try to make things up?

3

January 1 – Thursday

She shook her head; she hated parties, especially parties like this. She was an outsider and she wanted to go home. Amanda dodged a friend's husband who was dancing a little too amorously with one of the new office juniors. Bankers, thank God her Richard was not like that! It was irrational, of course, this panic rising up inside her. Richard had booked a room for the night, planned it all out. It would be a great night, he assured her as he sauntered off to schmooze some corporate bigwig, and she hadn't seen him since. She rang in the New Year, essentially alone, surrounded by people, none of whom mattered to her, nor, she suspected, she to them.

Her mind wandered home for most of the night, it was where she wanted to be on this last night of the year. She'd made muffins for the kids, well, kids? Casper and Robyn were sixteen and fourteen now, but they were kids to her. Before she left, she'd set out a midnight feast for them. She'd wondered, as she heard the ringing in of the New Year if they heard it also, or were they too submerged in whatever social media that pulled them ever further away from her to even notice. It seemed all wrong, to be standing on a terrace watching fireworks burst open the night sky; to be here surrounded by strangers, because essentially, that was what they were. Richard's work colleagues, their *friends*. To Amanda's mind, friends were people you counted on, not competitors you strove against. It was a long time since Amanda could call the people closest to her 'friends' in that old-fashioned sense.

She sighed, drained the champagne glass in her hand. It was still cool, which meant, she was probably drinking too fast. It would also account for the melancholy, wouldn't it? On the vista ranged about below the roof terrace, Amanda looked across at St. Mel's hospital, it seemed to shine ever brighter in the dancing brilliance of the city fireworks display. Perhaps, she thought, the celebrations might be watched from there too, marking out the end of one year and the start of the new. For a moment, she imagined, not so much a line of starched and kindly nurses, but rather, some old biddy in a bed, watching this display. The notion stirred something in her, as if she'd forgotten some important detail, but there was nothing she could recollect, so she put it down to too much champagne and resolved to walk about the grounds.

Anyway, it was no good regretting coming here at this stage, she thought as she walked around the front of the hotel. It was the best in Dublin – five big shiny stars, the kind of place that would import yak's milk from Angola if that were what you wanted in your tea. Surely, a taxi should be easy. She wanted to go home.

She turned on her ridiculously high heels and caught sight of herself in the polished glass opposite. For a second she didn't recognise herself. She actually nodded towards the dumpy little woman, with absurd copper rouge hair piled too high on her head. She stood transfixed, once she realised it was her own reflection. She studied the woman staring back at her with her expensive clothes and too much make-up. Amanda King was under there, somewhere. Her breath caught in her throat, she had been lovely, once. Where was that girl she used to know? A petite, porcelain-skinned girl with blue eyes and golden brown hair – what had happened to her? When had she become this primped and preened middle-aged hag? Of course, the real question was why she was trying so hard to be someone that she knew deep down she wasn't. Amanda wasn't willing to ask herself that question, because all of a sudden, she knew that if she looked at her life honestly, the foundations were rotting beneath her. Everyone knew, a house could only stand for so long on bad foundations. At the same time, Amanda wasn't sure what was wrong, apart from this deep-seated sense of dread that it was all about to start tumbling down around her. Maybe, if she held her breath, covered the cracks with expensive clothes, holidays and house makeovers, she might just make it to the finish line and everything would be fine.

'Hello, miss, are you okay?' She felt the steadying arm of the night porter at her back.

'I'm fine, just a little…' She looked into his concerned eyes. He was a short man, Asian, perhaps from the Philippines. 'Too much…' She fanned her face, felt that creeping heat travel towards her forehead, bringing with it a prickly rush of dread, she wanted to go home. She needed to get away from here, it was an irrational feeling of panic, but she would set out walking if she had to, just to make it back to her own house. 'I want to go home,' her voice sounded high-pitched, nervy even to herself. 'I need to get home, my children, you see, there's…' then she realised, this man was not interested in Casper and Robyn. In all likelihood, he just wanted to make sure the sad middle-aged woman did not keel over on the hotel steps. 'Can I get a taxi? Can you get a taxi to bring me home?'

'Of course, Madam, I will organise a taxi for you. Will you sit inside? To wait?' He put out his hand, gesturing for her to lead the way back into the hotel. 'Do you need to tell someone that you're leaving?'

'Richard?' she said his name as though it might steady her. 'My husband. I'll send him a text, there's no need for him to leave. It's a great party,' she lied. She was regaining some of her composure now. The reflection opposite helped in some dreadful way to sober and straighten her up. There was no point in calling Richard away. He would assume she'd left the party and headed off to bed. She could text him later and let him know that all was well. She had a feeling he wouldn't miss her for hours yet anyway. 'I'll just wait here, if that's all right.' She heard him scurrying back into the hotel to organise a car for her.

The taxi sped and it took only ten minutes to get home. The roads were clear. Amanda sat back and let the tired Christmas decorations wash over her. It seemed as if the twinkling lights had slowed down in preparation for their long rest until the following Christmas. Already, in the shops, January sales posters were tired, welcomed first, but soon ignored by greedy bargain hunters, gluttonous for more things that would all too soon be cast aside for new season fabulousness. Of course, it didn't make you happy, Amanda had known that before she married Richard. Tonight, she thought perhaps that everything had lost its sparkle just a little, was she getting too old for Christmas? It felt as though all of Dublin had gone home and decided to put a lock on December 31, to start a fresh new beginning tomorrow.

Amanda sank back even further in the cab to avoid catching glimpses of her reflection against the deserted streets. She had an odd sensation, as though suddenly she had come face-to-face with an ultimatum. As though, in that mirror image she saw everything about her life as it really was rather than how she pretended it was. Of course, she would wake tomorrow in her elegant townhouse, surrounded by her perfect family and they would settle into a new year and everything would go on as usual.

God, but here, in the anonymity of a Dublin taxi, that thought completely depressed her. What was she missing? Perhaps it was the change? It was time, after all.

She pulled out her phone, she would send Richard a text, explain that she had to leave, that she wasn't feeling well. He wouldn't mind too much, after all, it was *his* work do; she wasn't even sure if he'd wanted her there to begin with. She'd only tagged along to stop the other wives from talking about her behind her back. She sent the text, quickly, then she realised, she hadn't brought a key for the front door. The car keys were back at the hotel, in the room, beside the minibar. She'd have to ring the house, make sure the kids hadn't gone to bed yet so they could let her in.

'Hello, Robyn,' her daughter answered just as the second ring sounded. Robyn never missed a call.

'Hi, Mum, is everything all right,' her daughter shouted above the din of frenetic music, thumps and shouts of a teenage party on her daughter's end of the line. Panic prickled Amanda's skin, as though it was rolling over her, the champagne keeping it at bay, just for now. Her children should be tucked up in bed; they should be sleeping soundly in their grand Georgian townhouse on Swift Square.

'Robyn, what's going on there, I thought…?' Amanda heard a girl shriek in the background. God, they were having a party, in her lovely home, in Richard's house, dread tightened, catching the breath in her lungs, as if it was an arctic vice about Amanda.

'Mum…' Robyn sounded as if she was moving away from the girl and closer to the throb of base music. Christ, Richard would go ballistic if he knew. Amanda could see it all, in her mind's eye: teenagers shagging in every dark corner they could find, her lovely newly shampooed rugs covered in cheap red wine or cider, maybe that cloying smell of weed that he'd recognise immediately from long gone free and easy days. Oh, God, it'd take weeks to set the place to rights again, one night wouldn't be enough time to sort it out. Then, a sickly knot tightened in her stomach, Tess Cuffe would just love holding this one over them. Amanda wouldn't put it past that woman to call the guards. Could they be prosecuted for abandoning their children on New Year's Eve?

'Is everything all right?' Amanda felt a dribble of sweat race down her neck. She imagined it soaking into the unfortunate red satin gown that cost a fortune and still didn't fit properly. She couldn't give a fig about the gown now. 'Is Casper there?' In some ways, better if they were in Ronan's house, at least then she could just get them back, and….

'Mum, everything is fine.' Casper, her sixteen-year-old son, definitely sounded off when he snatched the phone from his sister. 'We're here, at home, where you left us. Enjoy your party, there's nothing to worry about.'

'Have you been drinking?' Amanda tried to keep the terror from her voice, but feared her lungs might implode between the cocktail of apprehension and the rush of cold night air now she'd opened the taxi window.

'Not exactly.'

She knew what that meant.

'Is Ronan there?'

'Yeah, he's here, somewhere,' Casper's voice moved away from the phone, in the background, as though looking for the friend she had for so long wished he'd grow out of. 'Why?' They both knew why. Ronan's parents were 'creatives' and Ronan smoked weed as other kids chewed gum.

'I'm on my way home, Casper.' She hung up the phone too mad to keep up a conversation, too scared to put into words what would happen if Richard thought they'd invited a load of kids to party and puke about his trophy home. She needed to make sure that her kids hadn't burned the house down. Worse, that they hadn't managed to kill half the kids from school with weed or the contents of the drinks cabinet. Had they pulled the house apart? Were two teenagers that she'd never met, at this moment, making out on her lovely French empire bed, crumpling and soiling her carefully constructed impeccable world? Had they emptied her expensive wine rack, knocking back bottles of prosecco until they were vomiting all over her Persian rugs?

She became aware of the thrumming again in her chest – it had been happening for months now. Her GP said it was anxiety, which was just crazy. After all, what did she have to be anxious about? Life was good, wasn't it? Well, she had to tell herself that now; otherwise, she'd go mad. The only thing that was truly hammering through her was the fear of what was waiting for her when she got to Swift Square.

But there was no party.

The house was in total darkness when she arrived and that unnerved her more than if there had been a hundred teenagers camped out in the garden. Where were her lovely twinkly Habitat lights? She looked up at the large drawing room window, dead centre above the front door. It was pitch black, as though there wasn't a soul nearby, never mind a light in the window. Where was her fabulous imported Scottish fir that she had dressed so carefully in Newbridge silver trinkets and candle-effect fairy lights? Amanda took great care with the Christmas decorations. Walking the fine line between generous and gaudy was always tricky, but she thought she managed to get the balance just right.

Her decorations all operated off a central timer, but in the event of them leaving the house, she had drilled in the basic safety rules. Unswitch, Unplug and Lock Up. The kids were rhyming it off before they even went to school. Robyn, was fanatical about it, Casper, not so much, but then, he was a boy.

The square brooded in an apocalyptic silence that made her panic even more. What was she going to do? Where were her children? She was locked out of her own house and her children were missing? God, but she was a terrible mother, first day of the New Year, what a way to start off? Her eyes trained up towards the first floor. A rustling movement in the shrubbery made her start, breaking the silence shortly about her. Amanda jumped back only to realise that it was just a cat, a big grey thing mooching about in the dark. 'Shoo. Shoo.' That cat was a complete menace. Robyn had always wanted a cat, had kicked up a real stink when she was younger to try to force them into getting one. It was out of the question of course, Richard hated animals. The memory made Amanda dislike the cat before her even more intensely. She hissed at it, but it strode past her in no particular hurry, and somehow, she got the impression even *it* knew that she wasn't really worth worrying about.

She paid the taxi driver, tipped him well for his trouble, then ran up the stone steps, heard her heels narrow sounding, as if they might easily crack beneath the weight of her heavy mood. She stopped for a moment before battering the door, she knew that her children were not here. Her home was empty. She could feel it as clearly as one does when they know they are completely alone. She wasn't sure how long she rapped on that door, but she kept going until her tears and panic had mixed so thoroughly that when the door below her swung open, she threw herself down the steps as though Tess Cuffe was the answer to all her prayers.

Except, Tess Cuffe wasn't there, it was just her door, left open and swinging on a rogue breeze.

As if the night could get any worse, she felt the crunch of broken glass beneath her feet. Reaching into her bag, she pulled out her phone again, slid down the menu so she could use it as a torch. The side panel window, as old as the porch itself, was shattered. It lay in smithereens in a splintered carpet, tracing out onto the little paved area before the door. She checked the inside door, it was locked and Amanda was certain that the flat was every bit as empty as her house upstairs. It seemed that everyone wanted to be somewhere else tonight except Amanda.

With a sudden sobering thought, Amanda knew, it was just as well Tess Cuffe was not at home. This damage could be cleared away in the morning. It was probably the work of some ne'er-do-wells, cutting a short cut through the square as they made their way home, with nothing more to do than throw stones or pitch themselves at doorways. For a fleeting moment, she realised that she hadn't worried that Tess Cuffe might be in some kind of danger. It seemed to her that Tess was the indomitable type, indestructible no matter what the trouble. Amanda leaned up towards the window, peered through the darkness, but could see nothing. There was no sign of her brown coat at least, hanging in its usual sentry position at the door. The only time that coat left its station was on Tess Cuffe's back and Amanda could not think of a time she'd seen the woman outside without it. She must have gone away for the holidays, she thought. Well, that was unusual, wasn't it? When she thought about it, Amanda never gave much consideration to what Tess did for holidays. It wasn't her concern after all, as she would have been all too quick to tell her so if she asked.

God knows, if she had been there, Amanda would have happily thrown herself at the woman's mercy if Tess could conjure Casper and Robyn back safely. Walking up towards her own front door, she pulled out her phone, dialled Robyn again. This time, across the square somewhere; she heard the familiar ringtone of her daughter's phone. Thank God, she thought as Robyn picked up the call. Thank God.

'We're here,' Robyn's voice came through, normal, calm; it reassured her now, because she knew her worst fears had not played out.

Then they were standing opposite her and Amanda

couldn't stop crying, but it was with relief as much as anything else. The fact that they'd lied, by omission, seemed so small now compared to the possibilities that had been running through her head earlier. Casper ran up the steps before them, his mood was black, but Amanda didn't care. Her children were home; she was where she belonged. She wanted cake, she needed cake, but she knew she could not have cake, not until she sorted out Casper and Robyn.

'Seriously, Mum, listen to yourself. It was just a party, everyone was there,' Casper said before she even got round to mentioning the lies, she knew he wanted to stomp off, the only thing stopping him was the fear that she might tell their father.

'That's not the point, you never asked, you never even mentioned it. What if there had been a fire or a…'

'Mum, there's never going to be a fire. Can't you see, our lives are so bubble-wrapped we are more likely to drown from the sprinkler system before any fire has a chance to get to us,' Casper huffed.

'Have you taken something, smoked something or…'

He sounded different, not like her lovely curly-haired boy. And he had been lovely, all dark curls, rosy cheeks and mischievous smiles.

'I'm bloody sixteen years old,' he was shouting and she could hear him becoming more and more like his father with every passing moment. 'What do you bloody think?' He was standing at the kitchen door, filling the space that so recently had framed him; not so long ago he had looked tiny in its grand surround.

'Casper, you can't speak to me like that… it's…' But her words caught in her throat. Her breath felt like it had trapped somewhere in the bottom of her stomach, so she stood there with her mouth open. Robyn just watched her with pity in her eyes, and then she sighed sadly before disappearing up the stairs. 'Robyn,' she called after her daughter, but all she heard was the gentle click of her bedroom door upstairs.

'What is it? Rude? Cheeky?' Casper brought his face up to hers so she could smell cigarettes on his breath, and for a moment, she wondered if he might hit her.

'It's not the way we talk in this house,' and as the words came out she heard them and she knew they made no sense. 'I mean, I'm not the enemy here, Casper, we're…' She stepped back from him a little, felt her voice become smaller, as though it was just about the size of a matchstick against his fearsome teenage anger.

'It was just a party, Mum, everyone was there.'

'So, why didn't you say that you wanted to go? I would have allowed you, if there was an adult there, someone responsible.' Of course, if it was in Ronan's house – the adults had even less sense than the kids.

'Oh, go eat another muffin, Mother, it's what you do best,' Casper said and then he ran towards the downstairs loo.

She heard him, inside, retch pathetically.

'Okay, so I'm drunk, ground, me,' he said, stalking past her when he'd finished.

'Casper, you can't talk to me like that,' she said, 'what's the matter with you? Don't you realise if your father had any idea that you'd come back in this state, he'd…' Her voice drifted off, because, really, what she wanted more than anything else was for her little boy to throw his arms around her as he'd done so often years before.

'My father? That's a laugh,' he shrieked manically, as if he might completely lose his grip. 'My father couldn't give a toss about any of us and you're the only one around here who can't see it.'

'You're grounded,' Amanda shouted, but Casper was already slamming the kitchen door behind him so her voice hardly wafted up the stairs to catch his angry step. Instead, she felt his derision echoing throughout the whole house. She dropped into the uncomfortable Scandinavian designer high stool that Richard picked to go with the distressed kitchen benches. She really couldn't decide which was worse, Casper's terrifying anger or the fact that his words had struck some invisible understanding within her.

4

Forty-eight years ago...

'It's perfect,' Tess said and she nudged Nancy in the side. Nancy hadn't said a word since they arrived on Swift Square. Probably, it was a combination of the decrepit state of the buildings and the poverty pervading even the stringy smoke rising from houses too big to find heat in just one miserable fire. Neither had expected the Ritz. No doubt, it had been grand – once.

Swift Square was situated on the right side of the city, but a hundred years of tenements and a lack of genuine fondness for the ubiquitous Georgian architecture had laid it prone. It was anyone's guess whether it would survive to glory once more or limp wounded into the annals of city history.

Tess loved its faded opulence, the houses, four storeys over basements, hung back like chiselled old men from a placid age. In the centre, a garden, perfectly square, the size of a playing field cut out into allotments, and in the afternoon sunshine, she could see threads of blackberries interlacing through the rusting railings.

Reaching up and over, apple trees gravid with this year's unripe hoard swayed gently on a late summer breeze.

Tess pulled her eyes back to the tall house that Aunt Beatrice had given them directions to. It was like every other house on the square, a little better, but no worse than most, the only difference seemed to be a small porch reaching out to welcome them on the drive beneath the main front door. It seemed the basement flat Aunt Beatrice had promised them was at ground level, the house built one floor up from the common hordes.

'Yes, it's...' Nancy was squinting at the darkened windows. 'It'll do just fine, I'm sure.' She sounded anything but sure. It was nothing like their home in Ballycove – a solid block, double-fronted, with a trailing footpath through the small garden to the road.

'Well, it's yours for as long as you want it,' Ted Smith lived up the stone steps, behind the once grand front door. 'I remember your aunt so well...' he said, smiling now at Tess. 'You're like her; you know that... she was a bonny girl, then.' He shook his head, as though remembering some long-told joke again. Then he handed them two fat black keys and pointed towards the little door opposite. 'You'll find it has everything you need for basic living, nothing fancy mind, but it should keep you going and it's a roof above your heads at any rate,' he said, making his way back up the steps.

'Aunt Beatrice could certainly pick them,' Nancy whispered when he closed the front door with a bang.

Tess thought the whole place had a faded bohemian look to it, but she decided not to murk the waters of Nancy's mood with any fanciful notions that might put her off even more.

'Come on, I'm dying to see inside,' Tess said. She'd never been in a grand Georgian house before and they'd be moving in properly in a week's time.

'I suppose, we do have things to do,' Nancy said half-heartedly. Today, their father had sent them on a mission to make a list of what they'd need to turn it into a home. In a few days' time, he would pack up all they needed in the back of their Ford Anglia and settle them in to their new lives.

'It feels like it hasn't been opened in a very long time,' Tess said as they pushed aside the porch door. She inserted her key into the inside lock of a once navy door that had faded to blue and was peeling slowly away.

'Well, we won't be bored, at least,' Nancy said and Tess was glad to hear some of her sister's resolve returning. 'Before you know it, we'll have that door looking as good as new,' she added, smiling at Tess.

Inside was every bit as dark and dusty as Tess had feared and she hesitated for a moment at the entrance to the main living area. 'It's very…' Then she caught Nancy's eye and they both laughed.

'It'll be okay, nothing that a bit of elbow grease can't

fix,' Nancy said, probably with far more enthusiasm than she felt and Tess loved her even more for it. 'We're not going to let a few spiders' webs finish your career before you even get a chance to start.'

'Oh, Nancy,' Tess felt for once as though she really was the younger of the pair. 'It will be great,' she ducked her head to avoid a particularly thick web. 'It's a lovely flat, once you look past the neglect.' Tess meant it, there was an unexpected homeliness about the place.

Of two small bedrooms at the front of the flat, one opened onto the main hall, the second into what seemed to Tess a large room that doubled up as a living room and kitchen – she could imagine blazing fires and hot chocolate here in winter, cosy and cocooned from the busy city beyond. At the rear, a small scullery and bathroom that smelled of mould and felt cold and damp, but even that was not enough to quell her pleasure. She walked to the furthest end of the living room and opened up the sash window, it looked out onto a long ribbon of garden, far more generous than their meagre strip at home. Immediately, a wafting fresh breeze began to infiltrate the years of stale neglect.

'Look,' Nancy called from the little scullery, 'we can start straight away. There's enough polish and soap here to clean the Taj Mahal.' She planted a sweeping brush in Tess's hands, 'Come on, you're not a famous singer yet, you can take the cobwebs from the ceilings and sweep up the floors.' She was running water across some old cleaning cloths, her eyes bright with the intention of making this little corner of Dublin a new and happy home for both of them.

They worked hard that day, but they hardly noticed that. They giggled their way through the work and, when the laughter halted, Tess sang whatever tune Nancy called to her. Soon it was almost five o'clock, their first day in their new flat over and so they finished up with barely enough time to make it to the train station.

'Thanks,' Tess said as they walked arm in arm along the platform, elated but tired from their busy day.

'Oh, don't be daft,' Nancy laughed, but then looked across at Tess. 'You know, this could work out very well for both of us. The last thing I want is our father coming down here and telling us it's all off because the flat is not suitable.'

'Do you really mean that?' Tess said. 'You're not just saying that because you want me to be able to take up my place in Trinity.'

'No,' Nancy smiled at her now, 'no, I really do mean it. I'm looking forward to this, in my own way maybe as much as you are.' She drew to a halt, for a moment, looked into Tess's eyes. 'The truth is, Tess, I've realised something…'

'Go on.'

'Well, I look at you and you're so… alive, where as I… well, I'm just wandering through life. I'm hoping that here, in Dublin, well, it might help me find something that really means something to me.'

'Like my music?'

'Perhaps, but it won't be music for me. I have a feeling that there's something, or someone, that I have to find and I'm not going to find whatever or whoever that is in Ballycove,' Nancy said shyly.

'Oh, Nancy,' Tess threw her arms around her sister, delighted that perhaps at last she was ready to take a brave step towards fashioning a future of her own making. That Nancy could have something that might offer more than all she'd ever known, it was all Tess could want for her sister. 'I'm so pleased. I have a feeling that you'll find it very easily and the future is going to hold all either of us can dream of.'

5

January 1 – Thursday

On first sight, it seemed Dr Kilker was still wearing the same shirt when he walked into the ward the next morning. Tess presumed it wasn't the same, because he smelled of aftershave and he looked as though he was the newly pressed, fresher version of the man from hours before. He also looked as if he'd rather be anywhere but on duty for the first day of the New Year.

'Morning, Tess,' he didn't lift his eyes from the notes before him. 'You've had two nasty falls – any woman falling about the place for no reason would want to know what was the cause of it.'

'Well, I feel fine now.' There was no point mentioning the blasted cat again, he had more to tell her, blood tests and urine samples don't lie.

'I'm sure you do. I've always thought the benefits of a good night's sleep are undervalued.' He scribbled something across Tess's notes and studied her. 'You know when you arrived here last night, your blood pressure was dangerously low? I don't need to tell you how serious having a stroke is, do I?' He sighed, perhaps he thought she would ignore him no matter what he said. 'You know, you're coming to an age where soon it'll be too late to change the course of your health. It's a new year, Tess, it might be an opportunity to take your health in hand before you are arriving back here with complaints that are not so easily cured.'

'Of course, I know, it's time to start cutting down on the finer things in life and moving about more...' Tess had heard it a million times already – indirect little comments, but all the same, she was a grown woman, she knew how to look after herself.

'Tess, this is serious,' his eyes bored into her. 'I know some doctors shy away from mentioning the fact that it's time to change things around. It's amazing, in a country that's marching towards an obesity epidemic, everyone talks around the problem. Mostly, I have a feeling that they are waiting until the patient develops diabetes or gout or take your pick of a plethora of other grim conditions.' He dropped down onto the chair beside her bed, lowered his voice. 'It's very simple, Tess. You have known for some time you have low blood pressure. Your own doctor has prescribed hefty medication. If you don't clean up your act, you are going to have a stroke and the reality is that could be any day now. And, if there's no one there to get you to the hospital...' He shook his head but his eyes silently conveyed more than any words could.

It was the truth. Tess had seen too many doctors and nurses dodge saying it.

'Of course, you're right; I've known it for a while.' There was no point arguing what was plain to see. Tess was a biscuit eater and a sitter. The one contributed to her high sugar levels the other to a telltale ribbon of additional belly that everyone knew was a marker for heart-related problems.

'Well, it's no good just knowing it, you have to do something about it, or mark my words, you'll be back here much sooner than you think and a stroke isn't as easily mended as a couple of stitches or a cast.' Dr Kilker looked at her for a moment too long.

'I can't help but think I know you from somewhere,' she heard her voice, soft and delicate on the sterile ward between them. It seemed so fragile, she wondered if it could be hers at all. 'Have we met before?' It was his eyes, they were drawing her back to the past, but she couldn't tell to where.

'You tell me,' he said and set off upon his rounds again with an infuriating smile that had not been there before.

The first day of the New Year might have been any other day, apart from the fluttery feeling in her stomach, when Tess left the hospital. They organised a taxi to bring her back to Swift Square. Moving determinedly, she decided that she would do something today. Something to mark out the first day of a new year, make a list or a resolution, or maybe both, if the painkillers didn't kick in soon.

Someone had boarded up the glass that shattered the evening before. They'd even swept up all the smithereens that she was certain must have spilled across the cobbles Mrs Snooty had insisted on laying right up to her front door. Tess looked about the square. She couldn't imagine Amanda or Richard King down here boarding up her windows, even less could she see them, hands clad in marigolds, sweeping up the shards of glass. Perhaps she had a guardian angel? She scoffed at that, must be the tablets – she decided. Sure they say painkillers can do mad things to the most sane minds.

The porch, when she let herself in, held that heavy air of home, the kind of aroma that marks out where you belong, mixed with a seasoning of neglect, because she'd left so abruptly. Her eyes were drawn upstairs, towards the Kings' above. They'd bloody love it if she went and died. That would be just so flipping convenient for la-di-dah Amanda, wouldn't it? She'd be in here in a flash, a one-woman decoration team, measuring up and ripping out before Tess had a chance to cool in her coffin. Well, damn that for a dozen tea scones – she wouldn't give them the satisfaction of dying yet. No, she flipping wouldn't, she would start walking, crawling if she had to. She would be a model of good health in no time.

She'd see the pair of them out, if it was her last piece of lovely revenge, she'd out-blasted-live those two yuppies.

In the little porch, she stopped for a moment before the faded mirror that hung there long before she had arrived to live here. She looked terrible, the mad stepsister, Frankenstein forgot to introduce to the world. Her face was a swollen mass of yellow, purple, blue and black bruises from her fall the night before. Across her forehead, they had placed a large gauze bandage to keep an oozing bruise in check. Her hair stood grey, white and brittle high from her scalp as though she had just been electrically shocked. Her icy blue eyes had the watery sad look that she remembered in her aunt Beatrice's. She was what her mother would have called a fine strong woman; towering and straight-backed, hard to believe, but she had been elegant, once. It was only in the last two decades that her frame had widened. She had settled into herself, lost the lanky look of her youth. She looked at her mouth, set in a determined line. She was not a smiler – perhaps she should try it, at this stage she had nothing to lose. She gave it a go. Just quivers at the corners, pulled her lips up further either side. It felt strange. It looked strange. Maybe, if she practised, a little. She peered closer. God – this smiling lark could be wearing. No. She would try something else. In that moment, Tess remembered she had smiled once. It seemed, suddenly that in her youth, she smiled all the time – perhaps she had used up her quota.

The day dragged and by half past three, because she had nothing better to do, Tess took down a writing set she never used and held her pen above the page to start.

She hadn't made a New Year's resolution, in… probably fifty years. The very idea had always seemed so absurd. Tess was not the kind of woman to think of turning over new leaves, pulling up socks or sweeping clean with new brooms. Her life just ambled along, some might say spiralled downwards, but she was still here. She sighed now, she had to start somewhere, that annoying Dr Kilker suggested exercise.

So, number one… God, this was harder than she'd thought.

Now, no dithering…

Tess got up from her chair, walked around the little flat, she felt a cold sweat film on her hands. What was wrong with her? It was just a piece of paper. She wrote things down every day, well, other people's words, typed and printed off, but still. Damn it, the harder it was, the more it seemed she had to make some effort. Did she want to make a change or not?

Yes, she most certainly did. Right, and so she wrote:

I will go for a walk each day. I will not miss my walk, even if it means getting wet or having to put up with irritating over-friendly news-bags who may assume I wish to keep them company. I will tell them to go away. Even if I am tired or hungry or in dire need of resuscitation, I will go for a walk around the square garden just so I can outlive the pair of them upstairs and pay my ten-bob rent to their surely awful offspring!

Gosh, she was getting into the swing of things. Of course, you had to do three, didn't you? Just two more to go and that thought filled her with the kind of dread an alcoholic must have surely felt on all Good Fridays when the pubs were closed.

The second one was much easier than the first.

Number two:

I will try to eat healthier foods and give up on biscuits with my tea.

Only one to go, she thought as she drifted off into a lovely afternoon snooze.

It was evening when she woke, the darkness of the square outside seeping in through windows a little too high for their lowered rooms. It wasn't the darkness that woke her though, and it took a second to get her bearings. Outside, it was the sound of a tin being lightly tapped, a murmuring as though someone was creeping about just beyond the porch.

Tess got to her feet as quickly as her dizzy brain would allow. Her legs were extra heavy, her body still catching up on her common sense.

'Here, puss, puss.' Near one of the large winter shrubs, Robyn King was scrabbling in the dark.

'What on earth are you doing there?' Tess hissed at her. 'You're lucky I didn't call the bloody guards.'

'Sorry, Mrs Cuffe,' the girl said and she made her way towards the porch.

'Is that bloody cat yours?' Tess pointed at the object of all her recent troubles. 'You can count your blessings I'm not the litigious type. I could sue you for that thing. I'm fortunate to be alive, he's a menace.' She began to close the door, then saw something in the girl's eye.

'I'm sorry, Mrs Cuffe, he's not my cat, but...' She put down a bowl of stinking cat meat and, for a moment, when Tess looked closely, she thought, *that furry nuisance is probably eating better than I am*. 'He belongs to the O'Hara's, I can't think how he's here on the square, they always book him into a cattery when they go on holidays, but this time...' She looked up towards the austere King residence overhead.

'Your mother isn't a cat person, is she?' It was too good – this girl, Robyn was babysitting a cat and trying to hide it from her mother. Tess loved the idea of getting one over on Amanda, even if she could have happily throttled this cat when he'd landed her in an ambulance only yesterday.

'Well, not my mother, but my father hates them and I suppose, by extension, that means my mother isn't going to be keen either – united front and all that.' Robyn shrugged her shoulders.

'So, you've taken him on, until the O'Hara's come back?'

'Well, he's a house cat. I don't know how he'd survive if someone didn't look out for him.' She looked down now at the cat, then muttered something that Tess didn't quite catch.

'Excuse me?'

'How's your arm?' Robyn asked.

'How does it look?' Tess eyed her now.

'Mummified?

'Nobody likes a smarty-pants, young lady,' Tess shot at her.

'Sorry,' the girl said, studying the pavement. 'I'm sorry about your fall. I told Mum, about the glass, you know, but it'll take a few days to get it replaced.'

'Did you…' Tess looked at the girl now. 'Is it you I have to thank for cleaning up the mess?' Of course, it stood to reason, it wouldn't be the mother. That kind of work would be beneath Amanda King.

'Oh, Mrs Cuffe, you don't have to thank me.'

'Well, I suppose it was decent of you all the same,' Tess harrumphed, oddly touched by an act of kindness that there would be no payment for.

'To be honest, I figured we wouldn't see you for a few days and I was afraid that Margaret might cut her feet.'

'Margaret?'

'Margaret, well, I should say, she might cut her paws.'

'Well, if it's that cat I've fallen over twice,' Tess pointed at her bruised face, 'she's a bloody scourge; it might be considered just desserts.' Of course she didn't mean it, the poor cat couldn't help being from the big house next door.

'You wouldn't want to see that? I think she's adorable.' Robyn looked out into the traffic before turning her innocent face towards Tess. 'I'd give anything to take her in, but...'

'No, well, they don't really go with fancy finery like you have in your house. I've never seen a deep-pile carpet yet that was improved with cat spray.' Although, for ten cents, Tess thought, she'd love to lock the cat inside Amanda King's pristine home and let her loose on her expensive carpets and curtains.

'Well, someone has to look after her, while they've gone.' Robyn held up a small shopping bag, 'Cat food,' she said triumphantly.

'Well I must say, you're doing a fine job. He's probably got more in his bowl than I have in my fridge.'

'I don't mind running to the shop for you. You know, if you need to rest over the holidays.'

'Hmph,' Tess said, because of all the things she'd expected at this stage in life, Robyn King caring that she was okay was probably the furthest down the list. Tess cleared her throat, she wasn't going to let on that it meant anything, though, not to a King, that was for sure. 'So, where are you feeding her exactly, anywhere near my front door, by any chance?' It would explain how the blessed thing was always in the way.

'Not now. No, I'm going to have to put out her

food somewhere else.' Robyn looked at her again, the penny suddenly dropping, 'Because I'm afraid of dogs swooping on her when she's having her lunch.'

'Oh, right, that'd be just tragic all together,' Tess said, not even trying to hide her sarcasm.

'Maybe…' Robyn stopped still, looked at Tess, 'maybe I could feed her in your flat?' She began to smile.

'Oh, really? No. No, that wouldn't work at all.'

'But why ever not? You like her, I can tell you do. And you'd be doing me an enormous favour, because if my mum finds out that I've been looking after her, well, to say she'd be furious would be an understatement.'

'Oh, no, I don't know.' Of course, there was no, '*don't know*,' about it. Except… God, but she'd love to put one over on Amanda King. 'Are you sure your mother wouldn't be keen on you looking after her?'

'Oh, yes. Mum is funny that way, supporting Daddy – it's her way of being a good wife. No, there are no pets allowed in our house. To be honest, I'd say if she realised that the O'Hara's had left Margaret behind she'd have called the cat refuge days ago.'

'Oh, well. I suppose we can't have Margaret going to the refuge, not this week at any rate,' Tess said seriously, although, when she fell over that damn cat, she'd have happily shot and skinned it herself given half a chance. 'You can feed her on my windowsill, if that suits you?'

'Well, it's not as good as inside, but it's better than in the garden where my mum could spot her dish and put two and two together.' Robyn shook her head solemnly and then smiled. 'Thanks, Mrs Cuffe, who'd have thought we'd be in cahoots over Margaret?'

'Who'd have thought, indeed?' Tess murmured a little surprised at herself as much as the turn of events while the cat furled itself about her legs. In the distance she heard church bells call out the hour, it was time to go shopping. Of course, Robyn wouldn't hear of it and offered to pick up what she needed, at least while the holidays lasted and she could rest after her recent fall.

'Really, I'd like to help,' she said and, in some way, Tess thought it made her New Year's resolution of healthy eating doubly satisfying. She was putting the temptation a little further down the road by handing the girl a shopping list with fresh produce and nothing that Dr Kilker could possibly disapprove. Best of all, she had Amanda King's daughter helping her to live a longer life, even if it was just to spite her mother, the irony of it tickled Tess in a wry way that made her lips almost curl into a smile.

Robyn returned quickly with the shopping, but Tess blocked her before she could make it any further into her flat. No doubt, the girl would have put away her shopping if she got a chance. Tess wasn't one for visitors, even if she delighted in the notion of getting up Amanda King's nose, the walls around her heart were too thick to allow for any kind of invader. It was a relief to close her door on the city and settle into what remained of the first day of her new life.

Tess put a match to the little fire she'd set earlier. She pulled out a knife and fork and poured herself a good three fingers of Irish whiskey – it was the one vice she had no intention of letting go. By the time she was ready to sit, the chill was just about deserting her sitting room, but she pulled on her drab old dressing gown anyway. There was something comforting in having it about her, like the contentment of being in the arms of a lover for many years. She sat on her battered couch, her dinner on her knees, the musical highlights of the previous year washing over her. Tonight, she could only think of one thing and it warmed her heart. Someone had swept up outside her door for her. Well, for her and Margaret that horrible cat, but it was an act of kindness, the likes of which she hadn't seen in a very long time. In a little while, she'd write her third resolution for the New Year.

I will help Robyn to take care of that mangy old cat – if only to annoy her parents all the more.

6

Twenty-five years earlier...

Richard King had a girlfriend. This week she was tall and blonde and the kind of girl who didn't want any other woman near. Amanda had worked that much out, as much from the way the girl put her arm proprietorially around him when they sat drinking their coffees, never mind how she gave dirty looks to every other woman who came within twenty paces of him. Amanda didn't know the girl's name, but she knew very well who Richard was, and when she caught him watching her, she guessed perhaps he'd noticed her too.

'So, this is what you do, is it?' he asked her one day when he slipped in on his own. It was after work, his tie was slightly askew, his jacket hooked about his thumb.

'I beg your pardon,' Amanda glanced over her shoulder. Her bateau top gave just enough of a glimpse of white unblemished soft skin, it made her curiously aware of herself. Her soft copper curls skimmed her collarbone and she knew she resembled Molly Ringwald at best, but that was not why Richard was interested in her, she figured.

'I mean, here, you're going to work in a bar all your life?'

'Does it matter?' She was playing with him, even though she had a feeling she was way out of her depth. She knew she was a challenge to him. Apparently, he'd dated every other girl in the bar, apart from her. They just seemed to fall for him, perhaps it was his Porsche that won them over. 'Beer?' she asked, bending towards the bottles of Mexican beer that he always ordered.

'No, not this time, I didn't come here for beer. What time do you finish up?' he asked, moving along the counter so there was only the shining black granite between them now. 'We could have a beer together...'

'Oh, I don't think so...' she'd heard all about Richard King. He wasn't the kind of bloke who settled for a kiss and cuddle. He expected girls to go the whole way and Amanda just wasn't that kind of girl.

'We could have it here, right here. No strings. Or coffee?'

'I'm really not that interesting and I don't think I'm your type. Don't you have a girlfriend already?'

'Darlene? Oh, she's a nice enough girl, but we're just having fun.' He said smoothly and she was tempted to tell him that she was sure Darlene thought it was a lot more than that. 'I'm not taking no for an answer,' he smiled at her. 'You can buy me a coffee, if that makes you feel better. I just want to talk to you.' Amanda almost buckled, perhaps it wasn't just the Porsche that won the other girls over.

'Well, I'm afraid you'll have to take no this time.'

'What time do you finish?' he persisted.

'When I do,' she smiled at him, enjoying his attention, 'I'll be going home and getting into bed alone.'

'Ah,' he said mock wounded, he placed his hand against his improbably breaking heart. 'Now you've really hurt me.'

'Don't take it personally. I'm just too busy with college at the moment to see anyone.'

'It wouldn't have to be a thing, with me…' his eyes crinkled and she was sure he'd had plenty of *no-things* all about the city before her.

'Well, here's the thing, Richard, it *would* have to be a thing for me.' She winked at him and then turned and left him standing there.

A week later he turned up sans scary girlfriend once again. And again, she sent him on his way, rejected. Soon, it became their *thing*. He showed up, begged to take her out and she flatly refused. Then, one afternoon, Amanda got word that her painting would be the centrepiece of the end of term show and she was just beside herself with joy. Richard turned up as usual, probably expecting rejection.

'Okay, I get a break in about ten minutes. I'll get us two coffees; we can have them at the bar.' She smiled at him, where was the harm in a coffee? It was all the nicer because he'd just stood there with his mouth open, probably in shock.

Amanda got a half-hour break. Usually, she walked around the corner to the National Gallery. She could sit there all day; half an hour gave her just about twenty minutes before one of her favourites. This week, she was working her way through the Ann Madden exhibition, Amanda could lose herself for hours before one of those charismatic works.

It surprised her that the coffee with Richard seemed to fly by even faster than one of her jaunts to the National Gallery. Afterwards, she couldn't think what he talked about, but she had told him more about herself than she intended.

'So, you're an arty-farty?' he said, draining his coffee. 'I'm impressed,' he took her hands, she scrubbed them clean each night before coming on shift. 'I bet you're really good,' he said smoothly and she reddened because she had a feeling that somewhere in there was an innuendo that had nothing to do with using charcoal or acrylics.

'I'm okay, I suppose.' Amanda figured she was middle of the class, but it didn't matter, she just loved art, always had. Everything about it just made her feel right. She loved bright colours, loved seeing the page transform and she adored the idea that something, hardly a germ of a notion, could come to life in a way that would never be forgotten.

'So, when you graduate – will you draw or…'

'Oh, I don't know. I mean, to make a living at it, you have to be really good, don't you?'

'I suppose that or just know the right people. You wouldn't believe the crap rich people buy. Don't you think, it's all about sales anyway? I mean, how do you know if something is good – it's only when some poor idiot parts with a couple of hard-earned notes for it that it gets a value.'

'Oh, I don't know about that…' Amanda wasn't sure if he was kidding her, so she decided, best not to rise to the bait. 'Anyway, if I did become an artist, *you* could buy them…' she smiled at him coquettishly, forgetting herself, just for a moment.

'Oh, Amanda, I think I'd buy every one of them, if I thought it'd make you happy.' He looked down at the table now, studied his hands for a moment, but she figured it was part of his act. It was how he drew girls in, she'd seen him do it a thousand times before. It was very subtle, but it was enough to make her realise that her break was over.

'Anyway, I must be getting back to work. They don't pay me for entertaining the customers, not even the regulars, I'm afraid.'

'Pity. Which college are you in, you never said,' he inclined his head, interested maybe as much to gauge how good she was.

'Oh, I'm in the National College of Art and Design,' she said, it still gave her a thrill to say that.

'The NCAD,' he made a little wolf-whistle, 'well, I'll be looking out for your end of year show.' Across the bar, his current girlfriend or at least this week's girl, had arrived, he put his hand up in the air, as though alerting a taxi to his whereabouts. 'Phoebe, have you met Amanda?' he said, his fingers resting on his lips for just one appraising moment. It was a trademark move for when he was about to tell a lie. 'She's sorting out some artwork for the apartment, you know, I must have mentioned her.' The fib tripped off his tongue so easily, but Amanda didn't care, she was much too busy at this stage trying to remember not to fall in love with him to register his only giveaway habit when he was economical with the truth.

7

January 1 – Thursday

Amanda King was at her wit's end. It was the first day of the New Year and none of her family was talking to her. It seemed that each of them blamed her for something and now she couldn't figure out what she'd done wrong.

It was as she was clearing up after lunch – a silent affair, with only the sound of cutlery, chewing and the incessant ping of messages on her daughter's phone – that she realised she'd eaten the whole Christmas cake on her own – how had she managed to do that? It was only six days since she'd cut the first generous slice – how could she have eaten the whole thing in under a week, for goodness sake it must have weighed at least four pounds. Amanda could feel herself sink into the kind of dark depression that only comes with a major sugar withdrawal. None of the other wives would have this guilt today, she was sure of that. For one thing, they wouldn't have celebrated with much more than a lettuce leaf and a stiff drink, or at least that's all that they'd have allowed to stay down. For another, as far as she could see, Nicola, Clarissa and Megan simply didn't 'do' guilt. Why was that? Surely the nuns had fair aim at all of them, how come Amanda was carrying the guilt for everyone. It wasn't as if they didn't have their secrets, after all.

God, but that was depressing. Other women her age were having torrid affairs with younger men or building up their offshore bank accounts, or hiding drinking habits that were out of control. Typical, Amanda King's dirty secret was she needed to eat less cake and make new friends!

As far as her figure went, the trick was, she told herself, to eat plenty this week. She might even eat enough to put her off food for life. God, wouldn't that be marvellous. To be reaching for the herbal teabags in a moment of crisis, instead of frothing up a storm of high-calorie caffeine and pairing it with doughnuts or chocolate cake. Sure, everyone knew, diets that began on the first of January always failed. No, she would start when everyone else was falling off the bandwagon, well, that's what she'd decided as she sat in her empty kitchen at four o'clock in the morning, polishing off the Christmas cake. There, you see, extenuating circumstances – she'd been worried, depressed... lonely?

Lonely, it was a word that she didn't want to think about too much. Life was moving forward, it was natural for the kids to draw away from her at this stage. Every other mother over time eternal had probably had to stare down the notion of being the most uncool person in the universe, as far as her kids were concerned. Nicola thought all teenagers should be sent away to boarding school. Nicola's kids were packed off as soon as there was the danger of a negligent hormone ripening to make her perfect life appear untidy. Amanda couldn't remember being anything like Casper when she was a teenager. Sometimes, when he looked at her, she wondered if maybe his disdain had turned to hatred. She'd looked it up, googled it so often it came up as a default search on her phone these days, even higher in the search engine ranking than Net-a-Porter and Habitat. Mothers across the world were experiencing exactly the same thing; it was normal, apparently. So why did sharing a house with them all feel like the hollowest place in the world? More and more, it seemed to Amanda that her raison d'être was being withdrawn; her primary role snatched stealthily while she tried to grip it even harder. She could fall back on being the perfect wife to try to fill the void, but Richard seemed to be more withdrawn than ever; working late nights and having business meetings over the weekend – there was no escaping it, she felt miserable and empty.

Today, even Richard wasn't talking to her. He arrived back from the party in a complete huff; he had hardly said two words to her since.

'How was it?' she asked when they found themselves alone in the living room that evening. 'The party, after

I left, did you get to schmooze who you needed to?'
She was trying to be funny, but the truth was, all the
directors looked the same to her. They were all young,
with glowing tanned skin and they looked as though
they'd been exfoliated to within an inch of their lives.
At the party, they were all in tuxedos, so Amanda found
it hard to tell them apart after a while.

'What's that supposed to mean?' He didn't even look
at her, but she had a feeling she'd hit a nerve.

'Nothing, I was just asking.' She guessed that Richard
had not made the big impression he hoped to on the
night.

'Well, if you were that interested, perhaps you should
have stayed around to find out,' he said, lifting the iPad
he was studying closer to his face. She passed across his
reading glasses, which he took without any comment.
He was still handsome, in a neat, squidgy way that
suited his age. He looked after himself, used male
grooming products so his hair was always slick, his
clothes were always perfect; Amanda knew he was still
attractive. His eyes were clear and piercing; he hadn't
fallen down the rabbit hole of booze or worse like so
many of his colleagues who couldn't handle the stress
of their careers.

'I had to leave, you know that.' There was no point
going over it again. Richard wouldn't have minded if
she'd stayed at home, probably. It was Amanda's idea to
tag along, well, it'd look very strange if she didn't and

Nicola Lennox had a nose for anything that seemed even a little bit peculiar. If Amanda hadn't gone to the New Year's party they'd have assumed it was because she couldn't find a dress to fit, or worse, that there was some kind of trouble between herself and Richard. 'Anyway, I hoped that you'd enjoy it. I really didn't want to spoil your night, if I could have sorted things out here and taken a taxi back I would have…' It wasn't strictly true. She'd come home because she couldn't stick it any longer. As it turned out, she was very glad she did. But, by the time the kids were in bed, Amanda felt as if the night had sucked the life from her. All she was fit for was her pyjamas, Christmas cake and a very large glass of liquor – well, it was still the season to be merry. She hated having fights, she especially hated that they always led to this cold war. That was probably the worst, for her, living in this atmosphere of rigid silence.

'Whatever,' Richard said and, for a moment, Amanda thought he sounded like a spoiled child. She dropped her magazine and headed for the fridge.

It was all very well for Richard, perhaps it was a man thing, but the kids, the house, absolutely nothing seemed to faze him these days. It was probably why he was so good at his job, she often thought. Richard worked very hard indeed, but you had to, as he kept telling her. Since Brexit, the Irish banking sector was under even more pressure than ever before. Everyone knew the financial services centre in Dublin was a hub of banking commerce and in the last few years it had become a portal between Europe and the rest of the world. So, while Amanda worried about cake, her husband doled out money to keep whole economies alive, drive planes around the world and establish power plants in regions she'd never heard of. Of course, with that came opportunities to make even more money, it was all about the bonuses and their divvying out was performance-related. Richard worked to get the best accounts and make the most profitable deals. His work, as he kept telling her, was not just nine to five, and so their whole lives had become trussed up in this thing he called success. Funny, but Amanda sometimes wondered if it was all worth it; as far as she was concerned, they had enough to live comfortably for the rest of their days. Of course, she'd never say that to Richard, or the girls, but it niggled at her, sometimes, it made her feel like she was completely out of kilter with everyone around her. She suspected it added to her sense of loneliness.

The following day, Richard was back at work and Amanda was getting his suits ready for the dry-cleaners. She always checked his pockets. He had a habit of leaving notes in them. Sometimes it was just fivers, but often enough there'd be a fifty hiding in the inside pocket, where he'd gone to buy lunch or dinner and thought better of it and put it on the gold card. They might be loaded, but Amanda could remember when fifty euros meant something to her. Fifty euros would put books in a child's school bag in September. There were people who had to save hard for that luxury. She laid the lot on their bed and decided she may as well get his tuxedo done too. It could be months before he took it out again, but it would need freshening before he wore it for a second time.

No fifties here, she thought as she checked the pockets automatically. Then something scratched her finger, a silver foil. She pulled it out, aiming for the wastepaper basket, but suddenly froze, stared at the packet in the palm of her hand; it was a condom. She felt the blood drain from her head, as though it was rushing out of her feet. She began to sway, catching her breath. In the room next door, the thump of bass music played on as though everything in the world was as it should be. Casper was studying for his exams; or supposed to be. For a ridiculous moment, Amanda wanted to scream. She wanted to wail at the unfairness of having her tubes tied when she really hadn't thought it fully through. She wanted to kick Richard in his bony, arrogant, vain backside.

All those years ago he'd been a player, but that had stopped the day they said 'I do'. Hadn't it? This condom was not for them and so her mind raced with the terrible likelihoods. *'For God's sake, Casper, turn off that noise, it's doing my bloody head in.'* Of course, she didn't say a word. Instead, she dropped onto her lovely French empire bed and examined the foil wrapper in her hand, working hard to even out her ragged breath.

It was raspberry flavour, she stifled what she knew was a frantic laugh. The thoughts of Richard – her Richard – he didn't even like raspberries. He was a strictly apple and orange sort of bloke; none of these girly fruits for her husband. Why in God's name had he chosen raspberry? And what on earth was her Richard doing with a condom in his pocket?

It rattled around in her head for hours. A raspberry-flavoured condom. It paced with her. It thrummed out a beat of its own. Soon it sounded like one of those annoying songs that won the Eurovision years ago, and somehow pops into your head and there is no way of getting it out again. A raspberry-flavoured condom. There it was again.

In the end, she took Richard's suits to the dry-cleaners, decided to leave the tuxedo back on the hanger and placed the offending silver packet exactly where she found it. Perhaps it had been some kind of prank. Yes, that would be it. It hadn't been used, so, really, it meant nothing. It was just a silly mistake. Some of the wags at the office playing a practical joke, she reassured herself with the sensible voice she once used when her children were young enough to take notice of her advice. Deep down, far down in her psyche, another voice whispered, but it was too low for her to pay it any heed. That voice echoed what had lurked within her for a very long time. *He's being unfaithful to you and no matter how you try to cover things over, you know, he's being unfaithful to you.*

There was no way, her sensible voice raged loud within her... Well, it was unthinkable. Her Richard. Not in a million years. She took down their wedding photograph from the dressing table before the window. They'd been so happy that day. It was the wedding of the decade. Everyone said so. They had Bollinger champagne flowing as steady as Irish rain and a week of celebrating with the best food and music for guests who travelled from all over the world to enjoy their hospitality. She looked into those young eyes, staring back at her full of eager expectation. She had so wanted to be Mrs Richard King. She had so wanted this life. To live in a period townhouse, have the perfect two children – they were living the dream. They drove nice cars, wore expensive clothes and holidayed in parts of the world that most people hadn't even heard of.

It wasn't enough though, was it? It mustn't be, not for Richard, not if he was... God, she wanted to curl up and howl at a moon that she wasn't even sure was there anymore. He wasn't having an affair, it was as simple as that and she wouldn't think of it again, she told herself sternly for the umpteenth time. She couldn't think about it. She couldn't think of him being with someone else.

God, suddenly it came to her. Standing there on the hotel steps, her reflection staring back at her. What was she? What had she become? It was another question she wasn't sure she wanted to ask or to answer.

She sat outside the dry-cleaners and cried for a full hour. A solid hour of wailing and huge wracking sobs that gave her body shivers as if she was blown through a hurricane of emotion. Eventually, she felt the shuddering subside. It was almost worse when the tears stopped, because then she felt something she didn't at first think she'd ever felt before. She was numb. She was a walking, emotionally void caricature of what she thought she should be. Somewhere, between the photograph that sat on her dressing table, taken all those years ago, and now, Amanda King got lost. Where was that girl she used to know? Had she known then that she would have to become someone else? Probably.

Richard was the first man she had loved, if you didn't count Rhett Butler. He was the first man she had slept with and she had always believed he would be the only one she slept with. Part of her knew then that she was stepping into a role. It was the role of her dreams. She was starring in the movie of her dreams, only today all those lines she'd said, all those costume changes, the beauty treatments and sly tweaks to stave off any signs of age, they all seemed to be completely inane. She was living a lie and the worst part was maybe she'd known it all along.

Okay, so she didn't expect to find a condom in her husband's tuxedo, but the rest, what she had become; it seemed suddenly she had an aerial view of her own life. Far from being a fairy tale, it was a tragic parody of the children's story, she had built a straw house and now it was starting to crumble when the wolf came to breathe on it. She wiped her eyes with a ferociousness that her beauty therapist would scorn. She would have to confront him, wouldn't she? She knew she would. However silly it turned out to be, however ridiculous she looked with a raspberry-flavoured condom as her only tangible proof, she had to ask Richard if he was having an affair – otherwise she had a feeling she would go mad.

Tonight, she would ask him tonight.

8

Forty-eight years earlier...

Tess and Nancy quickly settled into the flat on Swift Square. They had a bedroom each and a kitchen to prepare meals and sit in on afternoons when perhaps they should be doing other things. The square itself was a shambling Georgian monstrosity. Many of the houses were boarded up to keep out undesirables. On one side, a brave attempt at introducing commerce. A few fledgling offices treaded uncomfortably alongside the poverty remnants. If they stuck it out, who knew? Tess wasn't optimistic for their chances. It suited Tess and Nancy perfectly in many ways. College was just a five-minute walk away, the rent was cheap, more a token than the going rate and just around the corner there were vegetable stalls and a fishmonger. They may not eat as well as when their mother cooked, but Tess was too enthralled in this exciting new world to pay much heed to mundane things like meals or food or even maybe Nancy.

Perhaps it was just as well, because Nancy seemed to get on with things, in her own quiet dull way. Her first day of term passed without as much as a comment, until Tess drew her out. The secretarial college sounded grey, a bunch of nuns finishing off the girls of middle-class families. It sounded joyless, but there would be prospects, and at least it meant direction for Nancy.

'No boys, of course,' Nancy tempered a shy smile. 'But everyone seems very nice, they're all just like me, really.'

'It sounds like the kind of place Father would approve of at least,' Tess laughed.

'Yes, I suppose he would,' she said vaguely and Tess wondered if she might be homesick, but she didn't dare to ask. 'It'll do me, for now. I don't have your talent or ambition…'

'Don't say that, Nancy. You're going to make a great success of whatever you set your hat at,' Tess said warmly. In the few weeks since they'd arrived, it seemed Nancy's confidence was going down instead of up. Sometimes, Tess wondered if there wasn't some small resentment or jealousy at the bottom of it, but there had never been an angry word between them. They were just different, that was all. They wanted different things, or at least it seemed that way to Tess. Then again, she wasn't exactly sure what Nancy wanted these days, she played her cards much too close to her chest. Perhaps, Nancy didn't know herself?

Tess settled in a daily routine of her own making. The hours at college were much shorter than she expected, maybe than she'd hoped for. With so many others, between lectures, she hung about the library or the playing fields or, if she got away with it, the grand dining room that served coffee all day long if you could afford it.

She spotted Douglas Buckley on the second day. His shirt was white, almost iridescent among the sea of murky grey duffle coats and denims. Tidiness bordered on pristine about him, it marked him out instantly, as though he stood a little apart from the rest. He was not the tallest boy there, maybe he wasn't even the most handsome, but the minute Tess clapped eyes on him, she felt like she was being drawn towards him. It was first-class madness. It was the kind of ridiculous thing that happened in the movies or maybe even the kind of love story that Aunt Beatrice had been peddling for years. Whatever it was, Tess knew there was no changing it. The attraction she felt for this proud boy with angular features and ginger-blonde floppy hair was as steadfast and strong as the pull of the ocean. Tess knew from a lifetime looking out at the Irish Sea that there was no point fighting the tides.

Douglas Buckley stood over from her, unaware that she was even in the room while she felt his every breath. They stood next to each other in a line for something that seemed so inconsequential when she thought of it later. Then someone pushed her from behind and she found herself toppling up against him. He saved her from a fall and introduced himself as she straightened herself up. He was tall enough to make her stretch her neck when he spoke and something jangled between them so when she worked up the courage to speak she found herself smiling at him. Perhaps it was his eyes? Almost indigo, deep enough to dive into and lose herself forever, or maybe it was his hands, so familiar that she had to stop herself from reaching out and touching them. As they spoke – she couldn't remember what they said – she felt her insides churn about, as if the waves in Ballycove had nipped in the tide and then allowed the sand to shift so everything skewed, just a little. Something inside her changed forever when she met Douglas Buckley.

'You're studying music?' he tilted his head a little to the side. 'What do you play?' he asked.

'Oh, no. I sing.' She let the words flutter uncertainly across the space between them. 'Soprano, but my range is wide...' Tess wanted to impress this boy as she'd never wanted to impress a boy before.

'Really?' A tall boy, denim-clad with skin reddened from too much sun, spun round. He was the antithesis of Douglas Buckley's refined sophistication. Everything about him said poor, his callow roughness cobbled about him like a mantle, stuck on at the start and held in place seamlessly. He stuck out a hand. 'Stephen,' he said by way of introduction, 'I'm in second year medicine and, funny, but we're just looking for a singer.' He jabbed a thumb towards the noticeboard across from them.

'Hello, I'm Tess.' And suddenly they were three. 'I've only sung in choirs, apart from here, I can't imagine that...'

'Well, we do church weddings too,' Stephen said, rummaging through the notepad in his hand. 'Come along tonight,' he looked up at Douglas, taking him in, assessing the possibilities between them. 'Both of you, just for an hour.'

'Well,' Douglas looked at her uncertainly, then his mouth broke into a smile. They had only just met, but funny how two seconds can make the world of difference. Stephen thought they'd known each other a lifetime and it felt to Tess as though one day they might. 'Why not, if you can't enjoy an odd night out...' Douglas said and Tess wondered if he felt the very same.

'I'd love to,' Tess gushed but then remembered Nancy. 'Can I bring my sister along too?' She'd have her work cut out for her to get Nancy out the door, but it would be even harder to leave her behind.

'Seriously?' Stephen said as though his ship had just come in. 'Of course, the more the merrier.'

The flat had the still air of a question mark hanging about the place when Tess returned that evening. Suddenly, as she wandered through the rooms, everything seemed to have shrunk a little smaller, paled a little greyer. Her life outside this place had just burst into a delicious new adventure and the old familiar seemed so much duller than before. She should really make something for their dinner. Instead, she went to the little wardrobe that they shared between them in Nancy's room and rummaged through the meagre contents in search of glamour. There was a black lace dress that might look like something a mourning Italian grandmother would wear, but when Tess fitted it on, it clung perfectly to her so there could be no missing her slender waist or ample derriere. The dress had been in the flat when they arrived and Tess had halted Nancy in her zealous drive to clear each item out. From the moment Tess laid eyes on it, she knew it was a dress to wear on stage. True, she'd have to layer it up with jewellery to throw sparkles on a light she was confident would one day capture only her. For now, she drew out Aunt Beatrice's silken shawl. This was not just a sentimental piece, but it was more beautiful perhaps because of it. Aunt Beatrice was given it by an officer during the war for some favour she would never mention and maybe Tess knew better than to press. It was a sheeny forest of emeralds, jades, ivy; lush and verdant. A thread of lightest blue danced an azure path to a deep fringe that picked out Tess's eyes, making them even more striking above the black.

'Oh, Tess, you look divine,' Nancy said when she arrived back in the middle of the trying on.

'Do you think so? It's just that I...' Tess felt her cheeks flame pink, it wasn't something that happened very often and in the dim light of the flat, Nancy didn't notice. She was too intent on putting away the groceries from her basket.

'I've brought back some eggs and…' Nancy stopped, looked more closely at her sister. 'What? Has something happened?'

'No,' Tess said defensively and then she softened. 'Well, yes. And no,' a nervous giggle overtook her and she realised, this must be love. 'We've been invited to a club.'

'A club? What kind of club? Is that why you look so…'

'Fabulous?' Tess threw back her head and laughed.

'Well, yes, but different, there's definitely something different about you apart from all the finery.' Nancy shook her head and Tess had a feeling she knew exactly what her sister meant, because she *was* different, she felt like she was two inches taller and somehow changed since meeting Douglas Buckley.

'I've met someone,' Tess said, flopping into the seat.

'You've what? Tess, you've only just started college, how can you have *met someone*?' Nancy shook her head good-naturedly. 'And you're meeting him tonight?'

'We're both meeting him tonight,' Tess laughed. 'At the Sunset Club. Say you'll come?'

'Wild horses wouldn't keep me away,' Nancy laughed, but her expression had an anxious look that Tess recognised from childhood. She was meant to be looking after her little sister, perhaps meeting someone had not been something she'd really figured in.

'You can wear the grey?' Tess ran back to the wardrobe again, pulled out a silvery grey two-piece suit that probably dated from a decade earlier. It was fashioned beautifully, obviously expensive, and when Nancy tried it on, she might have stepped directly off the plane from Paris, such was her understated style.

'You see,' Nancy sighed. 'This is exactly why Father wanted me to stay with you this year.' True enough, the Sunset Club, was a complete dump. From the pavement, Tess felt the thrum of music linger long enough in her pulse to stir a steady commotion within her. She'd never been to a jazz club before. The darkness when she entered embraced her like a comfortable cloak of welcome. In this kind of place, she could imagine extinguishing the values that had been foisted upon her in Ballycove. It was a blackness that loosened ideals so the distinctions between responsibility and innocence; between liability and virtue, could be quietly snuffed.

Douglas found them as soon as they had left their coats; he led them to seats near the front. Tess did the introductions, had already explained to Nancy that they were guests of a boy called Stephen who played in the band. She didn't mention that they needed a singer, not that it meant anything really. After all, what did Tess know of jazz.

A group of five young men were playing on stage at odds with each other, and the noise, frenetic and grinding, seemed to expel a tension that Tess knew would make Nancy feel uncomfortable. This place, it seemed to make her sister even more washed out than usual. Here, Nancy faded to a beiger version of herself, as though her delicacy was lost within the smoky air, transforming her from butterfly to moth in a cruel twist that she did not deserve.

Douglas went to the bar and brought down three drinks. They sat for a while nursing warm Babychams, while Douglas ignored the cloudy glass of mottled beer before him. He sat between them, pulling up conversation when the intervals allowed. Tess could see that Nancy liked him well enough too. She couldn't think of anything worse than the people she loved the most not getting along together. Not that she loved him yet, Tess caught herself up on that thought. They'd only known each other for hours, she couldn't possibly love him yet. Could she?

The music was too loud for conversation and although it entranced Tess, she was all too aware that Douglas sat at odds with everything in this place. She decided they wouldn't wait for long, instead she would suggest that they leave here and perhaps walk through

City Green before she and Nancy went back to Swift Square.

It was while these thoughts were swirling about her brain that she suddenly found herself picked out in a shaky overhead spotlight, shining directly on their table. Then, from the stage, Stephen, the boy from earlier, was making his way across the floor.

'And now, please welcome, our special guest,' Stephen was standing over her, his warm solid hand on her shoulder, fighting to be heard above the grating of the instruments. 'Come on, Tess, you must know something the punters here would enjoy,' he shout-whispered in her ear. Then, a small stampede of feet began to beat out a demanding welcome. 'Something a little mellow?' he asked.

'Summertime?' she said loud enough for it to carry to the band and, of course, the crowd erupted. Everyone loved that old standard and everyone knew at least some of the words. So, Tess looked about the little club and stood uncertainly.

Stephen led her to the stage and when she stood beneath the single light and waited for the music to begin behind her, she felt as though she was standing just beyond herself. And then she heard a voice, at her side, 'one, two,' and they were off. The words fell easily, lazily from her lips, she closed her eyes to start, but then, she felt her hips sway, just enough to pick the rhythm. The crowd, the music, the feeling of liberation that overtook her whole body in those movements was like no other. She caught Douglas's unreadable eye – there was a flash of something she didn't understand – could it be desire?

All too soon, the music ended and the crowd demanded more. Tess bowed, enjoyed the admiration, but moved from the stage with resolve. The truth was, she didn't know any other songs that would work in this place.

'That was...' Stephen bounded up to their table in the break. 'It was...' he looked across at Douglas and Nancy for the words but he met empty stares. Tess hardly noticed. She was still on a high after the experience. 'Well, I think we have a singer,' he said to one of the other lads who'd joined him from the stage. 'If you're up for it?'

'I... well... I...' Tess wasn't sure what to say. She knew what she should say. Her father would want her to say, 'no'. She could imagine his disdain at the mention of them even being here, much less the idea of parading herself on the stage and titillating the crowd with her swinging hips and sultry dipping voice. This was a million miles away from opera in Covent Garden, and yet Tess loved it. She looked across at Douglas, waited just a beat, she spoke before he had a chance to comment, 'Yes, let's give it a go.' It would be good to let him see that she wasn't some artless country girl, but she was every bit as sophisticated as he was.

It seemed as they walked home that Nancy was even more subdued than normal. Douglas was brooding on the night they'd spent. Tess, for her part, filled with giddy excitement. She was high after the unexpected performance and animated at the possibilities creeping just ahead. They slipped through St Stephen's Green to make a shortcut, the autumn smells of decaying flowers and turf smoke seemed to be a symphony playing out the departing summer. If their moods were at odds with each other, the silence that tumbled between them was comfortable at least. Soon they were at the top of the square.

'And this bloke, Stephen? Well, he's a bit ordinary, isn't he? I mean he's hardly our type of person,' Douglas said into the silence as though the conversation was already in full swing, and just for a moment, in the darkness, the sentiment jarred with her.

'Oh, Douglas, you are funny. He's just a little rough around the edges, but he's in college too, I'm sure he'll be as successful someday as any of us. Anyway, it's just a band.' Tess laughed, he sounded a little like her father, it was too ridiculous to be true of course.

'I'll be glad to get to my bed,' Nancy yawned wearily as she let herself into the flat.

'I don't know how I'll ever sleep,' Tess said. 'I may just sit here for a while before I go in.' She dropped down onto the cold flag steps of the house above their little flat.

'I'll sit with you, for just a minute,' Douglas said,

brushing his hand uselessly against the steps to take the everyday dust from their surface. 'You know, Tess, if you need extra money – there are… better ways to make it.' His voice stitched across the silence of the night between them.

'Excuse me?' she looked at him now, pulling herself into the present, his eyes were a mixture of things she wasn't sure she understood.

'What I'm saying is, if you want to get a little part-time job, the city is teeming with them. My local post office is looking for a Saturday girl – they'd pay even better and it's respectable at least.'

'I'm a singer, Douglas, it's what I love to do,' she whispered into the night air, felt the words settle into her bones. All the same, she liked the idea that he wanted more for her, that he felt some need to watch over her, to keep her safe, chaste perhaps?

'Not that kind of singer though.' He spat the words out too quickly.

'What kind of singer is *that*, exactly?' she looked up at him playfully, held his eyes for just a minute too long, and then, suddenly, he leant across and kissed her. His lips were moist and, on the air, she caught the tangy scent of the glass of lager he'd nursed in the club. Tess thought she'd explode from the mixture of desire in this moment and rhapsody from earlier. Then, far off, across the city streets, a siren wailed out loud and obscene into the night and the spell was broken.

'Better if I go, I think.' His breathing was uneven and Tess thought she'd rip herself in two with longing for him in that moment.

'I'll see you in college, tomorrow, yes?' she called after him.

'Of course,' he said, moving quickly away from her.

She watched as he walked out of the square and thought it had been the most perfect night of her life.

9

January 2 – Friday

Tess had always been a morning person. Then again, it wasn't as if she was any more sociable at one end of the day than the other. Maybe it was getting older – but she preferred to get her day over with quickly, if there was a choice. Usually, if she could, she sat in the Square garden in the afternoon, but apart from that, so long as she wasn't falling over snotty office girls she chugged along unnoticed mostly.

Sometimes, on wet days, when she sat in the flat on her own, she dreamed about what her life might have been if she'd married Douglas. She'd have been a teacher's wife, certainly, Douglas would not have wanted her working outside their home. She tried not to think of it too often, but sometimes, well, in that flat, she could go mad if she didn't think of something.

'Ah, Mrs Cuffe,' the secretary called her name through her nose, as though it might keep the smell of something undesirable from pervading her lovely reception desk. Tess didn't usually work in the financial services centre. They were too far away to walk to, but the agency had promised double time and she never turned down easy money. Of course, double the hourly rate was probably what they felt would entice her back over the New Year break. Her bruises had died down a lot in so short a time and it was nice to have something to mark out the week. The holidays mean nothing when you're on your own. 'We've an outbreak of winter vomiting bug so there's lots to do. Mr Boyce has asked if you can go up to the third floor and get started on some filing.' She hardly looked at Tess when she spoke and Tess wondered if she'd ever know what it was to be old and invisible or would she learn too late?

'Filing?' Tess repeated, as though she would automatically slip into place like a well-oiled wheel ready for action. 'I'll have you know, young lady, that filing is a very specialised job, each business is different, so I'll be taking my time and I'll be seeing it in my wages.' She walked towards the waxy faux oak escalator doors, silently praying the filing system would be easy to follow.

But somehow, with all those buttons and directions, she managed to arrive in what she supposed was the executive floor. It was a sea of deep snowy carpet, modern muted artworks and heavy occasional tables partnering club chairs lining up between a series of arrogant maple doors. You could smell the money, raw and dangerous in the air. By the time she turned to make her way back to the third floor, the elevator doors had shut and she was left stranded and waiting for its return. To her left, she spotted the toilet. She decided to nip in; these cold days played havoc with her kidneys. They never warned you that it'd be the innards that would give you away first, as you grew older.

It constantly amazed Tess how the rich spent their money. Take this toilet for example, closed with a sign that said cleaners at work, when everyone knew that there was no place for cleaners during sociable hours. Air freshener pumped in so it smelled like the hairdresser her aunt Beatrice visited every week all those years ago. Mrs Mooney had converted her front sitting room into a little salon down at the very end of Ballycove. Her whole house smelled of hairspray and apple shampoo; sweet but nauseating after the first half-hour. Tess often wondered if it was why Mr Mooney spent all his days in the pub. There was something unnatural about a man living in such a perfumed atmosphere.

The music in here too throbbed as though it was a nightclub, then Tess heard it. Later, she'd wonder, had she really heard it? Had she heard anything at all, or had she just imagined it, but there it was, a scratching, thumping, grinding, breathless sound.

It was the sound of sex, of course, not one that Tess was what you'd call overly familiar with, but she was a woman who considered herself worldly, if not widely experienced. She'd grown up in the fifties – even if it was in Ballycove. It was definitely the sound of sex;

rough and ready, the kind that youngsters thought lasted beyond a first night – Tess knew different.

Well, they weren't running her out of the toilet. Now that she was here, with the sound of water flowing and the cool air conditioning hitting her anew, she really needed to go. The next loo could be a mile of corridors away. She rounded the cubicles, expected the lovers to have taken refuge behind a flimsy closed door.

But no.

There, in all his glory, stood her neighbour and nemesis, Richard King. He reminded her of a little haystack on his spindly thin legs. His trousers sank at half-mast, shorts standing valiantly about his knobbly knees and calves, pumping himself like a donkey into a red-faced woman who was leaning forward, white-knuckled against the sink.

'Find another loo,' the woman shouted at her rudely, but it was too late, it seemed, because Richard had obviously lost all motivation. He slunk away from her, trying to hold his balance, while righting his trousers too quickly for his pristine drawers to catch up.

'You could do yourself an injury with that kind of carry-on, Richard,' Tess said and managed to keep a straight face. Then she walked casually into the first cubicle, sitting comfortably on the toilet while she listened to the skirmish outside. Heated toilet seats, there was no such thing as cold bums in the Dublin banking world obviously.

When she'd finished and taken a deep breath so she was fairly certain she wouldn't laugh in their faces she went outside.

'It's not what it seems,' Richard King was white-faced, ashen didn't even come close.

'Really? Because I could have sworn you had your,' she looked down now at the offending body part safely tucked behind his closed zipper, 'little willie stuck in that woman, who I'm fairly sure was not average Amanda – or did my eyes trick me?' She shook her head, feigned bewilderment as only a woman of her years could.

'You know full well what I mean.' He rounded on her now and she could see again that rotten temper that flared so easily with her before. Of course, it had let him down then too. The judge was not impressed when Richard shouted brutishly at her in the court case, it had probably swung things in her favour as much as anything else.

'Oh yes I do, Richard,' she said calmly, keeping her eyes on him so she could enjoy watching him squirm. 'So, if it's not what I think, then I'm sure your wife won't mind one bit when I tell her about the most amazing coincidence...' She rubbed her hands thoughtfully beneath the tap, enjoying the feeling of expensive soap upon them.

'You wouldn't' He looked as if he could cry.

'Well, I mightn't...'

'Go on,' he leaned back against the sink, defeated.

Perhaps he was counting his breaths as Tess had counted hers each night when they first arrived and made it obvious they wanted her out.

'It's just, I suppose, I was going to mention...' she looked about this lovely plush bathroom, mentally comparing it to her own meagre-tiled, wet-rotted, damp-patched, apricot-coloured water closet. 'It's my bathroom, it's a bit... outdated, I suppose you'd call it. It could do with a good overhaul. I'm not getting any younger, you know. I need to look at things like a walk-in shower, a good immersion, maybe...' She stopped for a moment, it was now or never, she nodded towards the cubicle she'd just left. 'A heated toilet seat – it'd be a great relief to me, don't you know.' She enjoyed pulling the words out slowly, so he could just imagine her sitting there, on her lovely cosy toilet seat, and laughing her head off at the pair of them upstairs.

'I'll organise it,' he said before gathering himself up as much as he could manage.

Tess watched as he walked without any pep back to his important job.

'Yes, do that,' Tess said, but of course, she knew he couldn't hear her, he was far too concerned with the notion that Tess really had managed to get the upper hand at last.

After that, Tess felt lighter in herself than she had for

years. So much so, that when she got home, she decided to take herself out to the Square garden with her cup of tea and sit for a while. She put on her coat and wrapped her best scarf about her neck then chose a seat opposite her little flat so she could sit and watch the world go by.

The square was lovely at this time of year. It felt as though everything was sleeping, just beneath the surface, there was a calm about January that could fool you into thinking time was standing still in some arcane way. Sometimes Tess thought she could hear the bulbs moving about like an infant in the womb, waiting for their time to bloom. A lively game of start-stop football filled the air with roars of 'goal' and 'foul' and Tess fought down an urge to slug across the grass and kick the ball belligerently past the scrawny keeper. It was mad of course, this deep-buried desire to kick about a ball when she passed children in the street, slyly pick up where she left off before she even got the chance to start. Tess remembered being in such a hurry to grow up; she didn't realise then that growing up meant growing old.

She sat and watched as young mums wheeled prams with contented sleeping tots. Toddlers rushed about burning off energy before their evening nap and dogs strained on leads that probably their owners wished they didn't need. A woman, no doubt well-meaning (the worst sort of do-gooder, in Tess's opinion), pushed a flier into her hands and had the audacity to smile sweetly as she moved off towards the other end of the square.

Across the road, she saw Amanda King return with dry-cleaning slung across her arm. Tess watched as she marched up the steps and into her pristine house. Funny, but she never thought of that as being a home and she wondered absently why that might be. Then her mind flitted to Richard with that woman who would eat Amanda for breakfast, given half a chance. True, Tess felt no sympathy for Amanda King, but there was no doubting that Robyn might have the makings of a nice girl, one day. To give credit to the girl, she was looking after that cat as if it was a newborn baby. She could become quite fond of the girl, if she didn't watch out.

It was beginning to get cold and Tess knew she should go back to the flat soon. Night was drawing in early and they would lock the gates before she knew it. Still, she lingered, feeling an overwhelming sense of loneliness grip her. It was happening more often now; when she was younger, she put it down to Douglas. It was natural enough, under the circumstances, wasn't it? Now though, she knew it was everything in her life, and the fact that really, if she was honest, there was nothing in her life.

She watched as one of the young porters from the Swift Centre made his way through the park. He was locking the gates for the evening, checking that people had left. He nodded and had a word for everyone on his path, something mundane, forgettable. Tess knew, he could as easily have not bothered to salute the cross old woman on the bench. What if he was the last person she spoke to? What if she died here, on this bench, on this black night – all alone? The thought hit her suddenly, out of nowhere.

Was it out of nowhere?

She really couldn't fool herself on that one, could she? She looked down at the crepe skin on her hands and it seemed that they were prompting her to take stock of her life. Was that all she had? A mixture of temping jobs about the city that the younger girls wouldn't touch, a poky little flat filled with memories – mostly despondent at best – and the fridge of groceries Robyn bought that she would eat alone.

An overwhelming sense of dread cloaked her, wound itself around her so tightly, she thought that it might snap her shut. It was as though the square was closing in on her, but she knew that if she moved, the sensation would only get worse. It felt as if the darkness of night could snuff her out; extinguish her as easily as a wavering flame.

What was wrong with her?

She was having some kind of panic attack. That was it. It was simple. Life had gotten on top of her. Stress. She read about it all the time. Top executives got it, running on adrenalin, high blood pressure – she had low blood pressure; was that even worse? That frustratingly direct doctor had scared her at the mention of a stroke.

No, she wasn't stressed. That was just silly.

But she wasn't happy either, was she? She took a deep breath, exhaled long and weighty. For a moment, she stopped everything. Everything in the square, everything it seemed in this city, stood still. She knew that something was wrong and it wasn't just her blood pressure. It wasn't that she should be eating more greens or checking that she'd turned off the gas. She was missing something and it was something far more profound than just food in her fridge. She looked again at her worn-out hands and the crumpled flier for a choir recital that she would never see. In that moment, in the darkness, out of nowhere, Tess Cuffe realised, that not only was she alone in the world, but it turned out that now, in her sixty-sixth year, she might be the loneliest person on the whole planet.

This time there were no tears. She would do something about it, make something of all these wasted years and the empty ones that surely lay ahead if she didn't make some changes. She shuffled out of the garden, glared at the traffic as she crossed the road to her flat.

'If you so much as squeak, my lady, you'll feel the hard end of my foot,' she said as she passed the cat sitting stoically on the footpath.

'Do you think she knows that they've abandoned her?' Robyn asked her. She was standing in the porch, over a basket of suspiciously familiar clothes.

'Where did you get those?' Tess glared at them with the practical eye of a woman who knows she has been saved a lot of work in drying clothes that she'd hung out less than an hour earlier.

'Well, they won't dry in this weather, will they?' Robyn said, heaving the basket up into her arms and dropping it inside the hallway for Tess to sort from there. 'I mean, the air is so damp and cold, and there's no point hanging them about in your flat when I could just pop them in the dryer in our laundry room.'

'And your mother is happy to do that, is she?'

'Well, I'm sure she wouldn't mind, especially since your arm is plastered and you're still all bruised.' She stood back into the porch again, mildly putting aside that she was not welcome here, but perhaps she was happy to take what she could get. The porch provided some shelter for that nuisance cat she was so fond of. 'Anyway, she was out somewhere, so I couldn't ask either way,' she said casually, as though it didn't matter.

'Well, I suppose I should say…' Tess looked beyond the girl, couldn't quite think of a way of saying thanks without it sounding trite.

'It's okay, you don't need to,' Robyn said as she turned to gather up the cat who was wrapping itself affectionately around her legs and purring like a train. 'Come on you,' her voice softened even more when she reached to pick her up.

'I…' Tess began, but she wasn't sure what she wanted to say. 'It was thoughtful of you to take my washing in,' she said, looking towards the darkening sky, where rain loomed in heavy clouds. 'You've saved me a lot of time and trouble, very decent of you indeed.'

'Really it was no bother,' Robyn said into the cat's fur and turned towards the garden leaving Tess to watch from the silence of her flat.

'I don't think...' Tess called out, remembering Robyn's question of earlier. 'If that cat does realise the O'Hara's have forgotten, well, I don't think it can mind too much.' Tess cleared her throat, let her voice fall into a slightly gentler sound. 'I think it looks as happy as I've ever seen it.'

'Really?' Robyn said and when she smiled it lit up her eyes as Tess had never noticed them before.

The door closed with a soft and even click and with it, Tess thought she heard the world move just a beat too far away. All at once, it seemed her little flat and her life stretched further into abiding solitude. The familiar din of emptiness drummed louder than any other noise on earth and Tess thought she would scream if she had to endure another second. What was wrong with her? It had never bothered her before. Tess had no idea what she was going to do, but she had to start somewhere. Tonight she would begin to walk about the square, it would be a start in the right direction. Exercise for the sake of keeping her alive long enough to outlive Awful Amanda and Randy Richard. It may not be the answer to all her problems, but she had to start somewhere.

10

January 2 – Friday

Amanda checked the clock, it wasn't surprising, eight twenty-two, it was three minutes exactly since she last checked. She turned on the television in the front lounge, the music system in the kitchen and she lit candles in the hall. She picked up a magazine; threw it aside again. She was one step away from descending on the box of chocolates that whispered to her from the utility room where they lay expectantly, they knew she'd be back for them, eventually.

Richard was always late these days, but, she told herself, that didn't mean anything. It was hardly a crime to work hard. Richard wanted to be top dog, he would wipe Hugo Lennox's eye this year, and then, maybe Nicola wouldn't be quite so superior anymore.

Amanda was trying desperately to compensate. The truth was, at this moment, she didn't give much of a damn either way whether Richard got the job. As far as she could see, they had as much as they could want. A promotion would just mean more stress, when they didn't need any more money. It would mean she'd be expected to entertain people, and while there would be caterers and planners, entertaining Richard's work colleagues was about so much more than just putting food on the table. God, even thinking about it was getting her all worked up.

It was almost nine-thirty when she heard his key slip into the lock. Somehow, her senses heightened, she imagined she could hear the metal twisting in the barrel. The soles of his shoes kissing their lovely original parquet floor bristled along her nerves unreasonably.

'Richard,' she called as he passed the sitting room door. 'I'm here.' Funny, but mostly he just made his way to the kitchen, or his study – and those were the nights he arrived home before she was in bed already.

'So you are,' he called as he made his way into the kitchen.

'Can I get you something to eat?' She followed him.

'Ah, maybe something light,' he said, 'you can bring it through.' He walked past her, headed for the study and, she realised, if she disappeared now, he probably couldn't describe what she looked like, not really. He couldn't tell the police what she was wearing, or if she'd had her make-up on, or her rings. God, she could be walking about with whiskers and nose rings for all he knew, because, she realised now, he didn't really look at her anymore. Oh, he looked at her when they went to the New Year's party – not that he said she was nice. He managed to concede the heels balanced her out, so she didn't look so round. God, she'd been ridiculously happy when he said that six inches turned her almost into an oval shape. Was that all she expected now? And when had she turned into a maid or waitress for him? She looked down at the tray in her hand, was she going to carry his food into him and clear up afterwards?

She stood for a moment, alone again in her big kitchen. What was she thinking? Less than twelve hours ago, she'd found a condom in his pocket and even if she'd managed to convince herself that it was some kind of silly misunderstanding, she couldn't really be planning on pandering to him until she was sure it was just a mistake – could she?

Well, no she bloody couldn't.

'Richard,' she said a little too loudly as she rounded the kitchen door into his little study. When he looked up from his desk, she could see he was startled. Perhaps it was more than that, he looked really quite unwell. As though he'd had an argument with someone – she knew the look, a mixture of insult and upset. He didn't like it when he couldn't get his own way. She remembered it from when they fought with Tess Cuffe over the court case. 'Are you all right?'

'Yes, why? Why wouldn't I be?' he looked at her now as though he was waiting for her to supply an explanation for why he looked so worried.

'No, you look terrible and it reminded me…' She was distracted now, but it was as much with the present as it was with the past. 'Tess Cuffe…'

'Tess Cuffe?' He shot up. 'What about her? What's she been saying? Because whatever it is, you know what she's bloody like. Too much time on her hands, that woman – she's nothing but an interfering old busybody.'

'Richard, I didn't mean…' God, what had she mentioned Tess Cuffe for, she always annoyed him, although, not usually as much as this. Amanda decided he must have had a really rough day of it. 'She didn't say anything, no, I was just…'

'Well, that's all right then,' he said, lowering himself into his chair, as though the threat of attack had passed. 'Been a long day,' he said and Amanda wondered if that was meant to be some kind of apology for leaving any pleasantries somewhere outside the front door.

'I know, Richard. You work too hard,' she said, trying to smile. 'Actually,' she took the condom from her pocket and slipped it across the desk. 'Look familiar,' she drew up the corners of her mouth and managed a nervous smile, of course he wasn't having an affair, how stupid was she really? Her Richard, the very idea! He was far too busy to have an affair, far too worked up about his job and Tess Cuffe and a million other important things, to even have sex with his wife, never mind about an affair as well. 'I found it,' she said, moving it across a little further and dipping her voice, just a fraction. God, it was so long since they'd had sex, perhaps that was all they were missing. A good old-fashioned bonk-a-thon.

Once upon a time, it would have worked wonders for his stress levels, even if it did make her crave tiramisu.

'I...' Richard cleared his throat, picked up the condom, as though trying to figure out what was happening, he squinted for a moment, 'it's a... it's a... oh, my God,' then he dropped it, as though it might burn his fingers off. 'Where did you get this?' His voice was hardly a rattle.

'It was in your pocket,' Amanda said. 'After the party, I was getting your suits ready for the cleaners.'

'Oh, I see,' he said, flopping back in the chair. Then he sat forward and Tess thought the silence would swallow her up, he looked from her eyes to the condom and back again. 'God,' he said, his voice returning to a glimmer of its usual cockiness. 'Those jokers, you know what this is, don't you?'

'Well, I suppose, it's...' Amanda felt her temperature drop. Had she shivered?

'It's those blokes from accounts, they're such a crowd of wankers,' he moved his four fingers across his lips, left them there for a moment, and with that trademark move, if he never said another word, Amanda knew he was lying to her.

'Of course,' her voice echoed, 'the blokes from accounts, total wankers.' She took up the condom, automatically, felt it almost burn into her hands and somehow managed to get out of there without collapsing. She had to think this through, couldn't face the stark truth of what it all meant. One thing was certain, it was confirmed, for her at least, Richard was lying.

'A personal trainer,' Megan winked at her when they were having their weekly coffee in the Berkley a few days later. Then she added with a throaty laugh, 'You'd be amazed what the right one can do for your marriage as well as your waistband.' It was the worst kept secret that Megan was having a fling with a Mexican muscleman called Pedro.

'Well, I think it's very brave, deciding to give up the things you love,' Clarissa sniffed. Clarissa hadn't seen a jam tart in twenty years. She had developed a series of convenient food intolerances, so it seemed to Amanda that all she could manage now was water. Mind you, Amanda often reflected, it was doing wonders for her skin, if not exactly imbuing her with a sense of fun.

'I don't know about that, now, it is just cake and biscuits after all, but I'm thinking of going power-walking too,' Amanda chimed in, she could hear her voice going through the usual conversations, but they were outside of her. She was still in shock. She knew it. She hoped she was hiding it well.

She sipped her coffee in silence while the other women gossiped and it dawned on her that they might already know if Richard was having an affair. They usually did, when it was someone else. One of the husbands would always let slip on the other, so their coffee mornings had always been lively bitchfests. They gleefully swapped stories about the women who were not present. Each of them stupidly believed they would never be the one on the outside. Isn't that what Amanda had thought? Her Richard would never have an affair like Cordelia Pearse's husband. That had been truly scandalous. They'd all known about it for so long. He'd been shagging his secretary at every possible opportunity, while Cordelia kept a stiff upper lip. At least Cordelia had the last laugh. None of them realised at the time that Cordelia was siphoning off not only her husband's bank account but, in the end, his company credit card as well. Then, when it suited her, she hightailed it back to her well-heeled Boston family. She cheerfully left her hapless husband to face the music. Apparently, he was working in the charity sector now. Richard said it would take him three lifetimes to pay back what they owed.

She shuddered again, realising that comparing herself to Cordelia Pearse was something she never thought she'd be doing.

'Are you cold, darling?' Nicola examined her a little too closely through narrowed kohl-rimmed eyes.

'No. I'm fine. I think I'm just shaking off a touch of flu. I probably should be getting home, keeping warm.' Amanda began to shrug into her cashmere coat.

'I can drop you back, if that suits.' Nicola leaned over towards her. 'I thought you looked a bit peaky when you arrived.'

'As I said, I'm just fighting off the sniffles.' Amanda could hardly breathe. The last thing she wanted was to break down in front of this lot. She couldn't do that. She'd be the talk of the wives for a solid week. She could almost hear the phone conversations in her ears as she left, whispering about her marriage, about her home, her children and, of course, about the fact that she had let herself go so badly over the years. Oh, yes, that would be the pronouncement from Nicola. She could imagine the words tripping off those scarlet lips. *I told her, when you're forty, Botox is your only friend.*

Amanda made her way back to the jeep. Usually, after the Berkley, she trotted up to the National Gallery, wiled away an hour or two. She couldn't go there today, she knew, even sitting before one of her favourite paintings wouldn't soothe her soul. In her head, she hadn't left the women behind her at all. She could hear their cackling voices making up words in her ears. These women were supposed to be her friends. Friends, the people she could depend on and rely on when things went pear-shaped. Could she really rely on Nicola or Megan or Clarissa?

Suddenly she thought back to when news of Cordelia's marriage break-up became official. Amanda winced, she was no better than the others. She had greeted it with a mixture of interested curiosity at best, at worst, well… she'd hate to be talked about as they had discussed Cordelia. God, she was sorry now. And not just sorry because she found herself in the same boat. She was genuinely sorry for how they had spoken about and treated Cordelia. They had frozen her out. Well, they had frozen her out after they pumped her for any details she would give and then chewed over the carcass of her marriage as if they were vultures at a desert feast. They had been horrible. She had been horrible and really, she knew, as she drove back towards Swift Square, she absolutely had no right to expect anything better now that she found herself in the same position.

The house was silent when she arrived back, aside from the low hum of the alarm, clocking her movements, measuring every tremor that crossed its various trip points. Suddenly, she sensed the whole house was watching her. It was waiting to see what she would do next. Was it laughing at her? Did this overstuffed monstrosity that she had helped create see right thought her?

Amanda stood in her lovely bedroom for a moment. This house – she couldn't truthfully call it a home – had taken years to assemble. Years of her time and effort and the price of a dozen working-class homes to decorate. And what was it all for? She wondered now as she ran her hand along the wild organza drapes that she had imported specially from France. They'd cost the equivalent of a teacher's monthly salary just to cover the master bedroom window. She felt completely empty looking around the room that once made her so proud. Now, it represented something pinched from her. She wasn't even sure she wanted to live here anymore.

That idea filled her with complete panic. Her breath, shortening in her lungs, told her it was time to stop thinking and start moving. Only she didn't know where to move to or how to stop the maelstrom of emotions that had overtaken her since she found that...

She looked at the dressing room door again. She couldn't stay here. She couldn't stay in this room. She ran out, banged closed the door behind. In the kitchen, she went straight to the fridge. She grabbed a block of cheese and was about to cut off a large satisfying chunk when she caught sight of herself. Her reflection gaped back at her from the mirrored surface of the Danish TV that Richard insisted they must have installed across the opposite wall.

Amanda glared at the woman standing there. It was déjà vu, that woman who'd looked back at her only a few days earlier had sunk to a new low. She was a washed-up, overly preened, doormat of a woman. The image that stared back at her did not come near to matching the woman she once believed she could be.

What was she going to do?

Eat her way out of her collapsing marriage? Could chocolate and cheese really be the solution?

Ragroll her way to happiness? She had a feeling this wasn't a problem that could be sorted by Farrow and Ball.

Bury her head and hope it would just sort itself out? Convince herself that by keeping up the façade all would be well?

She knew it wouldn't. Nicola, Clarissa and Megan might be able to live that kind of life, but not Amanda. The silver foil packet from her husband's tuxedo had put paid to that. Now, standing here, looking into the depths of those achingly sad but familiar eyes, Amanda King knew that she would have to shake things up. She would have to make some radical changes and she'd have to figure out what kind of life she wanted to live. From today, she was living it on her own terms.

Amanda might have known that Tess Bloody Cuffe would be out lumbering about the square. As luck would have it, they bumped into each other just on the halfway mark. Well, Tess would have to behave herself out here. She couldn't just go around calling Amanda names or making a nuisance of herself, and if she did, Amanda had a feeling that she was in for a nasty surprise, because on this occasion, she might just bite back.

'So, you're out walking now, are you?' Tess said as they passed each other on their second time round the square. It was typical, of course, that Tess would have to walk in an anticlockwise direction, Amanda thought as she took a clockwise direction.

'Looks like it,' was all Amanda managed as they breezed past each other. Really, Tess Cuffe was too much, out wandering about with her face almost hidden beneath that huge scarf. She'd do herself a mischief if she fell over and then it'd be Richard that'd have to fork out for ramps around that little flat.

Oh, God, Richard, she wanted to wail her pain out here, right in the middle of the road.

Then, she saw Tess Cuffe rounding the end of the square. Had she managed to make it around the square with greater speed than Amanda?

'You'd need to be taking it easy, you don't want to end up doing damage to yourself,' Amanda volunteered as they passed each other for the second time. Amanda was almost out of puff, but she was determined to stay walking for longer than Tess and she certainly wasn't going to be walking any slower than her.

'Wouldn't you just love that?' Tess cackled. 'A nice clean heart attack to finish me off and then you could have my flat kitted out into a man cave or a sunken gymnasium no doubt.' And she seemed to pick up pace as though she was racing Amanda about the square, lapping her in some juvenile way. Amanda thought about her words. Of course, she was right, there was a time when Amanda thought she could do something lovely with the flat, but now in her mind she'd annexed that part of the house from her imagination. All the same, it was a shame they'd ended up with such bad feeling between them. Richard, with his bloody court case and his ranting and bullying – he'd turned her right off having anything to do with the basement, if it ever came up. Of course, she wouldn't go saying that to Tess.

She'd spent twenty years working on their united front – she wasn't going to let that woman know that they were anything less now.

'I suppose, you're trying to lose the weight for the new year,' Tess enquired as they met each other again, this time Tess had made even better headway and Amanda slowed down still further. 'Take the lead out of your backside, no harm,' Tess guffawed.

'Takes one to know one,' Amanda retorted, 'when it comes to having a big bum.' Beneath the glassy ray of the street lamp, Amanda did a double take. Was Tess's face bruised and battered-looking? She could have sworn as the old girl walked past that there were bruises and perhaps stitches too. The thought threw her off balance a little. She'd spotted the plaster on her hand before Christmas and for a moment she wanted to turn back and ask if everything was all right. It was what you did, wasn't it? Enquired after your neighbours? Well, not when your neighbour was Tess Cuffe and she was as likely to call you all the names under the sun as she was to engage in any kind of civilised conversation. So, instead, when she reached the point where she was opposite her house, Amanda crossed the road, leaving Tess to make her way round the square once more. Truthfully, she was out of breath anyway, if anything Tess had only spurred her on to work a little harder. God, there was a part of her that felt more determined than ever to get fit – well, fitter than Tess Cuffe anyway.

11

Forty-eight years earlier…

Tess knew that moment, the moment Douglas kissed her, was the axis on which her life turned. She dreamed of it, not just when she slept, but during classes when she really should have been listening to her lessons. She slept deeply at night and drifted through the weeks in a kind of wafting reverie. They ran into each other most days in college and even if he wasn't exactly thrilled when she told him she'd agreed to sing at the club again, he offered to chaperone herself and Nancy. She liked that he was a little old-fashioned; not a fuddy-duddy, he certainly wasn't that. Their kiss confirmed for her that he was everything that she wanted and nothing like the provincial types she'd dreamed of getting away from. Tess had never considered herself a romantic, but suddenly she was swept away on notions of happy ever after with Douglas Buckley, it really was quite wonderful.

True, he had very set ideas, but Tess admired that. He knew what he wanted out of life and so, if he didn't really like the jazz scene – they'd find more common ground when she was playing in the National Concert

Hall one day. He wasn't keen on Stephen either, but then they were very different people. Stephen had what Tess would call the common touch. His friends were all working class, and Tess had a feeling that it wasn't so much that Douglas looked down on them, as he didn't really 'understand' them.

He wasn't exactly upper class himself, but he had standards, he told her. He loved hearing about Ballycove and their father and the schoolhouse. Funny, but when Nancy spoke about it, somehow it all sounded so much grander than Tess remembered. Douglas's father worked in mills in a small town west of Dublin. His mother cleaned the Bishop's Palace and Tess had a feeling that Douglas saw this as a mixed blessing.

'It's not that I'm ashamed of them, but I've always thought I can be so much more,' he told her one lunchtime. They were sitting at a crowded table, the arts students always stuck together, and Tess had made her way across to join them. 'That's why I've worked so hard to get here. It's not everyone that gets a Bishop's Scholarship,' he said proudly and his chest puffed out a little further as he said it. 'Although,' he leaned in closer to whisper, 'I'm not so sure he'd be so keen to send young men from his parish if he knew the kind of ungodly carry-on that I've witnessed since I've arrived here.' Douglas shook his head and Tess knew he was talking about an American girl called Rhonda who it was rumoured had slept with four different boys since she'd arrived.

'Well, even the bishop will have read *let us not cast the first stone*,' Tess said mildly.

'Tess, honestly, you haven't got a clue, women like that are just bad news and even the men that they lead astray only end up hating them for it in the end,' Douglas said quietly.

'Oh, Douglas, I'm sure it's all just rumours,' she said. Her father would be impressed with Douglas's scholarship, she supposed it meant he had a good brain, but that wasn't why she was falling for him. She couldn't put a reason on what attracted her to Douglas, it was something magical, something within her that reacted to him. 'Nancy's making shepherd's pie this evening, if you fancy it,' she said as she gathered up her books for a history of music class that she had little interest in.

'About six?' he asked and looked down at his watch. 'I'll bring along my chessboard, shall I?'

'If you like.' Tess said, but she half wished he wouldn't. Chess bored the socks off her, but Nancy enjoyed it, so Tess listened to the radio while they played.

'The bishop is a great man for the chess, you know,' he said contentedly and she smiled, because she realised he was only doing what he thought would make a better life one day for him and maybe her.

Tess could see past the chess, the bishop and even the fact that he hadn't tried to kiss her again. Tess had a feeling that when things were right it would all happen and Douglas would sweep her off her feet and she would feel so happy then.

In spite of Douglas's reservations about the Sunset Club, he still insisted on tagging along with herself and Nancy each week. He always grumbled, just a little, but after the first few weeks it felt like they had a standing date. The jazz crowd were not her friends, not really. They might have been, she certainly enjoyed them, but she had college to think of and of course Douglas. While they stayed late in the club, she would happily make her way back to the flat with Douglas and Nancy. She pulsed with the expectation of what would pass between them, if Nancy went into the flat and left them alone in the darkness.

'Oh, really, Nancy, of course you'll come along,' Douglas teased her that evening.

'No, I don't think so, you'll take care of each other without me. I'm really tired, what with college and then shopping and making the dinner, I'm just beat.' She yawned delicately, just as Nancy did everything in life.

'Maybe you don't have to go tonight, Tess?' Douglas rounded on her and she thought it was rather sweet that he didn't want to abandon poor Nancy while they went out to have fun.

'I'm afraid they're expecting me, I can't just let them down, you know that, Douglas.' She had already changed into a dress she'd picked up earlier that week in the market. It was a midnight blue, shimmery, sparkly, clingy cocktail dress and as it rubbed against her skin, it awakened every cell in her body to the possibilities of Douglas Buckley. She suspected it might be a lot more expensive than the price tag, but she didn't ask if it had fallen off a lorry and the old girl selling it hadn't made a thing of it. 'Nancy doesn't mind if we head out, we'll be back early, promise.' She kissed her sister on her forehead and wrapped her coat about her shoulders. 'Come on, Douglas,' she called as she made her way out the door, a fizzing excitement rising inside her because she knew, deep within her, that this would be the night they kissed again.

The show had been like every other, apart of course from the fact that Nancy was not there. But Douglas was and Tess sang her heart out for him in every tune. Later, he helped her into her coat and, when she turned to face him, stood just a little closer than was usual, her face skimming past his chest for one enchanting moment.

They talked of all the usual things on the way home. Douglas complained of unfair rent and a miserable landlady, a useless professor and the approach of colder weather. He worried about Tess and Nancy and what would happen if the college should increase its fees, as rumour had it that this was a possibility. But then they stood at the entrance to the flat and suddenly it seemed as though they had run dry of things to say and the silence stretched tight as a demand between them. And then it happened. Tess wasn't sure which of them leaned in first, but soon, his lips were on hers and they were kissing, long, warm wet kisses that ran into each other so she thought she couldn't breathe. Her heart pounded in her chest and a delicious feeling swam somewhere deep inside of her and she knew that it was longing, sweet and wonderful and arduous. Between the kisses and the fumbling, he murmured so much in her ears that at this stage, she knew he felt the same. He was only holding himself back, really, she could feel it when she leant against him.

'God, Tess, it's not right what you've done to me.' His whispers played in her head for days afterwards. 'I always thought I'd be... you know, hold it for my wedding night, but this...' he had been shaking, trying to hold back the tension between them.

'Come on, Douglas,' she knew the risks, but she was playing with him, perhaps she was playing with fire if it was anyone else, but this was Douglas. She was in love with him and she could tell, even if they hadn't said the words, he was in love with her too.

'What kind of man would I be if I...' he shuddered, pulling himself away from her. 'No, Tess, it wouldn't be right. Our kind of people, we just don't. It's not right, carnal knowledge, before your wedding night, it's just so...' and still, she could hear his breath, forced, and it aroused her so much more than he even realised.

'Carnal?' she finished his sentence and laughed then. It was a game, really, to her. 'Okay, I'll go in to the flat and get my beauty sleep if that's what you want,' she said, kissing him lightly on his lips as she straightened out her dress around her. 'The next thing you'll be telling me is that nice girls don't kiss,' she was joking.

'Well...' he said and he stole another kiss before standing over her. 'Well, maybe nice girls do kiss, but good girls don't,' he said laughing and he made his way off out of the square.

It was Nancy's evening for doing the laundry, but when Tess looked at her sister, she sensed a lethargy that found no cure in rest. With each day that passed, Nancy seemed to shuffle further into a paler, smaller version of herself. Tess assumed her weariness had its roots in melancholy – she missed Ballycove and the familiarity of home.

Tess put her arms around her, 'Let me cook and take care of us tonight, while you rest.' She set about preparing eggs and warming up the slightly stale bread. While she cooked, Tess hummed the tune to one of the jazzy numbers she had agreed with Stephen.

'You're happy,' Nancy smiled as she laid the table for them both.

'I am. I've agreed that I'll start a second night in the club this week for the rest of the year, they're adding my name to the billing.'

'Oh, Tess, no. Not in that dive, I thought you'd be leaving it all behind you after Christmas. What happened to playing at wedding ceremonies?' Nancy dropped further into the seat, 'Tell me you're not going to let yourself get tangled into that scene, it's so…'

'So? It's money, just a job, and I think it's great.'

'But, Tess, you're so much better than that. We have enough money in what Father sends, you don't need the money, not really. What would Father think? And Mamma? It's not why they sent you here, they have dreams for you and those dreams never involved shaking your hips while old men leered at you. You could be…'

'What?' Tess turned towards her, it was better to have it out now, she knew that, otherwise, it would fester between them. 'What could I be?'

'Well, what about your dreams to sing in the National Choir or maybe even some day sing in the Royal Opera House?'

'Those dreams are still safe.' Tess dropped down opposite Nancy now, held her eyes with a little more coolness than she could ever remember between them. Before they came here, before she enrolled in Trinity College, Tess had conviction. She had been the best singer they knew. Back in Ballycove, no one could touch her voice. Here, she was in a sea of talented people. Instead of being the big fish, she'd turned into a small mackerel swimming among the shoal. The truth was, the Sunset Club had been her first chance to shine since she came here and Tess needed that just as Nancy needed air. 'And anyway, it was good enough for Ella Fitzgerald.'

'Ella Fitzgerald was black and she was so much more than just a...' Nancy said quietly. 'It's just so sleazy – can't you see that?'

'Honestly? Nancy, I see the chance to make about ten pounds a week and that will pay for clothes and hairdressing for both of us.' It was true, her sensible country girl clothes and long, home-styled hair was just another marker to separate Tess from the place she wanted to be. 'Just because I'm singing there, doesn't mean I'm going to be losing the run of myself or doing anything to put my course into jeopardy. This is just fun, if you let yourself enjoy it, it could be fun for both of us.'

'I'm not sure what's right anymore,' Nancy didn't sound convinced, but it had always been this way. They say there's usually a dominant sibling – they're not always the oldest, or cleverest, or the most beautiful, but they are the one born with the guts and Tess had always known she was that sister.

'Anyway, haven't I got Douglas to keep an eye on me?' Funny, but Tess knew instinctively that Douglas Buckley would look after her – she was still pinching herself that he had chosen her. She didn't have to say it to Nancy, her sister had to already know.

'Yes, of course. He's a good man, Tess,' Nancy said absently, 'I think I'll just go and have a little lie-down, I'm not hungry now.' Nancy left Tess standing with a half-cooked omelette that it turned out neither of them much felt like eating.

12

January 5 – Monday

The whining sound woke Tess before five o'clock in the morning. In the beginning, she thought it was the radio, normally the thick walls blunted any sounds from thwarting her sleep. Perhaps it was one of those disc jockeys who belt out questions and then wait for listeners to ring up to do their jobs for them. Tess hated them almost as much as she hated weather forecasters with their inane cheerfulness regardless of whether they were bringing news of sun, showers or snow. When she caught sight of the clock, she knew it wasn't the radio. Her room was at the front of the flat, normally the only thing to wake her was the postman, singing loudly out of tune to his Spotify subscription. In himself, he was a torture, but his racket was different to this. This noise grated on her nerves in its insistence.

The din outside now was so loud, she wondered if something was trapped in the outer porch. She'd never been keen on that porch. It served no real purpose, just more windows to be washed, at best a place to leave her umbrella. These days she didn't even bother locking it.

To her sleepy ears, it could be anything. There was no choice really. She had to go and investigate.

She cursed as she pulled on her thinning beige dressing gown. She padded over the plaited parquet softly, as though there was a danger of waking someone else at this ungodly hour. If it was a damn dog she'd march him to the pound herself. She solved the mystery as soon as she opened the door. The cat volleyed through her ankles and slipped around her sitting room door. Well, she thought, on this occasion, he's not going to do any damage and if it keeps him quiet, where's the harm in letting him sleep easy for a few hours. Outside, the morning looked like night. Still, it had that frosty dewy feel to it, where everything seems crisp, new and full of promise in the quiet before the day ahead. The stillness caught her up with an arresting optimism.

'Oh, look at you,' she stroked the soft coat and the cat looked up at her with the most soulful eyes she'd ever seen on an animal. In the kitchen, beneath the sink there was a large box, filled with recycling. She wasn't sure that he'd fit in it, but it was the best she could do for now. 'God, you're a bruiser,' and the cat gazed at her as though Tess was the best thing he'd seen in yonks. Tess felt her heart soften and lifted him as gently as she could into it. 'Mind you, I suppose, when it comes to heavyweights, I'm hardly one to talk.'

The flat at least felt warm as she moved through the kitchen. The stale smell of last night's dinner wafted from the top of her bin; a muggy colostomy of leftovers, dank mothballs and neglect, all permanently seeping within the fabric of everything she knew. There was an oppressive, if reassuring, feel to knowing that all was as she left it when she went to bed, even if it was shabby and meagre.

From the fridge, she took a half pint of milk, emptied it into a bowl before taking the cold from it in the microwave. 'Well, Robyn's certainly going to be missing you this morning.' When she looked at him now, it was hard to believe he'd caused so much trouble over the last few weeks. He'd caused all the bother with Tess's arm and then tripped her up so she ended up looking as though she'd done a few rounds in the ring. Only here, curled up in a pathetic ball Tess couldn't find it in her heart not to feel sorry for the poor thing. It was too late to be angry with the hapless little pudding. Nothing could convince her that those awful people hadn't just abandoned him, left him to his own devices while they swanned around the golf clubs and theme parks in the Florida winter sun. He was an inside cat, too expensive to be left roaming about – too cosseted to have the skills necessary for life on his wits. Just now, in that little porch, she'd seen him in his most pitiable moment and there was no going back to their old relationship of distinct dislike. Tess knew herself well enough to know, it was time to let bygones be bygones.

'Who would call a fine cat like you Margaret? No

wonder you've taken to throwing yourself in the way of grumpy old women, eh?' There was no denying that Margaret was not a lady – she had enough appendage for any Tom to be proud of. Tess much preferred male cats anyway, less needy, she'd always thought. She stroked his soft silky fur and, somehow, it seemed having him here made everything feel more opulent in some peculiar way. 'I think you're more of a Matt? How's that, Matt?' She scratched him under his chin and he purred agreement. It was decided, for as long as he stayed, he would be Matt and, with that, their past encounters were wiped clean as far as Tess was concerned.

Once he settled in, Matt was thoroughly reluctant to leave. Tess tried to encourage him out the front door when they'd had breakfast, just to stretch his legs, but his response was a decided no. She thought about popping him into her shopping trolley, for a little amble about the square later, but decided against it then. The last thing she wanted was to give him motion sickness. By late morning, she knew if one of them didn't get out the door, they'd be climbing the walls once it got dark, so she popped on her coat and decided to go for her daily toddle about the square while the weather held. The last few days, she'd been trying to time it so she didn't bump into that awful Amanda who seemed to have come up with the same bright idea as herself. Of course, being Amanda, she had to walk around the square backwards – well, clockwise perhaps, but it felt as though she was walking in the wrong direction. Truly, who turns left first?

Tess had a feeling that Amanda would be a fair-weather walker, falling out of the habit with the arrival of the first wet and windy night. Not so for Tess, she had a mission now. She'd made a command decision. She'd even weighed herself in one of the offices she temped in regularly – that had been an unpleasant experience. When had she grown so heavy? Then she realised, it was probably fifty years since she'd stood on scales. She couldn't expect to be the very same as she had been all those years ago. She wasn't exactly overweight, but she was brave enough to face the facts that it would do her no harm to lose half a stone.

Well, seeing Amanda King out there in her ridiculous sports clothes was just another stroke of motivation for her. She was damned if that snooty cow was going to be walking faster or further than her. If either of them was going to live a long and healthy life it was bloody well going to be Tess. She wouldn't give that pair the satisfaction of getting their noses inside her front door, much less their measuring tapes – unless it was refitting her old bathroom as a measure of Richard King's mortification and complete humiliation. The very notion of it made Tess feel pleased with herself all over again. So, when she ran into Amanda as she rounded her first circuit she was smiling and her greeting, instead of being bitten back, was almost pleasant.

Usually, she would have kicked herself for such a mistake, but today the look of complete shock and misapprehension on Amanda King's face almost made it okay. On her next circuit, she could say something a little less pleasant. Now, what to say… maybe something motivational. She settled on, 'It'll take more than walking to shift what you need to get off those hips.' Unfortunately, Amanda seemed to have ducked into the Square garden before she could follow it up with another motivational mantra to keep her going…

It struck Tess as karma in some offbeat way, the morning Matt arrived was also the morning that she learned about Douglas. It came as she'd always known it would. Out of nowhere, or more accurately, out of the letter box. It might have been there for days, Tess had gotten out of the habit of checking daily for letters that would contain nothing more than bills or fliers. A neat postcard, so she couldn't not read it, she supposed. It was a small three by five inches, with Nancy's flowing hand on the back. It was somehow obscene, to think that her sister would select an image of the sunrise in Ballycove to give her the news that Douglas had passed away. Tess sat with the card in her hands for she wasn't sure how long, the cat next to her, silently keeping time to her thoughts.

It was reassuring in some strange way to think that even though Douglas was gone, she was not entirely alone in this moment. Matt was here. Of course, he'd have to go back next door, but when she needed to know she was not on her own, he was here, doing as much as anyone could while the tears silently slipped down her cheeks. She had the strangest feeling that she was moving closer to her destiny, although she couldn't imagine how that might be. It felt wholly unnerving, but as with so many things in her life, Tess was too stubborn to make a move that might bring it closer just a little more quickly.

13

Twenty-two years earlier…

It was because her mother wouldn't be at her wedding. That was why, Nicola, Clarissa and Megan had become so important to her. Mind you, even if her mum had lived to see the day when her little girl would trip down the aisle with one of Dublin's most eligible men, Amanda wasn't sure that they'd have been able to organise the kind of wedding Richard and his family expected.

Ann Young had passed away tragically, when her daughter was just two years old. Amanda couldn't remember her mother, but she had a feeling they'd have been close. She had been close to her dad – growing up, before Line-dancing Linda arrived on the scene. Linda sashayed into their lives as a little gift for Amanda's fourteenth birthday. At the time, with her blue mascara and diamante-encrusted accessories, Amanda had almost believed that her dad had found Linda just for her. After all, she was coming to an age where having a woman about the place would be useful for conversations that a man like her dad just couldn't have with his daughter. They'd rubbed along, well enough. Linda certainly couldn't be described as a wicked stepmother, but at the same time, she was hardly maternal either. She was a platinum blonde, orange-skinned Oompa-Loompa of a woman who lived to dance and soon got Amanda's dad hooked on the country and western music scene.

'We'll be there, love,' her dad reassured her on the phone. 'I wouldn't miss it for all the world.' The line wasn't great, crackly and breaking up, but there was no missing his genuine joy for her.

'It's the heat,' Linda said. 'Summertime in the Canaries, it plays havoc with your highlights and the phone lines.' They'd moved over there as soon as Amanda started college. 'What does your dad want with farming when we can live for half nothing out there?' Linda had said and Amanda had a feeling she was reassuring herself as much as she was Amanda.

'Well, I'm just looking forward to seeing both of you,' Amanda said and she was, because even though Nicola had helped her to organise the wedding, she was not family. Although, in practical terms, she'd been as good as family. She had been very good – she'd helped with everything from the band to the orchid petals that would carpet the church. Nicola just always knew what was right and, more importantly, what was fashionably right. Amanda adored Nicola, really looked up to her. One day, she hoped, she would grow into a red-haired version of Nicola – not that she was all that much older than Amanda, but still, *one day*, she promised herself.

Even so, it wasn't the same as having her dad, stocky, soft, reliable and ordinary there at her side. Even Linda, yes, she could be a little embarrassing and Amanda was ashamed to admit it but part of her dreaded the Kings meeting her stepmother in all her garish glory. All the same, Linda was the nearest thing she had left to a mother and, in their way, Amanda knew that what passed between them was a comfortable kind of love that was easy and effortless.

'This time tomorrow we'll be in a nice old Dublin pub having a pint of the black stuff,' her father said to her just as they were about to catch their flight from Tenerife South Airport. It was six days before her wedding and that was the last time Amanda spoke to him. It turned out that Tenerife was good for keeping the arthritis at bay, but not so good for making her dad stop to think about the niggling pain in his chest in the run-up to his daughter's wedding. He had a massive heart attack as they set down in Ireland. He made it home, but not to the wedding.

'The show must go on,' Richard said gently, but she could see the stress of it all in his eyes. She wanted to marry him, so very much, but at the same time, it seemed wrong to come from burying her father to marrying her fiancé.

'It's what he would have wanted,' Linda said, but her

voice had lost all its lovely musical quality and rode out between them like a tired old dray. 'Don't think for a minute of cancelling it, he'd be broken-hearted if he thought that you'd...' she couldn't finish the words. Bless her, she wanted to say the right thing. She wanted to be brave and strong and hold it all together for just a few more days.

'I don't know, it won't be the same and it won't be right without him there.'

'God, Amanda,' Richard sighed and then he lowered his voice so it sounded velvety and smooth, 'I'm sorry, babe, but he's never going to give you away now. He's gone, but at least you have a future, a family to take care of you, my family.' He put his arm around her, squeezed her gently.

'You'll always be family too, Linda, you know that, don't you?' Amanda smiled a wobbly movement of her lips; she couldn't force anything more out and knew the photographs would be terrible. 'All right, we'll do it. Everything is booked; it'd be silly not to go ahead with it. Maybe Linda could give me away?' Amanda smiled at her stepmother, that at least would make her feel a little closer to her dad.

'Oh, really, Amanda, I don't think you can do that. No, we'll ask Nicola's husband, Hugo to stand in and do the honours, just for today, okay, Linda?' Richard smiled at Linda, but Amanda felt the loosening of the ties with her former life, with who she was and where she had come from. She was so head over heels in love with Richard though, what did it matter? After all, he was her future; as he said, she would have her own family now, the Kings. Soon, she wouldn't be Young anymore. It was the end of the line – the last of the Youngs would become Mrs Richard King.

14

January 9 – Friday

As Amanda came down the steps outside, a splash of colour from the Square garden opposite caught her eye. There were young mothers sitting on the benches chatting. Their small children made fun in the mini maze she had designed for her own children years earlier. The sunny morning, like a pied piper, had charmed them from the little streets that bled onto the square. They rocked designer prams laden down with all the paraphernalia of young motherhood. At the far end, Amanda noticed that two gardeners were hard at work. They were clearing back the remains of winter foliage around a large spring shrub decorated with huge wooden hearts painted in red and deep pink. With a sense of purpose, she made her way towards them.

'Hello?' Amanda called up to a young man who was busy cutting back ivy in its march along an ancient chestnut tree.

'Hi!' he said, turning to look at her.

'What's all this for?' she asked, a little put out because

she had put so much work into the garden over the years and it had left her feeling quite possessive of it.

'Oh, the city council. Apparently, this has been named the most romantic spot in Dublin this year and it's on the map for the "Love Dublin Festival,"' he said, smiling at her and she couldn't help but notice he really had the most enigmatic smile. It was broad and full, showing off perfect white teeth and it was somewhat contagious.

'Never heard a word of it,' Amanda said, not moving, but noticing the man's strong arms and shoulders as he leant towards a branch to hang the last of the hearts. She found herself unable to look away while he climbed down the ladder. When he stood opposite, he smiled as though he knew she'd been watching him, which only made her blush.

'Were we supposed to notify you, Miss…' he held out a hand and winked at her.

'Amanda,' she said, shaking his hand. 'And, no, I suppose not. But I've put a lot of work in here, so I keep an eye on it and I just like to know what's going on.' She felt foolish now.

'Amanda? Amanda King?'

'Yes, that's right.' Oh, God, had the younger mothers been talking about her? There was a time, not so long ago, when she used to march over to them and make their kids put back any tufts of grass that they'd kicked up. She wanted to die now at the embarrassment of what she'd let herself become. 'And you are?' She looked into his eyes which creased at the corners from hours spent in the sun.

'I'm Carlos. Carlos Giordano. My dad did some of the work with you?'

'Oh, God, yes of course, Antonio. How is he these days?'

'Retired. I'm running the business now, but you know, he still likes to keep his hand in. This,' he cast his hand about in the same dramatic fashion as his father might have done, 'he was very proud of the work you both did here. He wanted to come along with me this morning, but he's at a doctor's appointment for his knee.'

'Oh, I'm so sorry. Is he all right?'

'Old age and gardener's knees, it's going to come to us all with a bit of luck.' He laughed then, because of course the alternative to getting old was not so attractive. 'It looks as if he has arthritis, but he doesn't want to have the operation, he can be a stubborn old goat when he wants to be.'

'Yes, I remember, he certainly had spirit.' Amanda smiled thinking of the old Italian, they'd had some fantastic spats, but she had to admit, he knew his stuff, so she just had to concede when it came to plants.

'He liked you,' Carlos said softly and for a moment they stood shyly looking at each other. Then he smiled a rakish grin that made her feel giddy and a little scared all at once. 'And I can see why.' His voice dipped and Amanda wondered if he was flirting with her. His father had been the very same, incorrigible, she'd seen him with the older ladies and the younger ones, a charmer when he wasn't at loggerheads over the herbaceous border.

'Well, I'll have to look up this Love Dublin Festival, see if we can't be involved in it, here on the square,' she said, taking a step away from him. 'Are you finished here today?'

'For now, but we'll be back again. The council have contracted us to carry out repairs to the paths, benches and any of the beds that might be in need of it. Then, we'll take care of the spring planting. It'll be a sea of red and pink for the fourteenth.' He winked at her now.

'Well, then, I suppose I'll be seeing you again, Carlos,' Amanda said and even if she knew he was just flirting with her out of habit, she felt a little better as she headed back to real life once more. It was coffee morning with the girls again. God, it seemed to come round more quickly these days than ever before. Was it because she dreaded it for the six days beforehand, she wondered.

She had taken to doing an evening walk, just a quick stroll around the square before dinner and maybe to avoid Tess too, if she was honest. She wasn't exactly power-walking, but she was out of breath by the time she got back most days. She wasn't sure that being fit, or being thin, would win Richard back for her, she wasn't sure of anything much at all these days. The one thing she was certain of was that he would not have been so tempted away if, somehow, she'd just been a slightly better version of herself. Perhaps it was just once, a slip. If she convinced herself of that, maybe she could live with it? Did she want to live with it? With him? Would she always want to check his phone? Not that she was quite sure how she could. Yes, of course, she'd already tried, but it was password-protected and that in itself had made her stop. Maybe she'd think up a way of getting her hands on it, with plenty of time to spare, and figure out the password.

She was having conversations in her head all the time now. There were so many questions that she wanted to ask, but the truth was, she was frozen rigid by fear. She knew, she should find out if he had a mistress, or if this was a one-night stand. She just didn't know what to do next. It's not as though she expected him to tell the truth and, if he did, then where were they? At the end, that's where, she was sure of that much.

No, she wasn't proud of it, but she was too afraid to know the gory details yet. Too weak to face it head on, she wanted an easy way to find out, but she hadn't a living soul to confide in, so what was there to do? Try to pretend everything was normal and wait for one more slip. It was a cowardly approach but somehow better than seeing him leave her for some newer, thinner, maybe cleverer model. She couldn't blot out the girls he'd dated before they'd married. They'd all been the same: leggy, elegant blondes. He'd always gone for a 'type', until he'd met her. 'Gold-diggers,' Megan had said as though she'd married just for love.

It was funny, but back then, the girl he fell in love with – that girl she used to know – wouldn't have dithered for one second. That was probably more galling than anything else. Amanda had allowed herself to become weak and, in that altering of her very self, Richard had lost all interest in her. It was ironic and tragic all at once.

Either way, for now, she knew enough to put her off her food – and that was as much as she could handle. Into another day of starvation and it seemed like there was no more clarity than there was that day she had started calling condom-gate. Time would tell if she could hold onto him, she knew that.

The exercise was meant to make her feel better and maybe it was doing her head some good, but her body was ready to give in before she started. She wondered what people got out of getting sweaty, sore and breathless just for kicks. She couldn't see it herself. Funny though, perhaps it was the walking, more likely, it was the worry, but she'd all but gone off cake and biscuits – how had that happened? She always thought she'd eat her way through any crises. It turned out that the worst crises killed her appetite better than any gastric band. Tonight, most of the other buildings were in darkness. The office workers departed for the weekend, the only lights shone from houses that were still used as homes.

Amanda climbed the steps to her house, doing her best to ignore the little porch light that shone up from the flat below. Tess Cuffe had started walking too, she'd never thought of her as someone who might enjoy physical exercise. She really wasn't sure what to make of Tess these days. One minute she was smiling at her, the next she was sounding off as if she was some kind of corny fascist self-help guru. If she was trying to be funny, she certainly wasn't. Perhaps it was her idea of motivating. Really, it didn't bear thinking about, just something else to sap her energy, as if she hadn't enough already to worry about.

She would not think about Tess Cuffe now or her grotty little flat that Amanda had earmarked all those years ago as her state-of-the-art kitchen. She'd imagined a room that ran the length of the house and opened out into the garden, a place she could entertain with dining areas both inside and out. After all the trouble between Richard and Tess, she couldn't imagine having her dinner down there now. Instead, she admired the old glass in the Georgian windows of her lovely home that curved and wobbled so the lights inside seemed to glitter with more sparkle than they should.

In the hall, the kids had left their coats across the newel post. Amanda was starving and still she couldn't think of a single thing that wouldn't make her sick. According to the app on her phone, she'd covered almost eight thousand steps. Usually, at this hour, she'd open a bottle of red and keep herself topped up while she prepared dinner. Tonight, she threw some salad in a bowl. Took out a lasagne she'd prepared and frozen a week earlier and popped it in the oven. There was smoked salmon and a selection of cheeses. She piled them all on a board and filled a jug of water. Then she called the kids down for dinner.

'What the... Lasagne?' Casper said when he looked at his plate. 'Reheated...' he shook his head and, for a moment, Amanda thought he would push the plate away. Time was he loved her home-cooked lasagne, but these days it seemed nothing was good enough. Her children were used to freshly cooked and it seemed that everything was worthy of complaint to Casper, well, everything his mother did at any rate.

'Casper, if you don't like it, you can simply lump it,' Amanda said, feeling her temper flaring. 'It's home-cooked and it's healthy, up to you.' She kept her eyes on him, a silent ultimatum passing between them.

'Huh, well, Dad would have something to say about it,' he huffed, but picked up his knife and fork all the same. 'Aren't you having some?' He looked disdainfully at her plate.

'She's on a new diet,' Robyn said as she chewed her salad slowly.

'Seriously?' Casper said. He sneered at the jug of iced water, but it felt as though his attitude had ebbed. Amanda watched him, he really was the product of all around him. There was no doubting that there was a lot of Richard in him, but she had to take some of the blame for his sulkiness. She had pandered to his every whim over the years and, looking at him now, she knew it was time to stop. She took a deep breath, sat up a little straighter in her chair and forked some green salad thoughtfully onto her plate.

Eating salad and ignoring the lasagne was easier than she'd expected. She loaded her plate with lettuce, tomatoes and cucumber, and draped a little of the salmon across the top. Amanda had a feeling that whatever was on her plate would have tasted the same anyway – it seemed as if Richard had taken not just her spirit but her carb cravings too.

'When's Dad home?' Casper asked, as though Richard would have any interest in the power struggle at play across the kitchen table.

'I'm not sure. Ring him, if you want.' Amanda chewed her food without making eye contact and then she began to wonder. When had Casper become the new Richard in her mind? When had he morphed into a voice that constantly criticised and made her feel that whatever she did it would never be quite good enough? And then another question occurred to her: when had Richard stopped coming home for dinner? It had never been a thing. Not a real thing she'd noticed. Had it happened after the takeover? Or his last promotion? Amanda couldn't remember, but now she thought about it, it had been a long time since they all sat down to dinner together on a weekday. 'Yes. You should do that. Ring him. See what time he's due back,' she said.

Suddenly her lacklustre interest in her salad subsided and she sat back in her chair watching her two children. God, but she loved them so much. They had been delightful toddlers. Robyn had been such a sunny child, Casper serious but possessing a dry wit, he'd been too young to fully realise. Looking at them now, she wondered where those children had gone. These days she was lucky if they spoke two words to her, apart from when they wanted something of course. Mostly, she was lucky if Casper answered her with anything more than a grunt. Robyn was still sweet, if a little odd. She seemed to spend all her time hanging about the garden these days. Was that normal? Was it how other families lived around Dublin? Sharing houses with each other, but the only sound between them the blaring music or that strange silent world stifled by expensive Bluetooth earbuds. It seemed to Amanda that her family spent their time avoiding each other. Even car journeys now were an opportunity to make her feel as though she was somehow taking up their precious time. Invading the lives that not so long ago she'd been so totally central to. It struck her too, as she watched them flick fingers across screens while they chewed their food distractedly, that she didn't really know them anymore.

Her own children and it felt as though they were living in completely different worlds.

'Anyone fancy coming to the cinema tonight?' she said more brightly than she felt. The cinema had always been a popular destination.

'Seriously, Mum?' Casper didn't take his eyes from the screen in front of him, but she had a feeling that if he looked at her it would be with the blankness of a stranger. Robyn just sighed and smiled as though she knew her mother was making an effort, but really she was a little sad. Sometimes, Amanda felt she had turned into a 'Line-dancing Linda', without the sparkly shoes or the adoring husband. So, she sat there, willing herself not to cry, because she had a feeling if she let one tear drop now, she might never be able to stop.

15

Forty-eight years earlier…

'You look lovely,' Tess said when she saw Nancy emerge from her room. She wore a lovely red housecoat, but there was never any contest between the sisters. Tess had always been the beauty compared to Nancy's pared-down prettiness. They were alike, really, both tall, both narrow-framed, both with blue eyes and brown hair, but that didn't do them justice, because everything about Tess was so much more. Her eyes were cobalt blue, compared to Nancy's navy. Her hair was chestnut compared to Nancy's mousy colour. And Tess's smile was wide and bright, whereas Nancy hardly ever smiled at all. 'You really don't have to tag along every week though.'

'Well, we can't leave Douglas sitting on his own now, can we?' Nancy said and Tess wondered at the way her sister and Douglas Buckley sat each week to keep an eye out for her in a darkened corner where they still managed to look out of place. Nancy and Douglas together were, for all the world, like an old married couple, like her parents, really, sitting nursing drinks they had little interest in. But afterwards, alone within the darkness of the porch and in Douglas's arms, she felt he was nothing like her father.

The Sunset Club was a regular date. Now, Tess had a full set worked up and she and the band were taking on the occasional wedding ceremony too. She was making a nice little wage and the first thing she'd done was bring Nancy shopping. Tess thought they'd been transformed from their woollen tweediness to city girls. Tess had even bought some make-up and instead of cutting off her long hair, she'd set up a regular appointment to have it 'done' before the Sunset gigs. The most she'd persuaded Nancy into was jade bell-bottoms with a frilly blouse that cascaded down in ruffles around her neck. Her hair remained long and unbiddable – there was no talking her into anything trendier.

Soon, Tess's life took on a frenetic pace, she was happier than she ever imagined she could be. Moving between the college and the club, her world filled with new and exciting people. She sparkled her way through life and having Douglas in her arms and Nancy in the background was the foundation to her whirlwind existence. Far from losing its glitz, Tess loved the Sunset Club more than ever. She could see its seediness – she wasn't blind, but it wasn't about the place, it was about the feeling. The feeling when she got up on that stage and knew that every single eye was on her. It was about a new kind of power that Tess never realised she had before. Douglas drank her every movement in with his eyes and fought himself to keep them from consummating their relationship on the doorstep when they arrived back from the club. She might have done it, right there, in the open air, but for his reserve. There was something wanton about it, something euphoric about them together after she'd just come out of the limelight.

He was adamant. He would wait until it was right, she thought perhaps, he meant his wedding night. His sense of propriety, or maybe his fear of making her pregnant, worked to hold them both back and the longer it went on, the more promise reared in the ardent space between them.

The nights here in the club were when she knew she shone. While he sat with Nancy, in the dark, Tess could feel his eyes upon her. If she was truthful, she sang for Douglas – not for anyone else in that smoky little bar. He had taken on the mantle of protector – walking both herself and Nancy to the club and home again. Tess heard the rumours – these streets, the derelict tenements, crawled with underdogs – Ireland was at war – but it was not the Ireland of people like Tess or Nancy or Douglas. Dublin was just a few hours' drive away from the troubles in the North and, all too often, they had a habit of leaking into the city, albeit in a furtive, hidden manner. The Sunset Club was home to too many northern accents not to realise the danger. Tess loved

Douglas Buckley even more for that. Sometimes, she caught a glimpse of him through the darkened crowd, his eyes, or just the hint of a smile, and then she smiled in his direction, certain that their connection deepened with each passing moment.

And now the end of term dance was coming up. Tess knew it was her chance to firm things up between them. Tess and Douglas Buckley would be the most striking couple there.

'It's a grand ball,' he confirmed.

'I'm so looking forward to it,' she breathed as they walked home one night, and she was, although she was filled with dread at the looming exams. Douglas was linking both sisters. Nancy her usual quiet self, had no real plans to finish up the term.

Tess set about planning her gown, her hair and the way her new self-assurance would allow her to swagger in with more poise than any other girl in Dublin. She deserved Douglas – she had worked herself up to earn him, become worldly and shed the awkwardness of her rearing. Ballycove seemed as if it might be a lifetime away. Sometimes she thought of life there and it bothered her, not so much that Nancy missed it, but rather she feared it was the sort of place Douglas might adore.

She would ask him in college in a few days' time. It was silly to get so worked up about him asking her to be his date, perhaps he just assumed it would be so.

As it turned out, she didn't get a chance. The next few days were taken up with exams for the senior students. Douglas seemed to spend all his time in the library and when he wasn't there, he was not in the mood to talk about balls or gowns or even dates for that matter. So the arrangements settled on the unsaid words between them.

The following Wednesday she arrived back to the flat later than usual and stopped short to find him sitting on the grubby chocolate settee with Nancy.

'Oh,' she said and then remembered to pinch her lips back from the circle. 'I haven't seen you all week.' She cleared her throat; wound the long scarf away from her neck before hanging it on the hook that took their coats and hats and bags. There were just three hooks on the door, one of them held Douglas's coat and she saw it was dry. It had been raining all afternoon, but she left the knowledge to settle upon her. Perhaps he got a lift – or... then she noticed Nancy. 'Are you all right, Nancy, what's happened?' Her sister's ivory complexion had faded to an insubstantial grey. Her skin was a silky drape across cheekbones that seemed to sharpen overnight.

'They sent me home, early. I didn't feel well and they told me I needed to call someone so...' she looked up at Douglas, smiled the sort of serene smile that once they had both shared. 'He collected me in a taxi and brought me here. I'm fine now, really.' Her eyes sold out the vulnerability that she was trying hard to mask in her voice. 'I didn't want to bother you when you were doing your recital today.'

'Really, I don't mind staying here for as long as you're feeling under the weather.' His voice strained a mixture of affection and concern.

'It's probably just a bug, or something equally dull, you don't want to get it either.'

'It'll take more than germs to put me down,' he joked.

'No, really, you should go now,' Nancy said, catching something in Tess's eyes.

Tess walked him to the door. 'No Sunset Club this week,' she said as they looked out into the darkness, 'but at least we have the ball to look forward to.'

'Ah, yes, the ball,' he said absently. 'Are you going?'

'I...' she looked at him now and he seemed to be completely unaware of her plans for them both. 'I assumed we'd be going together, Douglas.'

'Oh, did you? Well, I didn't really think about it, not really my thing, you know, but if you want...' he said, smiling affably at her. 'Of course, we can go together. I'll pick you up here, yes? Will Nancy be coming along? She really doesn't look well at all,' he said now, looking back over Tess's shoulder.

'No. I shouldn't think so, it'll be just the two of us this time.' Tess leant forward and breathed into his ear, but somehow, without the caged-up energy of the Sunset Club inside her, it seemed as though there was some ingredient missing between them. 'Just us,' she said again, as he suddenly pulled away from her.

'Well, I'll pick you up about seven, here? We can walk to the college if the weather is fine.'

'Perfect,' Tess said as she watched him heading off into the evening dampness. 'Perfect,' and of course it was, because Douglas was the love of her life and, some day, when they were married and, who knew, maybe living in Aunt Beatrice's little cottage if that's what Douglas truly wanted, life would be absolutely perfect for them both. Tess shook off whatever daft notions had welled up inside her only minutes ago. She could be such a silly fool sometimes.

16

January 10 – Saturday

The rap on her front door startled Tess. It seemed in the last week it had been increasingly busy, between the glass fitters and the cat, it felt like she was suddenly popular compared to normal. Usually, no one ever called to visit. It took a moment to pick out its significance, once the sound itched her attention away from the cat in the small bed she'd made before her gentle fire.

Tess jumped up, then stood for a moment – perhaps she'd heard wrong. This old place was full of creaks and unexpected bangs, pipes and brickwork moaning and yawning for no particular reason. She'd gotten used to all of them over the years, even the new ones that arrived after upstairs had been ripped apart only to be put back together again.

No, this was definitely her door. She caught sight of herself in an old picture of the sacred heart – its light long extinguished. She might have moved it years ago, but she hardly noticed it anymore. These days she only used it as a nebulous mirror. It was good enough to check out all she wanted, but not so clear, that she ever had to look her reflection in the eye. She tried to smooth down brittle hair that stood on end too long to pay attention at this point, so she made her way to the door, a globule of irritated anticipation rising in her as she walked.

'Mrs Cuffe.' It was Robyn, her face even more anxious than normal. 'The most terrible thing, I can't find the O'Hara's cat anywhere.' She was close to tears, breathless and the tremble in her lower lip warned Tess that if she didn't get to see the cat she might crash into a meltdown right there on the doorstep. 'I've been searching for her since before breakfast, so really, she could be gone since last night. I can't think where she would go, but you know, she's worth a lot of money, if someone were to take her, well, I think I'd just die. I mean, I've looked everywhere.' She ran a hand behind her distractedly. It was four o'clock now, had she even stopped to eat anything? She seemed even more birdlike here today, cold and thin, her sparrow features pinched with fear and despair.

'You may as well come in. The cat is here.' Tess stood aside to let the girl squeeze past the narrow dim passage. 'He woke me, early this morning, and he seems to have taken up residence, for now at least.'

'Oh, thank goodness.' She rushed to the cat and fell upon him, the cat for his part remained stoic in his reserve. The questions tumbled out, some small relief just tangible in the air. Apparently, for Robyn, the least obvious scenario had been the cat, in all probability snoozing the day away in someone else's kitchen.

'He's fine,' Tess tutted. 'He's been here all day. I tried to let him out but he just came back in again at the first opportunity. He's probably been missing having a bed to call his own,' she said but suspected the girl didn't hear a word because she was still on the threadbare rug before the hearth and launching into the kind of babble others reserve for babies.

'Can I pick her up?' the girl asked after inspecting what she could of him.

'Probably best not to, he seems to be quite content,' Tess said, although he'd moved about the flat a little while ago, he seemed very happy to sit by the fire mostly.

'Oh.' She fell back on her knees, looking up at Tess now. 'What will we do with her?' Her face held that perplexity that Tess knew had long since been rubbed from her own, even if it wasn't wiped from her mind.

'Well, first off young lady, he can stay here.' Tess lowered herself into the most comfortable chair she owned, a scratched Queen Anne that had been here when she moved in and would no doubt be here after she left. 'And the next thing we're going to do is give the poor cat a proper name. She's a He.' Tess pursed her lips, it was all very well this gender equality, but the cat never asked to be part of this new trendy movement that half the country was caught up in. The cat was just a cat. 'So, I've decided that we'll call him Matt,' she said flatly, it wasn't her place to be teaching this youngster about the birds and the bees.

'Oh.' She had the grace to blush. 'Oh, I never realised. Matt?'

'Yes. It's a good name, solid, and I think it suits him. There are three other gospels, I could think of, but I think it's the best of the lot, don't you?' Anyway, the cat seemed happy enough with it, not that Tess would mention that to anyone.

'It'll take a bit of getting used to...' The girl reached forward again to stroke the cat. 'I'm just glad he's here to be honest.' She smiled up at Tess, 'It doesn't matter much what his name is, so long as he's okay. I've always fancied changing my own name. Robyn is so...' her words died off as her attention drifted back to the cat. 'I'm so glad he's here,' she repeated as she sat on the sofa opposite Tess.

They sat for almost an hour, just talking about nothing and everything and sometimes not even saying a word, but listening to the purr of a very contented Matt.

'It's just for a short time, mind. I'm not a complete softy,' Tess said, trying to keep her voice as firm and blunt as she could, because she did mean it. She had no place in her flat or in her life for a cat, much less for a teenager dropping down whenever the fancy took her, did she?

'So, Mrs Cuffe, how was your day?' Robyn asked and there was that unmistakable gentleness about her that made Tess feel relaxed and comfortable all at once. It was impossible to dislike her. 'Aside from the arm that is?' Robyn smiled, sipping from the mug of tea Tess had poured for her.

'Oh, dear, if we're going to get Matt's name right you may as well use mine too,' Tess said in a brittle voice, but she smiled at the same time, or at least it felt like a smile, it had been so long, it was almost hard to tell. 'Call me Tess, will you?' She waited until the girl nodded and then went on, 'My days are never anything special. It's the same old story.' What could she say? Tess was out of the habit of making small talk, but the card from Nancy that had arrived a few days earlier seemed to fill the silence between them, as though it was taunting her to be mentioned.

'Go on, tell me anyway,' Robyn said with the kind of open innocence that will accept as true everything you say. She waited until Tess told her far more than she ever intended to, and yet, all she spoke of was Matt and the gardeners working in the square that afternoon. The ordinary things of everyday life that seemed to come alive again simply in the sharing.

'Do you know, that's done me the world of good?' Tess said when she finished talking and she knew that there really wasn't much more she could say.

'You don't get to talk to many people so?' Robyn said gently.

'No, I suppose I don't,' Tess admitted. 'I didn't think I was missing anything; maybe I am too cut off for my own good.' She looked about her little sitting room and she couldn't tell if it was more precious knowing that Richard and Amanda had wanted it so badly or because living here put her in the way of people. Was she happy being here because being in the way was better than not being anything to anyone at all? She knew that if she didn't march up those steps once a week and drop her ten bob rent in the front door, sooner rather than later, ample Amanda would surely come down to check if she was still carrying on as the thorn in their side or if they had finally seen her out.

'Well, if it's any consolation, I'd say you're not the only person in this house feeling as if you're a little lost.' Robyn's eyes narrowed with meaning.

'There was a poster in the hospital, some do-gooder's idea of entertainment perhaps,' Tess mumbled, 'it said; *loneliness is an epidemic* and this last while, I'm beginning to think it's more dangerous than people ever recognise.'

'The worst is when you're afraid to admit it.' Robyn pointed over her head now, 'Some people don't even realise it.'

'Do you think? Maybe it's a touch of pride too.'

'Yes, maybe it is for you, but you'd be surprised at the people who are lonely into the depths of their souls and they can't even see it because they've worked so hard to block it out with everything money can buy.' Robyn said the words quietly and Tess found herself thinking of Amanda King and wondering if she spent her days thinking about what might have been, just over Tess's head, as she did the same here in this little flat.

'I think you're much too clever for your age, Robyn. You need to stop thinking about things and get yourself out with your friends,' Tess said and Robyn smiled at her in a half-hearted way.

Then, as the old carriage clock on the mantle began to call out the hour, Robyn jumped up suddenly. 'Gosh, I can't believe that's the time, my mum will kill me.' She rushed towards the door after nuzzling her face into Matt's fur one last time.

When Robyn left, Tess took down the little postcard once more. She had read it so many times already since it had arrived, but she was drawn to it. There was something pulling her to the curling font of her sister's hand. She tried not to think about Nancy anymore. Nancy and Douglas were the past. She'd learned to put them out of her mind over the years, but the truth was, they'd never really left her. They were, between them, the reason she was still here. It was all such a long time ago now, a lifetime really. God, she drifted into memories that for so long she'd tried to forget and again she felt that well of sadness open up within her. Douglas was gone and although Tess cast him from her heart so many years before, now it felt like old wounds were opening up once more.

17

January 12 – Monday

Amanda knew, she couldn't go on like this. It was as though she was running from a ghost, and the thing was, she wasn't even sure if the ghost was real. Richard seemed to be gone more often than home, since *condom-gate*, and when he was home, she couldn't breathe. It seemed he pulled the oxygen from every room. His presence was a leash on the air so she couldn't even make a cup of tea without producing a muddle. When he was gone, she rattled about the place waiting for his prickly silence to return. Their marriage was just going through the motions. They hadn't had sex in about six months. But then they were married for God's sake, surely the occasional slump was to be expected? All those things on their own didn't really strike any cords with her, or at least they hadn't before she found the condom in his tuxedo.

Funny, but now she could add another dozen items to the list of why her marriage was in trouble and the condom, while perhaps the most damning, seemed as if it was only the wake-up call she needed.

What could she do? Time was slipping past and it felt as though she'd done precisely nothing. Apart from the fact that she'd completely gone off cake and walked for what seemed like miles while listening to every self-help download she could find. She knew it was the demon of fear as much as her very real desire to make him love her again that pushed her in seemingly unending circuits around the square each evening. Sometimes, she wondered if Tess Cuffe had demons of her own because she appeared to be every bit as driven as she walked in the opposite direction. Her face was set in a kind of determination that matched Amanda's dread in ferociousness. Amanda wasn't sure how, but no matter what time of day or night she set off about the square, she seemed to run into Tess walking angrily in the opposite direction to her. God, she dreaded each time they passed each other. She was almost thankful when Tess insulted her; it was easier to deal with than her loaded silent glares.

Perhaps, all of that was good. She knew she needed to put everything she could into herself for now because the road ahead would be rockier than the Inca trail. She hadn't told anyone what was tormenting her. She couldn't bring herself to say the words. Richard had been unfaithful to her – how hard was that? But, she knew, it wasn't the saying of them that stopped her so much as the expectation that she would have to do something about it. That was what stumped her. She had no idea what to do. She knew what she wanted to do. She wanted to kill him, to rail on him and shout and scream, but she knew Richard too well for that. That would only result in him walking out the door for sure, and even if she hated him in this moment, Amanda wasn't sure that she wanted him in the arms of some new woman either. For now, all she could do was keep moving on that little wheel that had taken her to this point in her life. She kept making breakfasts, lunches and dinners. She brought her kids to school and collected them each day. She stopped nagging them about doing homework and started to really look at them instead. It dawned on her that as little as she knew about herself these days, perhaps she knew even less about her children.

Monday morning brought with it the added dread of the Berkley; she felt it looming about her shoulders. Even Carlos, the sexy gardener, whistling at her with a cheeky grin, hardly managed to lift her spirits. Nicola had invited her for an impromptu coffee morning with the other wives. *Coffee with the girls* was a ritual begun too many years ago to back out of these days. She was not ready to raise their heavily groomed eyebrows, at least not until she found her feet in these peculiar badlands of suspicion and fear. She looked at herself in the full-length bathroom mirror. Her roots were beginning to show, a whiter grey than she thought she deserved, she was only forty-six for heaven's sake; but the colour was completely beside the point. The point was that they would see it as a slip. It was enough to alert the others that something was amiss. She'd seen it before. A scuffed shoe – taken as confirmation of the first step on the road to fashion meltdown. There was no place in their set for anything less than perfection at all times. The scuffed shoe, it turned out later, was as a result of a flat tyre, which in turn, spun out to be the responsibility of the wife, who had been sauntering about the country electioneering on behalf of the Green Party. Everyone knew, the Green Party were hardly more than a hen's kick from the socialists. Yes. Grey roots would definitely cause a stir. Amanda would have to make sure they had something else to muse on for now.

'Oh, I'm thinking about growing out my colour,' she said it automatically, regretted it immediately, but it was the best she could do. Today, she had bigger secrets to hide than just her grey hair. The women looked aghast. None of them would be brave enough to go grey. They may never put a name on it, but they were well aware that being married to a wealthy man opened up too many possibilities for him to stray into the arms of a younger, blonder, better woman.

'Really?' Megan asked in a tone that left little doubt as to what she thought of the plan.

'Well, yes. I've been considering it for a while, since before Christmas, as a matter of fact. You know, you see so many of these stunning women our age and they've gone for a natural look that probably has very little to do with being natural at all.' She nodded towards Clarissa, who in a previous life had been a fashion editor.

'Hm.' Clarissa made a noise that was at best vague. She was probably the most diplomatic of the bunch, not that she was any less of a bitch. 'And you've thought this through? Fully?' She looked a little sceptical. 'It's just, most of those women, well to get away with that unstructured, natural look, they tend to have...' She drew her breath in, tapped her finger on cheekbones that looked sharp enough to cut, 'they tend to have very refined bone structures, whereas you...well, Amanda, you've a softer look. More gentle, you know. It's a good thing in terms of aging.' She was warming to her subject, looked across at Megan who had a heart-shaped face, but it was thanks to Botox and the surgeon's knife. Gravity, starvation and step aerobics had long since wreaked their toll on any elasticity in her skin.

'Well, that's nice of you to say so, Clarissa. Maybe I'll save on the fillers as well as the hairdressers,' Amanda said.

'Aren't you having a biscuit?' Megan asked, but Amanda caught a look shared between the women.

'Um, no. Not today thanks,' Amanda said and she could almost hear the nails hammering into her coffin lid. No doubt, she'd be the topic of conversation for the next week between the women. 'I've started working out.' She nodded over towards Megan. 'Not as serious as you, Megan, obviously, but I'm quite determined to shift some of this weight before the summer. You know, we're talking about a romantic cruise, just for the two of us this year.' Then, in an Oscar-winning performance, she whispered, 'Of course, Richard has to square it up at work yet. You know how things are,' and she looked meaningfully at Nicola who blanched. The other women followed her gaze and, for a moment, something hung in the air between them.

'I'm not sure I do,' Nicola's voice had risen an octave. Her normally cool reserve ruffled by the implicit suggestion that her husband was under some kind of additional pressure at work. Nicola always worked hard to make sure that she appeared to be completely neutral. It was part of the whole cool-girl chic she had going on. God, but Amanda had adored her when they first met. She had looked up to her, really, until this last week. Nicola just seemed to be so… everything Amanda wasn't? She was thin and stylish, that was for sure. It was more than that though; Nicola, with her dark hair and pale skin, was self-assured, she was never out of her depth. Rather, Nicola excelled at making everyone around her feel as if they had to make a supreme effort to please her. Funny, but it was only now Amanda realised that Nicola was a right old hag.

'Oh, well.' Amanda sat back in the chair and smiled as enigmatically as a gypsy behind a frenzy of smoke and mirrors. 'Never mind. Anyway, the point is, I fully intend to fit into the sexiest bikini I can find, especially if we're going on the yacht that Richard has promised.'

The women gasped. They were all vying to holiday with the CEO. Until now, with Amanda's subversive suggestion, they expected the first invite to go Nicola's way. After all, she was the queen of this little set and rightly so, because her husband was top dog in the last bonuses on the trading floor.

Amanda felt the delicious warmth of jiggery-pokery sneak through her. She had put them on the back foot and now they'd be hard-pressed to decide on who was the most worthy to gossip about for the coming week. It was a reckless move and perhaps she was making herself a hostage to fortune, but for now all Amanda wanted was to keep a straight face and not collapse in a sobbing heap before these witches that for so long she'd convinced herself were friends.

'Richard.' The coffee morning emboldened her and she dialled his number while she sat in the jeep waiting for the traffic lights to change. She called his cell phone before she had time to change her mind.

'Yes?' He was distracted, but he knew who it was, otherwise he'd have sounded interested. She wasn't sure when he'd started treating her as if she was the hired help, it had crept up between them slyly.

'Just thinking, I'm in town with time to spare, fancy lunch?' As far as she knew, Richard rarely had more than a sandwich, snatched between phone calls, emails and playing with Monopoly-sized amounts of other people's money. None of the bankers liked to take too long away from their desks, not if they could help it. 'I mean, I'll pick up lunch and bring it to your office, if you fancy it?' She felt her lip sting, where she had bitten down hard on it. When did she start biting her lip again?

'I'm not going to have time to stop for coffee, never mind lunch. Big moves in China, it's all got to do with a takeover in Minneapolis, but that's just an opportunity for the Chinese and I want to put in a finance bid for that takeover,' he said and she had a feeling that he was flicking through numbers while he spoke. She could imagine him, shirtsleeves rolled up, a thin film of sweat on his brow, his dark hair neatly combed. Maybe a stray strand or two fallen down on his forehead, his little pot belly hanging out over his expensive suit pants, while he did the maths to come up with the most attractive offer so he could swipe the business from beneath his competitors and his colleagues. Richard was two years older than she was, but he looked younger. He didn't suffer the usual aging complaints of greying hair or creasing skin. When Amanda thought about it now, he should look a lot older. He had a very stressful job. Of course, he also had a wife to take care of his every worry, so outside of work, life just chugged along around him. It guzzled along so efficiently all he had to do was turn up occasionally and everything was tickety-boo. The thing was, he was turning up less now and maybe that was something that could work in her favour.

'It's just a thought,' she said to the empty car, because Richard had already hung up the phone. 'So,' Amanda said to herself in the rear-view mirror, 'if he's not having lunch at his desk and he's not eating dinner, how come he's not fading off the face of the planet?' It was a question that wouldn't have occurred to her a month ago. Funny, but before this, she'd never have put together the whole idea that eating less made you a thinner person. Perhaps she'd just been blocking it out. 'It looks as if it wasn't the only thing I was blocking out.'

18

Forty-eight years earlier...

Douglas was, as she might have guessed, early. It didn't matter, because Tess was ready to walk out the door as soon as he knocked. He looked so dapper, his tuxedo jacket, flawless black, heightened the golden strands of hair that fell across his forehead.

'Borrowed,' he said, pulling down sleeves that might have been an inch longer, but not so short you'd notice. 'Nancy, how are you feeling today?' It was one of those questions that didn't really require an answer. She was back in secretarial college and Tess thought maybe she'd met up with some girls to be friends with. Nancy was arriving home a little later most evenings and she seemed to be much happier in herself. Perhaps, Tess thought, she was falling in love too.

Tess looked at her sister now, sitting with a magazine contentedly. They were so different, she couldn't imagine Nancy experiencing the sort of passion she felt for Douglas. She couldn't imagine her falling head over heels for some chap. In her mind's eye, Tess could see Nancy meeting some respectable young man and settling into the sort of boring domesticity that their parents had.

'Hello Douglas,' Nancy said, looking up from her magazine, as though she'd only just noticed him, 'you look very nice, try to be good, both of you.' She smiled serenely at them, but Tess thought she'd never seen her look more aloof, while at the same time something about her seemed to catch the air between them all. In an instant, her sister, normally so plain, had turned into an ice maiden and even Tess could see that there was something remote, untouchable and, yes, perhaps attractive about her indifference.

'I'm always good,' Douglas said and his voice held that middle ground where Tess wasn't sure if something had passed between them that excluded her.

'Come on, we'll be late,' Tess said, pulling him out the door as she wrapped her shoulders in the long shawl she'd picked up to match her ball gown. The bells across the city struck out seven chimes in night air that was chilly, but the overhead clouds held any frost at bay.

They walked along in silence for most of the journey to the hotel, both of them caught up in their own thoughts. Later, when they had finished dancing and drinking, she would forget the niggling fear that had crept up inside her in the flat.

Dublin, on a dry winter's night, heaved with a heavy spell that cast a net of uneasiness about the city. Tess felt it as they walked along the empty streets after the ball. It was as though they'd spent the evening at odds, as if they'd had an argument she had not been told about. So, she had drunk a little too much of the free punch and felt it go to her head in a woozy remote way that dulled the discomfort between them. Perhaps it clouded it just enough to give her courage to pull Douglas drunkenly to her when they turned into the square. The idea that something was amiss seemed as if it was a figment of her overactive imagination. She thought that he would kiss her wantonly, hold her and perhaps make some promise that would meld them in some way more than before. But instead he pulled away with a ferocity that almost sent her spinning.

'What is it, Douglas, what's wrong?' she asked, trying to meet his eyes, but he looked away and began to walk back towards the flat.

'It'll be bright soon,' he said needlessly as he hurried on.

Her shoes, cheap and uncomfortable, echoed their pointed sound against the pavements.

'Oh, Douglas,' Tess said, catching him up, not quite sure what to make of him, she linked her hand through his. 'It was a wonderful night, better than I'd ever thought it could be... you and me and the music, I'm so happy.' She did a little twirl, admiring how her dress swirled out and tapered back in again. Tess threaded her arm through his again, but he pushed it aside quickly.

She felt the rebuff, even more acutely than when she'd tried to kiss him. 'What is it?'

'We shouldn't have gone to the ball, not together. This, it's all wrong, the Sunset Club and all those nights afterwards, I'd never have...' He didn't look at her, instead he stared ahead at some unimportant point in the road.

'What do you mean, Douglas? It was...' her voice trailed off. 'But we're...'

'We're what?' He turned on her now. 'What are we, really, do you think?'

'I'm in love with you, Douglas, we're in love.'

'In love?' He laughed cruelly then. 'With you?' He shook his head, as though nothing could be further from the truth. 'Tess, we're not in love. I'm not in love with you. I'll admit, that first day in college, I thought maybe...' He ran his hand through his hair, pulled that thick flop of side fringe back from his eyes. 'Maybe when you seemed so pure, that first day. You were untouched, I could see it a mile off. You were innocent, different to all the other girls I met at university – they're all so easy, giving themselves away at the first chance, as though their virginity was something to be discarded like an old coat.' His expression changed now.

'But you kissed me, that night on the steps at the flat. You walked me to the Sunset Club every week, you...' Tess felt the reality of what had passed between them over the past few weeks and maybe what it meant to both of them. Had she let herself become what he seemed to despise so much? Had she, through loving him, managed to lose him?

'No, Tess. You kissed me. I'll admit, I couldn't keep away, but isn't that the thing with girls like you. You just trap men, you, with your swinging hips and your tight skirts and putting my hand places that would screw up a saint's brain.'

'You didn't have to kiss me back.' It was a cheap remark, but Tess could feel a sense of desperation rise within her. She was certain that if she lost him on this walk home, things would never be right between them again.

'No. You're right there and I'm...' He waited a moment, examined the footpath intently, and then she noticed something. He was the same as her father, he couldn't say sorry. Not that she wanted him to be sorry, not for any of it. No, she wanted something else from him, but it wasn't sorry.

'Well then,' she said as they turned into the top of Swift Square. 'So what now?' He had to lead the way. She prayed he'd chose to lead them where she wanted to go, even if she feared deep down that he had no intention of it.

'I suppose, we can't just fall out with each other, I mean, there's Nancy to think of too.' He shook his head and she knew he was just working to keep the worry from his voice. How had she not seen the way he felt?

He thought she was trying to trap him, in some way to lead him astray and now she could feel the resentment from him and worse, the shame. She shivered, realising in one sobering heartbeat that if she had found herself pregnant, Douglas would have turned his back on her.

'Goodnight, Douglas,' she managed before she let herself into the flat. Inside the door, she closed her eyes, willing for just a few seconds that she could find some way to turn back the clock. She knew that it would take going back weeks to make things right. She had a feeling that tonight had somehow confirmed for Douglas what he'd suspected for some time. He thought she was cheap – and Douglas would not want anyone who was cheap. She knew he was only half-right, because now, even if she was cheap, she was empty too, she flung herself onto her little single bed and cried until the sun came up – it didn't make things any better.

19

January 14 – Wednesday

'How would you know if someone was depressed?' Robyn asked Tess one afternoon when she dropped by to check on Matt. They were sitting at the back of the flat, overlooking the little yard as night drew in too fast for Tess's liking. Outside, the final drops of shadowy winter daylight sieved through patterned blocks that gave a teasing interstitial view of the lush forbidden garden just beyond. Tess was going through some newspapers she'd liberated from the office she'd been working in earlier that week. A wad of discount vouchers arranged at her elbow, a heavy pair of black scissors wielded for the next incursion.

'Well, I don't know, do I?' Honestly, the questions that child asked sometimes. 'I suppose they'd be very miserable. They'd look sad, wouldn't do a lot of laughing. Why?' It suddenly dawned on Tess that perhaps the girl thought *she* was depressed. After all, Tess could hardly be described as a jolly sort and she'd be hard-pressed to remember the last time she'd laughed; properly laughed that is. And, that wasn't just down to hearing about

Douglas. Funny, but that hadn't made her feel as she'd have expected at all. Perhaps those connections had been all too long ago, because rather than feeling bereft or grief, the news from Nancy made her nostalgic, not depressed at all.

'Oh, no reason, I was just wondering.'

'Well you must have a reason.' Tess looked at the girl now. She was an odd sort of a thing, really. She was both childish and advanced; she was what Tess would call, unconventional. She must be fourteen at least, but she was a scrap of a thing, perhaps not yet ready to grow up on any front. Tess didn't know a lot about teenagers; apart from having been one herself, she was clueless. The world was a different place when Tess was fourteen. The Ireland of her youth didn't entertain depression, drugs or even adolescence. These days, most fourteen-year-old girls were traipsing about the city making a nuisance of themselves around make-up counters where they could not afford to buy what they stuck their tacky fingers in. 'Do you think...' she couldn't finish the sentence, it might make it more real.

'Me?' Robyn looked at her, misunderstanding the concern on Tess's face. 'No, I'm not depressed, I'm just quiet – everyone says girls my age are meant to be moody, right? My mum says I'm at a difficult stage.' She screwed up her face as though wondering how well she was managing it.

'Do they now?' Tess shook her head, really some people know far more than what's good for them.

'I think my mum might be depressed.' The words were an undertone, murmured into the cat's soft fur. For a moment, it felt as if the noiselessness of the flat might swig them down into a hollow echoing of the words last spoken. Then Matt alleviated the awkwardness with the start of a loud purr that stretched on as though it might never stop. Silently, Tess thanked him, but she knew, she had to make sure that Robyn was okay.

'Why do you think that, Robyn?' Tess asked in the softest tone she could manage, it was one she'd kept stored away for a long time and it sounded unfamiliar as it slipped into the fragile kitchen air.

'Sometimes I hear her crying when she doesn't realise anyone is around. I watch her moving about the house and it's as if she doesn't really think about things, like she's on autopilot and then she pats her eyes and blames allergies, but she's not allergic to anything so far as I know.'

'I see,' Tess said and she knew she was so far out of her depth with this. God, there was a time she might have welcomed news of Amanda's misery, but now, well, things had changed, she felt a twinge of something close to empathy for the woman. Much to Tess's surprise, she really couldn't wish that kind of unhappiness on her. In Tess's day, that was what it was, nobody talked about depression. People didn't get depressed, they got a bit 'down in the dumps', and then they got told to 'pull themselves together'. Then they were either 'grand', or it was all down to 'trouble with the nerves'. No. Tess really didn't know a lot about being depressed. 'Well, there's probably no good telling her to cheer up,' Tess smiled at Robyn, the obvious solution now scurrying to the front of her mind. 'Have you told your dad about this?'

'No.' She shook her head slowly. 'No, I don't think he can help. You see, I think he's the reason she's upset.'

'I see,' Tess said, trying to catch the right thing to say before it dashed away from her too fast. Maybe she should feel a twinge of guilt, knowing what she knew, but really, Amanda King would not thank her for telling her what in all likelihood she already knew. 'If it's problems between them, you may just have to let them sort things out for themselves.' She reached out and placed her hand on the girl's sleeve, an automatic response that was so far from normal for Tess it made her catch her breath. All the same, it felt nice to reach out to someone who needed you, even if it was only for a moment. 'I suppose if there's anything that I can do, you know, to help...' Of course there wasn't, what did Tess know about depression or nerves, or Amanda King for that matter.

Robyn looked at her now with those searching blue eyes that seemed to see far more than was their due, considering how young they were. 'Could you talk to her?'

'I can't see what good that would do. She needs to get proper help, if it is what you think it is.' It felt strange talking about Amanda King like this, she might almost be a different woman to the person Tess had known for so long – it made her seem vulnerable, almost pitiable.

'Our school guidance councillor said that sometimes people who are suffering with depression do everything they can not to know it. You could find out if there's something wrong at least.'

'Oh dear. I'm afraid I'm the very last person your mother would tell if something was wrong.' Tess watched as a single tear slid down the child's cheek. It brought up in her the uncomfortable reminder that she'd seen Richard in the act, so to speak. While she'd laughed at the time, perhaps she had some responsibility to do something that would set things right, if only for Robyn. Tess had hung that notion on a peg far back in her conscience until now. 'It's not that I wouldn't help, if I thought it would make a difference, but I think I'd probably only make things worse.' Even though it was the truth, on this occasion Robyn was too young to understand.

'That's okay,' Robyn said and she stared hard at the charcoal evening drawing closer through the window. Silence yawned in the small space between them. It seemed to Tess she was willing the tears to stop. In the end, she wiped them with her sleeve and Tess thought her heart would break at the child's hushed misery.

When Robyn turned from the table to sit with Matt, Tess wanted to say something. There was nothing to say that wouldn't just give Robyn false hope and that would be a cruel thing to do.

The truth was, Tess had never seen more of Amanda King. Each day, it seemed no matter how she timed it, there was Amanda power-walking towards her as Tess took her daily constitutional. Typical Amanda, she was still walking in the wrong direction, even if Tess changed her track, she couldn't imagine walking alongside her. God, that would be a penance even Tess didn't deserve. No, she could no more hold out any help to the child's mother than Amanda King would take it from her

The following day dawned brighter and breezier than the weather forecast promised. It seemed there was no good reason not to keep her appointment at the hospital, so Tess set off early for St. Mel's. With a little luck, she might get there before the other appointments and have it over with quickly. She thought it was funny how hospitals never seemed to change, even if they added on extensions or built them from new; there was something in their fibre that remained the same. Tess looked about her now, the waiting room was little more than a corridor. A cream-painted, shiny-floored corridor. She watched purposeful nurses and doctors move to the beat of their own self-important steps, rubber kissing tiles in a telltale drawn-out squeak. They were all ants – grey and white on a constant rotation along corridors identical and unending. She wondered if it was just her, or did they move slower now than they had years ago? It felt that way with everything these days, as far as Tess could tell.

'Mrs Cuffe?' a young nurse looked about the waiting room, her eyes hardly falling on any of the patients waiting to be next.

'It's *Miss* Cuffe, actually,' Tess said as she gathered up her bag, coat and the plaster she intended to dispose of today.

'Of course it is,' the nurse, a whippet of a thing, murmured and then hardly under her breath, 'how could I have forgotten.'

'Pardon?' Tess said, but she wasn't really annoyed. Remembering her was a compliment in a place that saw hundreds of people pass through it every week. It was an acknowledgement of her unique personality.

'Ah Tess. So you came back to us, eh?' Dr Kilker said in salute. He had the look of a man who was ready to play a practical joke on her.

'Yes, well, fond and all as I am of your banter, we do have to take this plaster off sometime, don't we?' She was being facetious but he seemed to enjoy it.

'I suppose,' he said, but his eyes were twinkling. Surely, he wouldn't bandage her up again? 'How have you been feeling?' He looked into her eyes now with that intensity that made her feel he knew her too well for her liking.

'Well enough, I'm not one to complain, I just get on with things.'

'Yes, but I sense you enjoy a challenge.' Dr Kilker smiled now. 'And the arm, does it feel… better?'

'It feels as it always has, the very same, only now I'm dragging your big awkward plaster about with me.'

'Well, let's see if we can do something about that today, eh?' His voice was even and, for a moment, Tess wondered if anything ruffled him. He nodded towards one of the young nurses. 'Let's get this plaster off and then we'll take a quick X-ray before we make any big decisions.' Then he was off again, to the next patient, doling out his own particular brand of humorous treatment.

The rest of the day seemed to fall into the antiseptic haze of the hospital. They insisted on putting her in a wheelchair, which she absolutely did not need. 'It was my arm, you fools,' she said to their unheeding ears. 'Wheelchairs are for old people, for sick people,' she growled at them, but the orderlies didn't seem to have a word of English between them. The more she barked, the more they crashed her about, so she gripped her handbag tighter and swore at them even if they pretended not to hear. She might as well be on a roller coaster when they took some of the hospital corners at breakneck speed. They shunted her about endless corridors from the outpatients to the X-ray and back again. Two X-rays later and the junior doctors who were studying her slides were none the wiser.

'God, will someone bring back old Dr Kilker. At least he can make a decision,' she blew out the words, exhausted with half a day wasted and no nearer to getting home.

'Good job I haven't gone to lunch so.' Dr Kilker was behind her. 'Nice to be missed. How on earth will you get along when I retire, Tess?' he said, pushing his glasses a little further up his nose to study the slide on the light box before him.

'I'll try not to break any more arms,' she said drily. 'Now, can I go home?'

'Hmm.' His stomach rumbled loudly and he patted it for reassurance, but was non-committal in his reply. 'Let's try and put some work on it without the plaster,' he said, nodding towards an empty cubicle nearby. 'Have you used it, since the plaster came off?'

'Well… it's not as if I've had much of a chance what with the Stig driving me about the place like we're on a time trial.' Honestly, Dr Kilker was the most exasperating person she'd ever met. 'No. But I'm confident it'll be fine, I'm hardly going to be lifting weights or directing traffic,' she said, steeling her gaze so he knew there was no mistaking her resolve.

'Right, why aren't I fully convinced?' He nodded to the others who seemed happy to make a hasty retreat and leave them to it. 'Look, Tess, you've had a nasty fall and, more than that, a break at your age, which can lead to all sorts of things. Your blood pressure is not as low as it was, but I know it's been dangerously low. We both know that you're not in your twenties anymore,' he shook his head, good-naturedly, 'at our age, well, we have to be careful. That's all. I'm happy to see you walking out of here right now without a bandage or a further check-up, but if you feel any strain on that wrist, it could do quite a bit of damage.' He looked at his watch. 'Half an hour either way, should be enough to sort you out for sure.' He smiled to himself. 'Come on, you can leave the chair there, but bring your coat and bag.'

'I don't need to be talked to as if I'm an old biddy, Dr Kilker,' she said huffily, but she wasn't fooling anyone. She was just glad to be within sight of getting out of here for good.

'It's either me or back to the plaster room, Tess.' He stood, arms folded truculently, unmoving before her.

'Fine.'

'I'm bringing you for lunch. The cafeteria is a nice little walk from here. We can eat a sandwich, have a little chat and walk back again. You'll be able to tell me then how many compliments you got for my stitches.'

'How does it look? The arm?' She nodded to the light box as they passed it. The slides had changed now and the doctors were studying a ribcage, small and vulnerable. The heart-wrenching sound of a child's crying tugged at her for a moment too long. The feeling surprised her, she'd never considered herself a sensitive, bleeding heart sort of woman. Perhaps she was, at this late stage becoming a softie – there were, she realised, worse things in life.

Lunch was not the panic-inducing ordeal that Tess would have imagined. She found herself quite relaxed for the twenty minutes they were sitting.

'So, what is it you do with yourself, exactly, when you're not falling over cats?' Dr Kilker asked. He paid for her sandwich so she couldn't be too huffy with him.

'Well, I…' she smiled wearily, 'I make a lot less money than you do office temping around the city.'

'You're a secretary?' he said with his usual directness. 'An honourable trade, but what do you do apart from work?'

'I beg your pardon.' She found herself blushing slightly. To cover it up, she leaned over to put some more salt on her sandwich and he pushed the saltcellar from her.

'I mean, you need to be busy. At our stage in life, you need to have things to occupy your mind. You need people to take you out of yourself.' He put his hand up to stop her objections, then he lowered it slowly and rested it on her forearm. 'Don't go shooting the messenger; I'm only saying it because you know that it's the truth. Your bones and joints might be getting older, but you're a young woman in terms of what life has ahead of you, Tess, and your life could be great.' There was that familiar twinkle in his eye and she had a feeling they'd met before, long ago.

'So, I suppose you have the whole thing down?' she said flatly.

'No, I'm not saying that. My life isn't perfect. But I'm chasing it. That's the difference. I'm out there looking for my own contentment every day.' His words were gentle, perhaps too gentle because Tess could feel her heart softening.

'And I'm not?' She hated being so transparent.

'I suspect you are too argumentative to agree, and too proud to admit it, but you're on your own, Tess, I've seen it from the moment I met you. It's like a shawl you carry about you and it's going to kill you far faster than any cat or low blood pressure.'

'So, join a club? Take an evening class, is that it?'

'You're a smart woman, Tess, I'm not going to advise you on what to do.' He shook his head, looked about them for a minute, perhaps giving her time to think or make a plan.

'I've started exercising, just gently until I'm fully mobile,' she whispered. Somehow, it didn't seem right to add that she had only started to want to live longer so she could spite her neighbours.

'Well, good for you. That's the spirit,' he smiled. 'And does it leave you feeling fulfilled?'

'No. I mean, yes. Oh, I don't know.' She wasn't sure what she meant. The only time she'd known real joy was when she sang, but that was years ago and long gone now. He was throwing her thoughts up in the air as if he was a practiced juggler. It annoyed her because she never liked to examine how she felt too closely. What was she doing, explaining herself to this old codger?

She bent down to pick up her bag. She needed to be out of this café. It was suddenly claustrophobic, too hot, too packed and too intimate for her prickly nature. She could feel that tightening sensation in her chest again, as though she couldn't breathe. It pulled her like a marionette; strings of resolve drawn from deep behind her ribcage so her lungs fell hot together and she gasped for air as though about to drown.

'What is it?' He moved closer to her now. 'Sometimes, you need to tell whoever is there at the time, Tess, because if you don't... well, these things they only end up getting bigger.'

'There's nothing to tell,' she said, but her heart was racing in her chest, the same as it had a million times before, the same as it did a dozen times a day when she was home doing absolutely nothing. They careered into silence gravid with words she couldn't find.

'Just sit,' he said quietly and she found herself obeying him. 'You've the classic signs of hypotension.

That feeling, it's sitting probably in either your stomach or maybe even your chest?'

'I...' There was no point in trying to lie.

'The breathlessness? Hopelessness? You've been feeling all of those things?' He shook his head and she knew he was too wise to judge her and maybe too kind behind those mocking eyes. 'You're having panic attacks and you need to help yourself before anyone else can make you feel better.'

They sat in silence for a few more minutes. Tess felt her heart slow down, her pulse slackened to a rate where she didn't feel as if it might burst through every vessel in her body.

'So, what do I do?' Tess muttered once she was ready. Part of her couldn't believe she was asking Dr Kilker for advice, and especially for advice like this. It may be okay for the younger generation to bandy about their breakdowns, addictions and phobias as though they were a badge of honour, but Tess felt only shame. It made her feel weak and vulnerable.

'Do you sing?' he asked and she imagined herself like old Dancy, the handyman who hung about the square singing old rebel songs under his wheezy breath. 'Don't even answer that, Tess, because I know you do. I heard you, years ago – you were unforgettable.'

'I...' For once, Tess didn't know quite what to say. 'You heard me sing?' She felt an odd flutter, something rattle in some deep part of her, as though the very fact that someone remembered her from that time made it seem like it might have been real. 'You heard me sing?' she said again and, just beyond her reach, she thought she saw his shadowy figure many years before. That was all it was, a ghost, a bit player, one of many in that club perhaps, or churchgoers on a Sunday morning that she hardly recognised, then she'd been too lost in her own world. 'It was a long time ago.' Tess could hardly remember that time, she had spent too long sending memories scuttling like spiders into the crevice of her thoughts whenever they threatened to remind her how things had once been. It was so far back, but then, she had almost been a different person altogether.

'That's settled so,' he said, smiling at her indecision, and it felt to her as though she'd missed half a conversation, or maybe it was half a lifetime. 'I'll pick you up at seven on Monday evening.' From deep inside his jacket pocket, an incessant buzzing intruded on their conversation. He pulled out a pager and shook his head sadly then he looked at Tess. 'Your arm is fine, Tess. Go home, don't do anything silly, and we'll start working on that other thing straight away.' He waved a hand regally, to flap away her protests, 'It'll be good for both of us, I promise,' he said and then he was getting up from the table, hardly giving her time to catch her breath, much less wriggle out of whatever torture he had lined up for her on Monday evening.

20

Twenty-two years earlier...

Amanda found herself wondering if Claude had a second name. It was nerves, pure and simple, the morning of her wedding. The day that should have been the happiest in her life and all she felt was grief. They had buried her father two days earlier. The little grave, where her mother waited, seemed much too small for two, but it was what he would have wanted. Linda had hardly said a word since the funeral. Shock, Amanda supposed, it was all so sudden and now they were barrelling into her wedding day; it felt as if they were hurtling along with no brakes.

'So, ve agreed, ve vill go high to give you another inch or two, but not so high the groom is looking too much a shortie,' Claude said as he took strands of her hair upwards, inspecting it as if he'd never seen such a terrible mess. 'Non, non, non. This vill never do, it is the hair of a volfhound,' he was waving his hands theatrically. 'I can't vork on this, today,' he placed the back of his hand over his eyes and forehead, as though he might go into meltdown. Amanda could feel all stares upon her. She darted her eyes about the mirror, keeping her body rigid, as though Claude might yet resort to a guillotine to rectify the mess. 'Vax,' he screamed. 'Vax, I need vax,' he was shouting orders at the scurrying junior stylists. 'How could you expect me to vork on this... this...' He wrinkled his nose, looking down at Amanda's offending tresses.

The girl who took her back to the washing and conditioning area was a mouse, a lovely mouse, but she could see that Amanda was already teetering on the edge of disintegration. Across the salon, Claude hopped with temper, 'Imbeciles, I am surrounded by vork-shy, vomen. I am an artist, creative...' He darted behind a curtain covered in glinting silver stars and Amanda made a mental note never to come here without having her hair in tiptop condition first. It was cleaning for the cleaner, barking for the dog, but it was the cost of being lucky enough to be here in the first place.

'Don't be minding him. Sure, your hair is just lovely, this is Claude's way of getting at the juniors.' Then she smiled conspiratorially, 'It's not you, it's us!'

'Crikey, I'm just so nervous about everything today,' Amanda said as she sank down in the chair and let the girl rescue her hair so Claude could do his magic.

And he did, everyone said she was the most beautiful bride, even if her stomach growled louder than a bear after hibernation.

In some ways, it was a terrible thing to admit, but

Amanda felt her wedding ceremony, the church bit at least, passed over her in much the same way as her father's funeral had. Linda understood, she had smiled and stood in for photographs and waited for as long as it was decent and then she slipped away. Amanda knew she hadn't the heart to stick it out without him at her side.

Hugo Lennox walked her dutifully up the aisle and she caught sight of Nicola, Clarissa and Megan. They all smiled at her, if not with the kind of love that she would have had if her parents were there, but with a great dollop of encouragement. They wanted the wedding to be a success. They were her friends now and, in some ways, she had a feeling that her day was their day. They'd invested hours with her, picking out everything so it would be perfect. Nicola in particular had taken over all the details that Amanda knew would have driven her to distraction. 'All you need to do is be thin and gorgeous on the day,' she said every time Amanda gushed her thanks. In the planning, she'd just known it would be fabulous, but with the passing of her dad, well, fabulous just wasn't so important anymore.

Today, she had stood at the top of the aisle thinking of weddings and funerals and how people marked them out with rite and ritual. To be fair, the cathedral was a more gothic and impressive aisle than little St. Brid's where her father's funeral played out. Every so often, she'd looked across at Richard, just to check that this was really happening. And there he was, standing next to her, looking more handsome than she'd ever seen him, but he never returned her glance. Perhaps he was nervous too? His smile was set as if it was rictus, as though he might never return to the carefree playboy she fell in love with. Amanda was glad when the ceremony was over, she couldn't escape quickly enough to have a little cry.

Amanda had decided, the day of the funeral, that if her dad couldn't come along to her wedding, the least she could do was visit her parents grave on her wedding day. They would pass by the graveyard on their way to the reception in Dodder Castle.

'Not today,' Richard said when she asked the driver to pull in for just a moment.

'Oh, Richard, I won't take long, I just wanted to stand at their grave for a moment, I'll feel better going into the reception then, as if they'll know they've been included.'

'Amanda, listen to yourself.' Richard's voice was gentle but firm. 'We've done this, we've spent our week sorting out the funeral, when we should have been...' He bit his lip, maybe he knew that she was about to cry again. 'Amanda, it'll just upset you more. I'm thinking of you, really. Your dad wouldn't want to see you upset today, you've done all you can for him, but this is our day.' He sighed, looked out the window, they were speeding by the graveyard now and he turned towards her. 'This is our day and we need to get back to the reception, people are waiting for us to arrive.'

'I...' Amanda strained to catch sight of her parents' grave, she picked out the tallest yew trees and knew they were nestled just beyond them. 'I suppose you're right. It was a silly idea and my dad wouldn't want me upset.' She took a deep breath, she would not cry. She would not be one of those brides who spent the day bawling like a baby. The yew trees were passing out of site. She decided she would go back tomorrow, early, before any of their guests had risen from their beds, and she would sit at her parents' grave and tell them all about her fabulous wedding day.

21

January 16 – Friday

It seemed a shame to Amanda having all that lovely gym gear and not using it. So, on Friday night, Amanda decided she would head off around the city alone. She couldn't face Tess Cuffe again this evening. These days, there was something different about the old girl, but there was too much water under the bridge for it to really matter to Amanda anymore.

After dinner, she donned her ridiculous Lycra leggings, dayglo vest, sweatband and failed to convince herself she looked the part. She set off on a half-walk, half-jog, pant-a-thon along the city streets. She watched with envy as experienced runners glided by her. The women were the worst. They seemed to have a personal kind of happy going on and she wondered, if she jogged for long enough, could she ever achieve that too. It surprised her that she'd take happy over thin any day. She hoped, it would come, after the breathlessness, the racing pulse and the red-faced sweatiness had subsided. For now, she was accepting the fact that, for her, running was going to be more about pain than gain, but funnily enough, she was okay with this. Physical discomfort proved a consoling relief from the ongoing soundtrack in her head. *He's a cheat. He's a cheat. He's a cheat. He's a cheat.*

Amanda pounded down Dame Street, and came up behind two students straggling home after one too many drinks in the campus bar. They swayed a little uncertainly as she slowed down to catch her breath. She would have to sidestep them to keep her pace. There was a time when they would have annoyed her, sauntering home of an evening, living off the tax her husband paid. She would have automatically tutted as she passed them, assuming that they spent all their time in the college bar. Tonight, she caught a glimpse of something else. A young girl, wearing the ubiquitous student uniform – denims, parka and Converse – her hair straggly, her face bare of make-up apart from unfortunate HD brows that branded her desperation across her forehead. Her boyfriend, a slightly spotty, hair-gelled cocky little bloke walked with the assurance of a gunslinger in a bad cowboy movie. The girl was hanging off the boy's every word and she looked at him with the kind of open adoration that Amanda knew she'd once felt for Richard. The boy for his part looked a little younger; he was smaller, thinner and rather pretty compared to the girl's plainness. Amanda imagined them going home to some squalid little flat and having twenty-something sex until they fell asleep contentedly, each having fulfilled that thing they uniquely craved.

She missed sex. She never thought she'd miss it. If she was honest, she'd been a little relieved when Richard hadn't instigated it for a few weeks. Now, well, now she'd give anything to see longing in his eyes. For her. She shook her head at the correction; of course, he would desire her again.

She started to jog faster then, anything to get away from the thoughts. She passed the two students and puffed her way along the road. To take her mind off her own non-existent sex life; she let her thoughts wander to what might unfold for the students who were now walking behind her. Amanda had a feeling that he would break her heart, after he used her. Suddenly, she wanted to turn back and run right through them both. Stop it happening before it was too late. Then she thought of the girl's arm reaching around the boy's shoulder and she knew that she was the same as Amanda: she would not believe there was no hope until it hit her in the face like an icy bucket of water on a warm day.

Then something caught her eye. Just a little in the distance, a familiar figure. Dark suit, neat overall appearance and the telltale signs of a small middle-aged-spread tummy.

It was Richard. Amanda's breath caught somewhere between the inhale–exhale rhythm so she seemed to teeter on a precipice from within. He was on his way into a very expensive restaurant. She stopped for a moment; let the students pass her out. Not that he'd even notice her. For one thing, he didn't know she'd taken to running the streets of Dublin on dark evenings. For another, in her Lycra leggings, her sweatband holding back the shock of red turbocharged hair, out here, without a cream cake in sight, well, she was positively unrecognisable from the woman she had gradually turned into since she married him.

The students were moving far ahead and she doubled over, as though catching her breath for a moment, then she slipped into a doorway, invisible, watching, crumbling. He was waiting, for something. For somebody? Then, she spotted a taxi, pulling in, slowly, just a few feet from her. A reedy-looking woman, maybe thirty, tops thirty-five, got out. She glided, rather than walked towards the restaurant and in that moment Amanda knew for certain, this too tall, red-haired clothes horse was meeting Richard. Suddenly, Amanda thought she might be sick. Spew right there where she was standing, all across the path. Then she remembered, she'd hardly touched any food since breakfast. It was her new normal; somehow, her broken heart was overriding her empty stomach.

The woman greeted Richard with the kind of kiss that was a hell of a lot more than a sociable peck on the cheek. After a moment, Amanda wanted to scream, *let him up for air, for God's sake, let him breathe*. What she meant, of course, was, *let me breathe. Let me get some oxygen into my lungs. Some clean air that isn't tainted by the taste of betrayal.*

God knows how she made it back to the square. She couldn't remember most of the jog or walk, she may have crawled. Certainly, inside she felt that's what she was doing.

She rounded into the square, a sobbing, hysterical heap of a woman, unrecognisable from the Amanda who went about her business with the casual confidence that comes of being moneyed and stupidly content. The last twenty yards were the hardest to walk, as though she was coming to a finish line, except how would she know when she'd crossed it?

She couldn't face the house, plopped onto the bottom step and keened like a banshee. It didn't matter if anyone saw her, she didn't see them and being respectable was the very smallest of her worries now.

How could he do it to her? Selfish bastard, how could he do this to her, to their kids? Had he given any of them a second thought? After all the years they'd spent together, she'd invested everything in this life that they'd created. What would she do now? She couldn't think, she just couldn't think and then, a noise, the familiar dreadful creaking of a door nearby. What did it matter what people thought of her now, anyway? After all, she could see it was just a sham.

Her breath came out in pockets, hitting the air in doom-packed clouds. Each heave of her chest filled with fear for what lay ahead and as her body shook with sobs she didn't notice the door beneath her open. It closed and opened again with the trepidation of footsteps on a frozen lake. It was karma or the ultimate ironic payback that Tess should be the one to see her at her lowest point. Amanda finally heard those familiar footsteps move towards her in their owner's usual blunt manner. She wiped her eyes, not that it did much good, because all the wiping in the world wasn't going to change the damage done. *Of all the people to come upon her, why did it have to be Tess?* she thought. Some small part of her sought consolation that things couldn't get any worse and here was Tess bloody Cuffe to delight in her misery and add to it, if she could no doubt.

'Not you. Not now – I can't take it anymore. Not on top of everything else. Really. No.' Amanda held up her hands before her face. She couldn't look at Tess's sneering victory. 'Leave me alone, just this once.' The words came out broken between sobs. 'If you're going to say something horrible, just get it over with and go away.'

'Come on, you can't let Robyn see you like this.' Tess pulled her arm, yanking her from the step with a ferocity that jerked her without warning. Amanda had no choice but to tumble behind her into the little flat.

She found herself tripping onto a flimsy and

threadbare old couch in front of a dying fire. When she looked up, the old biddy was holding out a fat glass half-full with copper whiskey, the smell enough to bring her to her senses sharp and painful.

'Drink it.' Tess stood over her and it sounded more of an order than an invitation.

'I don't like…' Amanda shook her head, but she gulped it back and too late realised its burning aftershock. It slid menacingly down her throat, landed in her empty stomach and seemed to stretch its heat to regions that she'd forgotten could be warm. Amanda's eyes watered, her toes tingled and her breath struggled to free itself from the hold the panic of earlier had clasped around her chest. Old men, hardened up with years of drinking, would have had to catch their breath. 'What are you trying to do to me?'

'I'm trying to help you.' Tess sat opposite and sipped her whiskey easily from a matching glass. 'I heard you outside, if I hadn't pulled you in, the whole square would have heard you.' She shook her angry head. 'Robyn would have heard you,' she said more softly now.

'Robyn?' The name was out of kilter here. 'My daughter…' She shook her head, trying to piece together the bits she'd missed while she'd sat on those steps.

'She thinks you're depressed.' Tess studied the intermittent blaze escaping from around turf that looked too dark to discharge any real heat. 'Here, you're in shock.' She placed a crocheted shawl about her shoulders. 'I don't know, running about the place, and at your age? It's not natural, for heaven's sake. I've heard you panting when you walk to the end of the garden, never mind gadding about as if you're the bionic woman.'

'It wasn't the running that did it,' Amanda said flatly, looking about the little room. She might have stepped back in to the nineteen seventies. It was a relic of a room; a medley of lino, fluffy rugs, velvet chairs, embroidered cushions, a holy picture, lamp now extinguished, and yes, there was beauty-board to finish off the melange. It was like stepping into a time warp, but it was tidy, clean and loved, in every way the antithesis of the conceited, sterile house overhead. This room was cosy in a way her aloof and chic house would never be. Tess Cuffe in her beige dressing gown was the final touch, a remnant from a time fashion would never reinvent. Then she looked at Tess's face, something in her eyes had changed. Maybe it was because she was here, in this little flat, but her brown eyes seemed to convey sincerity, or was it just Amanda's warbled imagination? Nothing was right anymore. The world as she knew it had tilted into frenzy. Only a few hours ago, she could have convinced herself that she could paper over the cracks in her marriage. Now, after what she'd just seen, she couldn't kid herself anymore – there was no escaping the pictures that were playing out every time she closed her eyes. 'Robyn, how do you know that...'

Amanda looked about the room again, trying to take in the incongruity of it all.

'Well *are* you depressed?' Tess leaned her head forward, her voice soft, so Amanda wondered if she'd practised for this moment.

'No. I mean, I don't know. Something has happened and...'

'Your husband, he's made you feel like this?'

'How do you know?'

'Robyn thought it was down to him...' Tess Cuffe shook her head.

Amanda couldn't meet her eyes, so she looked into the bottom of the glass before her, as though it might contain wisdom worth sharing. She sighed, perhaps she knew better already.

'Robyn knows?' The words echoed through her and she began to sob again.

'Oh, God don't bloody cry, again.' Tess Cuffe moved in her seat, perhaps considering reaching out in some physical way. Thankfully, she knew enough to realise that wasn't going to give Amanda any great consolation. 'She doesn't know anything, not really. She's just worried about you. She's put two and two together and she's torturing herself wondering what's going on and if you're all right.'

'Really?' Amanda wasn't sure if that made her feel better or worse. 'Robyn said this to you?' Amanda wanted to be cross, she deserved the moral high ground on this at least, but then she spotted the cat. She was certain, it was the O'Hara's cat and suddenly it all fitted together. Robyn would go to the ends of the earth for a bloody cat. 'Oh God.' The words flipped from her lips, it was all too much to take in.

'You should be delighted she cares, plenty of young ones about the place wouldn't even notice if their mother was upset,' Tess said quietly, her finger circling the top of her whiskey glass, as though there was something else she wanted to say.

'You're right, of course you're right. She's a good girl.' The small part of her, the needy part of her, was happy that someone cared. God, that made her feel worse. 'I don't want her to be worried about me. I really don't.' She reached forward for another sip of whiskey. This time she only let it wet her lips, once burned, twice learned – she was still scorched from the last gulp.

'Of course you don't,' Tess said shortly. 'But you can't go up there like this. You're a fright. Honestly, I've seen better being carted off by the binman.' She shook her head. 'Just take a few minutes, pull yourself together…' Tess smiled, or at least the corners of her mouth lifted in an unfamiliar way, and for a fleeting moment, there was a whisper of the beauty she might once have been about her face. *Pull yourself together –* that's what we'd have said years ago.' Then she shook her head, 'Sorry, that didn't come out right, you know, if you're depressed.' She said 'depressed' as if it was a religious term – something she wasn't used to using and it wouldn't do to sully it by bandying it about the place.

'Look,' Amanda said and she took a deep breath, she could feel the despair flare up inside her again. 'I'm not depressed.' She stared long and hard at the fire in the grate. Small blue flames had taken off on one side and it reminded her of when she was young and convinced that the blue flames were a lucky sign. 'I…' Tears began to crowd up at the back of her throat again. She had to let it out. What was the point of keeping this a secret; Tess Cuffe wasn't going to see anyone or tell anyone, was she? 'Richard is… that is, my marriage is… not what I hoped it would be.' Funny, but even though she felt the emotional doors burst open once more, after blubbering and spluttering for a long while, she felt a little better – well, better than she had since seeing Richard and that woman.

'Well, that's hardly news, is it?' Tess said and then her posture yielded from its familiar rigid stance into something peculiar, something smaller and altogether more unassuming. 'I'm not very good at this. What I mean is, you're a long time married, aren't you, things change…'

'I just never thought that he'd… I never thought this would be us.' And that was it, Amanda had signed up for happy ever after and suddenly it was being snatched from her. 'I've just seen him,' she half gasped and hiccupped at once, 'in town,' Amanda tried to catch her breath. 'With someone else,' finally she wailed and somehow, it seemed like she had released some of the pain.

Tess handed her tissues, let her cry it out and in the end, she settled for a good old-fashioned cliché, 'plenty of husbands stray and your husband is very wealthy, there has to be a lot more opportunity, more temptation.'

'Well, that doesn't make me feel much better,' Amanda doubted this night could get any worse.

'Do you know for sure?' Tess asked, but there was something in her voice, as though she was placating her and it was all over anyway. Her eyes searched her as though checking how much she could handle.

'I'm almost certain.'

'Well, when you're sure, I mean, really sure, then you can make some plans. For now, you have two children up in that house and they need to know that you are all right. They need to know that if your marriage is over you're still there for them.'

'You're right, of course, you're right.' Amanda leant forward, sipped the last of the whiskey.

'Would you like another?' A smile played about Tess Cuffe's face, although, for the life of her, Amanda couldn't tell where it was exactly, since her features hardly altered.

'No, I think I'll quit while I'm ahead.' She could feel her head begin to swim, her thoughts taking on a soft furry feeling, as if there were guinea pigs padding softly about her brain. Guinea pigs could not do too much harm, could they? 'Thank you,' she said, inching her way to the edge of the couch, 'for taking me in, *pulling me together*.' Amanda pursed her lips; congeniality was unfamiliar territory for them both.

'If there's…' Tess stumbled on ending the sentence. 'Well, there's probably not much I *can* do to help, but, well, if you just want to come down and take a moment, I always have a bottle open.'

'That's very kind of you, but really, I should be fine now.' Amanda said, looking about the little flat one last time. Funny, but if it was a couple of weeks ago, she might have been mentally measuring the place up for her state-of-the-art kitchen and family room. Now, she thought that she'd never realised how comfortable it was, tucked safely away from all the expectations of empty perfection. God, it was scary how suddenly everything could change.

22

Forty-eight years earlier...

It was strange, this new imbalance in her relationship with Douglas. She still loved him, perhaps she always would. Now they bumped into each other and it seemed as if they were stepping into a new dance with each other. The Christmas holidays were coming up and Tess had a feeling that the break might do them both good. Secretly, she hoped that if Douglas didn't see her for a few weeks he'd be overcome with loneliness and realise that he loved her as much as she loved him. It seemed like her only chance at this stage.

At least Nancy was happier in herself. She left each day for her secretarial course with a real bounce in her step and arrived home later each evening. When Tess quizzed her about her new friends, she fobbed her off with 'Oh, just a bunch of girls from the course.' Tess was happy for her because Nancy had never been one to make a big circle of friends. She wondered, too, if maybe she'd met a boy. There was something about her, a new-found lightness and Tess recognised it as that same feeling she had in those first few days when she would run into Douglas in the university corridors. Sometimes she thought about those days, the world was a different place then, before they'd kissed, before they'd gone to the ball. It saddened her to think that life would never go back to those carefree days. As far as Douglas was concerned, it was as though, she'd completely lost her value.

The Sunset Club had grown smaller, warmer, duskier without Douglas. Tess felt something snake along her spine, a feeling that something had flipped within her since she last sang here. Stephen must have noticed it too. He handed her a tall glass of gin that burned her lips but imbued her with a sense of warmth that had nothing to do with the clamminess of the place. She drank the first half before she was due to sing.

When it was her turn, she walked to the stage with a lazy, sensual languor that fitted well with the cocktail dress that clung to her but sat at odds with the girl who came from Ballycove and wanted only the boy who once sat silently with her sister, disapproving, if only she'd known it.

She tried to put aside the fact that she felt more out of place in college with every passing day. Somehow, in that fuggy sultry music, the loneliness that had started to creep into her soul seemed to fizzle into a discontented energy that numbed the cloaking ache about her heart.

She heard the band behind her begin to rumble into the opening bars; it was time for her to sing, but nothing came. She stood back a little from the spotlight; searched out the eyes she hoped would push her on.

There was nothing. She was empty, there was no music – somehow it had deserted her. She waited until they rallied through a sequence that might have been a drawn-out introduction, but when it was time for her to sing, again she froze. It seemed she stood for an eternity, looking out into the anonymous darkness. There's no counting minutes when time stands still and a life is turned on the loss of something irreplaceable. In those moments, the tight-lipped conclusion of an unremarkable club choked the harmony from her. It was enough to let her know that she didn't want to be here anymore. She mumbled 'sorry' into the microphone and made her way into the wintry night outside.

Without her, they were just background music – she knew that. They needed her, but she couldn't do this anymore. It cost too much. She was failing every written exam she sat – the only one she knew she'd pass was when she had to stand before the class and perform. And now? She wasn't so sure of even that.

The fresh air served the gin more than it cleared her head. Each breath seemed to bring a new wave of unsteadiness to her. She leant against a railing, for a minute, tucked her collar up, buttoned herself in as much against the night-time roving crawlers as against the winter chills. She wasn't sure how long she stood. She thought of Douglas and how her life seemed to be suddenly changing. The knowledge that Nancy would move back to Ballycove only cemented the notion that she was, by comparison, adrift in some unfamiliar way. At this moment, she missed Aunt Beatrice and that common sense she could be relied upon to dispense in even the darkest moments.

'Hey, Tess.' Stephen was beside her. 'You all right? What are you doing here? You know all kinds are about this area, it's no place for a girl on her own, to be...' He looked at her now, 'Come on. I'll bring you home.' He placed an arm at her back; half held her up and pushed her along, all at once.

They walked in silence; he wasn't exactly full of sparkling conversation.

At the door, he stopped, just long enough for her to catch his eyes. 'You'll be fine, it mightn't seem like it now, but you know where we are if you want to come back to the club.' He put his hand up to her face and placed it gently on her cheek and then he was gone and Tess had a feeling that it would be a very long time before she saw Stephen again.

23

January 19 – Monday

Tess walked towards Dr Kilker's little car. It was too small for him, of course. Kilker was a bear of a man, with grey wiry hair and whiskers threatening to become sideburns. He was a tweedy, check-shirted barrel of a man. At six foot, he stood tall for his age, but then he wasn't as old as he looked. Tess had to remind herself that he could not be more than sixty-five. He was the sort of man who would have smoked a pipe, but gave up in time to keep his lungs clear and his vices affable. He arrived three minutes early and honked his horn loudly; it was just to infuriate her, but she decided she would not rise to the bait. She had been waiting for him, if not exactly looking forward to his arrival; at least she was ready for whatever might lie ahead. She'd spent some time getting ready, because she had no idea where he was taking her. In the end, she settled on a suit she kept for best, its light blue might have brought her eyes up once, but these days that was by accident as much as by design. She'd smoothed down her hair, glad the bruising had subsided, and found herself arranging strands about her face to soften out the years. She'd spritzed just a hint of perfume on her wrists and felt she was as *done* as she'd been in many years.

'I'm really not sure about this at all,' she said as she got into the little car. 'And what do I call you, I can't keep calling you Dr Kilker.'

'I'll wager it's a hell of a lot better than what you called me on New Year's Eve.' He laughed to himself and, somehow, when she caught his eye, perhaps she could see the funny side to his humour. 'Anyway, how are you feeling?'

'Well, there was nothing wrong with me that my own bed wouldn't have sorted,' she harrumphed, but caught his eye as he manoeuvred through the traffic. 'My arm is fine, you'd never know there was a break at all.'

'Yes, well, maybe there's some things we won't agree on. From here on in, I'm just Kilker, that's what most people call me, okay, and very soon, even if you do decide to go tripping yourself up, I won't be at the hospital to put you back together again anyway.'

'Kilker?'

'Yep, or plain old Doc.' They drove on in silence for a little while, but it was not uncomfortable and Tess found herself relaxing in the warmth of the car's soft leather seats. The radio played gently, it was tuned to a classical station, which surprised her a little. She would have assumed he'd be a news junkie or maybe a sports fanatic when it came to his car radio.

'I still don't know why we're doing this,' Tess said and it was true. They hardly knew each other and she had a feeling that she was more a cause of amusement to him than any kind of potential friend.

'We're doing this,' he paused, '*we're* doing this because I do it every week and I have a feeling that it'll be good for you. I also know that if I invited you to come along without making it clear that I had every intention of blowing my horn until the cows come home, you wouldn't come.'

'And where exactly is here?' she asked as he turned in towards the hospital and came to a jerking halt close to the little old chapel that hid in the grounds, far away from the comings and goings of the medical personnel. 'You're bringing me to church?' she asked.

'Not exactly,' he said, flicking his key fob towards his car and jumping slightly when it clicked closed. 'Yes and no.' He steered her towards the grounds expertly as if chaperoning her from the night air.

In the darkness, she could just about make out the narrow path. Kilker hurried ahead of her as they came towards the main door and looked inside as though to confirm something.

'Right, we'll go this way,' he said, leading her to the transept door.

He stood for a moment and it was the first time she thought she could see some indecision in those wily old eyes. In that moment, she heard beyond the door the sound of the choir starting up. First off, the organ and then, a hymn from her childhood that she could not name, but still the words as the soloist sang them came to Tess's lips.

'Shall we?' He was smiling at her now, that familiar nonchalant confidence playing about his lips once more. 'We can sit and listen, if you'd like.'

They stole unseen past the choir who were mostly concentrating on their music sheets. Tess picked out a seat in the dimly lit nave and eased herself down to listen. After a moment she closed her eyes, began to drift away on the hymns. For a long time she sat in complete blissful joy. In that symphonic cocoon, all was well in the world.

After the choir finished their practice, Kilker nudged her. 'You asleep, Tess?'

'No, I was just…' Tess knew there were tears in her eyes, but it didn't matter, it was emotion, a powerful awakening reaction the likes of which she hadn't felt in years. She looked at him now and realised he had known, how had he known? 'Thank you,' she said and if she was a touchy-feely sort of person, she might have reached towards his arm, but she had a feeling he understood.

'We should probably tell them how good they were, shouldn't we?' He winked at her and he was up and moving before she had a chance to argue.

'Kilker?' We wondered where you were,' the

choirmaster called to him when they approached. 'And, hello?' He held his hand out towards Tess.

'New recruit,' Kilker said and he looked at Tess with something of a challenge in his eyes, so she couldn't back out.

'Well, maybe.' Tess stumbled over the words. 'You're very good, I'm not sure I…'

'There's only one way to know. I'm Barry, by the way, and we're on the lookout for a mezzo-soprano, so if that's your range we'd be delighted to have you.' He was smiling now in a way that Tess found almost infectious.

'Well, I don't know. I mean, I haven't sung for years,' Tess said and she smiled back at him, a real smile that came from inside, not something forced. Suddenly she felt a warm blush spill into her cheeks and she felt no older than a foolish teenager. Then, she realised, they were both smiling and no one was speaking.

'Pearl,' Kilker called to an elderly woman seated at an electric organ. 'Tess here is going to give us a few bars; we're hoping she'll be our new mezzo.'

'Oh, yes?' Pearl cupped her ear and Tess had a feeling that she might be a little deaf. It might turn out to be no harm if they were all a little deaf, should she start to sing.

'Come on, Tess, no time like the present, up you go.' Kilker slapped her cordially on the back, but she knew he was pushing her forward. 'You must remember some hymns from way back,' he was goading her, insinuating that she was as old as Pearl. 'What about "Amazing Grace", sure everyone knows "Amazing Grace",' Kilker pressed her towards the lectern before she really knew what was happening.

'Well, that'd be just grand,' Barry was saying and he dropped his baton then handed her the sheet music and words to the hymn.

It all happened so quickly, Tess didn't have time to back out. One moment she was sitting invisibly in a pew and the next she was standing at a lectern looking out on the darkened church, punctuated by a line of expectant expressions. When this was over, she reasoned, she had grounds to murder Dr Kilker.

'Right, off we go so,' Kilker said and he moved back towards the pews.

Tess cleared her throat a little, it felt strange to be standing here, strange to think that she would be making any sound above a whisper. Then she heard Pearl, at her back, finger out the opening notes and knew in one awful, terrifying moment that it was her turn to sing. She looked down at Barry and took a deep breath. Then she opened her mouth and… nothing. There was no sound. Nothing at all. Not even a bark. Mind you, she hadn't sung in decades. What did she expect?

'Nerves, it's all right. Take your time,' Barry was saying and she didn't want to go over and strike him on the head with his baton. 'Let's go again.' He signalled to Pearl and once more Tess heard the opening bars of 'Amazing Grace' and she knew she desperately wanted to sing. She wanted to fill up this beautiful old church, hear her notes bounce off stone, timbers and mosaics that had stood for a couple of hundred years. She wanted to feel herself drift up to the rafters and float among the souls who'd passed through here. She wanted her voice to soar and make her feel alive as she once had.

All of a sudden, she was singing, shaky and thin at first, but then she closed her eyes for a moment, concentrated on where her voice was coming from. Soon, the tremble fell away; within a few bars she could feel the notes gathering substance and force. They were coming from deep within her, rallying momentum as her breath pushed them from the bottom of her lungs. It was incredible, liberating, she was at one with herself, and every corner of the old building was breathing with her, taking her in and pushing her notes higher up into the atrium. She could hear her words float away from her, could almost feel them touch Barry, then Kilker and finally Pearl on the organ, who smiled serenely as though it was the most beautiful sound she'd ever heard. She sang her way through the first verse, the second verse and was sad to come to an end, as though a part of her was going back to sleep. As she drew out the final notes, she closed her eyes again and the smile that came to her lips had, she knew, risen up from the deepest part of her heart. This was happiness.

The church was quite still when she opened her eyes. Along the wall to her left, she noticed a small movement and then she realised that some of the choir members had waited to hear her sing. From the pew before her, sitting at an angle, with his legs crossed jauntily, Kilker began to clap. Soon the choir joined in, then Barry and Pearl too. Tess felt that swell of emotion that had bubbled inside her from when she'd listened to the choir go through their hymns earlier and she knew she had found something. It was something that she hadn't realised she was searching for, but here it was, all the time, snuggled right in the middle of the city and all she had to do was open her heart to it.

'Well, Barry, I think we have our mezzo-soprano,' Kilker said when everyone stopped clapping.

'We do if you're available to come along on Monday nights to practise,' Barry said, confirming it with the nodding choir members gathered around the lectern.

'Really,' Tess said and she heard that distinctly un-Tess-like wobble in her voice, so she cleared her throat again. 'I'd be delighted,' she said and, truly, she was.

Kilker drove her back to the square at half past ten. The conversation in the car had taken on a mellow, friendly tone and they spoke of music and nothing else for the journey. Grudgingly, she had to admit, he could be interesting when he wasn't getting on her nerves. She was almost disappointed that the night was over when they pulled up at her front door and she got out of the car.

Matt was waiting patiently for Tess and so the niggling thoughts of Nancy and that card didn't make her feel as empty as they might have once. An unfamiliar feeling of sanguinity, just for tonight, cushioned them. In spite of all the years convincing herself that she had cut all ties, it was so obvious now that they'd always been with her, a background air to her every move.

She poured herself a small nightcap and stood for a moment before the little card. She should call Nancy, it was a chance to make some move towards putting to rights all that had passed between them so very long ago. She really should, but sipping her drink, she knew that would probably be the hardest thing she would ever have to do.

Matt was snuggled into the corner of the long narrow couch that had sagged a long time before he arrived, but it seemed to slump perfectly to his shape. These days, he ignored the little bed she made for him before the fire, but she didn't mind, he suited the room, somehow, made the place even more homely. She rubbed her chin as she looked around the little sitting room. It was strange having Amanda King here. It was three nights ago, but still it rattled her a bit.

Today, Richard King had sent in a man to measure up her bathroom. He could start as soon as she wanted, if she was happy with the plan. It had upset her, seeing Amanda like that, made her feel like a Judas, who sold out truth for thirty pieces of silver. Her price settled on a heated toilet seat. Of course, she reasoned, she didn't owe Amanda anything. Amanda King had stood by while her husband tried every trick to shift Tess from her home. It was funny, but before Robyn started to visit her, Tess never really gave any thought to the fact that they were actually real people, just the same as Tess, who felt the pain of betrayal every bit as badly.

If she was honest, Tess might have said she didn't blame him. Over the years, her many spats with Amanda had led not just to dislike, but to feel something close to hatred for her. So much so, that until she saw her here, trembling and despairing, she thought it was as much as Amanda deserved. God, but she really was a judgemental old cow sometimes.

The problem was, she wasn't sure what she could do to make things better, but as she stroked Matt's soft fur affectionately, she decided she was bloody well going to try.

24

January 22 – Thursday

It was almost three weeks. Three weeks now since condom-gate and Amanda was still undecided. One thing was for sure, she had to do something. Something more than walk around the square each night. God, last night she'd almost turned on her heel and headed in the opposite direction just so she could walk along with Tess Cuffe. Amanda took it as a sign that she was now, officially desperate. If she truly was that desperate, well, it was time to call up the men in the white coats and start chanting novenas to whatever saint took care of hopeless cases. At the same time, she had to admit that something had changed in Tess Cuffe, it was as though she'd softened, just a little. Maybe they were both changing, just a bit. So, now, rather than nasty comments and frosty silence, there was a tepid wariness between them that Amanda welcomed even if Tess might not.

She sat at her kitchen table with a small notebook before her and a pencil in her hand. She had plenty to be thankful for. No, really, she tried to convince herself, there was lots to be thankful for. She looked around her pristine kitchen. How many people would give a kidney to live in a house like this? The problem was, Amanda knew that the kitchen in itself really meant very little. By the same token, her lovely house and her lovely car – they were essentially worthless if you weren't happy. How had it taken her so long to truly understand this? Like Amanda and her life, they were empty. There was no putting it all back together. Like a priceless broken vase, Amanda couldn't see how it could be fixed. For one thing, they both needed to want it and Richard clearly didn't.

She needed a plan. She held her pencil over the notebook, circled the blank page for a moment. It was no good. She needed to do something now. She picked up her mobile. She would have it out with him. She would be brave and she would be strong. She hadn't really talked to him in days, beyond *pass the milk*, or *have you seen my keys?* Not really since she'd shown him the condom. They'd skirted around each other, two uncomfortable actors playing parts that no longer belonged to them. He left early, came home late and she was too cowardly to pretend she was even awake.

She dialled his number, her stomach doing backflips and somersaults in traitorous sequence. It went straight to mailbox. She held the phone in her hand for a moment. Perhaps, it was a sign? She was not meant to ring him now. Perhaps, he was with *her*? Perhaps, this very minute, they were…

Bastard. How could he do this to her? How could he do this to them? He was ruining her lovely life. This lovely, perfect life that she had constructed around them. They were already living the dream, why did he have to go and spoil it all?

She had to stop it – she was tormenting herself with these thoughts. She jumped from the table, no plan in mind, but found herself in the living room, staring up at the cabinet Richard had commissioned specially to carry his golf trophies. She didn't question, didn't think about it. Later, she'd wonder, is this what blind rage felt like? Is this how people commit murder and then get off with a plea of insanity? Had she really come to the point where she was no longer compos mentis?

Possibly, because in the next fifteen minutes she managed to take every single piece of crystal out of the cabinet and carry them carefully out the back door. A sense of what she was about to do may have fleeted in some deep part of her while she stood with the trophies at her feet. And then, she picked up the biggest, most important piece of glass Richard had won. A four ball with a political bigwig, a fat-cat CEO and a work crony. She remembered the day well. The wives had turned out to glide about the clubhouse, while their men competed on the greens. Truly, Richard wasn't much of a golfer, but when you have enough money, it's amazing how you get picked for all the best teams.

She lifted the crystal; it was almost two foot tall, a

deep vase with the all-important inscription. Waterford crystal – probably worth as much as a pair of Louboutin heels. Amanda pushed that thought from her mind easily. As she felt it fly from her hand, she smiled. A liberating sense of relief passed through her when she heard the crash of glass against the old brick wall.

It took only minutes to bring to smithereens a lifetime of golfing memorabilia. Did she feel bad about it? No, Amanda realised it was the first time in a long time that she felt she might be doing something to settle the score.

Later, as she swept up the shards, she knew it would take more than just a shelf of golf trophies to make her feel they were even, but she had every intention of making sure they were. Win or lose, Amanda had a feeling that she needed to somehow get the upper hand if they were ever going to be happy again.

All too soon coffee morning rolled round again. Amanda checked her appearance before heading out to the jeep. She'd made an appointment at the hairdressers to sort out her grey roots. Not Claude; not this time. She was finished with Claude and with his overpriced, exaggerated notions and attitude of infallibility around all issues follicle. No, this morning she was going to a little salon that had opened up just around the corner.

'Growing it out, are you, Amanda?' the girl – she introduced herself as Sonia – sounded as if she'd been brought up in the Liberties as she took strands of Amanda's hair in her fingers.

Even in this subdued light, designed to make all hair look good, there was no denying that the colour was awful. Amanda hadn't put her make-up on yet, so the overall effect was nothing short of tragic. In snapshot, she reminded herself of a strawberry muffin. Her bouncy bob was shocking red icing with a badger strip of white sugar grey hair. Beneath this, the bland invisibility of middle age, without the strategic application of primer, eraser and highlighter, not to mention foundation, blusher and lips, made her resemble half-baked muffin dough.

'No bad thing, change is as good as a rest,' the girl said, but she was nice, not like the stylists Claude unleashed on her.

'I don't know how it got to that colour, really. I mean, I started out colouring the greys, but the place I used to go to, well, they just seemed to keep deepening the colour, so…' Amanda picked up a strand between her fingers, winced. It was almost crimson, and a radioactive hue of crimson at that. 'I want something understated; something that'll be easy to take care of.'

'What colour were you? You know, before you let the rainbow fairies at it,' Sonia asked and they both giggled at that.

'Well, I was a redhead, a nice redhead – I used to get compliments all the time.' It was 'quite striking', was what Richard had said. 'Well, it was quite nice.'

'And do you want to go for something similar again or something a bit more…' Sonia wiggled her fingers as though she was ready to cast a spell on the disaster before her.

'I want something that's appropriate, low-key. I want something that gives me a bit of a break. You know, something that's classy, but not boring. Is that too much to ask?'

'Nope. Not at all. We could go for a nice, light brown, colour it all over and then, if you want, I can add in some lighter tones throughout. You'll look…' she scrunched up her face for a moment before smiling, 'normal. No, seriously, it'll look good. You'll look good and it won't take long.' Sonia looked around the salon. It was a weekday morning and although there was a steady stream of custom, it hadn't the same frenetic feel to it that Claude actively cranked up so clients always knew he was in demand.

Sonia mixed the colour expertly and Amanda felt herself relax in the faux-leather chair surrounded by the chattering of harried women who were just grabbing what time they could before getting back to busy lives. For an hour or two, the warm sweet-smelling salon and a mug of instant coffee provided a respite, and the fleeting camaraderie was enough to buoy Amanda for her meeting with *the girls*.

Amanda emerged from the salon looking and feeling better than she'd done in weeks. When her hair was blow-dried she'd applied her make-up, carefully and more subtly than usual. Then she paid a fifth of the price she would have handed over to Claude and headed off to the dreaded coffee morning feeling like Jackie O – without the strand of pearls.

She caught a glimpse of herself in one of the shop windows as she made her way back to the car, the image she saw there was a pleasant surprise. Critically, she could admit, she was hardly a supermodel, but she looked better; maybe even a little bit sophisticated with her new colour and tidied-up hairstyle. She had made an effort, nothing out of the ordinary for the set she was meeting, but compared to what she wore at home these days, she was decidedly glam.

'Oh,' Nicola sniffed, 'you've had your hair done.' She leant a little closer to inspect. 'So you weren't brave enough to go for grey after all?' She smiled smugly at the other women.

'I still might, just not yet. Anyway, I couldn't just let it grow out now, could I?'

'It's super,' Clarissa said, 'more chic than the red.' She nodded her approval.

'Anything is better than that badger strip you had last week,' Megan laughed. 'Honestly, we thought, next thing you know, Richard would be finding a younger model.' She glanced at the other two and for a moment, something cut through the silence that fell between them, then she looked back at Amanda. 'Not of course that Richard would ever do anything like that.'

'Well, obviously,' Amanda said as convincingly as she could. She had to front it out. Even if she was going to confront Richard, it would be something that she would never share with this lot.

'Still off the cake?' Clarissa asked.

'Yes,' Amanda said. Curiously this week, she hadn't even noticed the tiered plate before her, loaded up with biscuits, banana bread and cherry slices. 'It's really made a difference too, I can feel it already,' Amanda said with as much enthusiasm as she could muster. A few weeks ago, she would have been ecstatic at the thought of losing over half a stone in weight, now, well, it was the very last thing on her mind.

The conversation around her had moved on to gardeners. Apparently, you were nobody these days unless you had your garden redesigned and there was only one designer everyone wanted. Of course, Clarissa had him on speed dial. She passed the number along to Amanda, who didn't remember asking for it, but she smiled when she realised it was Carlos and she put it in her handbag without a word.

She sat back a little in her chair and watched the three women who had been her so-called friends for almost two decades. They were clones, each of them may look different, but they were clones. All of them prayed at the same altar. Was it desperation? Was that why they strived so hard for perfection? Was it fear? Perhaps they feared finding themselves in the situation Amanda had found herself in now.

She took a deep breath. Even the coffee sat precariously in her throat, threatening in its own spiteful way to damn her. This place, the Berkley Hotel, they had come here every week for years. Amanda could remember her first time. She'd been completely in awe of it all. This beautiful room and, of course, Clarissa, Nicola and Megan were enough to make anyone catch their breath. Back then, they really were all beautiful, full of life and expectations. Their smiles were genuine then – weren't they? Maybe they weren't. Maybe they had always been this bitchy and she just hadn't noticed because she was on the inside for so long. That thought made her feel disgust, not at them as much as at herself. They had been despicable. Cruel to people who were not faring as well in life as they were; when had she turned into someone who took pleasure in other people's misfortunes?

God, but she wanted to scream. Suddenly she wanted to call them out, tell them exactly how she saw them. She wanted to rupture their bitchfest and stamp out of here, she wanted to run down that street outside, find her car and drive... Where? Home was not the refuge she had hoped to make it. Since her suspicions began, she felt like an outsider in the beautiful house she'd spent so much of her time getting just right. Now, it was all wrong. Everything about it was wrong. She wanted a home where she could throw her coat over the stair rail, where she could leave her bag on the kitchen worktops without having to put it away immediately. She wanted a home that smelled as if her family lived there. She wanted a home where people sat together, not behind forbidding bedroom doors and beneath inimical headphones. She wanted a house that was a home. Could the house on Swift Square ever be that now? God, she couldn't answer that and the question as it hung over her carried in it a maelstrom of emotions from fear to regret and from sadness finally to anger.

'You're not even listening to us. Honestly, Amanda, you're in another world, it's as if you've something on your mind and it's completely cut you off from us?' Nicola was studying her, and although her mouth was smiling, those shrewd green grey eyes were assessing.

'No, just one of those things. I'm making biscuits for the Girl Guides and, for the life of me, I can't remember where I left my shopping list.' Amanda smiled what she hoped was an endearing smile. They had always seen her as a little ditzy. Over the years, Amanda had become the fat one. She was the one who could tell a joke and got frazzled by the various demands of having a fabulous life, but cake kept her on the straight and narrow.

'I was just saying,' Clarissa bent a little closer to the group and Amanda leant forward out of courtesy as much as out of habit, 'I have it on good authority that this new girl, Arial Wade?' She looked around at the women who were nodding like wind-up dolls. Amanda nodded automatically too, although she hadn't a clue who they were on about. 'Well, apparently, she's working her way through the trading floor. She's slept with every junior trader in the place and...' Clarissa smiled coyly, enjoyed having them hang on her next words.

'Oh, come on, do tell...' Nicola was practically gagging.

'Well, it seems that they're looking at promoting her, so she could yet be...' Clarissa walked her perfectly manicured fingers along the tabletop.

'No. There's not a chance that she's going to swan in from...' Nicola looked around. 'Where was she before? Japan, wasn't it?' She shrugged, 'It's never going to happen, not if she decides to shag Julian Fitzgerald himself. Everyone knows Hugo has...' she looked across at Amanda, 'well, either Hugo or Richard are entitled to that job.' *That job* was *the job*. It was the job Richard had set his heart on – the prize they were working towards for most of their married lives. The one that Amanda had always believed he'd pull from under Hugo and Nicola Lennox's nose. Now, well suddenly, it all seemed so worthless.

'Nicola, seriously, they haven't given it to either Richard or Hugo, maybe they are holding it open for someone...' she was going to say better, 'newer.' Amanda smiled with an ease that she never knew she had. 'After all, what do we need it for anyway? My family is taken care of, we have lovely homes, lovely holidays. If Hugo retired tomorrow morning you're still set up for life.' Amanda looked around at the other women who were staring at her now, all but open-mouthed. 'I mean, truly, quality of life, girls,' she said and she smiled to herself, sipping her coffee.

'You don't mean that,' Nicola said slyly. 'You know something we don't… about this job, have you heard something?' She was leaning forward so much, Amanda thought she might topple over.

'Heard something?' Amanda said innocently. 'Moi?' She was enjoying her moment of being the centre of it all, the one who seemed to hold all the cards. It was like a holiday from feeling so crap all the time.

'We're your friends, Amanda, come on, you've got to spill. You know the curiosity will just kill me if I don't find out for another week.'

'Do you think she'll start shagging the senior traders?' Megan's hand flew to cover her mouth, normally she managed to keep her reserve.

'I'd say she already has,' Nicola was aloof and Amanda knew that if she didn't play along, Nicola would be the first to shoot a poison dart in her direction.

'Look, I don't know anything about this Arial Wade, but I'm just saying, it stands to reason, doesn't it? They're looking for new blood, and maybe she's it. As a woman, we should be applauding her. I mean, better her to get it than some hotshot hardly out of his dad's school tie. Do we want someone who relegates everyone else to the scrap heap?'

'Hmm.' Nicola was thinking now. 'Maybe we should meet this Arial Wade?'

'Warn her off, you mean?' Megan was chewing on her lower lip and Amanda couldn't help but feel for her. It was amazing the clarity that arrived with knowing that your worst fears had materialised.

'No. Nothing as juvenile as that. After all, if she's made it onto the stockbrokers' floor, she's hardly going to be intimidated by a few ladies who lunch,' Nicola's laugh was sardonic, cruel almost. Was that all she thought of herself? Amanda wondered. Was it all she thought of any of them? Had they become little more than 'ladies who lunch' and supplicate themselves to second place because their husbands were super-earners?

'Well, I say good luck to her,' Amanda said with far more conviction than she felt. 'May the best man win.' She shivered then, a rattle through her bones as though someone had stepped on her grave, or perhaps they were just laughing at her.

Amanda was delighted to sit in the jeep once she left the Berkley. She switched off the radio. Its incessant chatter only added to the frizzle of agitation that the women had brought to her nerves. At the traffic lights, she turned left instead of right, headed for the underground parking close to the Stock Exchange. She hadn't a plan, just a need to not go home yet. At the same time as she was parking the jeep, she knew she really did not want to run into Richard. She could go shopping, that always worked well to soothe her nerves. After all, most of her clothes were becoming loose on her now; she'd begun digging in the back of the wardrobe for items that she'd saved for *one day*.

No. Shopping wouldn't do it for her. Not this time. Shopping didn't sort out seething anger and that was the emotion that she was feeling now. It came as a bit of a surprise, but today, finally, the shock and fear had begun to subside. Now she was angry. Furious with herself for feeling so weak and vulnerable and for becoming what once she would have despised. When did that happen? Had she always been such a wishy-washy wife? She had spent the last few weeks in mortal fear that Richard's affair would tear her world down. Now she was beginning to see that the world she thought was so pristine was far from being as perfect as she had believed. Today, with this unfamiliar anger searing through her, she realised, that tearing down the lot might be the best thing for her. At least then she could be free to take on the world on her own terms. At least then she wouldn't have to pretend, because that was what her life had become – pretence. It was the same for Nicola, Megan and Clarissa, only they couldn't see it yet.

Amanda took the exit furthest from the Stock Exchange. She was walking up Crown Alley when a key-shaped sign caught her attention. She'd never noticed it before, but it seemed to be drawing her towards the light green door emblazoned with the words. *P Boland, Investigator and Researcher.* Serendipity, wasn't that what they called it when things just seemed to fall into your hands.

The girl at the desk was lovely. A nondescript little thing, but her eyes were quick and she typed as if she was on a death mission. 'You're lucky. The twelve o'clock cancelled. If you could take a seat for a minute?' She made no move to ring through to her boss, but continued to type at breakneck speed for about four minutes. It was just enough time for Amanda to begin to come to her senses.

She was about to pick up her bag and make her apologies for being silly and that she should not have come when the girl got up from her desk and switched on the kettle. She tipped her head to one side and asked, 'Coffee or tea?' and Amanda found herself asking for a cup of tea.

The mug was hot and steaming in her hands and somehow it managed to taste a million times better here with this stranger than the coffee she'd just left behind at the five-star Berkley Hotel.

25

Forty-eight years earlier...

Sometimes Tess wondered at the blackness of this city as she stared at her reflection in the kitchen window before her. The patch of land outside, that might have been a grand garden once, only paraded the darkness further. Across the city, people picked their way home quickly, the promise of a turf fire and the six o'clock news perhaps enough to salve the inconvenience of the cold December evening.

Tess managed not to cry, instead she bottled it all up. She never spoke of Douglas or how her heart was breaking; how could she say that he had cast her aside because she was not quite good enough. She couldn't admit that to Nancy, it would make the rejection even worse. She hoped that if she left it just a little longer, he would relent and she would claim the happiness she had first assumed was hers. The letter sat uncomfortably on the kitchen table. Aunt Beatrice had taken a 'turn', her mother said. They hadn't worried, over the years it had become an annual event – Tess could hardly remember a December when she hadn't. Beatrice had led a band of women in the 1916 rising. She had played her part in the war of independence and later in the great emergency – Ireland's response to the Second World War. Her father said it was a relief she'd missed out on Cromwell – if, in his dry opinion, only just. Her mother played out all those conversations between the faded blue words in her letter and Tess knew that Beatrice was too tired for another battle.

Their final goodbye was so much less than Tess hoped it might be. Beatrice was unrecognisably shrunken and grey, an incongruous doll-like figurine splayed across starched pillows in the county home. How could she have aged so much in a matter of months? She wanted to believe there was the quiver of a smile upon her lips as Tess spoke of the new life carving out before her. Later, when they sat alone, she told her about Douglas Buckley and how she loved him, and Beatrice had smiled, just a fraction, but enough for Tess to know she heard.

She passed away an hour later and Tess allowed the paraphernalia of death to wash over her. They were shunted from the ward, the priest and doctors, nurses and other patients became a blur of words spent only to fill the awkwardness of loss. There was a pattern, a long-worn path of what people said and did at times like this. Even if her parents were unaccustomed to it, they seemed happy to track along and accept the handshakes and nods that were shorthand for words rhymed off in funeral homes and beneath graveside orations.

'She would want one of you to live there,' her mother said quietly as they made their journey home. They sat, all three, in the back of her father's car – and it struck Tess as odd that her mother chose to leave the seat in front free – their father captaining this sad journey alone.

'I would love to live in Ballycove,' Nancy said the words uncertainly. Tess knew Ballycove was where Nancy had always belonged. Nancy was hardly making a huge sacrifice, even if their mother counted it as such. She squeezed Nancy's hand, a muted message, unpicked by love and fear. Although they sat next to each other, Tess could not meet her eyes, instead she felt her sister's glance as it bounced nervously about the car – perhaps she had an inkling then that Nancy was about to bring her hopes crashing down upon her.

'Well, we've always known that, Nancy.' Her father's voice, pragmatic, reasonable from the front.

'She wanted me to have it,' Tess wasn't sure if she whispered the words, but her mother tutted beside her, so she supposed she'd said something, even if it wasn't fully heard. Not that she'd ever said she'd live there, in that wild and often lonely spot staring out into the sea – but Beatrice had wanted her there. It was funny, but suddenly, she could imagine Douglas wanting to live there. It made the cottage seem more important, in those few moments; it might be pivotal to her future.

'I think Douglas would love it,' Nancy murmured,

her eyes glued to the fleeting countryside that glided slowly past the condensation-shot window. It seemed to be such an odd thing to say, but it wasn't really, because they often shared thoughts and sentences with each other, as though they were reading the other's mind without even realising it.

Suddenly, all those dreams of music and Covent Garden and Carnegie Hall seemed to mist before Tess's eyes and she saw within them the emptiness stretched out before her, without Douglas. These last few weeks, the row with Douglas and the way Nancy seemed to be drifting from her, it all blunted her resolve. Unexpectedly, her heart was no longer in those dreams that she had once cherished. Perhaps she was just in shock – she'd loved Aunt Beatrice, maybe more than she loved her own mother? Beatrice wanted all those things for her, but she wanted more. Beatrice had a young man, once. A boy called Denny Larkin, who travelled to London in the war and soon found himself fighting for a king that not too long before he'd railed against. Beatrice never met another. Sometimes, Tess thought that if she had, if she'd married like the other girls in the village, perhaps the little cottage wouldn't have its faded sense of loss.

She looked far out to sea and felt the last vestiges of her aunt surround her in that place that was forever hers. She would return to Dublin, then things would seem better. If Nancy lived here – Tess could be happy for her, she might have some young man already. In these dark December days, everything just seemed so set. When spring bounced in and days were warm and bright – what could be nicer than a wedding? Yes, the more Tess thought about it, she had a sense that Nancy had met a young man and before they knew it, she'd be announcing her wedding.

She could imagine, living in Dublin, continuing with her studies and coming out to visit Nancy in Ballycove. She would get on with life. Douglas would work things out with her and they would be happy too. She would be glad then that she hadn't told Nancy about this falling-out with Douglas, it would be water under the bridge and some day they would both forget it had ever come to this. She would make a good life for herself. She would graduate and the world would be hers to make of it what she would. She clung to the idea, that one day soon, they would both find their happy ever after, knowing that everything was going to turn out well. It became almost a mantra, at night, Tess found she would wake, her teeth grinding to the words – one day soon.

26

January 26 – Monday

There had been no sign of Richard King, but Tess knew he had not forgotten her. It was just over two weeks since 'loo-gate', as she liked to think of it, when the builders arrived in her little flat. They were a nice enough old bunch, even if it took a bit of getting used to, tripping across broad-shouldered, pot-bellied men at every turn.

'In and out, Mrs Cuffe,' the contractor told her. 'We'll be gone before you know it.' Willie was from Wexford, a tea addict who talked more than he worked, but the others made up for him, so Tess supplied the tea and an occasional biscuit.

The first day had seen the lion's share of the work done. They parked a skip on Amanda's lovely Italian pebble driveway and filled it with a peach bathroom suite, plastic worn-out floor tiles, beauty-board and pipes that might have been of interest to the National Museum. That night, before she left for choir practice, they had put back half of what they took out, only this time round everything was the very best of quality. Tess stood in the little bathroom, which seemed much bigger and brighter when they left. It was gutted and sealed within a working day.

'You'll see it taking shape in a day or two,' Willie said now as he reached for his fourth spoon of sugar.

'That'll kill you, you know,' she said, stroking Matt, who kept tabs on all the comings and goings with a supervisory eye.

'Sure, something has to kill you,' he said, then he lowered his voice, 'this is costing them a pretty penny,' He smiled, 'Must be very fond of you.'

'Oh, yes, the feelings go very deep, all right,' Tess said, thinking to herself, it was time for her walk; after all, she needed to live a long life to get full value out of her bathroom.

'I suppose it'll be the kitchen next?' Willie said, leaning forward. 'We could do a lovely little job on that for you.' He squinted as he looked about her ramshackle collection of cupboards and drawers. It was a pathetic little corner; she could see that now, as she imagined it looked through the eyes of a stranger.

'Will you go on out of that, you'll have me robbed in tea and sugar if I get any more work done.'

'I'd say Mr King wouldn't even notice the price of getting this place done. He told our gaffer, it was to be only the very best here.' Willie shook his head thoughtfully. 'It's a drop in the ocean compared to what he makes in the year, I suppose.'

'I suppose,' Tess said thoughtfully. It would be tempting to go back to Richard King and tell him she wanted to get her kitchen updated too, part of her knew he'd agree, if it meant keeping her quiet. And he deserved it, he really did. But then, there was Robyn, and Tess knew she couldn't play a game that had the potential to destroy a family. She'd had her thirty pieces of silver, now it was time to do the right thing.

'It's going to be great,' Robyn said as she peered into the little bathroom; it was beginning to look much better already. Yes, she had all the modern conveniences she could possibly want. 'I wonder why my dad didn't think of doing it sooner? Mum says he should do over the whole flat, since he's in such a generous mood.' Robyn sighed and then added quietly, 'She's not herself at all these days.' Tess wondered exactly how much she knew about what had gone on between them all over the years.

'Well, I'm delighted, it'll be like living in the Ritz,' Tess decided to make light of it. 'And, I've joined a choir.' She had been dying to tell someone, well, she'd been dying to tell Robyn.

'Really, a choir? I didn't know you could sing.' Her eyes drifted towards the old record player, putting the clues together, maybe it made sense now. 'Of course, you love music, well, opera anyway.' Robyn made a little face, but Tess suspected she was growing to love some of the lighter more familiar pieces from *Madam Butterfly*. 'So how did you end up joining a choir?' She flopped onto the sofa beside the purring Matt.

'It's a long story, but I'm going to be singing mezzo-soprano, so I'll be doing my voice exercises every day now.' Tess cleared her throat, 'Just in case you hear it and think Matt is in danger.'

'And can we go and see you sing?'

'Well, I…' Tess didn't know what to say. 'I don't know. I mean, would you want to?'

'Of course I'd want to. That's what people do, isn't it? They go out and support their… friends.' She said the last word a little more softly, smiling shyly when she caught Tess's eye.

'Well, I suppose it is. There is a concert, but I'm not sure that I'll be ready for that. I mean, it is years since I did anything like this.' Tess pulled herself back from the past sharply, there was no point thinking of those days now. 'Anyway, who would you bring, it's not exactly the kind of thing your friends would be clambering to get to, I'm sure.'

'Mum would come. She'd love it and it'd be good for her…' Robyn's voice trailed off.

'Would she?' Tess found herself asking, not just to be polite – she had long lost that particular habit when it came to Amanda King. 'Are you still worried about her?' Tess passed Amanda every day on the square. They still walked in opposite directions, passing comments that were not so vicious anymore. It struck Tess, just this week, that maybe Amanda's comments never were spiteful. That had caught her up, so she'd stopped herself from being unpleasant to just being peaceable, if not quite friendly.

'Oh, Tess, I don't know how anything is now. It's as if she's changed. I suppose at least she's not crying anymore. In some ways, things are better; it feels as though she's really there, at least when my father is not around. But she's not the same, it's as if someone came along and emptied out her muchness and she's constantly searching for it, walking about the square. She even went for a run one evening, didn't come back until all hours.'

'But surely all that is good. I mean, she looks much better than she did a year ago. The walking and her new hairstyle, she looks a hundred times better,' Tess said, patting down her own hair. 'For someone, like your mother, looking well has to be important; it has to make her feel better in herself.'

'Honestly,' Robyn looked about the flat, then pulled up the little rucksack she carried everywhere and began to root in its depths. 'Honestly, I don't think she's walking for her figure. Not so long ago, she'd have loved to look so well. Maybe that's a bit shallow, but now, it's as if she's seeing past her looks, she's walking to find something that's deeper than just her waistline.'

She pulled out an old-fashioned hairbrush, held it up before her for a minute. 'Tess, can I brush your hair?' Robyn whispered.

'I...' Tess couldn't remember when she'd last had her hair brushed for her. For years, her hairdressing appointments were at the bathroom sink, she'd just tidied up bits as they began to annoy her.

'Please,' Robyn pleaded.

'Well, I suppose, it can't do any harm,' Tess said.

'No. What harm could it do?' Robyn murmured as she set about gently stroking Tess's long-neglected locks.

She brushed it silently, slowly and carefully. Not once, did she so much as pull or snag at Tess's scalp. And then, the oddest thing happened. Tess closed her eyes and it felt as though she was being transported, in the hush of their lovely cocooned contentment, to a place far away. She felt tension that she hadn't realised was in her body drain away as though it flooded out of her. Just one tear at first, a welling up of emotion that wasn't sad, nor was it happy, but perhaps it was a release of the emotions that for so long she'd buried. It was joy, she realised as one tear followed another, a steady stream that came from somewhere in her chest. She thought of Aunt Beatrice and Kilker, of her voice climbing to the rafters in that choir. She thought of Robyn and Matt and all she truly had to be grateful for right now.

'I'm sorry,' Robyn said when she noticed the tears.

'Don't be,' Tess said and she placed her hand over

Robyn's hand as she guided the brush softly along her hair, 'I can't remember when I last felt this happy.'

Tess made her way home slowly the next day. Moving fast was hard while she carried the weight of the city about her shoulders. Guilt is a shockingly heavy burden, she realised. Her hair sat neatly, she looked almost like the woman she'd been destined to become all those years ago, except that woman wasn't meant to end up here.

Richard King thought he had bought her silence with a fancy bathroom and she knew he had no idea what keeping his secret could cost her. There was Robyn to think of now and, grudgingly, maybe even Amanda. After all, Tess could remember how betrayal felt. How could she have believed it would be any different for Amanda King? She meant to stop off for biscuits for the builders on the way. She meant to run through her voice exercises, drink hot water and then relax with the local paper. Instead, she walked in a haze through city streets, teeming with faceless people, moving to a beat at odds with all Tess was feeling.

She sat in the Square garden for over an hour. Today she didn't notice the smug mothers or their puckish kids. She didn't catch the traffic rumble along the road outside, even a wren perched on a stripped branch close by couldn't drag her from her contemplation. Tess wasn't even sure what she was thinking. Everything she thought she knew was capsizing, turning on its head in a way that equalled and nulled all she had believed was real.

Across the square, she saw Amanda King, bent double, pulling weeds like they might root out the misery within if she caught them quick enough. A year ago, no, maybe as recently as a month ago, Tess wasn't sure that what she knew now might have even caught her breath. Today it felt as if it might suffocate her.

She watched as Amanda worked like a drowning woman against the tide. She never looked up, her hands and upper body moving like a machine, over and back, ground to weed bucket. It was rhythmic, hypnotic almost, and Tess could just about convince herself that this moment, here in the little Square garden, everything was as it should be.

But of course, it wasn't. Apart from Robyn, quite aside from the fact that she was really fond of the girl, she owed it to Amanda King to at least support her. Didn't she? Tess knew, even if she would never admit it, they both knew – Amanda King could have pushed her out years ago. She could have made it impossible for her in ways that only women could do to each other.

Even if her reasons for letting Tess stay were not founded on generosity or kindness, Tess had a feeling that Amanda was not all bad. Even if Amanda had lost her way a little in the gilded world she inhabited, there was compassion, Tess had always known that, even if she wanted to pretend she didn't see it.

Amanda King came towards her. She greeted her with a wave, almost friendly on both sides, and Tess wondered if there was such a thing as miracles. She sat in her seat until she was quite sure that Amanda would have let herself in through her front door. Then she got up and made her way back to her little flat.

She flicked on the kettle and brought the post over to the stove while she sorted through the unsolicited pile of advertising and general junk mail. It was the downside of living on the square – delivery boys never left her out; although, it must be obvious that she had no need of office equipment, executive swivel chairs, plant maintenance or courier services. Most of it could be set alight, it would help to start a fire and cosy up her flat more quickly on dark evenings.

The small envelope obliterated all thoughts of Amanda from her. She almost tore it in two, assuming it was some kind of clever advertising ploy to grab her attention. Just before she tore, something registered in the handwriting. Her name, spelled out in delicate script across the front, it was familiar, the curve of the S, the high dash across the T. There was no stamp, the sender had made a journey, especially to deliver it. Tess stood for a moment, her breath caught deep in her chest. She wondered if she should just discard it with the other rubbish, but her hand quivered and she looked about her modest kitchen. The stillness knitted her thoughts closer together, as though her nerves were thin needles clicking out the possibilities contained behind her sister's script. Outside, life bludgeoned behind the glass and Tess thought of the days she'd spent here when no one ever called to check on her.

Tess was afraid to open that envelope, and that was just silly. After all, it was just a card; she could feel the stiffness in her hand. It was probably just a note to wallow in the loss of Douglas – well, Tess knew what that was like. Nancy had always been the quiet one, the one who thought things through; 'soft as a marshmallow', her father called her.

Then the old feelings began to surge through Tess again. The pain, the betrayal, the loss, the hurt. Nancy had taken Douglas from her. She'd set her hat at him and come along with her charm and her delicacy and her soft hands and softer laugh and she'd swiped him from under Tess's nose. She had no idea how Nancy knew she still lived here, but whatever was in that letter meant nothing to Tess. She had long since left Nancy behind in Ballycove. That was where she always thought of her, in Beatrice's little cottage looking out upon the waves. Just because her sister wrote a note and came here to drop it through her letter box was no reason to open up old wounds.

27

January 28 – Wednesday

Did Nicola know? Amanda wondered, not because of what she said, but rather what she didn't say. Nicola never rang to talk about nothing, her every move had motive stacked behind it. The call on her mobile came when Amanda was out walking, ostensibly to ask how she was.

'Just thought I'd check in with you, darling,' Nicola breezed. 'You didn't seem yourself at all the other day.'

'Really?' Amanda almost squeaked. 'Well, I'm fine, just busy, you know. I've really taken to this exercise lark and I'm up to my eyes with committee work, but it's all good. Actually, it's great,' she managed.

'Oh, well, that's super,' Nicola drawled and Amanda expected her to add something about her 'bearing it all well', but thankfully she didn't. Nicola hung up the call with nothing confirmed but with Amanda being a little wiser than she was before. Like Jenga blocks, it began to add up; she realised, they'd been watching her. The last time they met, there had been no great bitching session and, from experience, Amanda had a feeling that meant they were gossiping about her.

Far from depressing her, the realisation was a release, as though, she was no longer tied to them in the same way. They'd cast her out, but maybe they would set her free. She realised that Nicola, Clarissa and Megan were not her friends and she wondered if perhaps she might have the making of better friendships much closer to home. She cut her walk short and raced quickly back to her house, there was something she needed to do.

Amanda searched the cabinet in Richard's study. It was where he kept the whiskey, too many bottles received over the years for them to get through. Richard pretended to drink whiskey, but he was a lightweight when it came to alcohol. Amanda peered into the hoard of unopened boxes and bottles. They stood to attention, sober soldiers in uniforms from around the world, gold seals and banners betrayed their fulsomeness. It was a shame to have these ridiculously covetous bottles held prisoner here when there was a malt enthusiast downstairs who might enjoy them. Amanda smiled, Richard hadn't noticed his golf trophies were missing until she mentioned that they were being cleaned, he'd hardly register a missing whiskey bottle.

Amanda selected a Scotch, reserve, oak aged and sealed with a black wax impress. She needed to thank Tess Cuffe and she had a feeling it was now or never. Something about her, when they met each evening on their opposite circuits of the square, had softened. Amanda couldn't go so far as to say the woman liked her, but it was as though much of the venom had been released between them. Perhaps it was time to make some kind of move towards a truce. Long gone was the hope that they might ever be friends, much less that Tess might step in as some kind of surrogate grandmother to her children. God, she'd been so naïve when she came here first.

She had a feeling the bottle of whisky probably cost more than Tess Cuffe earned in a week. She smiled at the notion that Tess would enjoy it at Richards' expense, then tucked it under her arm and headed for the flat beneath.

'Oh,' Tess said by way of welcome, 'what do you want?'

'I come bearing gifts,' Amanda said, producing the bottle from beneath her jacket. 'Well a "thank you" bottle at any rate.'

'If I said I was all gifted out, you probably wouldn't believe me,' Tess said wearily and Amanda thought she looked tired, as though she'd emptied half her fight out and stored it in a jar for another day.

'It's late, I'm sorry, I just wanted to say thanks, really for… you know, taking me in that night…' Amanda smiled, it was strange to be standing here, holding, what was, essentially a peace offering. 'It's whisky,' she pushed the bottle into Tess Cuffe's hands. 'One of Richard's, he never drinks them. Honestly, I could probably make a year's grocery money if I flogged the lot on eBay.' Her voice strung out between them, a nervous link chain she hoped Tess would grab hold of.

'Well,' Tess considered the bottle for a moment, then took it in her hands. 'You really didn't need to. I have plenty, it's not as if I…' her voice tapered off, as though she knew she might end up saying too much. 'Would you like to come in?' She stood back in the porch.

Amanda wasn't sure if she was asking because she'd like her to visit or because it was polite and they'd been standing looking at each other for so long she didn't really have much of a choice. 'Are you sure? I mean, I wouldn't want to impose.'

'Come on. We can open this and have a nightcap.' Tess's smile was just a little wicked, as though she might realise just how much more resistance she had to the stuff than Amanda could muster. In the light of her living room, Tess held the bottle from her to inspect it properly. 'It certainly looks expensive,' she said, then narrowed her eyes. 'It doesn't mean it's any good of course.'

'I wouldn't know.' Amanda flopped into the velvet couch again, noticed the sleeping cat on the end. A month ago, that cat would have been something else to get up her nose. After all, she would have reasoned, *poor* Richard couldn't stand them. Funny, but now she looked at the cat, it suited here, as though it had always been hanging about the place.

'Oh, he's not mine,' Tess said quickly as though reading her thoughts. She placed two glasses down before them, pulled hard on the cork, but it wasn't budging.

'Here, let me.' Amanda yanked it off with the ferociousness of one committed to liberating the contents, if not because she needed it, but rather, like a maître d', she wanted to gauge its reception with an expert. She watched as Tess poured the costly liquid into their glasses and then inhaled the contents for a moment. She looked different today, her hair somehow softened, her face held serenity at odds with her papery reddened hands. She closed her eyes as though she might fathom all its secrets from its aroma.

'That is good.' Tess smiled mischievously at Amanda. 'Taste it.' She pushed the glass forward and Amanda sipped slowly. This time, warmth radiated through her gently, pleasantly, as though it might smooth away the chill from her core.

They sat for a little while in silence, Tess broke it when she asked. 'How have you been?' There was an honesty to her words and the concern that lingered in her eyes struck Amanda as genuine.

'I could say I've been fine, but...'

'I saw you working in the square, remember,' Tess said. 'How are you really?'

'I did something. Something, I hadn't planned to, but I just sorted of ended up there.'

'Where?' Tess leaned forward now.

'I went to see an investigator.'

'That might be the wisest thing you've ever done,' Tess said quietly and studied her glass intently.

Amanda could hardly believe she had struck out and it had taken until she sat in this little flat before she told anyone about her impulsiveness. And that was what it was. A spur of the moment, not properly thinking decision to meet with a professional investigator and spill her guts out about her marriage. 'It's not to find out anything…'

'No. I mean, of course not.' Tess cleared her throat. 'You already know,' she said softly.

'Yes.' Amanda looked at this woman who she'd hated for so long and suddenly the penny dropped. 'You knew?'

'I…' Tess studied the glass in her hands. 'I came on them, pure chance, the kind of fluke encounter that could only happen in this claustrophobic city.' She shook her head and then looked at Amanda. 'What is it about Ireland, everyone knows everyone and if they don't then they're probably related?'

Amanda couldn't think straight, but she sipped her drink, sat for a moment trying to pull it all together. 'When?' she whispered.

'Just a few days before you ended up sobbing on your naughty step. I suppose, I was still in shock myself, I didn't know how to say it. I knew the last person you'd want to hear it from was me,' Tess said in a voice tinged with disquiet that made it unfamiliar. 'I just… I'm sorry, it was too hard and too convoluted. You and I, we've been so…'

'Horrible?' Amanda breathed. 'We have, truly. I've been the worst, just backing him up for a quiet life when I knew it was wrong.' She looked around the little flat, 'I couldn't understand how this place could mean so much to you.' She laughed now, a hysterical sound in her own throat. 'And yet, I wanted it so much – how could I have been so…'

'I thought you were an awful bitch. I didn't sleep properly here for months, afraid of what you both might do next to get me out,' Tess said and, for a moment, Amanda thought she might cry.

'Oh, God.' Amanda felt a shock of pain rise within her. 'Does he know you know?' It emptied her out, the idea that his disloyalty had almost come full circle. At the same time it all made sense. Why else would he have agreed to refurbish her bathroom? 'Of course he does.' The words tripped from her. 'He knows you know and he's… the work on the flat, he's trying to buy your silence. I've been such a fool.' Amanda shook her head and this time she thought the tears would never stop, because this was an even greater betrayal in some ways.

'No, Amanda,' Tess said and she reached her arm around Amanda's back until her sobbing ended. 'The real fool here is Richard; he's the one throwing away so much more than he knows.'

Amanda's love affair with spring began when she moved to Swift Square. Perhaps it was because she had given up work and she had time to watch the seasons, and while much of her day was taken up with renovating the house, it was the garden that drew her towards the end of each day. Back then, the square seemed as if it might be a project too large to take on. Rust-eaten railings, once painted black, chased about its perimeter. Then, it was little more than a shortcut, a maze of uneven broken paths through unofficial discarded allotments. Years of neglect and misuse rendered it a wilderness within the elegant if neglected square.

Amanda could clearly remember the first afternoon she'd walked into it. It was the day they'd finally re-hung her front door. Inside their home was still a ramshackle building site slowly mining into the derelict edifice she'd set her heart on. She had needed to get out. It was not yet a home, although she'd convinced Richard to move in to the two rooms that were just about sealed off from the cold Dublin air. Each morning she woke to a procession of plumbers, electricians, tilers and carpenters weaving through her grand plan.

The Square garden, when she entered it, felt like paradise, a wonderland she discovered through the rabbit hole of the broken railings. It turned out to be far bigger than she thought at first. It stretched out as far as a football field, but it was so overgrown, the weeds dwarfed out the space. If she'd known before she started work on it, she might have been more daunted. Woody lavender, lemongrass and honeysuckle shook off their scent after a summer shower and she sat, gingerly, on the edge of a huge curved rock within the perfume, listening to a city grumbling and losing itself in its own frenzy. The garden bit into some essential part of her, so she ached to bring it back to what it could be again. It was a chance to be creative, she only realised it after she had finished.

Over the years, she could honestly say that sitting on her much-loved bench on a spring morning, before the city rumbled into life, with a mug of tea in her hand, was as if she was sitting in heaven. For all the money they'd spent on their home, this little corner, surrounded by the bees in summer and the robins in winter, was her favourite place on earth. Richard ploughed a fortune into their own back garden, with an exterior designer on speed dial for every possible aesthetic emergency, but this remained a nirvana when she most needed to get away.

She had been happy here, with the old Italian, digging out beds, selecting shrubs, pulling in sponsorship from needy causes that hadn't stood the test of time like this place. They spent about nine months from start to finish. It took a full-term pregnancy to get it right. Of course, it wasn't perfect, not like the garden Richard paid so much for, but perhaps it was why she loved it so greatly. Every single plant here, she'd put her hand on at some point, either to save it or to set it. She and Antonio had tea and sandwiches on her rock each day, before the picnic tables arrived and they'd squabbled, laughed and watched the sun go down together, satisfied with a day well spent.

'You are smiling too much for it to be honest.' A deep voice penetrated her thoughts, Carlos Giordano regarded her with a smirk.

'I was thinking about your father and when we worked together here,' she said, shading her eyes from the morning sun intent on seeking out cracks in the heavy clouds overhanging the square.

'He will be glad to know he can make you smile like that.' He dropped down on the bench next to her, a little closer than perhaps he should, but the proximity only made her tingle unexpectedly.

'It was just a very happy time, doing this garden, I was thinking how much I enjoyed it all.' She found herself smiling at him and assumed he probably had the same effect on every woman he met. He was obscenely handsome and, more than that, unpretentiously charismatic.

'Well, you are welcome to start again.' He smiled at her. 'I can't guarantee the same charm as my father had for you, but there's certainly plenty of work planned if you think you're up for it.'

'I...' Amanda regarded him for a moment, was he insinuating that she was too old to take on the garden again? 'Of course I'm up for it. What is it that you're planning on doing to it?'

'Oh, the council have big plans,' he said, laughing at her and she couldn't help but notice how his dark eyes crinkled so you knew that there was warmth behind his smile.

'Well, we'll see about that, won't we?' They wouldn't be messing with her garden unless she was happy with it. 'When can I see the plans?' The last thing she wanted was some council official deciding they were going to pull her lovely garden apart only to come out and get their picture taken before applying for a promotion.

'How about if I call round to you later with the drawings?' He nodded across towards her house and she wondered for a moment if it wasn't some kind of crazy chat-up line.

'Well, I...' She could feel herself blushing, her new thing, damn it, on top of everything else. 'I'll meet you here, okay?' she said, getting up as quickly as she could before her face was completely scarlet. 'Three o'clock suit you?'

'Fine,' he said, getting up and calling after her, 'I'll look forward to it.'

28

Forty-eight years earlier…

They arrived together, Douglas and Nancy. Nancy looked different, the same, but transformed from when she'd left the flat earlier. She was radiant, glowing, suddenly grown-up, in a way that Tess couldn't put her finger on. Tess was standing at the kitchen sink doing her vocal exercises, trying to reach to the bottom of her diaphragm, but her voice just wouldn't behave. The exercises were meant to help, but really, the stress was knotting her from deep within. She hadn't sung properly in months, just limped through the Christmas assessments. The all-important end of year examinations were only days away and Tess was drowning beneath it all.

'Douglas,' she breathed when she turned around. He was standing with the light at his back, it feathered about him, as though he was a silver saint. When she looked at him now, he reminded her of one of those superheroes from the TV – a Simon Templar with a slightly taciturn glint when you fell into his bad books. His hair, golden and heavy, flopped roguishly across his left eye and, as always, she wanted to reach out and push it to the side. She was delighted to see him. What had she thought? That Nancy brought him back for her. A little gift to make everything right? 'What are you doing here?' And then she noticed their hands. Interlaced in a way that couldn't be easily pulled apart.

'Nancy said it would be better coming from both of us.' Douglas had the grace to keep his voice empty, even if his words were loaded.

'We're in love,' Nancy whispered in her tinny tiny voice. 'Douglas and I are going to…'

'You can't be in love with Douglas, Nancy. That's ridiculous. You know how I've felt. You've seen, these last few weeks, you've known all along, and even if I didn't say anything you knew that this can't be…' It was a bad dream, surely Tess would wake up now, laugh about it later.

'Tess, we're in love. Douglas has asked Father if he can marry me. We…' She held out her left hand, a narrow gold band sat on her third finger. Tess saw the glint of a small diamond, a cluster of glassy sparkles. For a moment, she held her breath, how could something so small destroy so much? It was just gold and gemstones, after all. 'We are getting married.' It was a statement of fact; all agreed before there was anything that Tess could do about it. They must have spent months planning this. Months of meeting behind her back, talking, holding hands, falling in love. Oh, God, Tess thought the room was going to tilt over, maybe the whole world was capsizing around her. Had Douglas been in love with Nancy while Tess was throwing herself into his arms for all those nights on the way home from the Sunset Club? There was no fear of Nancy letting herself down like that.

'But I loved you, Douglas...' the words fell from her, the last bit of dignity draining from her now. 'I thought...'

'Whatever you thought, Tess. I told you, in the end, I couldn't marry someone like you. I don't love you...' He looked then at Nancy. His bride-to-be had always been the second-rate version of Tess. She couldn't sing or entertain people with her lively wit, but she was ladylike, remote and it turned out, not quite so uncomplicated as Tess had always assumed. 'I've never loved you.' The words were cruel, not so much in what they meant, but more what she could see in his eyes. He despised her. She was little more than scum beneath his shoes even as she was turning herself inside out for him.

'You'll meet someone else, Tess. You'll meet some nice boy and fall madly in love with him and you'll look back on this day and laugh about how silly this whole mix-up was,' Nancy said. A small encouraging smile quivered on her lips, as though all would be well, if they just called it a mix-up. What did Nancy know of love, Tess wondered for a moment, what did she know of falling in love, was she capable of the kind of passion Tess had within her?

'This will never be right, Nancy. You knew how I felt about Douglas.'

'You never put it into words, Tess. You never said,' Nancy answered as quick as a flash.

'Honestly, have I ever needed to? You knew, after the Christmas Ball, you knew my heart was broken. You knew and you...' Tess thought, that this was the worst part of it all, worse than losing Douglas, 'you betrayed me. You betrayed me, whereas Douglas just broke my heart.'

'Oh, for goodness sake, there's no need for this melodrama,' Douglas said.

'Maybe you should leave, Douglas,' Tess rounded on him. It would be better if he left now, before she completely fell apart. Without him here, maybe she could talk to Nancy, explain why she couldn't marry him. If she knew how Tess felt, or what had happened between them all those nights, maybe...

'I think we should both leave,' Nancy said, turning on her heels. 'I'm going back to Ballycove, until the wedding. It's in July, by the way, the sixteenth.' And then, they were gone, pulling closed the door behind them.

Tess stood, rooted like a hundred-year-old oak tree, her feet planted in the ground, her heart gnarling at the betrayal. It was unthinkable. *Oh, my God, it was devastating*. For a moment she forgot to breathe and then gasped, but that only brought the whole horror of it into starker reality. *Douglas was going to marry Nancy*. Surely, she would wake up from a terrible nightmare at any moment now. She heard the tap trickle ruthlessly behind her and knew, in some deep part of her, that the terror choking the air from her lungs was real and it was something that she would have to live with every single day of her life.

She stood there, for a long time, waiting for the news to settle, trying to take it in. She had lost Douglas; worse, she had lost him to Nancy. Nancy, who never put a foot wrong; who had always been the plain Jane, goody two shoes of them both. Douglas had fallen for Nancy in spite of all of that, or maybe, he had fallen for Nancy because of all those things. Nancy was untouched, refined and, ultimately, wife material, whereas Tess apparently was not. Of course, there was no making sense of it, not there and then, not for a very long time afterwards.

29

January 29 – Thursday

It settled on Tess uneasily – the gradual realisation that perhaps Amanda King wasn't such a bad old egg after all. Once you got a measure of whiskey into her, she loosened out and she was quite tragic really, but funny too. It was late when Amanda tottered back up to her house. They drank down past the neck of the bottle, both pleasantly soothed, after confidences shared that tripped easily across the glasses of malt. If they did this years ago, the fissures of resentment between them might never have been so intensely mined. They could have seen each other for what they were – two lonely women in need of a good friend.

Could they be friends now?

After last night, Tess thought they might well be. Amanda obviously thought they were, in some way, of course, drink had a habit of loosening tongues, so it was hard to know where you were with people. Without the whisky, Amanda wouldn't have been so candid about her marriage, or her husband's affair or the Italian gardener who made her smile in spite of herself. Tess was glad she laid what she knew of the whole business out on the table. When she thought about it now, regardless of what her relationship had been with Amanda, the decent thing would have been to let her know immediately that her husband was having an affair. After all, they were both women and Tess more than any woman knew what betrayal felt like. That almost made it worse, because in her way, while she hadn't helped the affair along, she had to admit that it had given her some measure of dark delight. It was the notion, that, on some level, debts were being meted out between them. For too many years, it seemed Amanda had it all and, yes, maybe Tess was a little jealous, certainly she was resentful. But that she had been nasty enough to enjoy what could ultimately pull a family apart was disturbing at best; at worst, it made looking in the mirror a shameful experience.

'Seriously, you should try and get the kitchen out of him as well,' Amanda had said when they were sipping their second drink.

'No, really, the guilt of the bathroom has been nearly enough to finish me off,' Tess had said feeling the effects of the drink on her usual reserve.

'Well, no need to feel guilty anymore; you've got my full blessing to go right ahead.' Then she'd paused for a moment, looked about the flat, 'You know, it's lovely and cosy here, I can see why you didn't want to leave. I never really thought of this little flat as a home before.'

'Well, it's not so much about what it's like, it's just been mine for so many years I couldn't imagine being anywhere else,' Tess said and she'd bent to stoke the ends of the fire into a dancing flame. 'I probably should have taken your offer all those years ago, but...' Truthfully, Tess wasn't really sure why she didn't. Then she'd looked up at the card on the mantel.

'An invitation?' Amanda said, breaking into her thoughts.

'It's...' Tess sighed. 'It's from my sister.'

'Oh, I didn't know you had any family, still...' Amanda cleared her throat as if to double back on something she might have put her foot in. 'I mean, well, I suppose, I probably never thought about it, so...'

'Don't worry, you haven't said anything wrong,' Tess smiled sadly. 'We don't keep in touch, she just wrote to tell me that my brother-in-law passed away and then...' Tess had nodded to the unopened letter on the other end of the mantelpiece. 'Well, that arrived, dropped in by hand.'

'You haven't opened it?'

'No.' Tess sighed, 'You see, staying here, it was the only way Nancy could have gotten in touch with me, apart from that it would have been down to me and, well, you've probably noticed, I'm not one for holding out the hand of reconciliation all that easily.' She smiled sadly, but she was glad Amanda knew when it was time to change the subject.

'You look as if you have a lot on your mind?' Kilker probed. He had dropped in with some excuse a few days ago and she'd offered him a cup of tea – he seemed to view it as an open invitation ever since. He spotted the unopened envelope on her kitchen table. She should have dumped it, couldn't think how it hadn't gone out with the rubbish. Of course, being Kilker, being a man, a doctor and the most annoying know-it-all sometimes, he was aghast that she had lost contact with her own sister. 'Woman, do you need more X-rays, on your brain this time?'

'No, there's reasons for everything and there's too much water under the bridge to even try and make our way back to the same side.'

'Life is too short, if you haven't learned that yet...' He shook his head and she knew he thought she was as stubborn as she found him infuriating sometimes. 'Whatever you fell out over is probably long gone now,' he said and when he caught her eye, perhaps he knew he'd said the wrong thing, but he was at an age where he found it hard to leave things be. 'It's not as if you're overrun with family, that's all I'm saying.'

'Yes, well, it takes two to fall out and two to make up again.'

'She's sent you a card, woman. What more do you want? That's reaching out, right there, on your kitchen table.' It bewildered him that there could be such animosity, but then not everyone led his charmed life.

'Have you practised your hymns for Monday night?' Tess cut him off. Honestly, he was a right old woman when he started. The mention of family always got under Tess's skin and she had a feeling that Kilker knew it. It was all very well for him, his three sons scattered about America and his poor wife neatly put to rest up in Glasnevin cemetery. Kilker had been widowed in his fifties. Tess couldn't decide if he'd been happily married or not, and he was much too loyal to ever let her know. He'd asked about her family before. It had taken her spelling ESTRANGED, in long slow exaggerated movements of her mouth, for him to finally grasp that she was on her own and content with the idea of that.

Still though, since that envelope had arrived, she found her mind casting back to happier times with Nancy. They had been happy, once. They had been close, or that was what she had believed, time had taught her otherwise. Her mother called them 'Irish Twins', born eleven months apart; it was meant to make them closer somehow, perhaps it made the disloyalty a hundred times worse. They'd gone to dances, shared lipstick – oh, yes, back then, Tess even wore lipstick. God, but she really had been a different person then.

Robyn tried to talk her into make-up for the concert.

In the end, they settled on curlers to tame her hair and just the slightest dab of powder to dull away a shine. It was a spring recital, just a warm-up for Easter, really, but she was looking forward to it. Amanda and Robyn promised to come along to hear her sing. Tess wasn't sure if she was more nervous because of it, but still it gave her an unfamiliar feeling of warmth, at some level, she was no longer on her own. She was lucky, she realised, to have people who wanted to come and support her.

'I'm so looking forward to it,' Amanda gushed when she ran into them on the doorstep on their way to an extra practice before the big recital. 'I'll be looking out for you too,' she said to Kilker and Tess marvelled at how he seemed to put every woman he met at ease without even trying.

'Oh, I'm only cannon fodder – it's Tess here who's out front, carrying us all along,' Kilker said as he opened the door for Tess. He tucked in her skirt before closing it firmly and suddenly she realised, Kilker had become her friend too. As unlikely and all as it might have seemed to her just weeks ago, he made her feel safe, and with him she could be herself and she suspected he liked her all the more for that.

Later that evening, Tess closed her eyes after dinner, just for a moment, it happened all the time now. She felt her lids heavy and tired and then an hour or sometimes two later she'd open them to find that time had scurried from her like a fox into the darkness. She had to face it; her body was marching on in years and inconvenient napping, no matter how pleasant, was just another symptom. The knock that wakened her was loud and viscous.

Robyn's worried eyes cut through the glass when Tess opened the door to spit some light into the porch.

'What is it, child?' she asked, standing back to let Robyn trudge into the flat. She dived for Matt, who took the imposition very well.

'They're back.' Robyn's voice held that intangible note that tottered somewhere between distress and foreboding. 'The O'Hara's, I've just seen her at the door. They must have arrived earlier,' she snuggled her face further into Matt's fur.

'Well, that's that, I suppose.' Tess felt a wrench, but she had to be strong. She was the adult here, even if at that point, she felt like barricading her door and keeping Matt a secret for as long as she could. She had a feeling he'd be up for it, he was less inclined to go outside with every passing day. 'We should probably bring him back now.'

'Maybe we could leave it a little while longer...' Robyn's eyes were pleading and Tess didn't have it in her to gather him up and hand him over anyway.

'Okay, we'll give it an hour,' she said, sitting back

before the near exhausted fire. She bent forward and traded sparks with some dry fuel, content that it was set for a while longer.

'I don't suppose they've even noticed he's missing yet?' Robyn whispered into his fur while Matt purred loudly, oblivious to his imminent eviction. 'Normally they leave him in the cattery at the local vets.'

'Robyn,' Tess sighed, 'why didn't you tell me that sooner. If I'd known he escaped from the cattery, I would have marched him straight back there. I really thought he'd just been abandoned in the garden. They're probably going out of their minds with worry.'

'No, I shouldn't think so, they'll be insured.'

'That's not the point. Would you want to be the one to tell Mrs O that you lost her cat?'

'Well, he's been happier here anyway. It mustn't have been that nice if he felt the need to leave. Anyway, the main thing is, we have him here, safe and sound, and tomorrow is soon enough to return him.' Robyn smiled and Tess knew it was impossible to be angry with her. 'They only got him for Louisa and she went travelling last year. Mrs O'Hara told my mum she doesn't even like cats.'

'That's unfortunate,' Tess said and managed to keep her voice as neutral as she could. She'd never much warmed to the O'Hara's, but recently the goalposts had shifted on her horizon of appraising people. She wasn't sure anymore that her judgements were as accurate as she'd once believed. 'Still, you can't not miss a cat like Matt. Apart from the fact that he is their cat – he's probably quite an expensive old moggy if you went out to buy one.' Tess suspected that Mrs O'Hara would not entertain any old crossbreed cat in her pristine expensive world. A rescue dog might be good enough for a president, but Mrs O would have her eye firmly on a pedigree tomcat.

'She's a Burmilla,' Robyn said indifferently. 'They're probably a couple of hundred to buy, but that wouldn't mean a whole lot to Mrs O'Hara. She couldn't just go out and give Louisa a regular cat, now could she?' She was being facetious, but they both laughed when she threw her eyes up to heaven.

'Well, there you go. You don't want her to think we've catnapped her, do you?' Tess smiled, but she dreaded handing Matt back.

'You can't bring him up now. They've probably gone to bed.' Robyn couldn't quite hide the smile that played about her lips. Perhaps she was right; the house was in complete darkness when Tess checked from the porch window. They had a reprieve and Tess thought she could see a look of relief in Matt's eyes before he nestled deep into the crocheted blanket she left on the couch for him to curl into. There really wasn't much point in putting him out into the cold night. After all, what difference did it make to Mrs O'Hara whether he slept on her couch or beneath the bush in the garden?

'Well, first thing in the morning, my lad, you're going home,' she said in words that were far sterner than the sentiment he managed to tease up in her heart.

Tess went to bed that night and knew she wouldn't sleep. So she lay awake fretting in the bargain double bed picked up many years ago, it had taken on her shape so much it was uncomfortable in its familiarity. Tonight it refused to let her rest. Her thoughts swirling about so there was no getting away from the truth that tomorrow she'd be on her own here. She'd become used to having that great big ball of fur around. She was inured to him trailing her about the place and sitting on her newspaper when she wanted to read it. She'd grown accustomed to having someone else here, Matt needed her and she could admit it, here in the dark, she would miss him terribly when he left.

30

Twenty years earlier...

'It's too good to be true.' The words trotted off Amanda's tongue as she looked around the old house on Swift Square. 'No, Richard, I don't care what you say, houses like these, they just don't come up for sale anymore and at this price...' She walked over to the elaborate pink marble fireplace. 'This room is amazing; you can see it was a double sitting room.' She pointed towards the shoddy partition wall, and the room beyond with its matching fireplace. 'Oh, yes, I could see us growing old here, toasting our toes in front of a roaring fire,' she said, snuggling into Richard.

'That's a long way off yet,' Richard said, kicking his foot against a rotting skirting board. 'Anyway, we'll have underfloor heating here, no need to be dragging coal buckets around the place, we're having the very best.'

'Oh Richard,' Amanda walked to the window, 'it's such a lovely view.' She looked out across the square, she could imagine it once someone began to take an interest in it – it would be beautiful again. 'I could paint here,' she said, waving her hand to indicate the roomy bay window. 'There's plenty of space and light for my easel, maybe I could go back to using oils again,' she murmured, lost in her creative element.

'Oh, don't be daft, Amanda. You won't have time for any of that silliness anymore. You'll find very quickly you'll have much more important things to do than play around with paints and brushes.' Richard laughed and Amanda wondered at how he could see her art as so utterly meaningless, but then she supposed she'd never been as successful as him in commercial terms.

'It really is an exceptional property, so much potential and you won't come near it for price.' The auctioneer was standing in the doorway behind them.

'It's a bloody good price because there's a sitting tenant downstairs paying ten bob a week and refusing to move,' Richard said loud enough for the auctioneer to hear, but Amanda knew he wanted the house as much as she did. 'I'll offer twenty under the asking and if they want it they'd better come back to me before Friday, because I have my eye on another place out in Dalkey.'

'I'm afraid, Mr King, the sellers won't accept that. This house,' the auctioneer was warming up, 'it's a unique piece of Dublin architecture, it's…'

'It's a dilapidated standing ruin and you know it and unless the seller is a fool, he knows it too. My price is more than fair.' Richard put his arm around Amanda's back and they stalked towards the door. 'Let me know either way, I'm settling on a property this week, so it's either this place or…' Richard called over his shoulder.

In the car, they laughed about the estate agent. Richard called him a dimwit and Amanda crossed her fingers that they hadn't played it all too hard. They parked opposite the house and watched him leave. Once he was gone, Amanda convinced Richard to walk past the property once more. Amanda stood at the bottom of the heavy railings and it was then they met the woman who lived downstairs.

'So, you're thinking about buying this place, are you?' Tess Cuffe regarded them with the kind of practiced eye that said she'd seen plenty of potential buyers come and go over the years. 'This place has been on the market for nearly ten years now, no matter what they tell you.'

'It's a lovely house,' Amanda said warmly.

'It's lovely all right, it has everything you could want and more,' the woman, said casting her glance up towards the elevated front door. 'Oh, yes, there's any amount of dry or wet rot, ancient pipes, mice-chewed electric wiring and, of course, enough holes in the roof to give you an unfettered view of every jumbo jet that flies out of Dublin airport.' The agent gave an impression of a kindly old dear, but there was nothing old or kindly about her. Amanda guessed she was hardly forty-five and you would have to be naïve not to see that this woman was strong and smart and in no hurry to leave, no matter what Richard might believe.

'Nothing money can't solve though,' Richard said smugly, he was kicking his foot against the old rusting railings.

'Oh, well for some then,' Tess said. 'But there's one thing that no amount of money will buy you, sonny, and that's the basement.' She cackled loudly as she walked towards her front door.

Amanda stood, stunned for a moment. 'I think I see why this place is such a bargain now,' she managed finally, trying to make light of the old woman's comment.

'Don't worry about her, we'll have that basement too, just you leave it to me.'

'It's lovely without the basement, Richard, and you never know, she could be like a live-in granny someday, if we do end up here.' Amanda knew it was unrealistic. The old bat seemed far too prickly to be a grandmother, or a mother either, no matter how much Amanda might hold onto the idea. 'Yes, it could work out well for all of us.'

'You know what I learned a long time ago,' Richard waved towards the window where they could see the shadow of Tess watching them. It didn't seem a friendly gesture to Amanda and she had a feeling it wasn't meant as one. 'Money talks, and if that doesn't work, there are other ways to get her out.'

'Come on, we should be getting along.' Amanda put her arm through Richard's to guide him away from the house. It was as she turned that she finally really noticed what could be the jewel in the crown of this whole square. 'Oh,' she whispered, dropping Richard's arm distractedly, 'what a lovely garden.' She made her way over to railings that were rusted to the strength of lollipop sticks.

'It's a bloody wilderness,' Richard laughed as he tried to train his eyes through the thick growth of hedges and brambles.

'It needn't be though, this could be beautiful someday, Richard. Goodness,' she peered into the wilderness, 'we just have to get this house, I have the strangest feeling this is where we belong.' Amanda could suddenly see her children playing here someday. She could imagine being part of a family again and now she wanted this house more than she'd ever wanted anything in her life. 'God, I hope we get it.'

'I told you, leave it to me, babe, you just leave it all to me,' he said with confidence, and that's exactly what she did, she was happy to spend her life backing him up, they were a couple. Nothing could stop them as a united front.

31

January 30 – Friday

Four hundred euros, a damn sight less than thirty pieces of silver, paid to the private investigator – that was all it took and then there was no denying it. Her husband was having an affair with Arial Wade. The investigator, Patricia, had secured everything about her, short of her bra size, and Amanda had a feeling that she could probably have conjured that out of her bag too, if she asked. She had photographs, dates, times, addresses and even a copy of a credit card receipt that she'd managed to wangle out of some poor florist. It was confirmed and, in some ways, seeing it in black and white prints, ten by eights, made Amanda feel a little stronger, even though she suspected it was false bravado.

She sat, for over an hour in her kitchen, just leafing through the photographs, like a forensic voyeur, she had to examine every detail. It was amazing, really, they had the same taste in so many things from their expensive watches (they both wore Breguet with everything) to the same disloyal man. Then she noticed, sitting on Arial's doorstep, a great big hairless cat and it had been enough to tip Amanda into a kind of anger that she hadn't felt in decades. The blasted cat, bald or not, typified all that she and her family had conceded just to keep Richard happy. To be fair, she was extra-sensitive on the subject of cats now that she'd seen how much *that* cat in Tess's flat, meant to Robyn. She dropped the photos, it was eleven o'clock, plenty of time before she had to go and pick up the kids from school.

Amanda pounded up the stairs, two at a time, a rampaging elephant might have moved more elegantly, but she didn't care. She launched herself into their insipid, pretentious bedroom, flung every item belonging to Richard onto the bed. She had a plan, or at least she felt emboldened enough to stop torturing herself and do something about the tragedy she had allowed her life to spiral into.

It took only a few hours to set the stage. A call to an adventure centre in Connemara secured places for the kids for that weekend. They could catch the train this evening and be settled in before Richard even realised they were gone. Two days of pony trekking went down better than expected while she was ostensibly going to visit an old school friend in Wales. Richard for his part remained immune to any of this flurry of activity. His days had taken on the predictability of work, work and more work, or at least that was what she was supposed to think. When

Amanda thought about it, Richard had been going into 'work' for almost four months now, six days per week. Sunday was golf and he set off early for the club, had lunch there and returned in time to slouch in front of the telly with the papers, sometime after nine o'clock at night.

Well, not this weekend.

Amanda picked the kids up from school at the usual time. In the boot, she packed up two weekend bags. She suggested they all have dinner in the train station together before catching the train west. Then she would return to Swift Square and wait for Richard.

Casper arrived out of school scowling at the unfairness of having to miss his friend's birthday party but Robyn was genuinely looking forward to her weekend. They managed to get a table in the restaurant and ordered dinner and they sat, all three of them deep in their own thoughts while they ate.

'Is everything all right, Mum?' Robyn asked eventually, looking at Amanda's plate.

'Oh, yes, fine. I'm just not very hungry.' Amanda brushed away her concern.

'Well, exactly,' Casper said. He had pulled the buds from his ears and Amanda realised he sounded just like his father, judging her if she ate and mocking her if she didn't.

'Very funny.' Amanda tried to laugh, except, deep down, she wanted to cry. She wanted her little boy back, not this gangly youth who was turning into a sullen version of Richard. 'I've told you, I'm turning over a new leaf. Diet, exercise, I'm going to finally be a yummy mummy.' She smiled at her two children. They may be teenagers, but when she looked at them now, she realised they may drive her to distraction at times but they still needed her and she loved them with all her heart.

'Sure that's all?' Robyn said and she squeezed Amanda's hand.

'What else could it be? Aren't you always telling me I eat too much cake?' Amanda smiled, a little wobbly, but smiled all the same.

'I know we have, but it's only when we're mad at you. Really, we've never meant it.' Robyn looked over at her brother, as though they had something to tell her. 'It's just, we're…'

'What?' The last thing Amanda wanted was to have them worrying about their parents. She looked at her daughter now, caught something lurking in her eyes, an uneasiness that shouldn't be there.

'Robyn thinks you and Dad might be getting a divorce,' Casper said the words and managed to inject some cynicism into them, but all the same, Amanda caught something in his eyes.

'Why would you think that?' She managed to keep her voice even and her smile straight. Surely, they wouldn't see the muscles pull at it so it felt as if rigor mortis was setting in around her cheeks and eyes.

'It's mad, I know. I told her.'

'It's not mad at all, Casper. We never see Dad. He's never home and now you're gone all the time, and losing all this weight and changing your hair, it's like…'

'She thinks you've met someone,' Casper threw his eyes up to heaven as though nothing could be more ridiculous.

'Well, maybe not met someone, I don't know, but…' Robyn flushed. 'I did wonder if maybe you were, you know, going through,' she looked about her now, had the good grace to lower her voice, 'the menopause, but look at you,' her lips drew up into a quivering smile, 'with all the weight you've lost, you don't look… middle-aged anymore, so I thought maybe you…'

'I've met someone?' Amanda started to laugh. The notion of anyone looking at her with a view to romance seemed so wildly out of this world, it made her feel something very strange. 'Seriously?' she laughed a drum roll sound that teetered between the verges of giddiness and gloom. She dismissed the tears that threatened from the pellet of emotion sitting awkwardly in her throat. There was so much more here than she could even begin to put a name on. 'Oh, Robyn,' she moved her arm around her daughter. 'I'm sorry. I'm sorry for laughing and I'm sorry if you've been worried. I'm losing the weight for me, though, can you understand that? I'm losing the weight because I want to be healthy. I want to live a long and good life and maybe someday I want to bounce my grandchildren on my knees.' She held Robyn for as long as her daughter allowed and when she pulled away, she said the only thing she could. 'I love you, Robyn, both of you,' she looked across at Casper, she couldn't lie. 'And who knows what the future holds, but I can promise you this, we are a family and we will always be a family and I will always love you both.'

Amanda walked them to the gate at the train station, feeling a weight upon her shoulders that she'd never expected to feel. She stood for a long time, after the train pulled away, thinking about what they'd said. She was sure of one thing. They knew. She wasn't sure how they knew, or what exactly they knew, but they knew that it was crunch time and that made her feel as if she had even more to prove. She walked out to the car, dreading the weekend ahead. She was going back to Swift Square. She would wait for Richard to come home, even if it took hours, she would have it out with him tonight.

It was almost seven when she arrived back in the square. At least, she thought, she could go for a walk in the darkness. No one need see her face as she contemplated what lay ahead. She ducked into the house for a moment, grabbed her walking shoes and muffled up under a huge scarf and windcheater. The square was deserted now. Friday evening, most of the businesses closed for the night. Amanda loved it like this. She thought this is what it must have been like when the houses were built all those years ago. Of course, there would have been the occasional carriage pulling up in front of the fine houses, but apart from that and the hissing of the streetlights fuelled by gas, there would have been the same sense of serenity about the place. Tonight, she listened as life in the square settled in for the night. Behind the tall black railings, magpies, gold crests, robins and wrens called out their final good nights to each other. Amanda was lost in the sounds of them, carried away in the simplicity but loveliness of their song.

Moments later, the strangest thing occurred.

In the distance, she spotted Tess Cuffe walking towards her and for a moment felt that instinctual feeling of dread. But, of course, those days were gone, Amanda knew, the hatchet had been well and truly buried and if they continued to walk around the square in opposite directions, well – that meant they were different people, but it didn't mean they were enemies anymore. And then, it happened. Just as Amanda thought she'd left her behind for another lap, she heard the halting sound of Tess's footsteps. It was as though she pulled up fast to check something and then, she was catching her up. Tess Cuffe was walking alongside her, silently, awkwardly and willingly. Amanda felt herself smiling shyly, finally she was not alone.

32

Forty-eight years earlier...

It was one of those interminably hot days – the kind of day that seems to start too early and go on forever. The sun ripped heat through every layer, from blouses to windows to roads. The tarmacadam steamed and shivered its wavy warmth upwards. Sweat stickiness prickled insidiously, under clothes, hats, shoes, and made Tess feel trapped, even by the sea. It blinded, slowed her down so that she couldn't run and she couldn't hide. On days like this, her father always went with some of the local men to Ballydiffin bog. They would spend the day cutting fuel for winter, white slaves beneath the Irish summer sun. Not today, though, Tess thought, there would be no Ballydiffin bog today.

Tess stood at the bus station, biding her time in the cool of the darkened platform. That was the thing about buses and trains – everyone was in such a rush, you could sit here forever, putting off what you knew you had to do and no one hardly noticed you at all. Her eyes drew up towards the huge clock that struck out the minutes just a little faster than her watch. She had to go home, she was here to stand next to Nancy, to make it all look right, although, to Tess it clearly wasn't.

Most houses around here left their doors open, night and day. Her father thought this was a common thing to do and so, there was no barging in on top of *her* family. They kept themselves separate from their neighbours. Friendly and sociable, but with the kind of self-conscious restraint that comes from a peculiar middle-class snobbery – known mainly to the educated of small towns where history set aside the village master, priest and doctor as a breed apart.

Her mother welcomed her with the usual mix of gladness and inconvenience that was her way. 'Tess. We thought you'd missed the bus. Come on, it's almost time to go.' Her mother hardly looked at her, perhaps she knew of some of the damage being done. It was a funny thing, Tess realised later, Nancy hadn't said a word. Not a single word had passed between them for the day. Even eye contact seemed to be too much. It was a surreal thing for sisters who were so close before. Of course, there wasn't much to say. This was an occasion outside the normal rules of family etiquette. Well, it wasn't every day that your sister married the man you loved.

'I need to get back to Dublin tonight,' Tess said, though no one seemed to mind. She had a feeling that for Douglas it would be a relief, one less thing to worry about.

*

Even the swallows seemed sluggish in their flight as they dropped beyond the little church on the morning of Nancy's wedding. Their mother told Nancy to 'hurry up' and that she was 'beautiful'. Their father wiped unfamiliar moistness from his eyes as he sat beside Nancy in the long bench seat of McNulty's wedding and funeral car for hire.

Tess moved through the day in a kind of numb state. Doing what was expected of her automatically, she couldn't participate beyond those outward actions. She felt as if she was dead inside as Nancy glided softly into the life that had slipped like silken thread through Tess's fingers. For the first time, Nancy was beautiful, a tiny dollish figure in a ruffle of lace, puffed sleeves and her long veil unable to hide the unbridled joy of her eyes. Today, Tess was the taller, sullen version, plainer for the first time in their lives. Her eyes, if anyone looked too closely, gave away the secret her upturned mouth was determined to conceal. It was arranged within weeks. Nancy and Douglas had agreed on a summer wedding. Douglas could hardly wait and so as soon as his exams finished, they were married in the little church in Ballycove. Tess's parents paid for the wedding lunch and they would have a honeymoon holiday on the Isle of Man. They expected Tess to stand at her sister's side and Douglas's cousin, a pale, serious boy with glasses resting on his bony nose unevenly, was best man.

Nancy said the day flew by her as if it were a dream – a dream that she would remember forever. Certainly, her mother cried, but managed to maintain that contented serenity that was the closest her daughters had ever seen to happiness. Tess thought the day would never end. Standing in the church, the satin of her dress clung to her, making her imagine a steady stream of perspiration course down between her shoulder blades. A film of nervous sweat sat upon her upper lip. At least, at the reception, she could slip measures of the whiskey she carried in her bag into the endless cups of tea that would mark out the day ahead. She knew it was her only hope to keep her together for the day. The men made do with resting weary elbows on the long trestle tables, drinking tea from cups bleached white the day before. There were disgruntled snorts, of 'fine day', when what they meant, of course, was 'great day for the land'. Probably, the men would have given half the day up to get a run at making hay or moving cattle about to make the most of the fine weather.

When the meal was over, Tess could feel the alcohol begin to make her head spin. These past few days, its effects on her had changed, as though some part inside her was not content with whiskey to conceal her wretchedness. Today, rather than making her feel pleasantly woozy and removed from this emptiness she carried within her, it made her feel as if she was repelling some important part of her she did not yet know.

And of course, she hadn't sung in weeks now. The exams had been a catastrophe, every one of them, failed spectacularly, and there was no going back, how could she? What was the point? She failed them because her heart was broken. She couldn't sing with passion when it had been ripped from deep within her. Douglas was gone. Worse, he was gone with the one person she was closest to and, if that wasn't bad enough, it felt as though they both despised her now. She couldn't think of them living in Aunt Beatrice's little cottage – that was just the final betrayal because it made her feel as though she couldn't go back there anymore.

'So they are letting you go,' her father said after they had finished eating and just as a local fiddler began to stretch out the sounds of his bow across the room. 'The grand plan has come to nothing,' he said and, to her surprise, the disappointment in his eyes didn't feel like a reprimand, rather it felt like melancholy and that was almost worse. She could re-sit her exams, but everything about the college reminded her of Douglas. The disappointment was a physical pain so strong it halted somewhere in her gut, so hard it stole away the urge to sing.

'It's okay,' Tess lied. 'I'm not happy there anymore so, perhaps it's for the best.' Maybe it wasn't a lie exactly, how could you be happy anywhere when everything felt so wrong.

'You won't want to come back here, I suppose,' he

nodded towards the happy couple, as if he knew much more than she had ever said. 'We thought that once you got to Dublin you'd be the one to take flight, but it turned out to be Nancy who made the most of her year. Ballycove was never enough for you, was it?'

'No. I'll stay in Dublin.' She had made her mind up about that, she just hadn't expected him to agree. 'It didn't fall apart because of Dublin, Father,' she said, but she suspected that, somehow, he already knew. Not everything, but he noticed the uncomfortable looks that passed between all three of them, as though they were elements that would never work together now.

'Well, at least Nancy is settled,' he sighed, half a job completed. 'Douglas seems happy to step into my shoes in the village school and, God knows, Beatrice's cottage is giving them a great start.'

'Yes, it looks like they're well set up.'

'I…' his voice dipped a little further, as if he couldn't quite make up the words, but then he cleared his throat and said, 'I'm sure you'll find your corner too, Tess. You've never been happy to settle, but if the year has taught you anything, perhaps it's that having a dream is one thing, but keeping your eyes open and taking the right opportunities is what gets you what you really want.'

Tess looked at him now, this man who for most of her life seemed to rule their home with little in the way of tenderness. Had she missed all the love that was folded far behind his gruff and fractious exterior? It was too late now to find out, she wouldn't be coming back to Ballycove, not unless she had to and perhaps he knew that too.

'You could sign up for the secretarial college for a year, at least it would give you something to fall back on,' he said quietly. 'With Nancy here and taken care of, I could still keep up the rent and send a little extra your way, until you've found your feet.' He looked across the floor, Nancy and Douglas stood amid their wedding guests, oblivious to the breaking of Tess's heart so close. Then, his voice returned to its usual blunt tone, 'I think, it's the least we could do, since Beatrice's cottage has gone the way of Nancy.'

'Thank you, Father,' Tess said, and even if she wanted to reach out and embrace him, he was already moving away, back to join the men and complain about the cost of weddings.

By eight o'clock, she was sitting on the bus back to Dublin. There was nothing for her there, apart from a little part-time job she managed to pick up the week before. Still, she had her flat, somewhere she could hide away from all this pain. Yes, she thought as the bus pulled out of Ballycove, this was not home anymore. She belonged in that little flat, buried in the centre of a bustling city that gave her refuge from all this, even if it never gave her love.

33

January 30 – Friday

Matt watched Tess warily, with eyes that drooped heavily, but hooded suspiciously. She had been putting it off all morning, convinced herself for hours that it was too early to call on the O'Hara's yet. It was eleven o'clock now and she knew that if she didn't make a move soon, she could still be here at eleven o'clock tonight. She dragged herself about the flat, tidying things that didn't need tidying. In the end, she took down the supply of cat food she kept over the sink, placed it in a shopping bag and gathered him up in her arms.

'There's no good looking at me like that. I can't put it off any longer. You belong to the O'Hara's no amount of dolefulness is going to change that Matt.' She pressed her cheek into his fur and listened for a moment to the criss-cross patterns of his tiny heart against his breathing and the loud purr that had become an ever-present background noise in her home. God, but she was going to miss him so much. Robyn suggested getting another cat, but Tess knew it wasn't that simple. She and Matt, well, they simply clicked. It wasn't just having company around the place. It was about having Matt. He had managed to squeeze himself through the narrow opening so he filled up her empty heart, and now letting him go was much harder than she'd expected. It was some consolation when she picked him up and felt his healthy coat and the insulation that now covered his bones. He had thrived here as much as she had.

She laughed now, 'You rascal, you'll probably forget all about me once you go back to your fancy house and posh Mrs O'Hara.' She bundled him closer and slipped her hand through the carrier bag with his tinned food inside, grabbed her keys and pulled the door behind her. She made her way gingerly up the steps next door. Mrs O'Hara's house was more austere than Amanda's. It had the aura of a house that only accepted visitors by invitation. Tess had a feeling that if Mrs O'Hara could get her hands on a butler, she'd never answer the door herself.

It seemed to Tess that the woman had aged tremendously since she'd last set eyes on her. Her skin had that mottled look of too much sun. Her hair, expensively coloured, only added to the jaded look in her eyes, and her lips, dry and cracked, were so light they might have been brighter than the whites in her eyes.

'Yes, what can I do for you?' She had a habit of looking down at Tess, even though she was a good four inches shorter. Tess for the life of her couldn't understand how she managed it.

'I'm returning your cat. I've been taking care of him while you were away.'

'Oh, I see, the cattery is doing home deliveries now? Well, very good so, but really, there wasn't any great rush.' She sniffed and ducked out of sight for a moment before returning with her purse. 'So, how much did you agree?'

'Agree?' Tess looked at her now and felt for a moment like Judas. 'No, you don't understand… I…'

'I understand very well, you were taking care of him while we were gone, how much do I pay you.'

'Nothing. I hadn't made any arrangement with you. He was in the garden, you see, I couldn't leave him there, so between us, we looked after him.' She nodded back towards the King house just next door.

'I see, so I owe you both for taking care of him?' She shook her head, as though she knew she was being ripped off.

'No, you don't owe me a penny. I was happy to do it. He's a gorgeous little fellow, you're very lucky to have him.' Tess held him up before her once more. She had to hand him over while she could, couldn't let this woman see she'd become an emotional namby-pamby. 'Anyway,' she said, placing him into Mrs O'Hara's arms. 'There's some cat food there, I fed him already today, but he might like more later or some milk or…' She stopped. Matt's eyes pierced her with the fierceness of a child being left at school for the first day. She would have to tear herself away, otherwise there was no telling what she might say or do. 'Anyway, I'll leave you two to it,' she said and made her way back down to the flat.

There was a familiar emptiness about the flat when she returned. It reminded her of years ago, when life stretched out ahead a road full of nothingness with no escaping it here in the stillness of these lonely walls. She could go for a walk, get out, maybe when she came back later it wouldn't seem to be so cavernous. Then she saw the envelope winking at her from the mantle. Damn Kilker, he really was the most infuriating old goat, always thinking he knew what was best for her. She hadn't left it there. It had been rescued, no doubt by Kilker – twice now from the bin. Third time is a charm, and she reluctantly took it down. She opened it gingerly, as though something might jump out of it at any moment. She wasn't sure if she was more afraid of Nancy, or the past or herself, and her hands shook as she held the card before her.

It was a print of two young girls playing on a familiar sandy beach, a watercolour, simple and somehow touching. In the distance, she could see Poolbeg and, further out, the gulls dived off towards Wales. On the other side, Nancy had written her phone number, nothing more, the picture was enough to convey a thousand memories without words. The place seemed to be calling to her. What harm would it do to travel out there now? To walk along that stretch of beach she'd played upon in childhood.

Tess needed time and it was something she'd always found walking along the beach in Ballycove. There was no reason to stay in Dublin, not on a day that was winter-dry and bright – when she could just as easily take the train such a short distance and escape the loneliness of the flat.

When she was young, she would come out here, walk the beach for miles, with only the waves, the call of the gulls and the horizon to take her attention. She would glance up at the little cottage and wave at Aunt Beatrice; the memory filled her with even more loneliness. Tess tried to ignore it but the windows glinted down at her in the occasional flash of sun that penetrated the overhanging greyness; it stood prouder, pulling her attention away from the emptiness of her heart. The cottage was beckoning to her, somehow she felt compelled to go and get a closer look.

It was the oddest thing. She'd never felt anything like this draw before. She was moving towards the house, knowing that each step could bring her nearer to the kind of closure she'd have scoffed at not so long ago. To be – God forbid when she thought of it (at sixty-six years of age) – but to finally be on the verge of making peace. Was she losing herself in the process of becoming the person she wanted to be? Would it be such a bad thing?

Once she decided, she felt herself grow lighter, no longer trudging through the heavy sand, she moved quickly, spritely. On the narrow road, once she'd left the beach, she smoothed down her windblown hair, fixed her coat and scarf and then grabbed a posy of yellow flowers from the verge. She wasn't sure why she took them, but they seemed as if they needed to be picked. They meant something, far beyond being so much a part of this place, long before she came here and long after she would leave. She ran her fingers across the tiny petals, remembered picking up similar flowers when she and Nancy played here many years ago. It seemed they had been more plentiful then, like summer days and the smell of seaweed and the unmissable shrill tinkle of the ice cream van that passed by each day. On her walk, Tess did not question that she was doing the right thing. She didn't give herself time to think, she just kept moving. She had travelled here on the train, to Ballycove – the place it all began and had ended so long ago.

Tess pushed open the small wooden gate and her heart pounded, she put it down to nerves. She stopped for a moment, looked back towards the road; thanks to the foliage and the dip in the hill, it remained secluded. She stood for a moment, looking at her aunt Beatrice's little cottage. It hadn't changed, not really. They'd re-roofed it, done a little painting, put in new windows, but the structure remained the same. Tess almost imagined that her aunt might be inside, watching the waves far below, waiting for her solider to return.

With that she felt herself stagger and stopped short next to a woody rhododendron, catching her breath for a second. Her ears throbbed in ribbed tension, matching beat for beat the pounding of her heart. Rising up from deep in her stomach, she felt that nauseating feeling, as though she was being crushed and soon, she knew, she would struggle to breathe. Seeping from every pore of this house, she could feel the past surrounding her. It was too familiar, bringing her back to times first of great joy and then despair from which she thought she'd never recover. She could not stay here. She could not let those feelings overwhelm her now.

It's a panic attack, she tried to keep sight of it, *a panic attack, it will pass*. She leaned against the gate, prepared to double over, the waves beneath her echoed out the hammering of her heart, so she felt like it might explode in her chest. She closed her eyes for a moment, conscious that Nancy could be inside and watching and that only made her panic more.

'I shouldn't have come here. I don't belong here now…' Tess breathed the words on the salty air. With that, she hurled herself from the gate, pulled it open and the view down to the sea halted her, just for a second. It was overwhelming. She had always loved it, but now, it seemed to open like a raging beast before her and it felt as if she might tumble into its belly, losing everything she thought she knew. She had to leave here – maybe there was no going back, what was done, was done.

She stumbled away, back towards the safety of the village and on the air, she could have sworn she heard Nancy's voice call her back, but Tess didn't stop. Surely now, it was too late to pull back any connection from their shattered past.

Later, Tess waited until it was dark before she set off to walk around Swift Square. She half expected to find Matt loitering about the porch as he'd been doing weeks earlier, but he was nowhere to be seen. Of course, he would be tucked up in the lap of luxury and probably not giving her a second thought now and that just depressed Tess even more. Things had certainly changed; she missed him like crazy – she was turning into a silly sentimental old fool and there was nothing she could do about it. All the stern talking in the world couldn't hold her back from the loneliness that reached around her in that flat without him.

She was halfway round the square when she saw Amanda King. Something inside her flipped. For too long, she had allowed herself to wallow and let bitterness drive her into an existence of contempt and loneliness. Amanda with her untidy life, her candid honesty and her olive branch had claimed Tess from the abyss of loneliness that was her lot. In the last few weeks something had changed, they had shared a drink and loosened confidences, shared a house and allied over their love of the square, and Tess knew it was now or never.

Tess couldn't fight it if she tried, her legs stopped moving until she turned around and then she was walking round the square in the opposite direction. Walking clockwise as she'd always thought she'd never do. She was walking alongside Amanda King, both of them smiling silently like idiots, and it felt as though it was the most natural thing in the world – although she couldn't figure why.

34

It was almost one o'clock in the morning when Richard arrived home from the office. He walked through the front door like a man who had just run a marathon. He might have been doing the work of three men, such was his jadedness. Expertly, he fingered in the alarm code and flipped off his shoes as he came into the kitchen. The light from the open fridge door did not alert him to the presence of his wife sitting in the corner of their designer kitchen on the old-fashioned rocking chair she had picked up earlier in the day. Gone was the designer Nordic number that encouraged great posture and, Amanda suspected, skin sores from its unforgiving beach seat.

'Hello Richard,' Amanda said softly once he had the milk jug raised to pour.

'Arghh,' Richard shouted and, in a spectacularly slow-motion move, turned, slipped, grabbed the countertop before him, crashed the jug to the floor and sent his discarded shoes flying across the kitchen. 'Oh, my God, Amanda, you could have given me a heart attack.'

'Sorry,' she said, but she sank further into her chair and observed him dispassionately. This time, Richard could do his own mopping up. There was quite a bit of glass there too, she noticed, but she made no move to help. She watched him, impassively, as he scuttled around this family kitchen, checking various drawers and cupboards for cloths and a mop to help with the clean-up. She noticed that it seemed completely unfamiliar to him. Eventually, he swept up the glass and wiped the milk from the floor and units. His suit too, was sploshed, and while the milk no longer sat in white splats, Amanda could see the wet patches flecked across his legs and jacket front. 'So,' she said once he had done, 'I thought we should have a little chat.' Her heart was thumping in her chest. She smiled with a lot more confidence than she felt, but the fact that he was already rattled made her feel as if she had the upper hand.

'It's a bit late, isn't it?' He couldn't meet her eyes.

'No, I think it's the perfect time for what I want to discuss. You see, Richard, I've been waiting here for hours for you.' She patted the table across from her, indicating that he could sit while they spoke. He appeared to have lost his appetite now.

'Well, yes, well, I should have called, but work, you know, last-minute emergency, quite a few of us had to stay back...' He kept his eyes lowered, thinking up his excuse as he went along.

'Oh, right,' she said and then let the silence hang between them for a moment. 'What kind of emergency was it, Richard?'

'It was...' then he looked at her, perhaps he caught something in her voice. He suddenly became even more guarded, she could see it in the way he pulled himself up, folded his arms, knotted his brows.

'Go on, Richard, do tell, I'm interested,' she said, enjoying his discomfort now.

'Well, it was... just the foreign offices, they had a bit of a moment and it seemed the perfect opportunity to pick up some stocks at rock-bottom prices, so...'

'I see,' Amanda said, and when she caught his eye, they both had a feeling that this was just a game. He was the fly to her spider. Now he'd taken the first steps onto her web, they both knew there was no going back. On the table before her, she played with the envelope, running her fingers along its edges, knowing that it held the power to crack their marriage wide open if she was brave enough.

'What's that?' Richard's voice sounded more pathetic than she'd ever heard him before.

'This, oh, Richard, this is something very special. Would you believe me, if I said to you that this could be the passport to our happy ever after?'

'Don't be silly,' he laughed, but it was a high-pitched nervous sound that cut across the emptiness of their home. 'What is it?'

'Would you like to see?' Amanda pushed the envelope towards him, slowly, she was trembling with fear at what might happen next, but she hoped that Richard's nerves might make him blind to it.

'I... I'm not sure.' He looked at her for a moment, until he could not hold her gaze. 'Where are the kids?' His eyes flitted nervously around the kitchen as though they should be here now.

'They're in bed, Richard. In bed, it's where we should be too, but I had to talk to you.' That was true, they were in bed... on the other side of the country, but it seemed to her that if they acted as if the children were here, it might just keep them on the right side of civilised. Her voice sounded very far away even to herself, and when Richard looked at her again, she knew he knew that the game was up.

'Okay, I'll look in the envelope,' he said. 'Let's play this game you're so intent on playing.' His voice sounded harsher now. Richard played to win; he did not like to lose in anything. He opened out the envelope with a show of confidence that she had a feeling wasn't real. She could see his hands shaking as the 10 x 8s skidded across the table. They were face down. He gathered them like a deck of oversized cards, she almost expected him to shuffle them. 'Okay,' he said and then he turned them over.

He looked at each snap, lingered on them for a few seconds, as though he couldn't quite believe what he was seeing. He laid each one face down on top of the last. The silence in the kitchen seemed to stretch out into eternity, as though fate was hanging on each passing second. As though their lives hung suspended in this unreal bubble and, for Amanda at least, it was a bubble filled with fear. She was not sure what the next second would bring.

Richard exhaled loudly when he placed the last photograph down. He closed his eyes then and it seemed to Amanda that he shrank lower into himself. Never a tall man, she watched as his frame crumpled, so even his arms seemed shorter, his head sunk deeper into his shoulders. Was this shame, she wondered, or was it anger that he'd been caught out? She really wasn't sure as she sat silently opposite him for what seemed like forever.

When he cleared his throat, his voice sounded thick with emotion. He did not open his eyes; instead, he spoke soft and low, his eyes fastened tight shut as though he might keep the horror of this situation from being real if he didn't look at her.

'I'll go,' he said and then he shuddered. Two words and there was nothing else between them for an age. Amanda kept her eyes glued to him. He made no move to get up. He made no attempt to speak or to look at her; his ragged breath might have been anger as much as remorse, she really couldn't tell either way.

After minutes of sitting in this silence, Amanda knew she had to speak.

'I'm not asking you to leave, Richard. But this has to end, if you want to stay,' she said looking across at him. 'You have to see that; you can't stay here and be with her.'

'Yes of course, I can see that,' he said then, and when he opened his eyes to look at her, she could see they were filled with tears. He bent forward towards the table and put his face into his hands. 'God, I'm so...' he started to sob. 'I've been so stupid.'

'Yes. You have.'

'And you'd forgive me?' he looked up at her sharply now. 'If I end it, you think we have a future together?'

'I...' Amanda wasn't sure if she could forgive him. At this moment, she wasn't even sure if she wanted him here, if she told the truth. The only thing she was sure about was that she didn't want him anywhere near Arial Wade.

'You're taking it all very well,' he said then and his voice had returned to that weakened croak of earlier as though something worse was yet to come.

'Do you think so?' Amanda shook her head, wanted to be cool and laugh at him. She wanted to be as aloof as Nicola, but she was treading a fine line now between rushing to him and screaming at him as if she was a fishwife and having a complete meltdown. The last thing she wanted was for him to see how she really felt. She was still numb and hurt, but that was nowhere near forgiveness. More than that, she was raging, but thankfully, common sense was holding for now and, anyway, it was buried too deeply beneath her fears to really penetrate into the present moment. 'Honestly, I'm not sure how I'm taking it.'

'When did you find out?' He nodded towards the photos, perhaps assessing an opportunity around how much he could get away with.

'They are only from this week, Richard, I've known longer than that,' she said, shaking her head, thinking of that condom and his unenthusiastic response when she insisted on going to the Christmas party, so many things added up in her brain over the last four weeks. She wondered just how long it had been going on for, but Richard had already lied, there was no reason to believe she'd get an honest answer.

'So, what next?' he asked.

'Next, I think we get to bed. I've set up the spare room for you. The kids know that things aren't right, so it's not as if it's going to come as any great surprise. Tomorrow, Richard, we talk.'

'Right. Of course, we'll sleep on it, that's best.'

'And Arial?' she asked, couldn't help it.

'Arial…' he said softly and something lingered in his eyes when he looked at her and Amanda felt the most terrible fear grip her. What if this wasn't just a fling? What if he loved this woman? What then? 'Tomorrow,' he sighed a deep resonating sound that made them both shudder. 'We'll know better by then.'

Amanda watched him as he walked from the kitchen and she thought he looked for all the world like a broken man and then she stopped herself, because she knew she could not feel hatred for him in her heart, was it worse to feel pity?

The terrible fear that had gripped Amanda up to a week ago rose within her once more. What had she expected? That once she got through this, things would return to what they'd been before? She had been thinking that it would be down to her to forgive her erring husband, but now Richard was holding all the aces. He walked out as though there was a decision to make and it was not as clear-cut as Amanda had hoped it would be.

Amanda sat in her darkened kitchen for almost an hour digesting the words that her husband never uttered. He didn't need to say them, she could tell. Richard was in love with Arial Wade. What would she do if he chose to leave her? She knew it was a possibility. All the same, she hadn't seriously considered it until now and the sickening churn in her stomach told her that at this moment it was as likely as any other outcome.

Eventually, she looked at the clock, three o'clock, and she would have to get up and start a new day in a few hours' time. She hadn't cried in the time she was sitting here, perhaps she was too numbed by it all. She dragged herself up to bed, lay beneath her expensive goose down quilt; she didn't change into her lovely soft pyjamas, she didn't even take her shoes off. What was the point?

She lay for the next three hours, frozen by fear; her heart beating with the kind of trepidation that ancient man lived or died by. Far from feeling better, having 'gotten it all out in the open', Amanda felt much worse. As though she'd opened a Pandora's box of misery and she'd never manage to get the lid back on it again so her life could return to some kind of normality.

At six o'clock, Amanda heard Richard move about the house. He was always first out, there was nothing new in that. It sounded as if he was bustling about, making a greater effort to be silent, but still managing to make more noise. She heard him curse as he trod on the stairs; he didn't make himself his normal cup of tea. Amanda turned over and faced his empty pillow beside her.

It was only later when she decided to check the spare room for laundry that she realised, he was gone. Richard had packed up a weekend bag. He had left that morning without saying a word, it was why he had grunted and cursed as he made his way down the stairs. He had made his choice and Amanda knew she had lost in her gamble to save her marriage.

Too cowardly to have it out with her, he'd left a note. *I am in love with Arial.* There was no sorry. *I don't expect you to understand.* There was no remorse. *For months, fighting a passion so much more than...* Amanda felt herself retch, but held the note more tightly. *Once in a lifetime… too strong to walk away.* There was no goodbye. *We are meant to be together.*

She steadied herself; he was leaving her. He was leaving her with more cruelty than if he'd just managed to lie to her one more time. Amanda slid down off the bed he'd slept in last night. She curled up on the floor and cried until, eventually, her body could take no more and she fell into a wracking, sobbing sleep.

When she woke, she knew that there was nothing else for it. Her only recourse now was alcohol. The kids were gone and, God knows, there were enough decent bottles to inebriate the crews of several submarines. Instead of sailors, she would make do with Tess who had promised to check on her when the coast was clear. There really was no one else. By the time she arrived, Amanda had already almost finished a bottle of wine.

So, she ended up with the mother of all hangovers, true, but with Tess, she ended up laughing as much as she cried. Maybe she'd done her crying. After all, four weeks is a long time to spend your nights lying awake dreading what might happen.

Now it had happened and, Amanda realised, the world had not fallen apart. Her world was much the same as before, only now she had one less thing to worry about.

They drank three bottles of wine between them that Saturday evening. The truth was, it turned out that Tess had been just like her. She was lonely. They each needed company and friendship; luckily, it looked as if they had finally found it in spades in each other.

'You're better off,' Tess said, her words slightly slurring, but the intention was genuine. Tess really believed that Amanda could have a better life without Richard and all the crap he brought with him.

'Well, there are things I won't miss, that's for sure,' Amanda was sipping her wine now, the gulping desperateness of earlier subsided once she had calmed down. 'I won't miss my weekly coffee mornings, or the pressure of having to be the perfect hostess for all of his clients.' That was true, and it was only the start of it.

It dawned on her, as she looked around her untidy kitchen; she was in no rush to clean up. It didn't matter if she left a cup on the draining board, or if she burned rice so it stuck to the bottom of one of her expensive saucepans. Richard wasn't here to look at her as though she had failed. It didn't matter if she chose to dab on a dollop of Nivea cold cream to her overly preened skin and spend her day lounging with a magazine, Richard could not make her feel slovenly anymore. She could donate every piece of uncomfortable designer furniture and surround herself with pretty Laura Ashley or Cath Kidston or vintage finds if she felt like it. It didn't matter if her hair went grey, or if she didn't wear the most up-to-date labels. It didn't matter if she never had another filler or facial. It didn't matter if she bought her groceries in

Tesco or served up fish and chips in front of the telly occasionally. None of it mattered anymore and it took Tess to put it into words.

'You're your own woman; from now on you don't have to do anything you don't want to.' And that was when the resentment set in, because very quickly it angered Amanda that she had become someone she hardly recognised. No one had made her change. Richard may have expected that they live a certain way, but he did not make her into what she had become. No, Amanda realised that it had been all her own doing and the worst part was she hardly knew where she began and ended.

In her youth, Amanda had been the girl who sketched everything she saw. Four years of art college and she hardly owned a painting that she vaguely liked. Richard chose the art as investment pieces. She looked at the two prints that hung above their dining room table. They had come from a little gallery on Batchelor's Walk that was having a 'moment'. They were truly hideous, splotches of all the worst colours, overwritten with faux suicide-inducing lines of 'poetry'. Good taste had long deserted her when she allowed those to overlook her dining table.

'What are you doing?' Tess asked in a voice that wobbled as much with alcohol as it did with amusement.

'I'm getting rid of these,' Amanda said, pulling the vast kitchen table closer to the offending pieces. She climbed up, a little shakily and lifted them from the wall. They weren't large, but they were big enough to dominate the room with their dark themes. She laid them on the table at her feet. She would bring them back to the gallery; see if she could sell them on. She could donate the proceeds, if anyone was stupid enough to buy them. 'The emperor's new clothes,' she grumbled as she moved them to the hall. She tucked them out of sight in the antique sideboard that stood to attention beneath the stairs. By the time she came back into the kitchen, she had made a decision. 'I'm going to paint something for there. I'm going to paint something that is magical and hopeful and every time I look at it I'm going to remind myself that I've had a second chance.' And that was it, she mightn't be like Richard, off to start a new relationship with someone else, but she was going to make the most of life, starting right now. She smiled and mentally added it to her to-do list.

'What else are you going to do?' Tess asked, her eyes full of hope for a future that looked bright through the lens of a bottle and a half of the most expensive plonk she'd ever drank.

'I don't know, but I'm not going to wallow, I've done enough of that.'

'Well, good for you,' Tess said and Amanda had a feeling that she believed her and maybe that was enough.

*

Of course, Richard had only taken half of his belongings with him. Somehow, having them around kept her grounded in a kind of limbo. She moved everything she came across into the spare room, but Amanda knew she had to get them out the door. She thought it would be easy, compared to telling Casper and Robyn. When they returned on Sunday evening, she sat them down around the kitchen table and over hot chocolates; she explained that Richard had moved out. They took it quite well, but then, she'd given them the sanitised version. She told them that they'd grown apart. No big drama, just the love for each other had changed and they were both happy to be friends and be parents to their children. There had been no great rush to the phone, no outpouring of grief. The truth was, they hardly saw their father anyway. He'd always been *working* – especially since Arial Wade arrived on the scene. Amanda wondered if Richard would perhaps see more of them now than he had before, because there would have to be actual time put aside in his life for them. Perhaps they knew that too.

'Your belongings, Richard. There's quite a lot of stuff here and really, I'd prefer if they were out of the house,' Amanda kept her voice neutral, she had decided that she would not become emotional with him. At this point, she'd cried and worried enough to last a lifetime, there was no point in recriminations. He had chosen Arial over her. Amanda reasoned that, in some ways, she had stopped being Amanda a long time ago. She had come to the point, where she wasn't at all keen on who she had become either. All the same, it hurt as if it was a physical pain in her gut that he had chosen someone else over her. It was the ultimate betrayal; a public humiliation that shouted out to the world that she was not good enough. She put all those thoughts aside when she telephoned him at the office on Monday morning.

'Yes. Well...'

'Can I send them to Arial's place?'

'Well, no. I mean, I'm not staying with Arial at the moment, her place is quite small and...' he was whispering, trying not to be heard. 'Have you told Nicola anything about... us?'

'No, why?'

'Well, it's just... nothing is set in stone, you know. We still might...' Richard's voice broke off.

'What are you saying? That we might give our marriage another try?' Amanda was incredulous. One minute he was flying into the arms of the love of his life and making her feel as if she wasn't good enough and now this? 'I don't understand, I thought you loved Arial?'

'Well, I do, but...' Richard cleared his throat. 'Look,

we have things we need to sort out, you and I. This, our separation, is bigger than just the two of us, you know?'

'Have you spoken to the kids?'

'Em, no. I thought, you, I mean, we might…'

'I've told them that we've separated, Richard. You can't have thought they wouldn't notice.' Amanda sighed and, in that moment, all of the things she'd talked about over those bottles of wine with Tess seemed to come full circle. Richard was the expert on how they lived their lives, but Amanda was the one who had to do all the work around it.

'Did you tell them why we separated, I mean, about me and Arial?'

'What do you think, Richard? No. I didn't tell them that you're having an affair. I think it's enough for one person in this family to feel betrayed, don't you?'

'I…' he faltered, he still hadn't said he was sorry. Of course, Amanda realised, he wasn't at all sorry. 'We should meet up, you know, make a plan, so we can do this with as little…' his sentence hung in mid-air, other wives might have thought the missing word was upheaval, pain, hassle, but Amanda thought, he might just mean cost. All the same, she had a feeling that she was missing something. Could he possibly be playing her again?

'Yes. We should.' She was sitting at the bottom of the stairs. She had wrapped up the two paintings from the kitchen and was about to drop them off at the gallery.

She ran her finger along the bubble wrap, a longing to burst each bubble surged through her. She could never resist bursting each air pocket when she was a child. 'How's next Friday?' She knew, he could hardly say no. After all, it was their anniversary. Twenty-two years of marriage and they'd be spending it figuring out how to pull it all apart with as little fuss as possible. 'And I can bring along some of your things,' she said flatly.

35

Twenty years earlier...

Amanda pushed the bags far beneath the stairs. It was silly to hide them, but all the same it was a big week for Richard. The last thing she wanted was to upset him with art materials and canvases he saw as such a waste of time. She couldn't help herself, browsing in the galleries, she just... what was the word? Hungered for it. That was it, she was ravenous for some kind of outlet of her own. Of course, she had the girls, Nicola, Megan and Clarissa, she had her charity work and, heaven knows, she filled her days on the Square garden, but she wanted something more. Something just for her.

'But you have everything you could want,' Richard had said it so many times. 'Why would you feel you had to go plunging yourself in all that.' Richard thought the creative scene was shifty, obscure and lowly. He liked his art curated, delivered to his door without hassle or reckless browsing.

'It wouldn't be the same now, it'd just be a hobby, something to do on free afternoons,' she said lightly when they almost fought.

True, when they met first, she'd been so consumed by it. If she was in the middle of a piece, she could disappear for days, lost in the work, and Richard wasn't accustomed to that. Richard was used to his girlfriend being at his beck and call. Perhaps it had been half the attraction in the beginning. Certainly, when he came to the end of year show, she could see he was impressed, not with the work so much, but with the praise and admiration. She'd won the President's Prize. Her painting, an abstract called 'This Life', had gone on to sell for six thousand euros, a fortune for someone yet to graduate. It was a pittance for Richard, of course, and so it seemed diminished by his eyes.

'Have you ever thought about painting again,' Connor, a lecturer from that time, had opened a gallery on Fitzwilliam Street. Blue Canal carried an eclectic range of pieces, but they had one thing in common, they were each exceptionally good.

'Why, will you take some if I do?' She was kidding of course, she'd never create anything good enough to sit alongside the modern wunderkinds he carried here.

'I'd be the first to come knocking on your door,' he smiled and she thought he might be serious, 'if I could afford them.'

'Oh, it doesn't matter much anyway, I'm afraid I don't have time to paint these days,' she laughed, an empty contemplative sound.

'Amanda, everyone has time to paint.' He reached

behind the slim desk and pulled out a tiny canvas – it was no more than six inches square. 'Go on, I dare you to, just one.' He pressed it into her hands.

'Oh, I don't know, I really shouldn't…' She held it just a little away from her, as if to draw it nearer might infect her with the kind of desires she was slowly managing to quench. It sat on the passenger seat beside her as she drove home, her eyes pulled to it as she moved through rush-hour traffic. It was so small, just a half a picture really. Funny, but when they moved to Swift Square first she thought she'd paint all day long, but so much had gotten in the way.

Her mobile rang then, breaking into her thoughts. She'd never get used to having that thing in her bag all the time. Now, stalled at traffic lights that looked as if they were set on staying red, she dug deep into her handbag and pulled it out. Richard's name flashed across the dark screen. She pushed the button quickly before it went to mailbox.

'Hey babe,' she breathed, still thinking of their early morning sex, it brought a smile to her lips when she remembered just how lucky she was.

'Amanda, where the hell are you?' his voice had lost the silkiness of morning time. 'You need to get back to the house, now.'

'What's wrong? What's happened?' Suddenly, she could feel tension knot deep in her stomach.

'What do you think? Only Tess bloody Cuffe up to

her tricks again. She's called in the planning office, we have half of Dublin council in the back garden at this moment inspecting our geothermal heating system. Apparently, she's saying it's playing havoc with her pipes.'

'But we had planning permission for all that work, hadn't we?' she whispered, she hated it when Richard got angry; it felt like a dismal fog enveloping everything in her world.

'You'd think so, we certainly paid the architect enough to sort all this out,' he was ranting now. 'I'll bloody sue them over this. I'll take them to court and make mincemeat of that swanky practice. And, God, yes,' his voice had picked up a peculiar sort of venom, the one he reserved for Tess Cuffe alone, 'I'll bloody sue Tess Cuffe as well. I'm getting her out of that bloody flat either way and if she won't go with coaxing and hard cash, well then the courts can see her out. We'll see then what money can't buy if we have the best solicitor.' He slammed down the phone, leaving Amanda listening to the dead line in her hand.

God, she hated all this fighting, if only they could solve it all amicably, but she had tried. She'd tried calling down to the flat, when Richard didn't know, but all Tess Cuffe had offered was insults and threats. She was sorry afterwards, promised herself from now on they would be a united front, in everything. She and Richard, *'til death do us part*, the phrase rang in her ears.

Everything – did that mean a court case too? *For better or for worse*, she thought, as the traffic lights changed up ahead. She leant across and placed the canvas in the footwell; she had a feeling, it would only be one more thing to get on Richard's nerves.

36

February 7 – Saturday

Five o'clock in the morning and Tess wasn't sure what wakened her, but suddenly, she was wide awake, her senses keen to pick up something out of the ordinary. She lay, for a moment, trying to figure out what had woken her. It was a sound, something familiar and yet something that marked itself out as unusual enough to break into her sleep.

She looked around the darkened room, picking out the looming shape of her old wardrobe. The door beside closed tight to stop it creaking in stray breezes, was hung with her old dressing gown. She should really change that old thing, relegate it to the bin, she sighed happily. It was on her to-do list. After this concert was behind her, she would take herself into the city and treat herself to something soft, fluffy and luxurious.

There it was again, a familiar, scratching mewing noise. Matt. Tess flung back the blankets, turned herself quickly from the bed and dived to the door. Outside, it was still dark, cold and far too wet for a cat to be wandering about.

'How did you manage to get out?' she whispered as

she watched him jump from her windowsill and pad softly across to wind himself about her legs. 'I've given all your food away, you know that, Mrs O has all your treats,' although there was some ham in the fridge, but she knew he'd be more than happy with a dry bed and a saucer of milk.

When she bent to pick him up, his fur was wet and she wondered for a moment how long exactly he'd been sitting at her window. 'Come on, let's dry you off and give you a treat.' She closed the door with a soft click, leaving the darkened city behind them, and for the first time since he'd left, she felt like everything was just as it should be in her cosy little flat.

'I never thought I'd be so nervous,' Tess whispered to Kilker who looked as though he was ready for fight or flight. They were all a little keyed up. It was their first performance of the year and they weren't only debuting a new soloist, but they had a whole new repertoire of ambitious music. To make matters worse, someone mentioned there would be a delegation present in the audience from Choral Fest. There was a slightly nervous giggle from one of the women in the chorus line, which died wretchedly and instantly when Tess turned her coldest stare on the woman. For her part, Tess was relieved to see that she had not lost her ability to communicate effectively with just a glare.

'I think it's in Salzburg next year,' Kilker said a little too loudly. 'The Chorus Festival, you know, if we were to impress them…' his words petered off, it was too fantastic to imagine that they'd be selected for an occasion like that.

'Salzburg?' Tess felt the name on her lips. It was another of her regrets – the fact that she'd never had a chance to travel, that her life had ended so far off the trajectory that seemed destined so many years before. She'd said so, just last week to Kilker when he dropped by for coffee. He was doing that every other day now. Within a very short time, he'd managed to make his own of her sofa and leave space for Matt reverentially at the other end. Most surprising of all, to Tess, was that he had mastered a perfect cup of tea, just the way she liked it.

'Well, it's an honour that they're here, let's just do our best and see what happens.' Barry stood taller tonight than ever before. Tess noticed that his shirt collar was starched and white and when he tapped his baton, it produced the kind of stillness that goes far beyond quiet. The church, in that moment, was reverently silent and Tess loved it. They opened with two standard hymns, familiar pieces that would settle the audience.

Centre pews, Tess caught sight of Amanda and Robyn. She was no longer nervous, but still, it was nice to feel that they were there for her. When she moved to the front to sing her three hymns, she caught their eyes and nodded almost imperceptibly to let them know she was singing for them as much as she was for herself tonight. Those solo minutes seemed to last an eternity while at the same time floated away from her as an ethereal dream, time slipping; gossamer through her fingertips. She adored the precious freedom of her voice rising high above the heads of everyone in the church. She treasured the feeling that she was somehow at one with something far greater than she could have ever imagined.

At the end, she stood for a moment, revelled in the applause and yes, the admiration. She was basking in it. Her, Tess Cuffe – spinster and oddball. She was standing on this elegant podium and feeling as if she owned this city that for so long seemed to shunt her off. She stood for a second, dazed by emotion. The reaction of the audience, enchanted and applauding, drew each second fluently out, so she basked in every ounce of their admiration, then she bowed as she'd always known she would one day. Elated, she was moving back towards her place in the choir. Next up, the baritones moved forward and the music changed to something a little more upbeat, and a little less breathtaking. Tess could see it in the faces before her.

'That was amazing,' Amanda said when they gathered for refreshments at the end. 'You never told us you could sing like *that*.'

'So, how did you think I would sound?' Tess was

laughing at her, but she understood Amanda's confusion. After all, Tess herself had all but forgotten that she sang. She never imagined it was something she could find within her at this late stage. 'I suppose, it was so long, I just wasn't sure if I would ever sing again.' She sipped the prosecco and it felt cool and delicious against her throat.

'Why on earth did you ever stop?' Robyn rounded on her.

'Life, just life, I suppose. You have to be happy to sing, you know, to get up there and what is it you youngsters say, *put yourself out there*?' Tess sighed. 'I suppose, I just got to the stage where the joy had left me and I didn't have it in me to pretend anymore. I lost the courage to stand in front of people and praise God or anything else, because I didn't believe there was anything worth praising.' That was the truth of it, she'd never really thought about it before, but that was it. For most of her life, she had lost all faith in anything ever being right again. She learned to accept that she was only going to endure life, never flourish. But then, somehow, that had changed. She looked across at Kilker who didn't look so bear-like in his smart tuxedo now he'd tamed his whiskers and trimmed his unruly hair. 'I suppose, although it kills me to admit it, but it's down to you that I could get up there and sing tonight.'

'It took more than bringing you along, Tess, surely you see that.' Kilker was beside them now. 'You had it in you all these years, you just couldn't find it,' he said softly, enjoying that, for this once, at least, she was admitting he was right.

'How did you know?' It hadn't occurred to her before, but now she wondered.

'Ah, well.' He placed his finger at the side of his spirit-pocked nose. 'Now, that would be telling and I have a feeling that if I came clean, you might not talk to me anymore.' His eyes twinkled as he laughed and Tess thought he really could be the most infuriating man ever.

'Come on, you have to tell us, we'll burst now if we don't find out.' Amanda linked his arm conspiratorially.

'Maybe, someday, when I'm sure she won't be mad at me. She has a very volatile cat; I do worry that she might set the thing on me if I get on her nerves too much.' He laughed at that again and nodded at some of the other women in the choir.

'Not anymore,' Tess said but this wasn't the place to be sad, and anyway, she had learned the difference between home being a place and a feeling, and she knew that Matt would always be at home with her, even if his papers said he belonged with Mrs O.

'We won't let her set the cat on you. To be perfectly frank, he gave me the shivers too and anyway,' Amanda's voice dipped, 'he's not really fierce, he's all fur and no fangs. You must tell us now, Kilker.'

'Well...' he looked across at Tess, then leant nearer Amanda and Robyn. 'The truth is, I remember Tess from years ago. Oh, it took me a while to place her when she arrived at the hospital with her broken arm and giving out yards to the junior doctors, but she was the kind of girl you wouldn't forget. I had a real soft spot for her,' he said softly. 'Mind you, half the boys I knew were after her, not that she seemed to realise,' he cleared his throat and caught Tess's eye shyly, just for once. 'Of course, Tess was way out of my league. Anyway, she had a bloke and rumour had it they were getting hitched, so that was that.' He smiled now, thinking back to those days. 'Even then, she could have put St Peter to sleep, her voice was that heavenly.' He shook his head now and looked at Tess as though she might remember him. He leant in closer to her then, 'You called me Stephen then, back when we had the jazz band, of course, it was a long time ago. No one calls me that anymore.' He shook his head fondly, maybe a little sadly at the passage of time.

'Oh, dear God.' Tess felt her legs buckle beneath her, 'How could I not have known?' She peered at him now, trying to picture the gangly youth, with skin reddened from farm work and a denim jacket that never left his back. 'Stephen?' she heard the name fall from her on a breath. 'You were so kind to me, that last time, you said...' she felt herself fall back in time, 'you said it would all work out, in the end.' She felt a tear slide down her cheek, remembered too late the powder Robyn had pressed to dull away a shine.

'Oh, don't get so sentimental. It doesn't change anything,' he leant towards her now, pulling a great big cotton hanky from his pocket. 'I'm still the same, maybe wider and wiser, but we're here now, that's what counts.' He dabbed her cheek, held her face softly in his hand and their eyes connected, for just a moment; long enough to see the boy within.

'Time changes all of us, Stephen. I can't quite believe it's you…' Tess inclined her head a little, watching him. It all came flooding back, Stephen, he was in second year medicine at the time, a gangly, easy-going youth, she'd hardly given a second glance. 'After all these years, so much has changed.'

'I'm not sure about that.' He smiled at her now, his eyes creasing up so there was no mistaking the affection that had been there all along, if only she had looked more closely. 'Well, maybe some things have, but for the good.'

'Really?' Tess felt herself blush when she looked at him now.

'Of course, I'd say that your voice is even more enchanting here than it was in that club all those years ago.' He reached forward and kissed her gently on her cheek and she had a delicious feeling of something new and lovely stirring up within her. 'And of course,' he added smiling, 'it's never too late to be happy.'

37

Amanda had to do it. She had to front it out, if only to see what they knew, or if they knew anything at all. She marched into the Berkley Plaza wearing a navy blazer that was almost vintage, by Clarissa's standards. It was fifteen years since she'd fitted into it. A size twelve, hardly Twiggy, but it was a timeless design and she teamed it with a pair of fitted jeans, a Gap T-shirt and an oversized scarf she'd picked up for a song. It was amazing what a month of not being able to face a cream bun could do for you. This time, when she caught sight of her reflection in the plate glass she felt herself relax into a contented easy space within herself. It had more to do with how she was feeling about herself than it had to do with her appearance, but she had to confess that it didn't do her confidence any damage to feel she was looking much better than she had only a few weeks earlier.

'We thought you'd abandoned us, darling,' Nicola said, air-kissing her when she arrived.

'Sorry, it's just been so busy. I've been invited onto

the Love Dublin committee, so...' it wasn't exactly a lie. Carlos – the Italian love god – was transforming the square and she was helping out. She had spent the last few days clearing out beds and setting in spring bulbs that were already near full bloom. It was doing her good, her complexion was clear, her eyes were bright and each night she slept soundly, far better than she had for a very long time. Had she been worrying about Richard for years? It seemed now as if there had been a weight sitting in her heart for an age. It was an obscure time bomb ready to detonate and she had been anxiously waiting for the explosion that would spell the end of her way of life as she knew it for far too long. Funny, it turned out the end of that existence was no bad thing. She smiled now, a confident flicker of her lips that obviously rattled Clarissa.

'My goodness, we thought...'

'What?'

'Well, we thought...' Megan's eyes darted from one to the other women.

'You know how these things go, Amanda. You don't call your friends, you seem to have fallen off the social scene and look at you, you're positively fading away under all these, *new* clothes.'

'Oh, Nicola, I'm hardly fading away. I told you, I've started to overhaul my life. Make healthier choices around food and exercise and it's done me the world of good. I feel,' Amanda looked from one pained face to the other and began to smile broadly, 'I feel happy, really happy for the first time in years.' The word seemed like an alien concept here, among these women, perfection was the ultimate goal, happiness had long since lost any meaning.

'Happy?' Clarissa wrinkled her nose, an admirable feat considering her rhinoplasty and all the Botox that filled out deep lines that should now set it apart from her cheeks. Her eyes held some recollection of the feeling, perhaps there was a hint too that it was something she missed.

The rest of the morning filled with chatter about other people, mainly the wives, but as usual, Nicola had some juicy pieces of information from the trading floor.

'Apparently, Arial Wade has stopped sleeping her way through the junior traders,' she whispered, a little deflated that they could no longer gossip about her new conquests. She looked pointedly at Amanda, so perhaps she didn't know anything for sure, or maybe things had changed.

'Has something happened to her? Has she contracted some kind of sexually transmitted bankers' disease?' Megan was attempting flippancy. Amanda recognised the fear that had always been a part of marriage to a wealthy man.

'No, rumour has it, she's cooling off a bit,' Nicola threw her eyes heavenwards; love and romance were for fools as far as Nicola was concerned. Wealth and sex were two different currencies and the former was the one that dictated gratification for Nicola. 'Perhaps you were right after all and she's going after that promotion, Amanda.'

'But she was seeing...' Clarissa squeaked and then had the grace to blush.

'Well, who knows who she was seeing, but it doesn't matter now, because apparently she's free and single again and gunning for promotion,' Nicola drawled.

'Has she set her sights on Julian Fitzgerald?' Clarissa was bright red now, giddy with the triumph of knowing her marriage was safe, Clarissa's husband was never going to progress much further than the trading floor and so probably not worth shagging if you wanted to move higher up the food chain. 'Gosh, he must be seventy, ugh.' She shook her perfectly groomed hair.

'No, who knows? But, you can imagine, can't you. This time of year, the bonuses deferred for another month. No one is going to want to blot their copybooks, are they?' Megan said quickly. It was an unwritten rule among the partners. You could have flings and fun – that was just letting off steam, but a marriage breakdown was a weakness. The man who couldn't hold his marriage together lost integrity around his capacity to make a good choice. Invariably, divorcees stayed around just long enough to make sufficient money to mollify the family courts, but there would be no promotion, no garnering the way to fat bonuses. Mostly, they made their way to other firms or to financial institutions in other countries.

'The office gossip now is the divvying out of the bonuses, we ladies are the only ones thinking of love,' Nicola said drily. They all knew she spoke like that simply to remain above suspicion. Maybe if she convinced everyone else that her marriage was a contented place, she might convince herself. Amanda sat back thoughtfully, she was so sure they knew about Richard and Arial, and maybe they had. But now it felt like the ground was shifting once more beneath them all.

'You look...' Richard paused for a moment, as though trying to figure out the right thing to say, then begrudgingly managed, 'well. You've had your hair done, or something,' he said before drawing the menu up between them. Nevertheless, there was no mistaking, he'd been taken aback, perhaps he'd expected her to fall to pieces without him? Well, maybe that had been how she felt at first, but tonight, meeting him here, she was buoyed up by Tess and Robyn before she'd left the house. They'd bolstered her self-confidence as much as her new hairdo, trimmer waistline and sleek clothes.

Richard pursed his lips as he ordered the pâté starter and Amanda figured he didn't look all that delighted with himself. In a word, he looked awful. He looked as if someone had come along and washed him out. His hair had a newly salt and peppered look. An oily film covered his face and his collar appeared to have stretched to a size too large. Life had shaken him by his shoulders until his laconic calm turned to a nervy distrust she felt upon the air between them. It seemed his skin sagged more than before too, but she tried not to take pleasure in this. When had he gotten so old-looking? Good God, he'd only left the house two weeks ago.

'This is nice, very civilised.' Amanda looked around the restaurant. She'd never been here before. It was a busy French bistro buried deep off Leinster Street and she was glad it wasn't the kind of place she could imagine Arial Wade ever coming to. Arial would be more of a linen tablecloth girl, whereas, Amanda realised, she liked red check. It was the kind of place she'd love to bring the kids. When she said it, Richard made a sound that sat somewhere between a grunt and an agreement. 'So, how have you been?'

'Working, you know,' he said cagily.

'Where are you staying?'

'What is this, twenty questions?' he barked and she realised that a few months ago she'd have backed down, felt as if she was nagging him.

'It's a reasonable question, Richard. You are the father of my children and, on paper at least, I'm still your next of kin.'

'I'm staying at the Academy, it's down on Wicklow Street, busy spot and a nice walk away from work,' he said, tasting the wine the waiter had poured for him. Amanda had brought the jeep, it was the one way of ensuring that she didn't have too much to drink. She hoped it would stop her saying exactly what she thought of him.

'That's handy,' she said, but of course, he knew she was thinking, *so not with Arial Wade then.* Later, she'd wonder at how she could remain so calm, but of course, Richard had chosen this place to avoid a scene.

'It's giving me what I need.'

'And what's that, exactly?' she asked, sipping her glass of water.

'Time.'

'Oh, Richard, surely you can do better than that?' They hadn't spoken about Arial, not since that night. It haunted her still, the thoughts of him with her. And worse, now she knew, in her heart, that there must have been others. He had been playing her for a fool, she was sure of that with the instinct that she had for so long buried. 'You didn't leave me so you could have time, you left me so you could be with Arial Wade,' she whispered the words across the table, but there was no mistaking the ferociousness in her voice.

'I... It was more than that...' he folded the napkin unnecessarily before him then he cleared his throat, as though to rally himself for what was long overdue. 'It was more than that, I wasn't happy for a long time. You have to admit, things have been dead between us for much longer than this…' He sipped his wine, too fast perhaps, because it turned into an uncomfortable gulp.

'Maybe, Richard, but I've done nothing wrong…' she let the words slide out between them and they were true. At the same time, she couldn't help but think of that night on New Year's Eve, that strange woman looking back at her from the plate glass window. She wasn't familiar, she had turned into a stranger to herself, no longer the girl she used to know. 'Well, we've both changed.'

'I can see that,' he said shortly.

'What does that mean?' she snapped.

'Well, look at us here. Who'd have thought you'd turn into such a cold bitch?'

'That's rich. Do I need to remind you, you're the one who's been unfaithful, not just to me, but I bet you haven't even thought about what this could do to your kids? Don't you dare sit there and start blaming me. True, we've both changed, but I've always thought of you. I've always done things to make you happy, where as you…'

'Oh, now we're hearing all about it. I suppose, you're going to throw the old accusation about missing out on being a great artist,' his voice tasted of bitterness and reproach and it didn't suit him. 'Seriously, Amanda, I've given you a great life, a beautiful home, sophisticated friends and the kind of credit card that means you never have to think twice about what you buy. And what have you given me in return?'

'God,' she sighed, 'so two lovely kids, a home that rose out of the wreck we bought and supporting your career at every turn counts for nothing, I suppose?' A nervous tension released with her resentment, so she knew she didn't give a damn anymore about Richard's idea of what was good and what was worth having. 'You really think that money is the answer to everything?' She shook her head.

'You can make all the faces you want, it's easy to be blasé about it when you don't have to depend on tips in a bar anymore, or have you forgotten where you came from?'

'No, Richard, I haven't forgotten at all. I'm prouder than ever of where I came from and the fact that I could paint, and will again, makes me even more proud. True enough, your money, it's been great, not to have to scrimp and save, but don't for a minute think that I wouldn't have managed on my own. And as for your friends, God help you if you think that those back-stabbing bloodsuckers are anything more than waiting to take first shot at you as soon as they find out about Arial.' She sat back on her chair now and looked him dead straight in his eyes; he was the first to look away.

'Well, that was a long time coming,' he murmured at last. 'I had no idea that you felt so angry.'

'What do you expect, Richard? That I'll just fall into line and sit quietly by while you head off into the sunset?' She looked around the restaurant, took a deep breath and for a minute the silence between them bristled. 'You still haven't said you're sorry,' she said flatly.

'No. I didn't, did I?' he said then and nodded towards the waiter for more wine.

'Well, this is getting us nowhere.' Perhaps he wasn't sorry, maybe he'd never say it and maybe that wasn't the end of the world. 'Anyway, we are where we are now,' she said eventually. She knew they couldn't move forward unless it was something they both wanted and now, sitting here opposite him, she couldn't imagine going back to the way she was on New Year's Eve.

'No, I had hoped we could be civilised. This isn't easy for me either, you know?' he blanched when he caught the look of hatred that flashed across her eyes.

'Richard, we can be as civilised as you like, but you've hurt me and I won't be playing your games anymore, so you might as well get used to the idea that I won't be pussyfooting around you any longer.' She sipped her sparkling water and sat back in her seat, determined to let him take responsibility for filling the silence between them.

'Anyway, how are the kids?'

'Haven't you been in touch with them?'

'On the phone, but you know it's all one-word answers.'

'That's teenagers for you.' She didn't want to push him meeting up with them, what was the point? They weren't bothered, she knew that for certain. 'They're good. Actually, they're great.' It was true. Their house was much happier without Richard around, now there was no longer the constant need for perfection, the feeling that you were always on stage. Robyn had started to bring friends over after school. Last week, Casper set up the old potting shed as a practice room for the band he talked about forming for so long. Amanda wasn't sure the neighbours appreciated his *music* but she certainly loved having them around. The only one who wouldn't complain was Tess, but then she dropped in with Stephen in the evenings to listen to their efforts and drop off biscuits or join in some old-fashioned melody if they could knock one out for her. It seemed, these days, Amanda filled her fridge five times more often than she had before. Every time she turned around there was another gangly teenager helping himself to a doorstep-sized sandwich, but she knew where they were and she knew what they were doing. Of course, she didn't tell Richard any of that. The only things that mattered in Richard's view of the world were school grades and achievements he could brag about at work.

'And you? How are you?' he asked and he met her eyes really for the first time that night. For a moment, they seemed to linger on her face before he topped up his wine glass. He drank deeply as though to quell his anxiety at the ordeal of having to spend time with her.

'Me?' Amanda almost said, *seriously, you want to know how I am*? But she didn't. Instead, she said, 'I'm great.' It was what he wanted to hear after all. Richard didn't want to hear that she felt as if he'd discarded her like a child throwing away a toy he no longer wanted. He didn't want to hear that he had made her feel used and dirty and that sitting here, looking across at him was depressing the hell out of her. He certainly didn't need to know that she had every intention of going home after this and emptying the contents of one of the most expensive bottles of red wine he'd bought in the last five years into a large wine glass and drinking it until her teeth were stained a deep and dirty mahogany red. She had been angry, maybe even still there were flashes of it, but the weeks when she'd kept silent and bottled up her fears were a down payment for how miserable she was going to feel later. The worst was over. It had happened, and she was still here and she was not going to let him see her be anything less than this new, improved version of the woman he had left. 'Yes, I'm doing fine.' She thought of Carlos Giordano and the way his jeans seemed to trap the hardness of his legs and shapely bottom as he worked each day alongside her. 'I'm doing great, considering, so we're both good?'

'Oh, you know, things aren't always what you expect...' He had a faraway look in his eyes. Perhaps things with Arial were not so rosy now that they were no longer playing away behind the stupid wife's back. Amanda took what little joy she could from that fleeting notion.

'Well, this is lovely,' she said as she tucked into her warm chicken salad. She certainly was not going to put herself through listening to him whine about life not turning out as he had hoped now he was free to shack up with his fancy woman.

In the end, after they ate dinner, neither was too pushed about dessert, they agreed that Richard could pop over and take what he needed from the house. The rest, Amanda would organise into storage. She had every intention of putting the lot into a lock-up and handing him the keys. She had no desire to see anything belonging to him lying about the house.

They hadn't even talked about the house, or money or any of the practical things that she knew they should be sorting out. There was money in her account every week, the house was paid for and Amanda knew he could keep her more than comfortably on a small fraction of his annual bonus. No court in the land would see her going without; especially when they looked at his earnings. When they left the bistro, they stood awkwardly at her jeep for a moment. Oddly, it felt, to Amanda at least, as though they were parting again, for the first time. How many times had they gone out for a meal and she would drive them home together.

The way Richard lingered, she had a feeling he felt the same and if neither of them wanted to change things, perhaps it didn't make them immune to the sadness and waste of it all.

'Hey,' a warm voice called from behind her. 'Amanda, it *is* you.' Carlos Giordano came up alongside her and suddenly Richard seemed to shrink.

'Oh, hi, Carlos. Fancy seeing you here,' she smiled and, for a moment, it felt as if it was just the two of them standing on the street, he really was quite the hunk.

'Ah, yes. My uncle, he has a restaurant, just around the corner from here, not as… French, as this place.' He winked at her and only then noticed Richard. 'Hello…' he smiled and instantly Amanda could see Richard wither up into the shell of a man he truly was compared with the open, friendliness of Carlos.

'Carlos, this is Richard, my…'

'Husband. I'm her husband,' Richard said and he set his jaw at an angle and looked Carlos up and down as though measuring the man by the expense of his clothing. Of course, there was so much more to Carlos than just the label on his jacket and it seemed Richard was painfully aware of that.

'Oh, well, good to meet you,' Carlos said, letting the unfriendliness brush off him, it was truly meaningless to Carlos. 'And you, senorita, I will see you soon,' he said and then he took her hand to his lips and kissed lingeringly, giving her the cheekiest wink before heading off into the night.

When Amanda got home, she was still grinning like a six-year-old at a sugar party. Richard's incredulous expression had been enough to make her night and, as for Carlos, he had certainly made her blood rush in a way it hadn't for a good many years.

38

Forty-seven years earlier...

Mostly, Tess tacked through life – making her way to and from work without looking up from the cracked Dublin footpaths. She became a shoe studier – one of those women you'd never recognise if you met them straight on. The problem with that is that sometimes you can walk straight into the last person you would want to meet. And so it was that one day, cutting through St Stephen's Green, she almost tripped when she heard a familiar voice call from behind her.

She had walked right past Nancy and Douglas. The so familiar voice that called her back sounded much younger than her own. As though it was still bouncing through the first flush of youth Tess had cast aside for Douglas. Tess found herself halted stubbornly on the path, her feet would not move forward, but nor could she turn to face them. Instead, Nancy stood before her, heavily pregnant; her face much fuller than before, her eyes so filled with eager anticipation for all that surely lay ahead.

'How have you been?' Nancy asked almost shyly, it seemed to Tess.

'You know.'

'No, Tess, we never hear from you these days, apart from the occasional phone call to Mamma and, even then, she can't tell us much of what you're up to.'

'Well, I'm sure it's not half as interesting as your lives,' she hated that she sounded so bitter.

'You've left the music behind, then?' Douglas moved forward.

'Yes. I… thought it best.' The words slipped from her tongue. She tried not to think about that time now, it was all wrapped up in the cost of losing Douglas and Nancy too. She couldn't find any more words to sing, she doubted there was anyone who would listen even if she could.

'But, that's such a shame…' Nancy said now. 'You can start again, perhaps, try another way… perhaps in the club?' She let her hand rest upon Tess's arm and Tess feared she might disintegrate beneath the weight of guilt.

'I don't think so,' Tess said flatly, moving her arm away. She didn't want their pity and even less their remorse. Instead, all she wanted was to get away from them. It was overwhelming, seeing them, knowing how much everything had changed and knowing too, when she looked down at Nancy's stomach, that soon she would have the happiness that had might have been Tess's if things had worked out differently.

'Oh, Nancy, can't you see, Tess has no interest in

singing or in having anything to do with any of us and it's probably just as well,' Douglas said coldly now and there was no mistaking the hatred in his eyes. 'After all, what is there in Ballycove for a girl like Tess?' He said it as though she was nothing to anyone, but of course, she was worse than that, because she was a reminder of his past weakness and maybe if she did go back, she'd cause more harm than good.

'That's not right, is it, Tess, you'll come back for Christmas, perhaps, won't you?' Nancy's voice was brittle as though she knew that the rift had widened too far to bridge it with the social niceties of holidays or birthdays or anniversaries. 'It's your home, Ballycove will always be your home...' her voice petered off.

'Goodbye, Nancy,' she said and then she turned before they saw her tears.

That day, she walked for miles; heedless of the concerned looks of people she passed by. Her face, when she got home, looked as though she'd taken four rounds with Cassius Clay. Its tenderness almost bruised through from crying – Tess had rubbed it viciously to dry the salty tears away, but it did no good because they just kept streaming down her cheeks.

It was funny, but she'd never thought that far ahead. A baby, but now, it consumed her – the idea that someone could cement two people even more. The emptiness did not go away, if anything it dug into an even larger gulf within her, so everywhere she went and everything she touched seemed laden with a gloom that was all her own. In the end, she hardly noticed, it was only when she caught sight of her reflection without warning, unrecognisable and jaded compared to her old vivacious self, that it would strike her once more that she had somehow jettisoned her life on a whim for Douglas Buckley.

Did she love him then?

As the months went on, after that day in St Stephen's Green, she really wasn't sure. What would have happened if things had turned out differently? Could she have been happy as Mrs Douglas Buckley? Living in Ballycove, looking out over the Irish Sea for the rest of her days?

Soon, that thought began to haunt her too – she knew it was a way of putting aside the other demons that threatened to overtake her and throw her body and soul into frightening depths.

Then, one sunny May Tuesday morning she woke – the early rays skipping across her eiderdown from the streets above. She somehow felt lighter, as though there was the promise of something better ahead today. Perhaps, she thought, she'd visit her mother? Or just walk along the beach at Ballycove?

She pulled herself from the bed, with slightly less force than she had to employ most other mornings. Applied a tint of blush to her cheeks and brushed her hair back so it sat a little higher on her head. She drank a cup of tea and left the cup deliberately on the drainer, perhaps to remind herself that she would have to return to wash it at the very least.

She walked to the bus stop – if not light of step, but certainly with a surprising sense of expectation, as though she might deserve to hope, just a little more than she had in quite a while.

Today was going to be a very special day. She could feel it in her bones. As though she was coming home, but not so much to Ballycove, rather, in some feverish way, it felt as if she was coming home to a girl she used to know.

39

February 14 – Saturday

For the days after the concert, Tess woke up lighter than she had in years. True, it felt as though she had dreamed a million dreams, but in daylight, she sifted through them and realised that all the good ones had been real.

Funny, but now, even if she tried, she couldn't see the grizzly doctor that she'd known for the last few weeks. He had, in a moment, transformed into Stephen, and with it, she knew something fundamental in their relationship had softened. Perhaps she had softened too, because some of the memories that had once stirred her so deeply were letting go their grip. It was as though a lifetime of regret and bitterness was slowly ebbing away from her. So gradual she hadn't noticed it at first, but now, the tide so far receded that it made her feel as if she'd come much further than she'd ever have dreamed possible. So, why didn't she feel as if everything was as it should be? After all, things were a million times improved on what they were only a month earlier.

'You have more to do,' Amanda murmured as they walked around the square together that evening.

'I think I've done very well,' Tess was defensive. She had lost almost a stone in weight. Even more importantly, because she was exercising and taking better care of herself, she'd transformed in a way that couldn't be measured in inches or pounds but was much more profound. Most astonishingly, for the first time in fifty years, she felt good about herself. Undoubtedly, there was a long road ahead if she wanted to be fashion-model slim, but at sixty-six years of age, all Tess had ever wanted was to even out her blood pressure and reduce her risk of diabetes.

'We both know I'm not talking about your weight. Yes, you've done splendidly to achieve your weight loss, even better because the changes you've made are ones you can stick with for life, but there's something else?'

'I'm sure I'm just tired.'

'Tess, it's up to you. As you've said, you've done well already, but I have a feeling you know, you'd be crazy not to want more for yourself.' Amanda's eyes were dark and penetrating. Although she spoke softly, it seemed to Tess her words had the brutality of righteousness. 'You have bridges to build and only you can build them.'

Later the words were still lingering in her mind. Tess

tried to ignore them, but everywhere she looked there were reminders. Amanda and Robyn coming to the concert, that in itself, while she was thrilled they were making the effort – well, it had just underlined the absence of any family. Family? She'd thought about that word so often over the last few months. What did it mean anyway? She'd had a family. Nancy had been even more than a sister – had they somehow betrayed each other? It was all so long ago.

Everything was so very different now. Stephen Kilker was unrecognisable from the stringy youth who'd encouraged her to sing the blues. Nancy would be changed too, she'd lost Douglas, lived a life so different to Tess. And their child? What had become of him? Tess hadn't thought about that baby for many years. It was only in these last few months that she could begin to entertain thoughts of that terrible day.

'You look as if you're a million miles away,' Amanda said softly. She dropped by every day for a coffee and a chat. It seemed as if they had established a routine. These days, after Amanda left the kids to school, she'd come back and help out in the communal garden. Then, she'd pop across to the flat for a natter before going out to brave the cold again with the spunky-looking Italian, who it seemed, to Tess at least, had a bit of a crush on her.

'No, just about forty years away,' Tess smiled and shook her head. It was silly to become so wrapped up in the past when the future was turning bright and beckoning.

'Well, maybe you have things to sort out?' Amanda said as though she could read her mind.

'It seems that way, doesn't it?' Tess said and somehow here, with Amanda, the notion of having to face up to the past was not quite as terrible as it was before.

'Is it a man?'

'It was, sort of, and a woman and a…' Tess felt a small tear scud down her cheek.

'I'm sorry.'

'No. Not your fault. Mostly it's my own fault. You're right, of course. Maybe I need to resolve this before I move on.' Tess placed her hand on Amanda's arm, glad that her friend had not pressed her for answers.

Perhaps it was the week for facing up to things, or maybe, the concert had just given Tess that added brio she needed. She knew it was time to do the right thing. It was time to spring-clean her entire life and, sometimes, it's easier to clean up dust that's newly fallen.

The following afternoon, as she sat on a bench, watching Amanda and Carlos working hard, she made a decision. She was sixty-six years old, retirement age. It was time to start living and stop drudging her way through life. That night, she wrote her letter of resignation to the temping agency. They'd hardly notice if she left anyway, there was always a steady stream of girls just waiting to get a foot in the Dublin door. Office temping was the easy way to start earning cash and make some kind of life in the underbelly of this grey city.

Early the following day, she woke, her decision was already made. Taking her time for once, she placed the rollers in her hair as Robyn had for the weekend concert. This could become her thing now, taking care of herself. She had enjoyed the compliments on the day of the concert, noticed it in the other women's eyes, she was a transformed woman when she took a little care. It was time to become visible again; Tess felt she was ready to be beautiful once more.

She sat, peacefully with a cup of tea on her little sofa next to Matt. His purr was comforting, steadying her. These days, he seemed to spend more time in her flat than anywhere else, slept cosily on the couch for most of the day and trailed her about the flat when she was here. He had taken to darting in through her kitchen window as soon as Mrs O let him out to tinkle. Poor Mrs O, he really had rejected her, Tess had a feeling that she hardly even noticed and perhaps that made having him here blameless.

She arrived at the temping agency with no intention of working one more day. She should give them two weeks' notice, but she was an old woman and they expected her to be bad-tempered. The girl, an unpronounceable name on her breast, took the letter and smiled, as though it made a difference to Tess either way.

She stood in the doorway for a moment, her heart thumping wildly in her chest, hardly believing that she'd just resigned. A measure of panic rising within her, but then, in her mind, she heard Stephen's voice guiding her through her breathing exercises and so she inhaled deeply, taking in the cool Dublin morning. She walked out of the temping agency that day a free woman and only wondered why she hadn't done it sooner. Across the road, she noticed a small art supplies shop, funny how she'd never spotted it before.

An old-fashioned bell on the front door rattled when she let it close behind her. The man; a youth with dark hair that hid his eyes, turned out to be the most obliging boy. He filled a bag with a large sketchpad, charcoal and acrylics. He tossed in two small canvases for free.

Tess walked home lighter of step than she'd felt for many years. She reasoned, if she could sing in front of a hundred people, there was no reason why Amanda shouldn't paint again.

'He's a child.' Amanda laughed at the very idea of Carlos Giordano fancying her.

'Thirty years old is hardly a child,' Tess said. They were sitting in the square, drinking steaming instant cappuccinos that Tess had brought across for them. It was time for Amanda to take a break, and Tess had brought along a lovely gift of artists supplies to mark a new start for them both.

'It *is* when you're forty-five years old, Tess.' Amanda had lost the thread of what she was saying. Of course, it was Carlos. They had been working every day together for the last week and this afternoon he invited her out for a drink.

'I've never been to a salsa club, though I did love jazz, back in the day,' Tess said and it sounded like nostalgia on her lips. She looked at Amanda now, 'He's not asking you to marry him. Where's the harm in going out dancing with the bloke? You might really enjoy it.' Tess winked at her. 'And if a chance should present itself to kiss him or,' she lowered her voice, 'something more, well, you could see it as a perk for all that gardening you've done free of charge.'

'He might not want me to do any more gardening now,' Amanda said.

'What exactly did you say when he asked you?' Tess asked.

'Nothing, I just laughed. I thought he was joking, I really never imagined…' They had been talking about her separation. She assumed he'd just felt sorry for her, but then, when she laughed, she'd caught something else. Probably not desire, she wasn't silly enough to think that, but she could have hurt his feelings.

'You've been lusting after him for weeks. Did you not think that maybe the feeling is mutual?' Tess asked.

'Come on, Tess, you've seen him. The body of a god, face of an angel – men like that don't fall for middle-aged frumpy women.' She knew she was nowhere near as frumpy as she'd been a year ago. Robyn had dragged her into what seemed like every high street shop in Dublin one weekend and now she had a whole new wardrobe of clothes that fitted her and made her feel like she had shed her middle-class, neurotic, vanilla dullness.

'So, he's a man now, not a boy anymore?' Tess teased. 'Well, I'll tell you this for nothing, if he so much as winked at me, I'd have my best linen on the bed and I'd be inviting him in for a stiff one before we got down to business,' Tess said and Amanda struggled to keep her laughter under control. 'You'll march across that garden tomorrow and tell him you'd love to go to a salsa bar with him, and anywhere else that might be on the cards, or I'll be looking at you as if you lost the run of yourself. What are you waiting for – Richard King to ride across the square on a white charger?'

40

February 17 – Tuesday

It took the whole morning before Amanda managed to pick up the courage to broach the subject with Carlos.

'Carlos, remember you asked me to a salsa bar?'

'Yes,' he hardly looked at her and she had a feeling that maybe she had embarrassed him with her reaction, which was not what she would have expected or wanted.

'Well, you sort of caught me off guard and I'm not sure that I gave you the answer that I should have.'

'So, you want me to invite you again?' he looked up from the row of plants before him.

'Yes, or maybe I could ask you?' She was feeling more courageous now as she looked into those delicious brown eyes. 'Not that I would have a clue where to find a salsa bar, or even…' she smiled now, hoped he'd find it endearing, even more that he'd see she hadn't meant to hurt his feelings.

'I think I could sort that piece out. Mrs King, I would love to go on a date to a salsa bar with you. Would I be free on Friday night? Yes, as it happens I would, and it also just so happens that I was going along anyway, so that's handy.' He ran his fingers through his thick black hair, 'Pick you up around eight?'

'I don't mind driving, I could meet you there.'

'No, it's fine. Getting you there is the least I can do, now you've invited me out for the night.' He shook his head and she wondered again, between all the banter, if he had asked her on a date or if it was just a casual drink because soon this job would be finished and he would be moving on to the next commission.

'So, he's a landscaper?' Casper asked on the Thursday and Amanda felt like he was considering whether to give his permission to meet Carlos or not.

'We're just going for a drink, Casper, I'm hardly running off with him,' she laughed a little nervously.

'No, of course not, I know that.' Casper said, but he dropped into a stool all the same, his tea steaming from the mug in his hand. 'It's just that you're my mum and...'

'Exactly, I'm your mum, you're not my dad!' She smiled at him and sat next to him. 'Really, it's just dinner. I think he feels he owes me for helping out in the square.'

'Right,' Casper didn't sound convinced. 'And if it was something more...'

'It's early days, Casper and I really don't think I...'

'I know, I know.' He studied the mug before him intently for a while. 'It's just that, I know I've been a bit of a nightmare these last few years, but all of this,' he looked around the kitchen, as though something had fundamentally changed. 'I mean, Dad leaving and everything, well, I feel like it's time I grew up a bit, took a bit of responsibility as the man of the house,' he blushed a little.

'Casper, there's no need to feel like that.'

'But there is, I've been horrible to you and you didn't deserve it, if anyone deserved it, I think it was Dad, but...'

'No, you can't talk like that about your father, Casper, he's being the best man he knows how to be and that's all any of us can do.' Amanda said quietly.

'Well, maybe, but...' he looked at her now, held her eyes for longer than she'd remembered him doing for years, 'I just wanted you to know that I intend to be a better son from now on.' He started to get up off his seat, take his mug with him, 'and, by the way, I think I've decided on what I'd like to study in college,' he nodded up towards the forms that had been sitting for weeks in a neglected cubbyhole above the fridge.

'Oh, really?' Amanda didn't mind what he did, but of course, his father had aspirations for him in the banking sector.

'Yes, I'm applying for the National College of Art and Design,' he smiled at her and for the first time in a very long time, she could feel he was coming back to her in some indescribable way.

'You don't have to worry about me, you know that, don't you?' Amanda said to him gently. 'All of this, with your dad, it's fine, you know.'

'I know that,' his smile reached all the way into his eyes, 'we're better than *fine*, I think, with all my friends being able to come and go and Tess popping in and out, this place has never felt more like home.'

'But you wouldn't fancy a strapping Italian hanging about?' she laughed at him, then, biting her lip, she added happily, 'not that I think that you have much to worry about on that score.'

'Well, that would depend on how nice the Italian was to you, wouldn't it?' He put his arm about her shoulder, just for a moment and squeezed her gently and Amanda thought she might melt with happiness.

By Friday, Amanda had almost made herself nauseous trying to second-guess if this was an actual date or if it was just a casual drink among work colleagues.

Carlos arrived bang on time and he looked even dreamier in his white shirt and black jeans. She realised it was the first time she'd seen him clean-shaven. His skin seemed so soft she wanted to reach out her hand to caress it as you would an exotic fabric that was enticingly touchable. She managed to resist, but tingled warmly when he leant in to kiss her cheek. Robyn had selected a simple pair of black leggings for her and a pussy bow blouse that, teamed with her highest heels, made Amanda feel sexy but at the same time demure. She shelved her pearls and opted for drop earrings and Casper's large watch on her wrist. Her leopard-print clutch and a spritz of perfume finished off the outfit.

Camino was a heaving, sweaty basement club. The music sent an anticipatory shiver through Amanda as they headed away from the dancing to a small tapas bar upstairs.

'Hungry?' Carlos asked her.

'Ravenous.' It was as though she hadn't eaten all day long, then when she thought about it, she realised, what with nerves and time, she hadn't eaten since breakfast.

'Let's order something here and then we can go dancing?' Carlos showed her to a long table that filled the length of the restaurant. They squished up at the end and joined the group conversation there. Carlos seemed to know everyone. Later she realised that most people there had arrived in smaller groups and some on their own, but everyone was welcomed just the same. The wine flowed and conversation was lively. There wasn't a mention of designer labels or the right place to holiday or anyone else's dirty laundry. It was liberating to be among people who had no expectations of you or of the night before them, only that they were all intent on eating, drinking and being merry. The wine certainly made things easier and soon she and Carlos were chatting away as if they did this every weekend. No one seemed to notice that she was a decade and a half older than he was and, if they did, they were far too diplomatic to make it obvious that they had an opinion about it or perhaps they really just didn't care.

'Come on, let's go dancing.' He smiled at her and she thought she might turn herself inside out with desire for him. The music didn't help either, nor did the movement, soon they were like two extras from *Dirty Dancing* gyrating their way across the floor. Amanda was throwing her hips and shoulders around with the best of them. After they had managed to sweat themselves into a fever of what Amanda knew for her was desire, the music slowed. Amanda thought she'd never heard such slow music and she felt herself blush as she leaned in close to Carlos. When he kissed her it was full and warm as if she was diving head first into heaven and she never wanted to come out again.

'You're happy?'

'God, Carlos, this is…' She was divinely happy. In this moment, she'd have traded everything with Richard – apart from her children of course – to stand here and feel the longing that pulsed between them. 'I think it's time we were leaving, don't you?' His eyes met hers and, although they didn't speak, in some ways they'd exchanged a lifetime's worth of words. 'Let's go.' They went back upstairs and she grabbed her bag.

Outside, the air was icy cold, so her breath held on tight to it, warm, lingering and erotic.

'So, you want me to drive you home,' he said, looking at her from beneath his slightly too long fringe.

'Well, maybe, unless you have a better idea?' She leaned in close to him for emphasis. God, when did she turn into such a tease?

'As it happens I do,' he said and he pointed to the door behind them. It was a non-descript green door, same as any number of other old shop doors all around the city. 'That's my building, I live at the top.' He pointed up to two small dormer windows that peeped out three storeys overhead. 'Fancy a...' he pulled her close, 'coffee?'

'God yes, and maybe more than one, if you're up to it.' They laughed their way up she didn't know how many steps of stairs. There was no coffee, because once they got inside Carlos's flat there was just a frenzied discarding of clothes and lovemaking.

Later, he woke her from deepest sleep and this time their lovemaking was slow, sublime and achingly zealous.

'Richard?' her phone rang just after seven.

'Where are you?'

'I'm...' she tried to rub the sleep from her eyes, looked back towards Carlos who was stretching down the length of the bed, his tanned skin even more olive against the stark whiteness of his sheets. 'Is there something wrong?'

'No. Nothing, except that I'm here on Swift Square and my family seem to have left without even letting me know.'

'Yes, well, we had plans for the weekend.' The last thing she was going to do was tell him that Casper and Robyn had decided to sleep over with friends or that she had spent the night in the arms of a hunky Italian. 'Why are you there?' She watched Carlos make his way around the room, admired his muscular body move with the grace and fluidity of someone much lighter and daintier. God, but he was even more beautiful this morning.

'I've come home to you. I've come back.' Richard's voice held an uncomfortable note of earnestness that sat at odds with the offhandness she'd grown used to over the years.

'You've what?' Amanda felt the words splutter from her mouth.

'I'm moving back in. Things didn't work out between Arial and me and I want to give us another go.'

'You can't just...' Carlos was putting on a bathrobe. He moved as quietly as he could from the bedroom to give her some privacy. 'Richard, you can't just decide that you're going to swan back into our lives.'

'Why not?'

'Are you serious? You can't just move back in and expect...' Amanda started to search for the clothes that had been fired off so quickly the night before.

'Of course I can, this is my home too after all, Amanda. I should never have moved out. It was a stupid thing to do, for so many reasons.' She could hear him moving about, imagined him looking around the kitchen, seeing the cups stacked high in the sink and wrinkling his nose in disapproval.

'Richard, I'm on my way home now, please, don't think that this is okay. This is not okay, you can't do this...' But the line went dead in her hand.

She scrabbled into her clothes as quickly as she could manage. In the tiny kitchen, Carlos was making them both coffees. It seemed the coffee maker took up most of the kitchen and the cup he handed her smelled heavenly. She looked around his flat. This was very much a single man's domain. Framed cinema posters, an enormous L-shaped sofa – she found herself wondering how on earth he managed to get that up the flights of stairs and a huge television in the corner. What she wouldn't give to stay here for just another few hours, but Richard's call made that impossible. So, she drank her coffee, kissed him lightly on the lips and made her way back to real life.

Carlos had been a little present just for her; but now she had to go and finally sort out her husband. She knew, as she sat into a taxi, she had let things slide for too long. She needed to sort out her life and finally, sort out her marriage.

41

Forty-seven years earlier...

Ballycove had shrunk, the way places do when you've been away for a while. Tess could see no other great changes – there were no new shops and all that were there before were still the same. It seemed as if the lines of washing blowing in the early summer wind had not been touched since she last walked past them almost a full year earlier. But, of course, that was ridiculous, everything had changed. Nothing could remain unaffected and Tess was walking, breathing evidence of that.

She skirted about the little village, careful to avoid the schoolhouse where Douglas would surely be setting scholars to rights. He had taken over where her father left off; would he have his cane in one hand and perhaps his Bible in the other? She planned to call in on her mother, but it seemed her feet had other ideas and instead of heading down Plunkett Road past the only three substantial houses in the village, she made for the cliff path. It was a narrow boreen; grown tighter with time and weeds that edged ever closer to the middle before the local council culled back growth for another year. She capered along, the roar of the sea below, a mellow blue and frothy white, lapping up on the rocks with the gentleness of a lullaby to soothe her wayward thoughts.

Soon, she was standing at the last house on the road. Aunt Beatrice's little cottage looked much the same as it had when she had spent so much of her childhood here. It had drawn her in then, pulling her out of the way of her father's temper and her mother's nerves. Aunt Beatrice and this little house had soothed her when she was sad and gave her courage when fear raged within her. When she looked back on her childhood, she would remember this little plot and the humble home upon it. She would remember cold days with hot chocolate made on the little stove, or warm days sitting in the garden, home-made lemonade and patchwork quilts spread across the grass. Perhaps she stood too long, but soon she felt a shiver seep from deep within her bones and it shook her out.

Somewhere, behind the house, the sound of a baby crying cut through her thoughts. She must have been imagining it, she decided, but all the same, she moved fast through the garden gate, up the narrow paved path. It was a baby, crying inconsolably. Douglas and Nancy's baby, the child that might have been hers had they not cheated her out of the life, the husband and the house that might have made her feel complete. She never had the chance – the thought crushed Tess as she heaved about the corner of the house.

There, in the centre of the little garden, was a large grey silver cross pram; the sort of pram that Tess might have bought in the January sales. It was a pram to push about the city streets, proudly looking down on the beautiful child within. She raced over now but pulled up short before the pram, held her breath while she peeped over the pile of summer blankets. The little face within was peering wide-eyed and distressed at her. It seemed to Tess, there was no choice, she had to take the baby out, console it. As she lifted up the little one, it struck her how much he resembled both Nancy and herself. It was a boy, all dressed in blue, with eyes that were just a little too large and soft skin that smelled of powder and purity. The baby wore a blue bonnet and someone had crocheted a small blue cardigan that was still too bulky for his tiny body.

For those moments, time stood still, Tess walked about the garden, comforting the baby, and everything in the world felt right. She was meant to be here. She was meant to come here today, to pick him up and look out upon the sea. She was meant to look after him. She held him from her, inspecting him; every crevice of his face was so familiar, as though she might be looking at a reflection of herself and Nancy years before – and for a moment, the light glinting off the sea made everything perfect. Tess blinked again, pulled him close, the crying had stopped now, perhaps he was just too warm.

She looked back at the house. This was silly. She was being silly, but she couldn't put him back into the pram. She took a step towards the back door, then another and another. Before she knew it, she was walking quickly to the front of the house, past the front door, out the narrow path, through the gate. The baby was gurgling, happy. The sea, far below, was calm and, for once, still. In those few surreal moments, the whole village had been cast under a spell. Her sister lay sleeping, as did the McNultys at the end of the road.

Up and past Plunkett Road, Tess walked, her head held high. She should have brought the pram, then she might have been just walking round the block. That was it, she had taken the baby to stop it crying, to ease its discomfort, and it was working. She'd just walk back the way she came and knock on Nancy's door and everything would be as it should be. Then, she looked down once more at the child in her arms. She never knew that something so small could stir so much within her.

There was no time to think. Suddenly she became aware of the traffic rumbling past at the end of the road. Turn left and she was at the bus station. She kept on walking, one foot before the other, and then she nodded towards a woman who was familiar. In her anxious, giddy state, she couldn't put a name on her. She saw the bus, the driver idling while the engine ran. She pulled out her ticket, told herself to stop thinking. She had to do this. She knew she had to. In those moments, she could convince herself that this was fine. This was her baby and she was taking him home.

The smell of stale cigarettes on the bus caught her breath as she stumbled to the leather upholstery too heated by the sun to welcome her. She sat in the furthest seat from the driver – six seats in a row – and prayed that no one joined her.

The baby had settled now. Soon she'd have to get it food. Tess thought of all the things she did not know of babies. There was so much, but then what did anyone know when they set out on the path of motherhood. She willed the driver to start up the bus. Sweat trimmed uncomfortable bands of damp along her back, it was guilt, of course, but she could live with that. Her eyes locked with the baby's as though they'd made some secret pact. She would never leave him in the garden.

'Be a while yet, if you want to take a walk about,' the driver shouted back.

'No, we're fine. We've done our walking.' They sat, for she wasn't sure how long, in a contented reverie, the baby and Tess. All the rhymes and songs she'd ever known waited for this moment and soon they were ensconced in their tiny little world while she sang those familiar tunes.

Tess hardly noticed the commotion on the street. It was only when the bus seemed to shake that she looked up, maybe expecting the engine to have started, but not really expecting anything at all.

'Tess,' Nancy screamed from the front of the bus. 'I've been frantic, what were you thinking?' She launched her normally insignificant self along the aisle, was beside them in a breath. 'Oh, my God, is he all right?' She went to take the baby from her, then faltered as she caught something in her sister's eyes. 'Oh, Tess, I was so scared, I thought I'd lost him. Surely you can understand, you can't just steal my baby?' Nancy's face was blotched with tears and panic.

'I didn't… I mean…' she held the baby close for just a second longer, felt Nancy rip him from her arms then and knew that something fundamental had severed between them. There would be no going back – ever.

'You're lucky we don't have the guards on you,' Douglas was standing over her now, his wife and child shepherded safely towards the front of the bus. 'Whatever you think you're playing at, Tess, this is not a game. It's over and if I set eyes on you anywhere near my wife or child again, so help me…' The hatred on his face made her flinch far more than any fear of getting hit.

Behind him the bus driver laid a hand on his shoulder. 'Come on now, Master Buckley, there's no harm done. Let the girl go back to where she came from.' The driver's eyes held disgust and pity in equal measure when he regarded Tess, but his calm voice was enough to defuse

Douglas's anger. Tess watched, bereft, her hands still warm from holding the baby, she brought them to her face, could still just catch the scent of him, a mixture of baby powder and summer days. Her heart broke open once more, as their perfect family made their way back to that charming cottage overlooking the Irish Sea.

When the bus pulled out of Ballycove that day, Tess had a feeling that she wouldn't be coming back here for a very, very long time.

42

There was no excuse, no reason to put things off any longer. Tess knew where to find Nancy, and Stephen persuaded her to let him drive her on a sunny Saturday afternoon. They arrived in Ballycove, for all the world like two day-trippers.

'So, this is where it all began…' Stephen said when they were sitting outside her parents' house.

'It's a little tragic, isn't it?' she said and, truly, looking at the house she had grown up in, she felt a pang of something close to loneliness. It was rattled by years of neglect, the roof in need of repair and the windows yellowed and dirty. 'My fault, of course,' she said and she dug into her bag; she had brought along the key to the front door, it was her house after all, but she couldn't bring herself to go inside, not today. 'I think it was my mother's way of making things right. They left it to me, since Nancy inherited Aunt Beatrice's cottage. To tell the truth, it was another thing to make Douglas hate me all the more. He'd have preferred the Master's two-story village house, to the little farm cottage at the end of a one-track road.' She smiled now, it was so obvious how very different they'd always been, pity she'd learned that far too late to change things any sooner.

'So this is yours?' Stephen lowered his head to look out the passenger door window. 'Do you want to go inside?' He smiled at her, but he didn't ask the questions that she dreaded most. It was too obvious what had happened anyway. She'd just left the house to die of its own accord and it seemed like that was what it was doing, even if it was taking three and a half decades to get on with it.

'Yes. I didn't know it straight away. I just turned up at my father's funeral and left when the clay was scattered on his grave. They sent me a letter, well, the solicitor did at any rate.' She smiled, could see now it had been Douglas's hand behind those tense lines on a taciturn page. Nancy's letters had been different, a flowing deluge of sentiment and sorrow, the first sent when their mother died. It was filled with grief and love and loneliness and it was, in its own way, an attempt at mending bridges. They both knew, that behind those words, Douglas would have none of it. Then, a decade later, with the passing of her father, Nancy wrote once more. This time, the sorrow was more demure, time had settled between them and they both knew there was no room for reconciliation, but still Tess caught something in the flowing hand. 'My father wouldn't have wanted a scene, so I just arrived and left. I shook hands as mourning daughters do, but then I travelled back to Dublin on the evening bus and kept my grief my own. This house meant nothing to me and, if I'm honest, maybe I liked the idea of it embarrassing Douglas as it slowly decayed before his eyes every day.' She was not proud of how she had allowed herself to feel for far too many years.

'It seems to me that Nancy has been looking to make amends for quite a while so,' Stephen said. 'Maybe she didn't get quite the prize that you thought she had.'

'Honestly, looking back, I think she married our father and that probably suited her.'

'You speak about your father as if he was… something terrible… but he left you this house…'

'No. He wasn't terrible, he was just so very middle-class. He was like a lot of men back then, so taken up with what the neighbours thought, cripplingly so. I suppose, I just wanted to get away from that, whereas Nancy was like my mother and she needed someone to take care of her and make her safe.'

'Nothing wrong with that, Tess, if someone loves you,' Stephen said softly.

'No, not a thing, so long as they love you as you are and they're not looking to make you into someone else.'

He squeezed her hand and his eyes said more than his words could. They pulled away from before the Master's house and Tess directed him towards the little cottage that she'd loved so much. The road seemed to have shrunk, the colours much less vibrant than she remembered, but of course, this was February and all her memories of Ballycove seemed to rest in summer. He pulled in on the grassy verge and said, 'Take as long as you need, I'll be here, waiting for you.'

'You don't have to; I can take a train back, if it's…'

'I want to wait,' he said gently, 'God knows I've waited long enough for you, I think you might even be worth waiting for a little longer.' He laughed at her now, but his words warmed her deep inside. 'Go on with you now, you silly songbird, and take your medicine.' He touched her face, as though he expected there would be tears. 'You're doing the right thing.'

This time, she took in the details of the little cottage on the hill differently. This time, she noticed more, it made sense that Nancy should have lived out her days in this place. It was everything she'd always wanted. Even the door, tastefully faded to just the right hue, it was so Nancy. She rang the bell. She hadn't a notion what she was going to say to this woman, connected to her on one level and removed on every other.

'Oh, Tess, you've come back,' Nancy flung back the door and threw her arms around Tess when she saw her. 'I've thought so much about you, come in, please, come in.' She was walking her into the little sitting room they'd spent many of their childhood afternoons in. Now it opened up into a large reception room that volleyed back into a modern kitchen. 'I can't believe you came back, I wanted to call to you, but I was afraid. I didn't want to intrude, but I wanted to put things right. It's time.' Nancy had the flushed look that Tess remembered vividly from youth.

'I don't know how to put things right,' Tess said evenly. 'I'm not sure how we can do that, Nancy, but I have a feeling we have things to say, things to hear and if...'

'It doesn't matter now, none of it matters now, Tess. It was all so long ago, but we're sisters, we're linked and we shouldn't have let...'

'No, Nancy. I have things to explain, what I did, it was a terrible thing to do to you.' Tess moved back towards the kitchen, it was bright and new and free of any memories for her.

Nancy followed her automatically. 'Let's make some tea, it could be a long afternoon,' she said and they both knew the making of tea had a lot more to do with settling their nerves than it had with anything else.

Tess was glad of the cup in her hand. It gave her something to hold onto, perhaps something to pull her back from the abyss she'd always feared if she faced up to the past.

'Of course, it was inevitable that this day would come – where else would we both have ended up if not here.' The words fell into the chasm between them. 'Ballycove is probably the last place we were really happy together,' Tess said.

'It's the only place I was really happy at any rate,' Nancy's smile didn't quite reach her eyes and Tess wondered how long that had been the case.

'With Douglas, you had a good life?' Certainly, that prospect had eaten away at Tess for many years.

'Douglas never loved me, Tess, not the way you thought he did. I suppose we both made the same classic mistake.' She smiled sadly now.

'Oh, what's that?' Tess asked, blowing the steam from the top of her tea.

'We fell for our father. Oh, don't look at me like that, I knew you were in love with him too, how could I not? Of course I knew how you felt about Douglas,' Nancy whispered now, then she held her hand up to stop Tess from interrupting her. 'I know you don't believe me, but I wouldn't say it if it wasn't true. He loved me, of course he did, on one level. He took care of me, long after I should have been taking care of him. He was a good man. He was trying to be the best man he could be, but he couldn't make himself anything other than what he was.'

'I'm sorry, Nancy,' Tess said the words, couldn't quite believe she was saying them, but then something of her sister struck her that perhaps that fragile look had as much to do with inheriting their mother's situation as it did with inheriting her looks. There had been very little joy in her life, Tess could see that now.

'It doesn't matter now. It was all a long time ago. He

never got over the baby.' Nancy walked over to the old sideboard that had filled the sitting room once, leaving only squirming room behind the sofa. She pulled open a drawer and took out a small old album of photographs, handed it across to Tess. 'Danial died just weeks after that day. They said it was natural causes, cot death. Nothing to be done about it. But...' Nancy looked away.

'I know,' Tess said and maybe she had known all along, because she'd never searched for him in the sea of faces that she met each day in Dublin. She'd never expected to see him again.

'Douglas blamed me.' Nancy shook her head. 'After that day, with you, he watched me all the time. He thought I wasn't fit to mind the baby, leaving him in the garden on his own, but he wasn't an easy child. He cried all night and, that day, when you came here, I was so worn out. I lay on the bed for just a few minutes and when I woke, he was gone. I must have slept for two hours, but...'

'I'll never be able to tell you how sorry I was. It wasn't...'

'I know. I knew it then, but everything was so bound up. Our father, Douglas, the baby and I knew, of course I knew, you would never have hurt him, you'd have brought him back.'

'I...' Tess couldn't say a word, she'd often wondered if she would have brought him back. When she remembered that time, it was as though she'd been looking on from outside. As though, she'd watched another person take that baby, sing those songs and feel that fleeting happiness that she knew wasn't hers to feel. 'I don't know, I've never really known. I was like someone else that day. I suppose, after everything, I just couldn't handle the reality of it all. Everything was just a little further away from me and I've gone through most of life feeling cut off.'

'In the same way as our mother?'

'Perhaps, I hadn't thought of it like that, but…' Tess realised Nancy was probably right.

'You never spoke to me at her funeral, you were gone before I had a chance to say that it was all right, that we should try and…' Nancy said then.

'I didn't think you could really forgive me for that day with Danial, maybe I didn't forgive myself,' Tess said sadly. It had hurt at the time, not being able to stand at her side by their mother's grave. 'And, maybe, I was afraid of being properly cast out, and ashamed too. I'd acted so badly.' She shook her head.

'It wasn't just you. It was everything. We were brought up in a house where we were afraid to let ourselves down. We couldn't say how we felt or even explain, in case Father found out we'd made a mistake. That's not normal, Tess. You must realise that.'

'Of course.' She sat back now, looking out the slender windows that faced south, catching the final echoes of winter sun on the water beneath the cottage. 'Maybe, now, I do,' she said and she felt a lifetime of tears cascade down her cheeks, but it felt good, as though with them she was finally letting go the past.

'And you never married? You made a life for yourself in that little flat?'

'I don't know that I'd have chosen to spend the years as I have… But life is good now.' Tess said firmly. She wouldn't talk about the days she regretted throwing away the opportunities she'd once had. She'd spent a lifetime feeling sorry for herself, it was time to start enjoying life now.

'I'm glad to hear that,' Nancy said quietly, and Tess knew now that her sister's life had not been the idyllic fairy tale she'd always imagined either. Maybe, no one could have made Douglas happy, it would be hard to live up to his expectations.

'You could have told me, I would have…'

'Ah, don't be daft. I made my bed. I thought I knew what I was getting into. I really thought, I'd won the jackpot.'

'I thought you had too,' Tess said quietly, embarrassed now at her jealousy all these years.

'No.' Nancy shook her head with the finality of one who has thought things through many times over the years. 'No, as it turned out, it soon became apparent that Douglas had very set ideas and very high standards. I spent a lifetime not being quite good enough. And then after Danial… we tried, don't get me wrong, we made the best of things, but there were no more children. You and I, we both ended up in the same boat, even if it didn't seem that way to you.'

'God, it's a terrible mess, isn't it?' Tess looked across at Nancy, she wasn't sure if she'd said the words or not, but she must have, because Nancy was nodding at her, slowly agreeing with the inevitability of her reaction. 'I'm sorry, Nancy, I'm so sorry for everything that happened to you, that day and…' she never thought she'd be the one apologising, but then, she'd never expected this. 'I'm sorry for all of it.'

'You didn't know.'

'I turned my back on you – on both of you. I assumed that I had come out the worst and you had made the better life at my expense,' she cast her hand about the cottage. 'I should have let him go and been happy for you both.'

'Well, you were right about this place, I shouldn't have asked for it, we both know, Beatrice wanted you to have it.'

'God, no. It wouldn't have suited me at all,' Tess said and she knew it now in her heart. She couldn't have lived here, in this lonely spot. Dublin was her home; holding this place in her heart was just another thing to blame them for. 'But you're right, I know that Beatrice wanted me here and I'm glad I've come back, at last.' And she was, because apart from putting things right with Nancy, it felt as though Beatrice was here too, silently looking on and approving of her courage in finally facing up to the past.

'The thing is, Tess, it's not too late for us. We still have time to make things right.' Nancy whispered the words and when Tess looked at her now, she saw something she hadn't seen before. This was her sister, her flesh and blood, holding out all these years for her to come back to her. Tess knew she could walk away now, their war settled. She could go back to Swift Square with a clear conscience and never see Nancy again. She could do that, or they could truly put the past behind them and try to build something for the future. She sat still for a moment; it was hard to change the habit of a lifetime.

'I want to visit Danial's grave,' she whispered, it was the right thing to do. She had to go and make peace. That is what she should have done years ago. 'Will you show me where he's buried, I need to spend some time with him.'

'Oh, Tess.' Nancy began to cry again, only this time the tears were a mixture of relief and joy. She threw her arms around Tess and, somehow, Tess had a feeling that the world was settling to where it should be for her now. It was more poignant to think she'd passed this graveyard when she travelled out to Ballycove. It was a small old gated burial ground that stood mostly neglected because the village nearby was all but derelict and people were being buried in a new graveyard a couple of miles closer to the next town.

They stood now, only metres from the main road, but completely out of sight, thanks to the mounds of earth built up to block off the motorway. Tess could hear the traffic in the distance and it seemed wrong that Danial should be left here. She'd have preferred somewhere with yew trees, where birds could nest and the seasons marked out with the departure of the swallows and the arrival of the butterflies. Nancy had chosen a simple cross with his name and the dates that marked out his coming and going from this life. Next to him, Douglas's grave was marked with a similar cross and Tess could see Nancy had made sure the plot on the other side of Danial was free – it seemed she had it all planned out. By the time Douglas was buried, he didn't belong to Tess anymore, not even in her imagination and she'd never truly belonged to him.

'It had been too easy, in some ways,' Tess confided in Nancy as they stood at the grave.

'How's that?' Nancy was buttoned tight against the biting cold.

'Well, I've spent all these years blaming you both, when really – it was easy to let Douglas go. I'm not saying I wanted to, but if I had truly wanted to hold onto him, surely I'd have fought harder for him?'

'I often wondered about that,' Nancy nodded, but she never took her eyes off the little cross.

'I never really tried to win Douglas, I just walked away – I could have tried to get him back. If I'd really wanted him, letting him go wasn't something I would have done.' The sad thing was, it took her over forty years to realise it was the truth.

'So, perhaps you can make peace with what has happened?' There was hope in Nancy's eyes, just a glimmer but enough to cast off the heavy darkness.

'I'm saying, I think I already have.' Tess popped her arm through Nancy's and linked her to where Stephen parked the car. She would come here again, to spend time with Danial, maybe to make her peace with Douglas too. 'I think things worked out as they were meant to, in the end.' Tess sighed as she looked back at the simple crosses where they lay. It was a pity that they didn't get the chance to put things straight between them, but she had time to put things right with Nancy. She paused, drinking in the stillness of the neglected cemetery. Tess felt the warmth of her sister beside her, it was comforting, it was right. 'Yes, perhaps things *have* worked out just as they were meant to.'

43

February 21 – Saturday

Richard was sitting in the kitchen studying the *Times* when she got home. He looked at her over his reading glasses, surveyed her as though she was an errant teenager who had outstayed her curfew. 'The kettle is just boiled, if you fancy a cup of tea,' he said, as though it was normal for him to be sitting in her kitchen at nine o'clock on a Saturday morning.

'Right, make a pot, will you while I run up and get changed,' she said and she pointed towards the kettle as though he might need reminding which step came first. It was true, she couldn't remember the last time he had made a cup of tea for her, never mind a pot. As she walked up the stairs, she realised he had washed the dishes that had been left sitting in the sink. Maybe he just dumped them in the dishwasher, but either way the effort represented something momentous, even if it was just a little too late.

In the bedroom she closed the door tight, caught a glimpse of herself in the full-length mirror. She looked exactly like what she was; a woman who had just spent a passionate night in the arms of a thirty-year-old Italian stallion. It was a look that suited her. Even after she had a shower and changed into a cotton blouse, jeans and Birkenstocks, she still had a wanton look about her. It was as though Carlos had unearthed a new sexiness to her. With the glow in her cheeks from working outside and the recent changes to her diet, she was unrecognisable from the woman she'd been only weeks ago. She wasn't all that much thinner, it had to be said, but it was something else. It was something that had changed deep within her. She dumped the towels in the laundry basket, and it struck her, it was something that made her an ample adversary for Richard. She threw her shoulders back and marched into the kitchen.

'Tea?' he offered in a meeker than usual voice, he was pouring out a steaming mug for her.

'On second thoughts, Richard, no thanks. I've changed my mind, I don't want your tea and to be perfectly frank, I don't want you anymore either.'

'Hold on a minute now, Amanda, I'm the one who has put this roof over your head. I'm the one who pays the bills. Without me, do you think you'd be having coffee with your friends at the Berkley every week?'

'Honestly, Richard, I don't care if I never see inside the Berkley again. As for your colleagues and their wives, they are not my friends. They never were, it's just a shame I didn't see that until recently. So I can survive without them.' She didn't add that she felt she'd probably thrive without them clawing at her to hold her back in the place they believed she should stay. 'And as for this house and your bill-paying capacity, I could live with a lot less. Of course, I won't have to. Any family court in the land will make sure I have plenty to live on and this house for as long as I want it.'

'Don't be like that, Amanda, we don't want to go down that route,' Richard's voice held a nervous quaver that gave him away.

'No? But you must have realised that by taking a mistress, it was something that might happen? Surely when you left here to be with her, it crossed your mind?'

'That's not how it was,' he was almost squirming now.

'Hah,' Amanda felt a surge of temper rise within her. 'Like hell it wasn't. Richard, we both know that the only reason you're back here is because things didn't work out with Arial.' She put up her hand to stop him lying. It was enough to be betrayed, but to be treated as if she was some kind of simple imbecile a second time round really would be too much to endure. 'Even though you hurt me, Richard, I'm glad it happened.'

'I...' he looked down at the table before him. 'I'm sorry, Amanda, I didn't think... I...'

'That's the first time you've said sorry, Richard, and it's long overdue. Not just for the betrayal, but you know, it's only since you left that I realised you have so much more to be sorry for.' She held up her hand again, there was no point going over it. It wouldn't do any good trying to explain to him that she had let him stifle her. That each time he had shrugged her off, wrinkled his nose or compared her disparagingly to someone else, he had only made her try harder to be someone she wasn't. In the end, that night at New Year's the truth was that she really didn't know that dumpy little middle-aged woman who looked back at her from the plate glass window. She couldn't find herself in her own eyes anymore, much less in the clothes she chose, the colour of her hair or the mounds of skin that had accumulated all across her body. It took Tess and Robyn to show her that the mounds didn't matter. What mattered was finding who was hiding beneath and then everything else would fall into place. And they were right, that was what had happened. Amanda had made friends, real friends, and through the galleries, once she started painting again, she'd make plenty more. With Tess and Stephen at her back, she was beginning to see the wood for the trees. She was having fun again, not just with Carlos – but with herself. She had walked into her beautiful bedroom this morning and seen a woman that she liked. She wanted to get to know herself better because she had a feeling that she could really grow to love that woman in the mirror.

Amanda took a deep breath, what she was about to do now was going to take far more courage than she'd ever given herself credit for. 'Where are your bags?' she looked wildly about the kitchen, but there was no sign of a suitcase or any kind of travel bag. 'Did you bring your things with you?' she asked him now, eyeballing him so there was no room for him to fudge.

'Yes, I put them in the spare room, for now...' he said almost against hope.

'For now?' Amanda threw her eyes up to heaven and darted through the kitchen door. She took the stairs two steps at a time and rounded into the spare room. She had the contents of the drawers emptied into his bag before he made the landing. The whole lot was packed before he could make an argument to stay. 'It's very simple Richard. This is my home now. This is the children's home. We've told them that you've left. I've told them that we don't love each other in the same way anymore. They understand that. They get it. I'm not having them confused for one thing and for another...' She heaved the bag towards the door, took a final look about the room, checked she had everything in. 'I don't love you anymore. Maybe I haven't loved you for longer than I realised when you left, but I'm sure of it now. There's no way for us to go back, Richard, not now.'

She shook her head. She felt no sadness, only a tinge of regret at all the years she'd wasted being someone she wasn't meant to be. She realised, had it not been for the fact that she hadn't wanted him to end up with Arial, she might not have felt as much sadness before either.

'And, in case you're wondering,' she said as she yanked the bag down each step, bump by bump, 'this is not about Arial, it never was. I stopped loving you long before you took up with her, I just didn't realise it.' She pulled the bag out the door, noticed that she'd torn her lovely expensive wallpaper along the stairs, but really, what did a scrap of wallpaper matter in the greater scheme of things? She didn't like it much anymore anyway.

'You don't know what you're saying, Amanda,' Richard said and he found his second wind. 'You've been drinking? It's affecting your decision making.' She tossed him his jacket and half pushed him out the door. 'You're seeing someone else, is that it?' He was clutching at straws, trying to make sense of all this. His voice sounded as though it was verging on tears as she banged the door behind her. She knew if she looked out at him now, she might just crack. He would look vulnerable and pitiful standing on the doorstep in the cold, his bags at his feet, his face shocked and his expression defeated. Amanda chose not to look out the window at all. Instead she made her way back into the study that had until now been Richard's. She decided that she would make it into a storage area for her paintings.

It really was a little haven of a room. Admittedly, it was west-facing, cut off from every sound, with only the evening sunlight to illuminate it, but you could do so much with artificial lighting these days. She stood with her back to the door for a long time, imagining what it would be like to fill it with canvases. It would be cathartic, emptying every bit of Richard from this room. She would have fun putting her own stamp on it. First off, she would paint a nice big canvas for the kitchen. Something cheerful and bright? Or perhaps, something sultry, sexy – Italian?

Amanda threw her head back and laughed a throaty chuckle that was new to her. She felt alive, ready to take on the world and, with Tess at her side, she had a feeling it would be quite a ride.

44

It took Tess a moment to place Stephen's voice when he rang much too early one morning. He sounded different – taller if that was possible on the phone.

'I had to ring you,' he was almost out of breath. 'I've just come off the phone with... um, well, that is, I've heard something marvellous... and I had to tell you...' his excitement was contagious.

'You're being very mysterious, Stephen,' she laughed, in spite of herself, he had that effect on her all the time, she found herself smiling when he spoke to her. Funny how she hadn't noticed it before.

'No. Me, never,' Stephen said mildly.

'Oh, yes you are, what's up?'

'Okay, well, if I tell you, will you promise not to tell anyone else. I mean, we really should wait until it's official and tell the whole choir together. After all, it's...'

'I promise, it'll be our secret,' she laughed again now, had a feeling this could only be good news.

'We've been invited to perform in Salzburg, next

year. I mean, we are being officially invited. They made overtures that night, you know, when I spoke to them after the performance, but I was afraid to say anything until I heard more, just in case, but today it arrived, an email from the president himself. They'd want us to be part of their closing performance; it's a great compliment to the group.'

'Oh my God, Stephen, how did you manage to keep it under your hat for this long?' It was weeks since the concert. Tess had a feeling that she would have burst if she had to hold in this kind of news.

'Not easy, let me tell you.' He laughed now, a real belly laugh. 'I suppose now we're in cahoots, are you sure you can keep it a secret until I tell the rest of the choir, you know how some of the other members can be a bit precious about... things.'

'Oh, Stephen, you know, I've kept bigger secrets than this, if you can get them to meet without spilling the beans as easily as you did to me, then I can keep quiet on my end.'

'Ah, it'll be easier not to tell *them*, that's why I rang you first.'

'Well, thank you.' Tess knew in there he had managed to include some kind of compliment. 'Do you want a hand to gather them up? I've an hour here to spare; I could make half the calls for you?' It was such a joy to have the days to herself, she felt outrageously fortunate to be liberated from the nine to five. Her bold move into sudden retirement had goaded Stephen to finally do the same. She knew that for all his talk, he'd been as scared as she at the idea of being alone if he did not have a place to go each day. She suspected he was the kind of man who would have been 'good' at being married. The fact that he hadn't rushed back up the aisle again made her wonder if she really knew him as well as she sometimes thought she did. He set her straight on their journey back from Ballycove that day. There had been opportunities to settle down over the last few years, but something always held him back, and then he'd winked at her and she had known more than if he put the words between them. She was very glad he hadn't.

'Would you do that for me?' Stephen's enthusiasm brought her back to the present.

'Of course. I'll call the women and you call all the men, how's that?' It was the least she could do, after all, things were different now.

'And, maybe in return…'

'There's no need for any return, Stephen, I'm only helping you out.'

'Well…' she could hear him fumbling, as if perhaps the phone had fallen from his hand. 'Here's the thing,' his voice was clearer now, 'I wondered if you might come along to see *La Bohème*, I've managed to get two tickets for Sunday night and… just us, you know…' his voice turned into a mumble.

Tess held the phone away from her for a moment.

A deep blush travelled from her neck to the top of her forehead, then she took a deep breath.

'You're asking me to the opera?' she had to check, it was so long since anyone had asked her anywhere. 'On a date?'

'Well, yes, that is I want you to come with me, I thought we might...' Again, he seemed to sink into a bashfulness that was so unlike the person she knew him to be from the moment they met, but Tess found it oddly endearing. It was easy, not threatening or judging. 'Well, would you, go on a date with me?' Yes, she liked it very much.

'I'd love to come,' she said and she could almost hear him exhale his relief on the other end of the line. 'Let's make a plan after we've contacted everyone about Salzburg.'

Tess put down the phone and whooped. The sound brought Robyn running from the porch a startled expression on her face.

'What, what is it, is everything all right?' She stood nervously at the door; even Matt looked a little scared.

'I'm going on a date. A proper date, to the opera!' Tess flopped back in her chair, she was ready for this, finally ready to start living again. 'No, I'm definitely going on a date.'

Epilogue

Salzburg

In June, Salzburg was much warmer than Amanda expected, but perhaps that had more to do with being surrounded by the people she loved than it had with the blazing sun or the vivid colours of the Mirabelle Palace and Gardens. At the same time, there was something of a light breeze that held upon it an optimistic whisper that the winds in her life had changed direction, something she didn't realise she'd so badly needed, not long ago. When Amanda turned to Carlos, she could see he felt it too; it was more a sentiment that floated between them than something she could put into words.

'I will go back to Dublin, inspired,' he smiled, catching her hand in his. 'Thank you,' he kissed her fingers gently.

'Oh, don't thank me, I'm still a little surprised that Richard wanted to pay for us all to stay in the best hotel in the city.' Amanda shook her head. Funny how things work out. Here she was, strolling through Salzburg with Carlos, while Richard was still on that treadmill, running furiously to catch the promotion; he thought would make him happy. At least he had Ariel. They seemed to be bumping along together, if not exactly contentedly, then at least resignedly. Amanda had greeted the news that Ariel was pregnant with much more enthusiasm than Richard had. She had a feeling that becoming mired in nappies and night feeds had not been part of his original plan. Ah well, c'est la vie, she thought. Richard had handed over their tickets to Salzburg with a wistful smile, knowing perhaps that he was in for another decade of theme parks and water slides. It made it even easier for Amanda to count her lucky stars at how their lives had changed.

'We'll both be inspired going home,' she said and she meant it. She'd taken hundreds of photos over the last few days and she was dying to get painting as soon as she got back to Swift Square. 'We should be getting back,' she smiled at Carlos, 'they will be waiting for us.' It was fifteen minutes to the hotel and Amanda intended to walk it slowly, drag out their last evening in Salzburg, times like this, she knew were worth treasuring. So, they walked along hand in hand, admiring again the baroque architecture, carried away on their own fizzing happiness.

'You know, I want to ask you again...' Carlos pulled her close to him, his dark eyes still had that stomach flipping effect on her. Still, occasionally, she wanted to pinch herself that he'd fallen for her every bit as much as she had for him, 'but I have a feeling that I already know the answer.' He smiled, they were happy, it was all that mattered.

'Not yet,' Amanda felt his arms snake around her back, it was a good feeling. She knew where she was with him and the fact that he wanted to marry her was enough for now. 'Anyway, you don't want to take Stephen's moment of glory, do you?' She laughed.

'True enough,' Carlos agreed. 'Speaking of which,' he kissed the tip of her nose, before checking his watch, 'we really should be getting back.'

Stephen picked the restaurant, months before they'd arrived. It wasn't the most expensive, but it was a perfect blend of stylish and homely and the hotel manager said the food was the best in the city. A table for seven, by the window – they had a view of the river and the cathedral in the distance. The festival was the most magical experience of the trip so far. Tess was invited to sing solo and perhaps it made up a little for all those missing years, but Amanda had a feeling that Tess was too happy to feel she'd really missed anything at all now. Perhaps it was being with Nancy also, it turned out that her life had not been so charmed as Tess always believed. That cemented the sisters' relationship even more. Mostly, though, it bloomed because Tess was ready to forgive and move on and Nancy poured every ounce of love she had into it until Tess could measure up to her.

Amanda couldn't help looking around the table; she was lucky to have all of these people who between them meant the world to her. Casper, her lovely bright son, who smiled all the time now, had applied for art college. It turned out, far from being like his father; he was becoming more like Amanda with every passing day. All he wanted was to paint and play music. Robyn loved to paint too, and maybe, she could study design, but she'd set her heart on becoming a vet, so Amanda had a feeling that she'd be seeing more than just the neighbours' cat wandering about the place. Nancy and Stephen had become her friends, far better than Nicola or any of the others that believed they had cast her out of those torturous coffee mornings at the Berkley. Carlos, dark and sexy on her left was part of her family now too. He'd managed to wiggle his way in, slowly but steadily, winning over first Tess and then the kids with his open, easy ways. He was generous and funny and it seemed that these days he spent more time in Swift Square than he did anywhere else. But, it was Tess, sitting opposite her who had come to mean so much to her and so she smiled across at her, excited and happy about the future that was spreading out before them.

Tonight, it felt to Amanda, as though they were all holding their breath, waiting for something and it was hard to believe that Tess didn't feel it too.

'It's such a lovely place,' Tess murmured looking around the restaurant and when she smiled at Amanda it seemed she had transformed into the kind of woman she was always meant to be. Everything in her life had changed so utterly. Here tonight, Tess glowed. The woman that Amanda used to know was gone and in her place, Tess beamed at her modern, if somewhat unconventional family. 'Champagne?' she looked at Stephen curiously and Nancy giggled. It was a nervous, girlish sound and it reminded them she was happy to be here, counted as one of them, her family too, she belonged with them now. Robyn reached out and held her hand; they were as excited as each other at what lay ahead.

'Yes, I think so,' Stephen said handing her a glass. 'I think we have plenty to celebrate, don't you?' It was true. Within a year, Tess and Amanda had settled around them the kind of family they'd both always wanted.

'Stephen,' Casper elbowed him, handed him a small round box containing the ring that Nancy, Amanda and Robyn helped him find for Tess.

'Oh, yes.' Stephen stood, pushed back his chair and dropped to one knee. He'd spent the last few days practising this, since Robyn told him he'd have to do it properly. 'I have something to ask you, Tess.' He cleared his throat and Amanda felt a tremor of emotion rise up within her. 'Would you do me the honour of becoming…' he opened the box to show an antique emerald ring that looked as though the jeweller had carved it with Tess in his thoughts. 'Becoming my wife?' He finished between a nervous smile and tears of happiness.

'Oh, Stephen,' Tess said leaning forward and putting her arms around his neck. 'You silly old thing,' she mumbled into his ears, 'of course I'll marry you.' Then she pulled back a little from him, a tear escaping down her cheek. 'I'm so happy,' she said helping him to his feet, but the tears were hardly noticed because the whole restaurant was cheering and clapping and Amanda thought, this is surely what it means to live happily ever after.

Acknowledgements

All books begin with an idea of some sort, be it a person, a place or a question. To make the journey from an idea, to a story, to a book, it takes not just writing, but buttoning up, ironing out and a damn good editor. I've had the best – Caroline Ridding, who took my final draft and managed to find two weeks of solid work within it – thank you, it has catapulted the story to a whole new level, it was very much worth every dotted 'i'!

The Aria girls – the nicest bunch around – Vicky, Nikky, Sue and Geo, it is such a joy to work with each of you!

Thank you to Judith Murdoch, for your keen eye and sound advice. You have been, as always, full of editorial wisdom, funny stories and strategies to brighten any day – it is very much appreciated.

This edition of *The Girl I Used to Know* has much to thank Hannah Smith for. It is always scary to move editors but I'm very lucky to have landed on your desk – I'm really looking forward to seeing what comes next with my favourite Jedi Master.

Thank you to Helen Falconer who looked over this

story when it was still a baby and saw within it what it could become.

Thank you to all the lovely people who have in any way helped to bring this book into the world, all friends in the guise of colleagues, reviewers, bloggers and readers – I've loved talking books with you, each and every conversation makes it all even greater!

Particular thanks must go to early readers: Ailish Munnelly, Fiona Brady, Marcella Hogan, Ann-Marie Mc Loughlin, Mabel Snee, Orla Holmes, Teresa Canavan, Mary Devanney and Ann-Marie Durcan-Gilvarry. Thanks to Silke Kauther-Ginty and Michelle McGovern for reading and generally putting up with me!

Thank you, Bernadine Cafferkey, (super sister), for enthusiastically reading the drafts and being so very much more clever than your average fashionista.

Thank you, Christine Cafferkey, who has kept us all going through kitchen mayhem, telly blackouts, and so much more as well, you truly are Magic Mammy!

Thank you to Seán, Roisín, Tomás and Cristín – always be the ones who turn can'ts into cans and dreams into plans xx

To James, my PR guru and most enthusiastic supporter, still counting my blessings – here's to the next fifteen x

Finally, thanks to you the reader for choosing my book, I hope you enjoyed reading it as much as I've enjoyed writing it!

Hello from Aria

We hope you enjoyed this book! If you did let us know, we'd love to hear from you.

We are Aria, a dynamic digital-first fiction imprint from award-winning independent publishers Head of Zeus. At heart, we're committed to publishing fantastic commercial fiction – from romance and sagas to crime, thrillers and historical fiction. Visit us online and discover a community of like-minded fiction fans!

We're also on the look out for tomorrow's superstar authors. So, if you're a budding writer looking for a publisher, we'd love to hear from you. You can submit your book online at ariafiction.com/we-want-read-your-book

You can find us at:
Email: aria@headofzeus.com
Website: www.ariafiction.com
Submissions: www.ariafiction.com/we-want-read-your-book

f @ariafiction
🐦 @Aria_Fiction
📷 @ariafiction